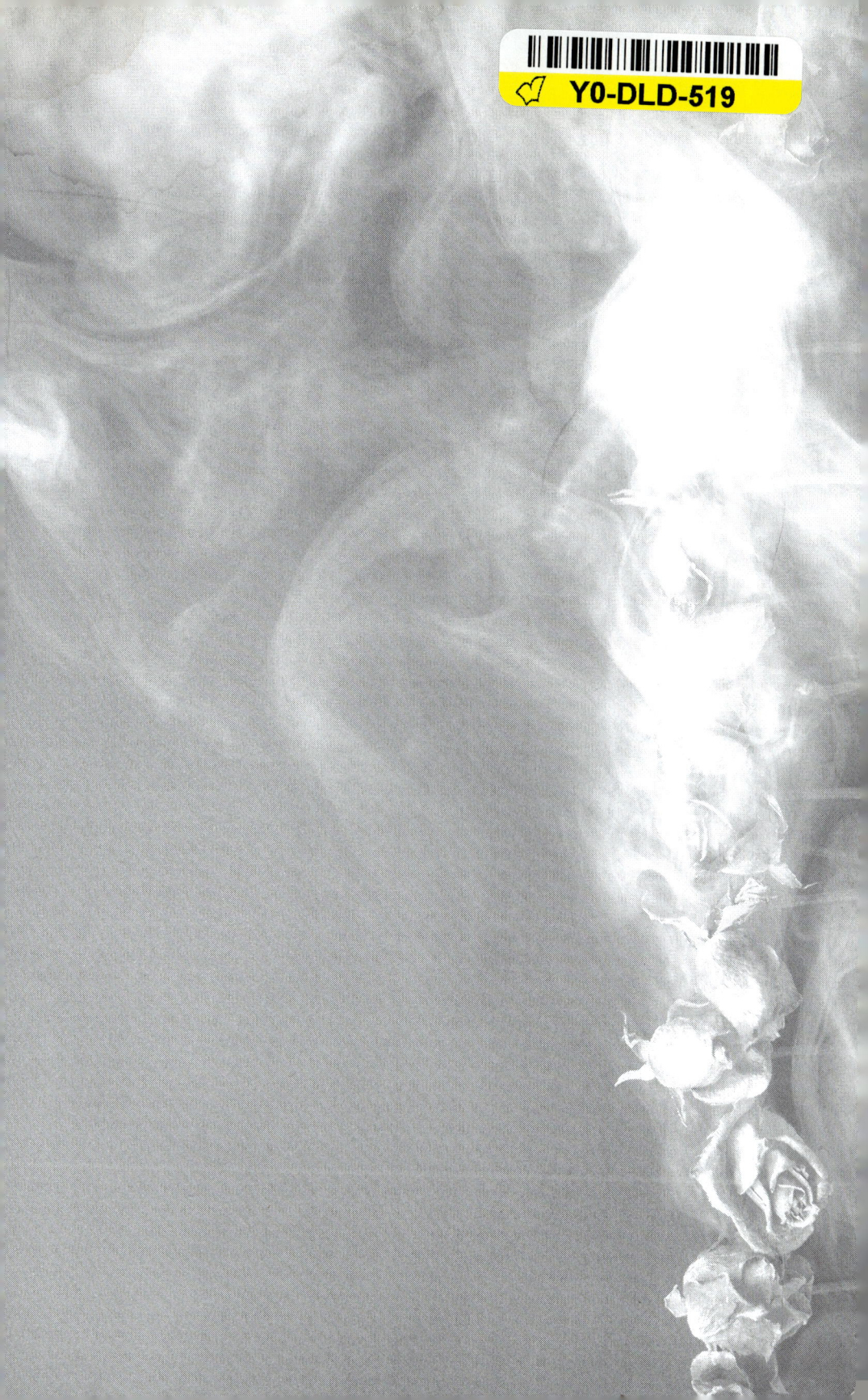

POSSESSION

THE AGENTS

BRYNNE ASHER

Text Copyright
© 2023 Brynne Asher
All Rights Reserved
No part of this book may be reproduced, scanned, or distributed in any printed or electronic form without permission from the author. Please do not participate in or encourage piracy of copyrighted materials in violation of author's rights. Only purchase authorized editions.

Any resemblance to actual persons, things, locations, or events is accidental.

This book is a work of fiction.

POSSESSION

The Agents

Published by Brynne Asher
BrynneAsherBooks@gmail.com

Keep up with me on Facebook for news and upcoming books
https://www.facebook.com/BrynneAsherAuthor

Join my reader group on Facebook to keep up with my latest news
Brynne Asher's Beauties

Keep up with all Brynne Asher books and news
http://eepurl.com/gFVMUP

Edited by Hadley Finn
Cover Design by MSB Design - Ms Betty's Design Studio

ALSO BY BRYNNE ASHER

Killers Series

Vines – A Killers Novel, Book 1

Paths – A Killers Novel, Book 2

Gifts – A Killers Novel, Book 3

Veils – A Killers Novel, Book 4

Scars – A Killers Novel, Book 5

Souls – A Killers Novel, Book 6

Until the Tequila – A Killers Crossover Novella

The Killers, The Next Generation

Levi, Asa's son

The Carpino Series

Overflow – The Carpino Series, Book 1

Beautiful Life – The Carpino Series, Book 2

Athica Lane – The Carpino Series, Book 3

Until Avery – A Carpino Series Crossover Novella

Force of Nature - A Carpino Christmas Novel

The Dillon Sisters

Deathly by Brynne Asher

Damaged by Layla Frost

The Montgomery Series

Bad Situation – The Montgomery Series, Book 1

Broken Halo – The Montgomery Series, Book 2

Betrayed Love - The Montgomery Series, Book 3

Standalones

Blackburn

CONTENTS

1. Forever and Ever, Until Death — 1
2. Red — 13
3. Blood-Stained Bride — 27
4. Mrs. Torres — 39
5. Boz, Brian, Boss — 47
6. Whacked — 57
7. Disrespect — 65
8. Beauty Queen — 75
9. Six Feet Under and Chipper As Fuck — 85
10. Bikini Police — 93
11. Annihilated Boundaries — 105
12. Funeral — 117
13. My Heart — 125
14. Bonding — 137
15. A Regency Romance Gone Wrong — 149
16. Good One — 161
17. Initiation — 173
18. Trinket — 183
19. Brian — 197
20. Inferno — 203
21. Cross The Line — 215
22. Nothing and Everything — 221
23. Fake — 235
24. Reverse Sexual Psychology — 245
25. Grounded — 255
26. Asshole — 261
27. Tongue-Twister Family — 275
28. Kill — 285
29. Bare — 299
30. Two Days — 309
31. Milf — 319
32. Pleasure — 327
33. Blinding — 335

34. Jittery	343
35. Reality	351
36. Go	357
37. Déjà-Fucking-Vu	367
38. Choose Good	375
39. Gone	381
40. Offer	391
41. Flames	397
42. Coincidental	401
43. I'm A Guest on Your Merry-Go-Round	409
44. Jammed	415
45. Lucky	421
46. Alone	431
47. Morning Person	437
48. Breaking Up The Band	441
Epilogue	445
Acknowledgments	453
Also by Brynne Asher	455
About the Author	457

For Hubbalicious.

1

FOREVER AND EVER, UNTIL DEATH

Landyn

I never dreamed my life would be over at the age of twenty three.

I stare back at my empty, dead eyes in my reflection.

The white couture gown fits like a second skin. I don't know how they managed it. I never laid eyes on the dress until thirty minutes ago, let alone tried it on or dealt with alterations. My makeup is heavy, but it looks like I'm barely wearing anything other than pink gloss on my lips. My hair is twisted into a complicated updo and whisps tickle my face. It's youthful, perfectly imperfect, and appears effortless even though it took over an hour to create.

I'm a work of art.

A team charged into our suite hours ago to work their magic. I've never met any of them, and they didn't ask what I wanted. In fact, they murmured amongst themselves in their native language about their project. They only spoke directly to me when giving me orders in English to *sit up straight*, *turn*, or, the most embarrassing of all, *suck it in*.

They didn't care what I wanted. I guess it isn't their fault. They had their orders.

His orders.

I look like a dream in the middle of a nightmare.

"Dennis, do something. Anything but this. You're ruining our lives! It's embarrassing. This is your last chance to fix it. Find another way to pay the debt. Work it off somehow. Do something—just not this. What will people think when she marries him?"

My father paces back and forth behind me in his smart black tux—in and out of the reflection like a pendulum. His strides are so violent, he's sure to wear a path in the Persian rug. I can't bear to turn and look him in the eyes. I haven't been able to since that dreaded day.

When he stops, the room rumbles around his roar. "You think I have a choice? I fucking don't! We'd be dead right now if I hadn't given into his demand. Dead, Nellie. All of us!"

Dead.

And the thing is, I think he's telling the truth.

"Damn you. I told you to stay away from the Marinos. They're too dangerous—Damian especially. He's evil, and you're handing our daughter over to him on a golden platter!" Every muscle in my body tenses when Mom screams, "Look at what you've done!"

It was only five days ago that Dad sat Mom and me down and explained what happened.

How Dad fucked up in the worst way with his scariest associate.

I'll never forget the moment. Dad sat there with his face in his hands, tension clouding his warm brown eyes as he admitted what he'd done.

A debt—one he can't begin to repay even if he took out every possible loan and called in every favor and marker owed to him on the West Coast.

My father is not a small player, but he isn't a big one either. Though, he was trying to be.

As normal a life as my parents pretend to live, it's anything but. To most people who know us, Dennis Alba is a successful businessman, but I know how my father makes his money. Very little of his income that supports our lavish lifestyle comes from legal or legitimate ventures.

It feels like that dark day played out a lifetime ago—the day he looked me in the eyes and told me what was to happen so we didn't all end up dead.

That I'd be the one who would ultimately pay the price for his fuck up.

I'd be the one to pay his debt.

And I'd do it with my own life.

I argued and refused. When it finally sunk in that there was no way I'd get out of this, I shed enough tears to rival an old woman who lived through more heartbreak than any one person deserves.

But as the days have dragged on bringing me to this moment, I've become numb.

I didn't even have the chance to run. One moment my father was informing me of my demise, and the next, we were taken from our home in our up-scale neighborhood and brought here.

We haven't stepped foot outside of this suite since.

Dad agreed to a deal.

Me.

In exchange for millions he doesn't have.

Alamandos Marino is one of the wealthiest men in Mexico. Unlike my father, Alamandos is a big player.

Huge.

Actually, he is *the* player that all other players are measured against.

He's also ruthless.

But if rumors in the underworld we live in are true, his son, Damian Marino, is worse. So much worse.

Damian hides that side of himself from most of the world. When you have that much money, it's easy. And Damian lives and works in the U.S. He likes to play on Wall Street and has found a way to keep his hands clean with a very defined line between him and his father's cartel.

But we know who Damian really is. And his father, Alamandos, is said to be on his last leg, demanding that his son produce a *legitimate* heir.

Insert me.

I might throw up all over my couture wedding gown.

My father breaks into my nauseating thoughts. "Landyn."

He's barely spoken to me since Damian Marino's people collected us from our house by gunpoint and brought us here, to a resort on the coast just south of the border. Apparently, this is what happens when a cartel leader believes you're a flight risk.

I don't move and continue to stare back at my reflection. I look like a stranger—even to myself. I'm not the same person I was five days ago.

"Landyn." My name is laced with desperation as he grabs my bare arm and flips me around to him. I finally look into his creased face and desperate eyes. Guilt bleeds through his features. "I'm going to fix this. I promise. Let's get through today, and I'll talk to Alamandos. I'll find another way to pay him. I'll get you back."

I've gone through the motions, because I've had no choice. The only other option is dying. I can't run and I can't hide. They're watching us constantly.

But as I look at my father and listen to his empty promises, I can't ignore the emotions I've buried deep since we arrived here. I'm out of tears, and I'm done begging and pleading. Nothing is left besides resentment and anger, but I can't afford to go off half-cocked.

I have no one to count on but me.

My father handed me over as payment. He can't undo this or make it better.

I swallow over the lump in my throat and speak for the first time today, as I yank my arm out of his hold. "In twenty minutes, I'll be forced to walk down an aisle to marry Damian Marino, the son of the biggest cartel leader this century. He's twenty-one years older than me, and everyone knows his reputation."

My mother whimpers into her tissue.

My father's face turns ghost white. He has the audacity to try and make me feel better about what he's done. "He promised he would be good to you."

I'm no idiot. This is a Marino-owned resort. Guards haven't hidden their presence since we got here. We're surrounded by armed men—all of them work for the Marino Cartel. I'm not betting against video surveillance in every corner of this place, so I lean in and lower my voice to barely a whisper as I glare at the man who used me as a pawn to save his own ass. "Let's not pretend what I'm about to do isn't another form of death. You're the one who botched a shipment for the biggest modern-day cartel leader. I'll never get out of this. I'll never be the same. I'll never live a free, normal life, and it's all your fault. You might as well slit my throat yourself before I'm forced to walk down the aisle."

This is the first time in days I've allowed myself to say the things that have been simmering below the surface. A car will be here to collect us any minute—this might be my last chance. I have no idea when or if I'll be able to see my parents again after today.

"Landyn," my mother cries and tries to reach for me, but I step back from both of them.

"Don't. Just don't." I motion to the wedding dress that was picked by someone other than me and do my best to manage my emotions, because I've been warned what would happen if I'm not completely compliant. "If you think you're getting me out of this once the deed is done, you're more demented than I gave you credit for. I hope you both enjoy the freedom my life sentence is about to buy you."

A strong, efficient rap at the door breaks through the tension that's thick enough to cut with a knife.

My heart seizes.

Mom dabs at her eyes so her tears don't mess up her mascara. She shakes her head dramatically. "There has to be something we can do. There has to be."

Whoever is on the other side doesn't wait for us to answer. The door opens, and a man I've never seen stands there, filling the space with complete and utter authoritative force.

His tailored suit fits his large frame as perfectly as his expression that screams business. He's tall and broad, and looks more like a GQ model or an NFL player arriving for the biggest game of the season rather than a drug dealer. His hair is clipped short, his manicured beard is even shorter, and his dark skin is flawless.

He's gorgeous.

He also doesn't look like he's in the mood for dramatics.

I guess begging for my life is off the table.

His deep voice rumbles through the room. "Two cars are waiting outside. Damian won't be happy if we're late."

Well then.

That isn't good.

That is all kinds of bad.

Damian Marino is buying a twenty-three-year-old college dropout who is always late.

As if it could get any worse.

My dad picks up my mother's purse and grabs her wrist. He tries to put up a show of decorum and lifts his chin, like he's somehow important. "We'll ride with Landyn. We'd like to spend the time with her on the way to the church."

The muscled man in a suit shakes his head once. "You and Mrs. Alba will go in the first car. The bride will arrive last, on her own. It's what Mr. Marino ordered."

I turn quickly to look back at my parents. As angry and frightened as I am, I didn't think this would be it.

The man steps aside and motions to the door. "Let's go."

"Wait," I beg. The need to drag my Jimmy Choos is overwhelming. "Will I see them after the wedding?"

The man reaches for my elbow, as if I might run in this tight-ass dress. "No. You'll be taken straight to Damian's home after the wedding."

My expression falls, and my knees go weak.

This is it.

Holy shit.

This is it.

The man who looks like he can take down brick walls while

wearing a custom suit gives me a little yank. I have no choice but to move, and my parents follow us out the door.

The moment we step foot outside, the sunny day is a slap across my face.

It's warm and bright and beautiful—technicolor spreads as far as I can see. After my shot of Novocaine to the heart that has lasted days, all of a sudden, every nerve ending in my body is hyperaware.

The flowers are brighter.

The ocean breeze is crisper.

The sun is hotter.

And the hand on my elbow becomes tighter.

Twin black Escalades greet us like the Devil himself on doomsday, sitting side by side outside the villa that has become a holding cell.

My chariot awaits to deliver me to hell on earth.

My new reality.

I'm forced to swallow down the taste of bile that bubbles in my throat. I don't say goodbye to my parents.

"Sit in the middle," the man demands before lifting me with no issue and pushing me into the icebox of an SUV. He shoves the train of my dress at my feet and slams the door.

My blood pulses, echoing in my ears.

This is it.

Another man sits behind the wheel. He's also dressed for my demise in a crisp black suit.

And now I wonder if everyone is wearing black but me. Even my mother is donning a black dress.

Fitting, I guess. This might as well be my funeral.

The driver doesn't acknowledge me, but he does turn to his partner who climbs in the passenger seat. "We're late, Boz."

Boz.

What a name.

Boz produces a handgun from inside his suit jacket and rests it on his thick thigh. He doesn't mince words around me. "Shit show in there. Alba looks like he might crap his pants at any minute. His wife is a fucking mess."

My weight is pulled back into the smooth leather as the SUV takes off. I'm not sure if it's instinct or purely a reason to keep my hands busy, but I pull the seatbelt across me and click it. My new prison guards don't do the same as we exit the resort property and enter the streets of Tijuana.

Growing up in San Diego, I've been here more times than I can count. It's packed and colorful, just like it always is. People are carrying on about their day as we speed through the streets in a caravan. I've never been here when the traffic wasn't congested and bumper to bumper.

I wonder if my fiancé had the streets closed for us.

Only a government official or cartel could make that happen.

Boz and the driver don't speak as the world flies by. I wonder where we're going and how long it will take to get there, but I don't dare ask. I'm afraid to open my mouth for fear of what will come out.

I also wonder how badly it would hurt if I opened my door and threw myself from the moving car. Surely Damian Marino wouldn't want to say *I do* to a bloody bride standing before him covered in road rash.

Maybe I wouldn't survive.

I can think of worse things.

Like marrying the evil son of a cartel leader who will take over the helm someday.

Damn.

I should never have hooked my seatbelt.

I'm rocked to the side when the driver takes a sharp turn. We're leaving the touristy area and moving off the beaten track. The roads are narrow and bumpy. These are areas my friends and I never ventured in all those times when we'd come for the day and think we were brave and daring, getting drunk on tequila because no one cared how old we were. When we were here, we were out from under the control and protection of our parents.

That thought is laughable now. The protection of my parents is a joke.

If I only knew what my future held back then.

I should've run for the hills.

Or Canada.

The farther we move out of the city and from the Pacific, real-life Mexico appears. I will time to stand still, but as the days and hours have turned into precious minutes, very little is on my side, least of all time.

The SUV carrying my parents comes to an abrupt stop first, and ours follows. We're parked in front of an old church. It stands tall and beautiful on the city street, with so many steps leading to its grand entry. I wonder how I'll maneuver them in my spiked heels and tight dress. Sucking it in will have new meaning.

Boz turns to me. "Don't move. We'll get your parents in and seated, then it's your turn."

"But..." I hesitate as I look out the windshield. Men are standing guard around my parents as if they'll make a break for it. I look back to the man named Boz who's still casually palming a gun on his thick thigh.

His profile is intimidating as he studies our surroundings. But he's the only one of Marino's people who has spoken to me today, so I decide to take a chance. "What about my father? Isn't he going to walk me down the aisle and give me away?"

I've never been angrier at my father as I am now, but being with him is better than going it alone.

Boz shows his first emotion that isn't stoic or deadpan and looks back to me with a hiked brow. "Chica, he already gave you away."

Shit. He's right.

Time and options. I'm completely out of both.

I watch my mother cling to my father as they climb the stairs to what's waiting for me inside.

I still haven't officially met my fiancé.

He's not famous—he's notorious. He's the legitimate face of the Marino family. I've heard my father talk about him for years.

It's all I've been able to think about since I was told I'd have to marry him in order to save my family.

Damian has never been married, but he's rumored to have multiple children by just as many women. All illegitimate, and he doesn't claim any of them publicly. Unlike his father, who unofficially rules most of Mexico and lives on the coast of the Baja Peninsula just south of the border, Damian lives in San Diego in Del Mar Heights.

He might run the legitimate side of his father's business, but he's also said to be ruthless and willing to do anything and everything to get what he wants. Many hushed words go hand in hand with my fiancé, including the biggies.

Torture.

Murder.

Rape.

Case in point, threatening death to an entire family to land himself an unwilling young bride such as myself.

The driver turns and aims his cold eyes on me. "Every Marino has been married in this church for the last century. The priest knows you're not Catholic, but go with the flow. Repeat what he tells you to say and take communion like you've done it every week since you were eight. There are some important fucking people in there from all over the country. Act like you know what you're doing, like you're in fucking love, and ready to rip that dress off to jump Damian's bones in front of his friends, the priest, and God. That's what he expects. The sooner you learn to give him what he wants, the easier your life will be. Got it?"

The blood drains from my face.

"And don't fucking pass out," the driver warns. "That'll make us late. Trust me, you do not want to piss off your husband-to-be on your wedding night."

I can't form words.

And I definitely can't force my body to move.

The driver gets out and slams his door.

Boz looks back to me and aims his impossibly dark eyes on my blue ones before doing the same. "Let's go."

He opens my door and holds out a hand for me.

I don't move a muscle and sit here buckled into my seat like a freak. "Am I really going to have to walk down the aisle by myself? I've never even met him."

Boz looks me up and down, but not lewdly. I think he feels sorry for me. He reaches in and presses the button on my seatbelt. "Come on, Landyn. I'm not shitting you when I say the boss doesn't like anyone to be late. I'm trying to do you a favor. Let's get this done. Later, you can numb yourself from the inside out. Focus on that, and you'll get through it."

Get through it?

Holy shit.

This guy works for Damian, and even he realizes how horrible my life is about to be.

Boz grabs my hand, and instead of trying to pull away, I grip it like it's my last lifeline.

Because it is.

"Please," I whisper. "Don't make me do this. Let me go."

He shakes his head. "Sorry. I don't want to get dead."

Lord. How many lives is one girl expected to save by marrying the devil himself?

I have no choice but to climb out of the car. At this point, I need to try not to make my fiancé wait longer than necessary, since it's been insinuated more than once that I'll pay for it later. I can't think about what that means.

On shaky heels, I maneuver my way up the stairs clinging to a man named Boz. The big doors creak when they open, and we enter the vestibule. A bouquet that weighs more than a gallon of milk is shoved into my hands. It's dozens of red roses the color of blood and wrapped in the color theme of the day—black. As if on cue, an organ bellows throughout the old church.

I have no idea what piece it is other than the anthem to my demise.

Boz dips his face to the side of mine. He's probably eight inches taller than me. His low, gruff voice vibrates down my spine as his breath tickles my ear. "Keep your wits about you. Good luck."

He tries to pull away, but my grip on him tightens. "Please, don't leave me by myself."

"I'm the best man. Damian is waiting."

I pull in a shallow breath, and just like that, he's gone.

Before I have the chance to exhale or run, the doors leading to the sanctuary part.

Every pew is filled, and guests line the walls. And exactly like I thought, this may as well be my funeral rather than my wedding day. Besides the priest, there's nothing but a sea of black in front of me.

Why are there so many people? And why are they all wearing black?

This has got to give "shotgun wedding" a new meaning. Everyone really came out of the woodwork on short notice to see Damian tie the knot.

Or to get an eye full of the victim in this charade.

Me.

Standing at the end of the long aisle, is an ostentatious wedding party. Young women who I've never seen before are dressed in long evening gowns, the color of the night.

When my eyes land on the perpetrator himself, I take him in for the first time in the flesh. He's not much taller than me. Acne scars pebble his cheeks above his facial hair, and the button on his tux strains around his belly. I guess when you're as powerful and wealthy as him, you can let yourself go in your mid-forties.

Damian's glare cuts through the vast space and slices me wide.

I'm frozen to my spot.

His evil eyes narrow as the organ hits a low note. The man who just told me to keep my wits about me steps in beside his boss. Boz towers over Damian and looks more like a guard than a best man.

But my gaze flicks back to the man who will be my husband as he flexes his fingers before making a fist.

Shit, shit, shit.

2

RED

Landyn

I swallow over the boulder in my throat as my sweaty palms fight to keep hold of the bouquet.

It's worse than I imagined.

All eyes are locked on me. I can't make myself move as my husband-to-be's leering eyes rake over me in the flesh for the first time.

He doesn't look happy.

Well, buddy, the feeling is mutual.

I've never been less happy than I am at this moment.

The music continues to vibrate up my spine, looping the overture for at least the third time as the church waits for me to make a move.

"¡Vamos, muévete!" I glance to my side where an older woman is standing in her best funeral garb motioning for me to get on with it.

I look back down the aisle and force a Jimmy Choo forward.

One step.

Then another.

The closer I get to Damian, the darker his sneer becomes. My heart sprints, and my desire to turn around and run for the ocean grows. I'd rather be swallowed by a real undercurrent than the one who's about to suck the life out of me forever and ever, 'til death do us part.

I'm over halfway to the altar and feel every curious eye in the place glued to me. There's no way I can make it another step if I look at Damian, so I allow my eyes to wander...

The priest ... I wonder how much he was paid to care that I'm not Catholic?

My maid of honor ... who is she?

My mom ... she's still crying.

And then, Boz.

His expression is void of emotion as he stares at me. My mouth feels like cotton, and my eyes sting with unshed tears, but Boz never breaks his stare when he brings a hand to his face to drag a thumb across his full bottom lip.

It occurs to me as I walk toward the short, round, horrendous man I'm about to marry, that Boz is hot. Literally a beauty of a man.

Someone clears their throat. My gaze shoots to Damian.

Shit. He's angry.

Three pews separate us.

I swallow hard and shift my focus to the marble at my feet.

That's when it happens.

The organ screeches to a halt.

For a mere moment, the church goes weirdly still.

Then ... shots.

Gun shots.

The acoustics in the old structure go haywire. Not just gunfire this time—it's a barrage.

Commotion breaks through the congregation.

The sea of black undulates as a whole. It begins with confusion that morphs into screams and bellows and a tidal wave of running.

Some drop to the floor. Dad is pulling Mom by the arm, his eyes ablaze with panic as he searches for cover.

I should do the same, but I can't because my fiancé is in my face. With a gun in one hand, he grips my arm so tight I scream when he flips me around, fitting my back to his chest.

He's using me as a shield.

"You're not going fucking anywhere," he growls in my ear through the chaos. He wraps his arm around me—my neck is caught tight in the crook of his elbow. He's holding me so close, the stench of his breath seeps into my already haywire senses.

I yank and pull at the sleeve of his jacket. "You're choking me!"

Though, I doubt he can hear. People are fleeing, yelling, or have fallen into piles around us. Shots continue to echo through the centuries-old church.

Blood.

So much blood.

"Boss, get to the side. We need the wall at our backs." Boz is crowding us and grips Damian by the shoulder, shoving us against the flow of guests.

I'm bumped, prodded, and fight for oxygen.

Shots continue to rain from the balcony.

I drop the bouquet to the floor. Damian trips over it and almost takes me down with him, but Boz has a death grip on him. I try to scream but the noose Damian has around my neck is just too tight.

"Did your fucking father do this?" Damian bellows in my ear through the commotion.

I can't speak, but I try to shake my head.

"He's fucking dead, you get me? I'll still marry you and make sure he knows I'm gonna make his precious daughter's life a living hell right before I kill him myself. No one fucking goes back on their word to a Marino." He shakes me from where he's holding me around the neck. Pain vibrates down my spine. Bullets are the least of my worries because my future husband is cutting off my oxygen. "You're not getting off easy, you little bitch. I'm going to make sure you personally pay for this in every way. Your family will never cross mine again."

I gasp when we hit the wall with such force, the side of my head bounces off the stone. I yank and pull at his arm with what little energy I have left. He's going to suffocate me before he has a chance to make me pay for anything, because I'm sure this is not my father's doing. There's no way he could pull off something like this. This requires more manpower than my father has.

Damian shoves me against the stone again as his malevolent words pierce my eardrums worse than the gunshots. "You'll never be the same once I get my hands on your sweet body. I'll use and abuse you any way I want. Because of this, it'll be even worse. You're mine and will be forev—"

Then...

Another gunshot.

This one stands out among the rest.

My ears ring.

It's close and loud and...

Holy hell, I can breathe again.

But ... red.

I'm covered in it.

So much blood.

I push away from the wall and turn in Damian's hold that's now loose and weak.

His eyes are frozen wide, and his expression is set to shocked.

The side of his head is also blown off.

I shriek.

Boz looks from me to Damian as he lets go of his boss, and we both watch him fall at our feet.

He's dead.

The horrible man I was about to be tied to forever ... is dead.

Shots still echo around us, and no one cares about me anymore, which means I have one goal.

I need to get the hell out of here while I have the chance.

I kick off my stupid shoes and step over my dead fiancé, but Boz moves in front of me.

His chest rises and falls with deep breaths that I'm sure has nothing to do with his physique and everything to do with his emotions.

"Get out of my way," I demand.

Boz is about to say something, but that's when I lose sight of him. I actually lose sight of everything. Something is thrown over my head, and my bare feet lose all purchase on the floor below me.

I scream when arms circle me from behind. My arms are pinned. A hand clamps over my mouth.

The chaos surrounding me is muffled.

I writhe and fight, gasping to breathe the air that leaves nothing behind but the taste of death.

And just when I didn't think my day could get any worse.

I'm jostled—my bare feet dragged against the floor. I can't see anything, but if I were ever to be in a rush mob, I bet this is what it would feel like.

Until…

A whoosh of fresh air hits my exposed skin as my captor pulls me into their arms as my wrists are bound in one hand behind my back.

There's more shouting, but this time the dialects are different.

"That turned into a bloodbath." A deep voice rumbles against me right before I land on my side. I scramble to yank the cover off my head, but a hand grabs my wrists as I hear a car door slam. "Get the fuck out of here."

Something cuts into my skin around my wrists. Shit. I'm cuffed.

"Stop fighting and you won't get hurt."

Given everything that has happened, I doubt that.

My heart clenches as my emotions catch up with everything. Tears betray me, but I do everything I can to stay still. I know, growing up the way I did, that if I don't cooperate, whoever this is will hurt me.

I need to focus.

Brax

I cross my arms as I stare out at the parking lot. It's littered with trash, potholes, and cracks. We're far enough outside of town, we might as well be in the desert. Gone are the views of the ocean, mansions on the water, and luxury that drips in money. We're back at the shithole motel that has become one of the long list of our meetups. We have them under surveillance to make sure no one follows us, but we still switch it up just in case. Habits and routines will get you burned.

And I'm dancing so close to the fire right now, I'm sure I've lost all fingerprints from being singed. Which is good, I guess. One less identifier.

"This was not part of the plan, Cruz. Start a war. Take the girl. Find her and bring her back so you could ingrain yourself deeper. We needed Damian Marino alive. I want to know who took him out."

I turn to the men standing in the room behind me, but focus on my boss, Tim Coleman. I haven't seen him in months. This operation was thrown together in a matter of days when the transaction with the Alba girl was announced. The op was solid. And given the fact everyone in this room is standing, living and breathing in one piece, proves it.

When Tim's wife, Annette, hears about what went down, she'll kill me and then she'll kill him for jumping into the action. She's the shit, but she also appreciates Tim's job as a supervisor which usually involves sitting back to manage operations like this, not participate in them.

Even the best plans are subject to last minute changes. Damian might be dead, but it doesn't change the end goal.

"For some reason, I don't think my main man here gives a shit," Carson drawls.

My eyes shift to CIA Officer Cole Carson. He's my other boss. The DEA doesn't do this anymore. No one goes this deep undercover for this long, but the CIA does this all the time. Seeing as how Carson's wearing a shit-eating smirk while splattered in blood is a testament to the fact I chose well two years ago when I took a chance and approached him about this case. He's a crazy fuck who doesn't mind pushing the boundaries as much as I do.

Which makes me the perfect asset for him. I had no problem taking this assignment between the Drug Enforcement Administration and Central Intelligence Agency. It's the only way I can get this shit done the way I need to.

Professionally and personally.

I shrug. "Bullets were flying, Tim. Half the people in that church pulling triggers aren't trained in firearms. You think they're good shots? How am I supposed to know who took him out? I'm just glad it caught Damian and not me again."

"This changes everything," Tim bites. "Without Damian, you lost your main advocate. He's the one who trusted you, and he's the reason you got as far as you have. You lost your leverage."

I look around the room that's just as wired as it was when I got here even though it's closing in on midnight.

"I'm not leaving. I've got two years invested and one hell of a scar. The way I see it, we're in a better position than before."

Cole crosses his arms and loses the smirk. "You know I'm down for anything, but you'll need to convince me we're in a better position than we were. Damian was one of our main targets."

"And we still don't have enough on Alba to take him down for good," Tim adds. "His books are tight. If we move on him now, his attorney will have him out on bail and the charges dropped within days."

After everything went down at the church, I didn't move from old-man Marino's side until he gave me the order to find the Alba girl. I fed Alamandos the information I needed him to believe. In his state, it wasn't hard to convince him this was a war on his family. Dennis Alba is a slimy fuck, but the attack at the church today isn't his style. Not to mention, he's a pussy. Any man who'd auction off his only daughter to save his own ass is.

"It's taken a long time to get to this point. Too fucking long," I argue. "Alamandos may hate Dennis Alba, but I was able to convince him that the attack on his family today was orchestrated by the Lazadas, and he bought it. This is what we need, and I'm in the perfect position to see it through with Damian out of the way."

If Alamandos Marino hates anyone in this world, it's the Lazada Cartel. They've been flirting their way into Marino territory for years. The Marinos keep delivering warnings in the form of shallow graves, but that hasn't stopped them.

Alba's deal for his daughter was the catapult we needed. We created a war that will distract everyone's attention, so they won't see what's going on right under their own noses. Blaming today on the Lazadas is brilliant.

"You still haven't explained … how the hell are you in a better position?" Tim demands. "Without Damian, you've lost all access."

I look from Tim to Carson. "Damian might've been my advocate, but he was also my biggest barrier. I spent hours this afternoon with Alamandos to make sure I'm cemented in the family. He might be old and distraught from losing his son, but he's not stupid. He needs his business up and running in the U.S. I convinced him I'm the person to make that happen until he finds a more permanent solution. Damian's death might not have been the goal today, but this puts us in a better position than we've ever been in. Everything will go through me."

Tim gapes. "No shit?"

The two men glance at one another.

Carson whistles as he crosses his arms and rocks back on his heels. "Why the fuck did you wait to tell us? This changes everything."

I shake my head before angling my eyes to the neighboring room where the next topic of conversation is being held. The woman in the bloodied wedding dress is the bomb that could ruin years of work and fuck up my one and only chance to do what I need to do. "Alamandos might be mourning his son, but that didn't soften him. He lost millions because of Alba. Just because Damian is dead doesn't mean the deal is off. He wants the girl, and I was tasked with finding her. And just to throw a wrench in the plan, I need to return with the girl if I want a chance to run his business in the U.S."

"Fuck," Carson bites.

"What the hell is he going to do with her?" Tim asks.

What I did not anticipate was for the girl to get wrapped up into the deal. That's a problem none of us anticipated. We planned to grab her, get her out, and turn her against her father.

I shake my head. "That's the million-dollar question. I tried to convince him she would be a pain in the ass, but he wants her. What he really wants is to fuck over her father. There's no way he'll let her go, and there's no way I can finish this if I don't bring her back."

"If we let her go, they'll find her," Carson says. "And if she goes home, her shithead dad will hand her right back over like a dirty five-dollar bill. He did it once, and that was to marry Damian fucking Marino knowing what he was capable of. He won't blink an eye doing it again."

I cross my arms and turn to look out the window. I shouldn't give a fuck about Landyn Alba. I have to watch my back twenty-four-seven. I don't need anyone else to worry about. With the shit I've seen since I've been under, nothing shocks me anymore. But the last thing I need is an organized crime boss's high-maintenance daughter to babysit.

Fuck that.

I'm a man on the clock with one goal—revenge. And even though I just hit the gas pedal on my personal project doesn't mean that the figurative clock isn't a ticking time bomb that could blow up in my face at any moment.

"The way I see it, you have two choices," Carson says. I know my choices, but since the man likes to hear himself talk, he spells them out for me anyway. "One, you leave her fate to chance. The Marinos will find her eventually. They've got the track record to prove it, and it's not like the sorority dropout looks like she has the wits to run from a cartel or her father. Two, you take her back, let them sing your accolades for finding her so fast, and do what you can to make sure they don't make her life a living hell. If you really think this could be wrapped up sooner rather than later, she can try to live her shallow life on her own without Daddy's money since he'll be in federal prison and everything attached to him will be confiscated."

I turn back to the men in the room and state the obvious. "Those aren't great choices."

"No shit," Tim agrees. "But it's your ass on the line. It's up to you."

I drag a hand down my face as I contemplate the woman in the next room.

Fucking hell.

Landyn

AFTER I WAS TOLD to stop fighting back, they never said another word to me. But at least they told the truth. Besides moving me from the car to this lumpy mattress, no one has laid a finger on me.

Not even to remove the cover from my head. I'm thirsty and I'm starving.

I have no idea where I am. It feels like we drove halfway across Mexico, but I bet when one is kidnapped from their own wedding, time tends to drag.

Since this is my first rodeo, I can only assume.

If I'm honest, slamming the door and leaving me alone was a step in the right direction. But I need to go to the bathroom, my body is stiff, and whatever they bound my wrists with is cutting into my skin.

I had to force my muscles to relax, but not anymore. When I

hear the lock turn and the door open, every nerve in my body goes haywire.

"Shit. You're a fucking mess."

That voice.

That deep, rumbly tone. It's the same one that told me to keep my wits about me. The same one that reminded me my father sold me. And it's the same one that refused to help me because he didn't want to *get dead*.

"Please, don't hurt me—" My panicked tone rises as a touch hits my neck.

He interrupts me immediately. "There's no one around for miles. Scream if you want, it won't help."

Then, for the first time since I was in the church, I gasp a breath of air that isn't stale. He rips the hood off my head, and I blink away the low light.

All I see is him.

Boz.

He's bent at the waist, leering over me as his gaze rakes over my face. "You okay?"

I shouldn't be relieved to see a familiar face. This is the man who delivered me to Damian at the altar, and he did it with no remorse. He did it knowing my fate—I could tell at the time.

I shake my head, and my voice is shaky as I try to control my tears. "No. I need to get out of here. What if the people who took me come back?"

He stands and digs a hand into his pocket. When he flips open a switchblade, my scream fills the room.

He puts a knee to the bed and a firm hand on my hip, rolling me to my stomach. "Told you no one was around. Chill out, chica. I'm trying to cut the damn zip tie from your wrists."

Blood rushes through my arms, and I'm twisted in this damn dress trying to scramble away from him. I have my back against the headboard as I look around for the first time.

The walls are made of cinderblocks. The carpet is thin with holes worn in a path from the door. An old tube TV sits on the dresser that's missing a drawer pull.

And Boz stands tall and wide between me and the door. He's in the same black suit he wore to my wedding, but he lost the tie and his shirt is unbuttoned at the neck. He's covered in as much blood as I am, and it just dawned on me it's probably blood from the same person.

My dead fiancé.

I'm not at all upset about that turn of events.

"Where am I?" I whisper.

I jerk when his knife snaps shut and he slips it back into his pocket. "Mexico."

I swallow over my dry throat. "Mexico is a big place."

His dark eyes never shift from me. His only answer is a lazy shrug.

"Who took me?"

He still doesn't answer. "We've got a drive, and it's late. Alamandos is anxious to get you back."

My face falls. "I don't want to go back."

As Boz gives me a chin lift, I wonder what's wrong with me. I'm proud of myself that I'm able to freak out while contemplating how he's hotter now than when he was standing at the front of the church.

Him wearing Damian's blood is a constant reminder that I could be in a worse position at this very moment.

I need to focus on that.

"Please," I beg. "Don't make me go back. Damian is dead. What do they want with me now?"

The man leering over me shakes his head. "I have no fucking clue. My orders are to find you and bring you back."

Panic—real, heart-racing terror—is an instant hit to my system. I shake my head and there's no controlling my tears any longer. "Please, no—"

"We'll figure it out. All I know is they're going to get restless and the last thing we want is for them to come looking for both of us. If you don't get up and come on your own, I'll restrain you again if I have to. But we're going, and it's happening now."

I look down at my wrists—my skin is red and angry from the

zip tie he just cut. I can't handle that again. I certainly can't handle being suffocated by that damn bag.

Gathering the material at my legs, I slowly scoot to the side of the bed. I feel every spring and lump beneath me shift as I force myself up.

Standing on bare feet, Boz is impossibly big. There's no way I'll get away from him. "I ... have to go to the bathroom."

He tips his head to the door at the side of the room. "Make it quick."

The man can threaten me all he wants, he can't make me move faster. The moment I click on the light and shut the door, I gasp when I get a look at myself in the mirror. The last time I saw my reflection was at the villa. I was fit for the cover of the June issue of a bridal magazine. I would know, my friends and I used to flip through them in high school, planning our dream weddings.

Dream wedding.

That's a joke.

I look away and use the bathroom before flipping on the water. I grab a folded towel that's threadbare and unraveling and soak it in water. Willing my hands not to tremble, I wipe dried blood from my face, neck, and chest. I'd do anything to get out of this dress.

I can't rub hard enough and do everything I can to get the smudged makeup off my face as I go. Then I pull every pin from my hair and massage my scalp, trying to pull in deep breaths.

I jerk when there's a rap at the door. "Chica, speed it up."

I flip off the water and squeeze my eyes shut. I can't remember what my life was like just a week ago. I never understood what it was like to be out of choices.

I've heard stories of human trafficking. I've read about it. We were even warned when I was at San Diego State. But no one thinks it will actually happen.

And for the whole thing to be started by my own father?

I hate him.

There's another rap at the door. "Landyn."

I open my eyes and stare at the stranger in the mirror. I wonder what will happen to her.

I put my hand on the knob and open the door. Boz is standing in the open space with a cell to his ear.

His impossibly dark eyes stare into mine. They're not evil, and that surprises me. I wish I could figure this man out.

"Yeah, I've got her." He never looks away from me. "I'm bringing her back."

And with that, my fate is sealed.

I'll never escape this man.

3

BLOOD-STAINED BRIDE

Brax

We've been driving for over an hour.

Landyn's asleep.

She hasn't uttered one word to me since she disappeared into the dirty bathroom.

She downed the bottle of water I handed her after she walked barefoot across the rocky parking lot. I've lost track of time and I'm starving. I bet she is too. I know she hasn't had anything to eat since she was kidnapped.

Before she passed out, she not only gave me the silent treatment, but wouldn't even look at me. She stared out at the dark night and massaged the welts on her wrists as we passed the world by.

I, on the other hand, have looked at her plenty in that damn blood-splattered wedding dress. It doesn't matter that she's covered in Damian's blood, I'll never forget how she looked when I opened the door to the villa and took her away from her asshole father.

I thought Damian Marino was the scum of the earth, but Dennis Alba handing his daughter over to a psychopath is one of the craziest things I've seen since I've been under.

And I've seen some bad shit.

I knew when I gave the signal for things to go haywire at the church, it would be a bloodbath. It was perfectly timed. Every eye in the place was on Landyn Alba. They were nosy as fuck to see the woman who would *willingly* tie herself to a Marino.

Especially Damian.

The assault on the Marinos went exactly as planned. We had the element of surprise on our side while everyone was distracted by the beauty in white.

There's nothing better than organized mayhem.

But Damian catching a bullet through the skull was not in the plan. Hell, it wasn't even a part of my personal plan. But since the deal was made, and the Albas were brought to the resort so they wouldn't run, Damian hasn't shut his fucking mouth about his fiancée.

About his plans for her.

His sick-as-fuck plans.

It made me ill. I felt like punching myself in the face when I had no choice but to egg him on. Be his fucking cheerleader.

It was bad enough learning what he'd done in the past and knowing what he was capable of. I never laid eyes on Landyn Alba even though I'd heard everything about her.

She lived up to the hype and more.

I tried to separate myself from the situation. I thought I did...

Until she walked down the aisle. I saw the way Damian looked at her like she was a wild animal he planned to beat into submission.

Which I know was a part of his plan since he laid out his wet dreams to me in horrid detail.

I glance over and watch her tits rise and fall in that damn dress. I don't care if her reputation is being a spoiled princess of a dried-up mobster. No one deserves what he had in store for her.

And here I am, taking her right back into the lion's den. I have no fucking idea what's going to happen, but at least Damian's out of the picture.

For good.

I pull over onto the side of the street and put the Escalade in park. "Landyn."

She doesn't move.

I reach over and brush the side of her arm with my knuckles. "Chica. Wake up."

She jerks and shrinks away as if I woke her up with a knife to her throat.

She looks from me to our surroundings. "Where are we?"

"Look at me." She turns her icy blues my way and frowns. I shift in my seat and take her in from top to bottom. Her hair is falling around her face in a mess, and her eyes are framed in dark circles. I wonder if it's from the stress, tears, or leftover makeup.

"What?" she bites.

"Damian's dead," I state.

Her eyes widen as she motions to our blood-covered clothes. "No shit. I still have his brains splattered all over me. I might've been kidnapped, but I haven't forgotten that highlight of my day."

I put my finger up to stop her. "Drop the attitude. I'm trying to do you a favor. Again. Señor Marino does not play. I tried to get him to let you go, but he's mourning the loss of his only son and blames your dad. He wants you back, but I have no fucking idea what his plans are. There are people all over Mexico looking for you. Consider yourself lucky that I'm the one who found you. No one else would be coaching you on how to handle this shit."

Her expression is set to freaked the fuck out, but she still says, "You haven't coached me on anything."

"I'm getting to that part." I tip my head and take her in. Even in her state, she's got a backbone. She's going to need it walking into Alamandos' compound, and now I wonder how devoted she is to her father. "I have a feeling you might have a fire inside you that could get you in trouble. That attitude isn't going to do you any favors in this life. Keep your mouth shut when we get in there. I have no idea what we're walking into since I've been gone for hours looking for you."

"Who took me?" she demands. "And why? There's no way my father could have done that back at the church. That's what Damian thought. If you take me back in there and they think my father had Damian killed, who knows what they'll do to me."

I glance at my watch because we need to get back. I can't control the situation when I'm sitting on the side of the road arguing with a blood-stained bride. "No offense, chica, but they know your father couldn't pull off that bloodbath if he tried. He doesn't have that kind of pull in Mexico or the U.S. Alamandos knows it. What happened today is business that has nothing to do with you or your family."

Her blue eyes disappear when her lids fall shut and that backbone of hers gives out. Her voice comes out in a whisper over the quiet hum of the engine. "But I'm still caught in the middle of it."

I tell her the truth. "You have your father to thank for that. Landyn, look at me."

She drags her tired eyes open. She's raw and looks like she might give up or snap, which is why I need to get this through her head. "I don't know what's going to happen when we get in there, but whatever you do, don't say shit about Damian. Not to Alamandos and not in front of the family. Got it?"

She gives in after too many moments of hesitation, and now I wonder how much I can trust her. "I'm heartbroken that my asshole fiancé was shot in the head. Got it. Maybe they'll let me wear black now."

I narrow my eyes and wonder if I should kick her out of the damn car and let her go it alone in Marino territory. I have a feeling this woman will be a pain in my ass. "You pull that shit in front of Alamandos, you're on your own, Landyn. Trust me, you don't want that."

She crosses her arms over her chest and turns to stare back out the passenger window.

The silent treatment.

Fuck me.

I wasn't kidding when I said I can wrap this up faster with Damian out of the way. I knew it the moment that bullet cracked his skull.

I thought I saw a light at the end of the tunnel, but with the roadblock sitting next to me, my task just got harder than it should be.

Damn the girl.

I put the car in drive and pray she doesn't do anything stupid.

Landyn

WE DON'T STOP or even have to knock. The massive double front doors part like magic as Boz leads me into the home of Alamandos Marino with his big hand wrapped around my bicep. He hasn't taken his hand off me since he rounded the SUV to open my door.

The property goes on forever, and we've passed so many guards with guns, I've lost count. The entire complex is painted white, from the perimeter walls to outbuildings to the mansion. It sits like a beacon in the dark, lined with lush gardens and palm trees that wave in the night as the waves hit the rocky shore below the cliff where it's perched. It's more beautiful than the resort where my parents and I were held the last five days.

But as we enter the world of the Marino Cartel, it couldn't be more different.

Gone is the light and airy feel of the resort-like fortress. The colors are heavy, the intricate ironwork reminds me of prison bars, and the mood reeks of death.

Much like the vibes I got from my fiancé for the short moments we shared before his demise.

But it doesn't matter how bleak my future looks, I'm still single. Score one for Landyn.

I'll cling to that small victory like it's my last lifeline, which it is. My last bit of freedom.

We approach a man in a suit. He must have fared better than us or had time to change out of his bloody clothes. He's standing outside a set of tall double doors in an intimidating, wide stance that screams *it's the middle of the night and I'm not in the mood to fuck around*. "He's waiting for you."

Boz gives him a chin lift as he pulls me on bare feet over the cold tiles and turns a door knob.

Alamandos Marino rests in a leather wingback chair behind a massive desk. I didn't see him in the church earlier, and before now, I've only heard of him. My father wasn't kidding when he described him as one broken hip away from his deathbed. He sits in shriveled skin, which makes me wonder how much he's shrunk over the years. Even though the grand office chair swallows his frail figure, power rolls off him in spades.

It might have to do with all the armed guards standing sentry around him. There are others in the room standing to the side—ranging in ages from me to my father. One of them is the priest from the church. Gone is the elegant robe he wore at the altar. He's dressed in black from head to foot other than his white collar. He looks as tired as I feel. Boz and I are the only ones out of place in our bloody clothes.

Alamandos might be old, but that doesn't mean he's lost his ominous reputation. By the way he's looking at me, no one would guess that I'm the innocent victim in the middle of a nightmare. Instead, his glare on me is dark and accusing.

As if I was the one to put a bullet through his son's head.

If I could have, I would have.

Alamandos' gaze shifts to Boz, and his tone sends a chill down my spine. "Where was she?"

Boz comes to an abrupt halt in front of the desk and pulls me to his side, never letting go of my arm. "An hour and a half south-west. Once I started asking in town and talked to Damian's main contact at the department, I knew which direction they went. It took hours, but I checked every Lazada safehouse in that area. She was alone."

Mr. Marino's tired, dark eyes shift to me, taking me in from my messy hair to my bare toes. It's all I can do to stand my ground and not hide behind the man who delivered me back to ground zero.

I shouldn't trust him.

I can't trust anyone.

Not even my own father.

Alamandos Marino's gaze hesitates on my dress stained with his only child's blood, before it moves to my face. "Is that true?"

I swallow hard over the lump in my throat, but don't say a word.

Boz gives my arm a firm squeeze. I guess when Mr. Marino asks a question, I need to answer.

"I..." I force myself to clear my raspy, dry throat. "I was bound and hooded the whole time until he found me. I have no idea who took me or where I was. I honestly have no idea what happened today or who—" Boz gives me another squeeze.

Shit.

How am I supposed to know how much to say or when to keep my mouth shut?

Alamandos tips his head and glares at me. "Your father had the balls to ask for you back."

My heart skips a beat, but when Boz's fingers squeeze my bicep, I clamp my mouth shut. I can't say the same for my expression since tears instantly threaten what shaky demeanor I'm trying to hold onto.

The tips of Alamandos' fingers drum on the leather arm of his throne. "After today, your father has more problems than auctioning off his only daughter to pay his debt to save his own ass. I'll find out who was behind today's attack and Damian's murder. If it's the last thing I do, I'll find out who pulled the trigger on my son. And when I do, I'm not going to kill him. I'm going to keep him alive for as long as I can. He'll be tortured so badly, he'll beg to meet his maker. If I find out that your father ordered the attack today, he'll experience the same. Do you understand?"

My knees wobble when I nod. I sway, and Boz yanks me against him tighter. I'm grateful. Otherwise, I might land in a puddle on the floor.

"Now I need to decide what to do with you," Alamandos states.

Yes.

The same question burns in my gut too. Especially since he just announced he's not giving me back, like I'm some sort of ugly heirloom, valuable enough to keep just to piss off your greedy, long-lost uncle.

Still, I've learned my lesson. I keep my mouth shut and send up a silent prayer that torture isn't in my future.

"Nic," Alamandos bites.

I'm confused at first, until one of the men standing to the side steps forward. He doesn't look as old as Damian was, and he's in much better shape.

But I do not like the way he's leering at me when he answers, "Yeah?"

"You'll marry the girl."

I pull in a sharp breath. My eyes jump back to Alamandos.

What?

No.

No, no, no!

Nic pulls a hand up to his mouth and drags a thumb over his bottom lip. "Fuck, yeah, I will."

If I had any food in my stomach, I'd throw up all over my bloody wedding gown.

Boz holds up a hand as if to stop the proceedings. He raises his voice, and when he does, he doesn't even look at the man named Nic. Rather, he speaks directly to Alamandos. "Whoa. He couldn't even fucking find her. He might be your nephew, but Damian sent him back for a reason and promoted me instead. Why him?"

Why anyone?

That's what I want to know.

Alamandos' answer is swift. "Because he's a Marino."

Boz doesn't let go of me, but steps forward and jams a thumb into his own chest. I not only feel his anger in his hold, but it's rolling off him in waves. Whatever he feels for this Nic guy is intense, which makes me want to marry him even less than I did Damian.

Which was none at all.

"Have I not proven my loyalty to the family? I have the fucking scar to prove it. I was the one Damian trusted. I was the one he thought of like a brother. You damn well know it, because he told you. Nic doesn't deserve shit."

Nic moves, and an electric charge shoots through the room. "You're not family. You're a fucking imposter—"

Boz pulls me behind him, and armed men appear between us and Nic. I wasn't wrong about Nic being in better shape. It takes two men to hold him back.

Boz lifts a finger and points at Nic over the shoulder of a guard who's restraining the second man I've been told I'm supposed to marry today. "You fucking stole from Damian and you know it."

"I didn't!" Nic tries to fight off the guards, and two other men enter the fray. "Damian made that shit up and tried to frame me. He was my cousin—my blood! I didn't take a fucking thing from him."

Boz glares at him. "Right, a hundred Gs went missing while you were in charge of the books for no reason, asswipe. The only reason you're still standing here is because you *are* blood." Boz pushes me forward to present me to the leader of the largest cartel in Central America. It's all I can do to silence my wince. "Are you really going to reward your nephew with this when he stole from your son? From you? Damian would come un-fucking-done, and you know it. This is the way you want to honor your only child?"

Alamandos places his trembling hands on the desk and painfully pushes himself upright. "Lost my son today."

"I lost my boss and my friend. Don't taint his memory by giving his bride-to-be to a man who stabbed him in the back," Boz growls.

I look between Alamandos and Boz. I'm an outsider looking in. I have no clue what the history between Boz and Nic is, but I can tell it's not good. The energy in this room is charged with red-hot, emotional anger.

Alamandos uses the desk to support his frail body and never takes his stare off Boz, mulling over his options.

He drops his head and stares at the old wood before he shakes it. When he looks back up, his expression is tired.

Exhausted.

"You want her?"

"No fucking way!" Nic yells. "He's not a Marino. He brainwashed Damian and—"

Boz ignores Nic and states, "I'll take her."

All the air escapes my body.

I slowly turn to the man who hasn't taken his hand from me since we got out of the car.

But Boz doesn't break eye contact with Damian's father.

"No!" Nic bellows.

"Fine," Alamandos mutters. "Let's get this done."

I don't turn to look at Mr. Marino. I can't take my eyes off the man who just said he'd take me, just to spite another man. The way he said it, I might as well be a day old, leftover wilted salad.

"Now?" I whisper.

"Father," Alamandos bites. "Do it and get it over with. I need this day to be over. We have a funeral to plan."

Boz shifts his stare to me. It's empty and cold and sends a chill down my spine. I shake my head and want to protest for the millionth time today over my fate.

My future.

But I'm stuck.

Nic is dragged from the room, yelling obscenities and insults about the third man today I'm offered to as a bride. The guards pull him out of the room kicking and screaming that he didn't steal from anyone—how he was set up.

The priest appears at our side holding a book.

"Wait—" I start but Boz's hold on me finally loosens only for his large, warm hand to land on the side of my face.

His hold is firm, and his gaze is hot and intense as it seeps into me. His expression screams *Shut up!* but what comes out of his mouth is heavy and laced with finality.

"You're mine now."

4

MRS. TORRES

Brax

Turmoil.
You can get stuck in it, or you can create it.
I'll choose the latter every time.

For two years, I've managed my turmoil like a well-oiled machine. I've treated it like a delicate and intricate war plan. When to strike. When to sit back. And when to let the plots you've laid play out like an action movie climax that just never ends.

Sometimes I have to tweak it. Sometimes I have to massage it. But I'm always the puppet master. If I lose control, it'll eat me alive. I'll get sucked into its tornado and never make it out.

If I have one fear, it's that.

Not making it out.

When I committed to this, I knew it was going to be a long haul. Playing the end game is never easy or quick. But then again, nothing in life is. It's worked until today—all of it. I haven't taken one step that wasn't well thought out, planned, or where I didn't know what the five steps following it would be.

Until just now.

This is not me. Working against who you are is hard. The only way I've been able to manage this life—this operation—is discipline over my true nature, one that never shows restraint or control.

Today, I not only threw that out the window, I shattered the glass and am left as figuratively bloody as I am literally.

Fucking Damian. I'm not sorry he's dead. None of us would be in this situation if he hadn't insisted on the payment standing barefoot and terrified in front of me.

Nicolas Decker is Alamandos' nephew—his sister's son. If Damian was a sneaky, evil bastard, then Nic is a plain evil one who lays his shit out for the world to see. In the matter of twenty-four hours, I've stopped them both from getting what they want.

And this is where it got me.

Talk about taking one for the team.

But I was the one who dragged her back here for the sole purpose of getting her back to San Diego to wrap this shit up quickly. I never thought I'd be standing right here to make it happen.

"The quick version, Father. She's a reminder of my son's murder. I want her the fuck out of my house."

"Wait, do we have to do this right now?" Landyn's petrified blue eyes flare in desperation. They're begging me to give her a break. She has no fucking clue. "I don't even know who you are."

I claim her arm again and turn her to face me as the priest takes his place at our sides. "I was Damian's right hand in everything. I'm taking over his duties with the family and managing his interests. And since you were his main interest, that makes you mine. You're paying the same debt you were earlier today, just to a different man. The sooner you realize this isn't about you, but about your old man, the better. Nothing has changed, and you're expected to cooperate."

She sucks in a breath. "Cooperate?"

I narrow my eyes on her. "You know the consequences, chica."

"For fuck's sake, shut up," Alamandos bites. He hobbles to us on his cane and comes to a halt next to me, never shifting his glare from the woman who's about to become my wife. "No one was as loyal to my son as this man. You'll marry him in honor of Damian, and be fucking happy to do it."

I do my best to ignore Landyn's glassy eyes before turning to Alamandos. I need to cement myself as deep as I can. "My first son will be named Damian. We might not share blood, but he was my brother. I'm sorry I couldn't save him twice."

Alamandos brings a shaky hand to grip my shoulder but turns to the priest and gives him a nod. "Deliver the sacrament so we can be done."

I turn to the woman I have no fucking idea what I'm going to do with. Her tits rise and fall in her stained dress quicker than what should be natural for a twenty-three-year-old healthy woman. She's white as a ghost.

The priest opens his Bible, and I dip my hand deep into my pocket. Without looking away from Landyn to make sure she doesn't fall over sideways from anxiety or lack of food, I produce the rings Damian gave me first thing this morning for safe keeping. After I toss them onto the open Book, I grab her hand just in time. She was about to take a step back.

Alamandos wasn't wrong. We need to get this shit done and get the fuck out of here.

I pull her body to mine and wrap an arm around her narrow waist. Her arms are pinned between us as her hands land on my bloody shirt.

I'll never forget this moment or the look on her face. Maybe, someday, when this shit is over, and I've done what I needed to do, she'll realize this is for her own good.

"Dearly beloved," the priest starts. "We have gathered today to join these two in marriage. We ask you, oh Lord, to strengthen them with your sacred seal."

I feel every swell of her body pressed to mine.

"Brian Torres and Landyn Alba, do you come here today to enter into marriage without coercion, freely, and wholeheartedly?"

"I have," I answer.

Landyn trembles but says nothing.

I narrow my eyes.

Silence.

"Señorita?" Father presses.

My arm tightens around her. Besides our bloody clothes, our bodies are one—in every sense but the fucking kind.

She pulls her bottom lip between her teeth and bites down. Hard.

Landyn

Freely and wholeheartedly?

Is the priest shitting me?

And who learns their future husband's real name at the moment of saying *I do*?

Brian Torres' arm is a vise around me. I feel every plane and muscle of his body pressed into mine, proving my earlier thoughts from today—this man is capable of backing up every imposing threat with real muscle.

I'm no challenge for him. In any way.

So when he growls my name as everyone waits for me to consent to this farce of a marriage as if I'm not here as payment in exchange for keeping my family alive, I feel it everywhere. "Landyn."

A single tear matches my unstable tone. "I have."

"Brian, repeat after me…"

Boz's eyes are dark and hard as his empty promises hit me like a boulder. "…faithful…good times and bad…sickness and health…love and honor…"

It's everything I can do to repeat the same terms, knowing they mean nothing except for the last ill-fated ones. "… all the days of my life."

The priest keeps talking, but I block it all out.

This is it.

As horrible as the day has progressed, I still can't believe I'm here.

I snap out of it when Boz shifts me into his other arm long enough to grab the rings off the Bible.

"Hand," he demands. I slowly hold out my left one as he slides the most ostentatious ring on the finger that's supposed to have a vein connecting straight to my racing heart. But that's just some ancient belief that's a crock of shit.

Just like this marriage.

I look down at the ring. The diamond is huge and is surrounded with baguettes lining the band. Nothing has ever been so ugly. I instantly hate it and everything it stands for.

Boz slides a gold ring on his finger—one that was meant for another man.

"Let us humbly invoke God's blessing on this bride and groom as he bestows the Sacrament of Marriage."

The room around us rumbles with mutters of "Thanks be to God."

"I now pronounce you husband and wife."

Holy shit.

I'm fucking married.

"Brian, you may kiss your bride."

My heart seizes.

Boz gives the priest a chin lift before settling his dark eyes on me.

I'm frozen in a way I might never thaw.

I didn't realize how much he was supporting my weight until he lets me go. His hands are warm on my clammy skin as he claims my face with force. I'm pulled to my toes when he lowers his face to mine.

Then our lips touch.

No.

But they don't just touch.

This is no simple kiss.

It's a declaration. He's proving he's entitled to me.

And, probably sooner than later, all of me.

His tongue presses through my lips to taste mine. Firm. Demanding. Audacious.

He's proving to me—and everyone else in the room—that I'm his.

I'm nothing more than a barter.

He takes, and he takes.

I begin to lose myself in more than one way when he finally lets me go.

His stare lingers as I settle back on flat, bare feet to catch my breath.

I haven't breathed easy since the day Alamandos Marino's men took my parents and me from our home in San Diego. And now I'm married to a different man than the one I was promised to.

"Congratulations," the priest mutters.

"That's done." Alamandos exhales as if my new marriage was one thing to check off his to-do list.

It occurs to me that this is it. I've lost myself. I'll never be Landyn Alba again, but even worse, I'll probably never be myself again. I might not be married to a Marino like I thought I would be right now, but I am married into a cartel, nonetheless.

Boz turns to Alamandos and claims my hand in his big one. "I've got to get back to Damian's, make sure whatever attack today didn't extend to the business. I'll call if there's a problem. Until then, get some rest. Let me know if you need help with funeral arrangements. I'll be here for anything you need."

Alamandos grips Boz's shoulder again. "The only thing I want is revenge, Boz. Fast. You're my number two. Make it happen."

"You know I will."

"We'll touch base tomorrow." Alamandos drops his arm and shoots me a glare before Boz pulls me toward the double doors of the office.

With a firm, possessive hold on me, Boz gives every man we pass a simple chin lift. I'm not surprised no one congratulates us on our new marriage.

I'd accept condolences.

And just like that, we leave through the same heavy iron gates. Boz opens the passenger door of the Escalade and watches me climb in. I don't know where we're going, but it can't be worse than this place.

I turn to look at him when he doesn't shut my door. He says nothing.

"What?" I demand.

He pulls in a big breath before turning his head to look out into the darkness. When he looks back at me, he mutters, "Fucking unreal."

Then he slams the door in my face.

Well.

Finally, something I can agree with.

5

BOZ, BRIAN, BOSS

Landyn

I've decided, from here until the end of time, silence is my friend.

That was after I riddled Boz with enough questions and complaints to fill a town hall meeting during election season. Here is a sampling...

"Where are you taking me?"

"Can someone get married in Mexico without a marriage license?"

"I'm starving."

"I swear this day will never end."

"Is your real name Brian?"

"Seriously, is our marriage even real? I didn't sign anything. I'm sure they have marriage certificates in Mexico, right?"

That's when he pulled over on the side of the road, got out of the car, grabbed a bag from the back, and got back in. He dug through it and tossed me a clean T-shirt. "Put that on. And, I swear, chica, if you keep asking me questions, I might lose it. We've experienced the same day, and it's been a helluva one. Can we not ride in peace until we get to the house?" I was about to ask whose house we're going to, but he didn't give me the chance. He tore off his jacket and bloody dress shirt, yanking his own clean T-shirt over his dirty, white undershirt, before he turned and pointed a finger in my face. "We're going back to San Diego. I've got your passport. If you make one peep to Border Patrol when we go through, you'll have bigger problems than you do now. Answer yes when they ask who you are and keep your mouth shut. Do you get me?"

I got him loud and clear. So, I nodded, pulled the T-shirt over my head to cover Damian's blood, and kept my mouth shut.

The shirt swallows me whole and smells like lavender, which is weirdly comforting, given the situation.

Crossing the border was easy and fast. But then again, I've never crossed the border at four in the morning. And as much as I don't want to go anywhere with Brian "Boz" Torres, I feel a little bit closer to home, even though I have no clue if I'll ever get to go back to the house I grew up in.

Other than my nap on our way back to Tijuana, I haven't slept. We're in the early morning hours, the sun will soon rise on a new day. I need a shower, food, and sleep. Then I can focus on what comes next.

Next...

I'm married.

I know what comes next. By the way Boz kissed me after I was forced to promise him my undying love forever and ever, until death, I try not to think about what comes next. In fact, I can't think about the future at all.

Surviving the present is hard enough.

Which brings me to my current state of silence. I've decided I don't need to know what's going to happen next as long as no one else kidnaps me.

Being rescued, on the other hand, sounds really good right about now.

The farther we drive north, the more I recognize. I didn't grow up in La Jolla, but that doesn't mean I didn't spend time here. I have friends who grew up here. I've been to countless weddings here. Shopped here and dined here and acted like I was from here.

The closer we get to the coast, lots start to sprawl, houses become estates, and the opulence climbs higher and higher up the Joneses chart.

Boz finally slows enough to turn into a wide drive and pulls to a stop in front of a solid black wall that's manned by an attendant.

Though, from the last twenty-four hours, I imagine he's no attendant. This is an armed guard, he's just not out in the open about it as they were in Mexico. When he approaches our car, he looks as serious as the attack on my first wedding yesterday.

Boz rolls down his window and the attendant drags his eyes from me to my new husband. "I don't know what to say, Boz. No one was closer to him than you. Sorry, man."

Boz lifts his chin. "It's been a day. What's happening at the house?"

When the man rests a hand on his hip, a holster and gun peek out from under his sport coat. "We went on full alert when we got word. No one was allowed in or out. The housekeepers are freaked, but they were told to hold steady until you got back." His gaze wanders to me when he adds, "I hear congratulations are in order."

"Yeah," Boz says with zero emotion. "It's a turn of events."

"I hear you're not just Boz anymore, but boss. You've got my respect."

Wow. From Boz to Brian to boss. I wonder how I should address my new husband?

He doesn't bother introducing me and continues talking to the guard. "I need to get into Damian's office and check on things. After I grab a couple hours of sleep, I'll meet with the team."

"Got it, boss."

The massive wall is really a gate. It slides apart, and even through the dark, what appears in front of us is nothing short of spectacular. A long, lit drive winds its way down a steep hill. Even the filthiest rich of my father's friends weren't as dirty as this.

This is something else.

The modern mansion sprawls on the grounds that sit behind the privacy wall. The estate is only open to its gardens and the Pacific. And the level of security is no secret. Cameras are everywhere.

My stomach sinks. There will be no escaping this place.

This was Damian's home. I guess it would have been my home, too, if his brains weren't blown all over my wedding dress. I should feel bad that I don't at all feel bad about that turn of events.

I can't take it any longer. I turn to my new husband. "You have a lot of names. Boz, Brian, boss ... what should I call you?"

He pulls to a stop in the circle drive in front of the structure made of mostly windows and trimmed in natural wood and stark black paint. It's a one-eighty from Damian's father's home. He barely throws it into gear when he turns to me. "I don't give a fuck what you call me as long as it's not Brian. When we get in there, keep your mouth shut. They expected you to walk in there as Mrs. Marino, not Mrs. Torres."

I frown. "They?"

"The staff. It's going to be an adjustment for everyone, but really, they need to get used to me being in charge. I'll take the lead—keep your mouth shut."

He turns for his car door, but I grab his forearm to stop him. "How many times are you going to tell me to keep my mouth shut?"

He turns back to me and leans over the console. Before I know it, his hand is wrapped around my neck and I'm almost nose to nose with Boz-Brian-boss. "Chica, I'm thinking you don't understand the severity of the situation your father sold you into. Damian Marino is dead. A war is brewing. And you could be married to Nicolas Decker right now instead of sitting here with me. You don't understand what that means, and given the day you've had, I'll spare you the details for another time. But trust me, be grateful for who you're sitting next to. So when I tell you to keep your mouth shut, it's for your own good."

I try to pull away, but he holds tight. "But—"

"No buts, Landyn. You're mine until you're not. Do yourself a favor and obey. You'll understand soon enough. I want to end this fucking day once and for all."

Wow.

So dreamy.

Just what every woman wants her new husband to say on her wedding day.

He lets me go, and I put as much space between us as possible. I'm already out my door, and my bare feet hit the pavement by the time he's rounded the front of the car. He says nothing more, but grabs my hand. I have to fist my dress so I don't trip over it when he pulls me up the many steps to the grand front doors.

I wonder who's watching, because just like at Alamandos' house, the doors open exactly in time for us to enter. Cool air sends a shiver down my spine, and we're greeted by three bodies lining in the entryway.

One man and two women in varying ages and sizes.

And they're all staring at me.

The doors shut behind us, and I stop when Boz does, since my hand is still held tight in his. And there's the fact he yanked me to his side.

Boz greets them in a gruff tone. "Good morning."

The staff looks like they're about to face a firing squad and mutter in unison, "Good morning, sir."

"You've been informed about Mr. Marino?" Boz asks.

"Yes, sir."

Nod.

"Very sorry, sir."

Chin lift.

"Our condolences."

Boz nods. "Thank you. It was shocking, to say the least. My job now is to carry on for Señor Marino. I'll be in charge until we hear otherwise."

More nods.

"This is Mrs. Torres." Boz lets go of my hand and wraps an arm around my back, pulling me to his side. My breath catches when his hand slides down to the small of my back and settles on the swell of my ass. "My bride."

Silence.

Shit.

My hands instantly go clammy.

"You'll make sure she's comfortable and welcomed while she settles in. We will be taking over Mr. Marino's wing. Mrs. Torres' things are already there." Boz pauses to glance down at me before turning back to the staff. "I want my things moved in with hers."

"Yes, Mr. Torres," the older man says.

"A light snack and bottle of champagne to celebrate would be nice," Boz adds.

My stomach almost growls at the mention of a snack. A snack right now is the only thing worth celebrating.

The older and rounder woman nods. "Right away, Mr. Torres."

"We'll meet tomorrow to discuss the future." Boz looks down at me as he gives my ass a squeeze. "Come. I'll show you to our room."

Our room?

Holy shit.

He doesn't glance at the staff again and keeps his arm wrapped around me as he leads me through an enormous great room to a set of stairs. I have to double time it to keep up with him and not trip on my dress as I vaguely wonder if they had my things moved from my parents' home.

When we get to the top of the stairs, he drops his arm and catches my hand once again. We walk silently down a long hallway, passing so many doors, I wonder what in the world can be behind all of them.

At the end of the hall, open double doors await us.

All I can think about is this is the same spot I was fated to end my wedding day, only with another man.

I pull him to a stop. My feet refuse to take another step.

Boz stops and turns to me. "What?"

"I..." I swallow over the lump in my throat. "Maybe I can take another room. You know, until we get to know each other better."

Boz hesitates before looking up and down the hall. Then he lets go of my hand to claim my face like he did right after we both said *I do*.

But he doesn't kiss me.

At least not on the lips.

He tips my head back and drags the tip of his nose up my jaw. His lips touch the skin below my ear. This time it's gentle and warms my cool skin.

But there's nothing warm about his words when his lips move against my ear. "Chica, shut the hell up. I'll tell you when you can talk, and now is not the time. I'm also not letting you out of my sight."

Shit.

He pulls back enough to look into my eyes before his stare drops to my mouth. He drags a thumb across my bottom lip before leading me the final few feet into what is now *our* bedroom.

It's huge and dark. Rich brown mahogany furniture fills the space and sits on a blood-red backdrop.

Fitting. It matches my dress.

I barely get to take in the sitting room to the side that's flanked with floor to ceiling windows that overlook the ocean. It's still dark, but I can see the moonlight bouncing off the whitecaps of the waves. There's no serene beach here, only a rocky shore below the cliff the mansion sits on.

Boz doesn't let me go, dragging me farther into the room to another set of double doors. My bare feet hit black marble, but he doesn't stop. Beyond the vanity and enormous freestanding tub, Boz pulls me around the corner and into a walk-in shower with no door.

"No!" I fight to twist my hand out of his, but he pulls me to his chest and wraps a muscled arm around my waist, holding me tight. I push and jab and struggle, but I'm no match for the man who's now in charge of Damian Marino's business.

He reaches around me and flips on the water. I jerk when an ice-cold stream hits us from the side. Boz fists my now wet hair and tips my head back.

I brace for what's to come.

But he doesn't do anything that I feared. He doesn't kiss me or rip my dress off or hint to the fact our marriage will be consummated right here in the shower.

He pushes me against the wall but leaves enough room for Jesus between us when he lowers his voice. "There are hidden cameras in Damian's bedroom. Don't ask me why, because I won't tell you. Don't act like you know they're there, either. I'm going to have those ripped out as soon as I can. Until then, don't do anything in there you don't want anyone else to see. Do you understand what I'm saying?"

I lick the water from my dry lips. I'm not sure how much more I can take today. Learning that the man I was supposed to marry has cameras in his own bedroom is…

"Cameras?" My chest heaves with shallow breaths. "That's sick."

Boz nods. "Your closet was stocked before the wedding. Find what you need and dress in there. There aren't cameras in the bathroom, but you do need to watch what you say. Watch what you say everywhere in the house. And until shit calms down after what happened at the church, stick close to me."

"But—"

He takes a step back and yanks both wet T-shirts over his head. They land on the tile floor with a heavy splat. His suit pants cling to him like a second skin. But from the waist up, he's bare and …

Holy shit.

Beautiful. More so half-naked.

His shoulders are wide and muscled, strong enough to carry the weight of the world. I can't help but stare at his rippled abs that flow down to a narrow waist. He has that deep indentation of the V that is rarely seen in real life. I assume it's normally photoshopped on models to enhance what's difficult to achieve in the gym.

Boz standing before me is proof it's possible.

But low on his abs to the side of his V, is a pink, puckered scar.

"Get his fucking blood off you and get dressed. You look like shit. Then get some sleep. Trust me, you'll need to be on top of your game to live here."

And with that, he sloshes off and leaves me alone in the shower. The water is finally hot and steaming up the marble space.

I'm not surprised I need to be on top of my game to live here, but I am surprised Boz confirmed it for me.

And cameras? I can't think about that right now.

Boz is right. I need sleep. There's nothing I want more than to wash the last twenty-four hours off me and forget it ever happened.

I never want to see this damn wedding dress again. If I were able to light it into an inferno just like the Marino family has done to my life, I would.

6

WHACKED

Brax

For the first time since I worked my way into the Marino family, I'm able to sit at Damian's desk and do it knowing I'm supposed to be here. I don't have to manipulate the cameras to steal minutes here and there. I don't have to sneak in on the rare occasion he left the house and didn't demand that I drive him. And I don't have to worry about making an excuse if someone walks in.

I'm here. I can work freely. And I'm not leaving until I have what I need.

My *wife* is asleep in Damian's bedroom. She barely said two words to me when she came out of the bathroom fully dressed in sweats and a tee with wet hair. Not that I was worried about her stripping down in front of me—she doesn't want to be here anymore than I want her here—but I sure as hell don't need the guys manning the security cameras jacking off to the sight of her.

Who am I kidding, she wouldn't have to strip down for them to do that. That's why I'm going to trash the cameras the minute she wakes.

She downed a bottle of water and stuffed her face from the platter of food that June delivered while she was in the shower. By the time I got cleaned up and came back, she was passed out on the sofa in Damian's bedroom.

I ignored the cameras, left her there, and took the bed. I was too fucking tired to worry about anyone watching me sleep.

I'm used to people watching me at this point.

They're always watching. It's their job.

What they don't know is, I'm watching them right back.

When Landyn wakes, not only are the cameras going, but so are the bugs I planted last year. Damian was a sick fuck. He enjoyed watching what he did in that room, whether it was consensual or not.

And often, it was not.

He didn't give a shit who saw it. In fact, he got off on that too. It was his chance to prove to everyone around him he was powerful enough to do what he wanted.

And he did a lot.

But not anymore.

I look up when there's a knock at the door. "Come in."

The double doors from the upstairs hall open. "Hey, Boz—I mean boss. Sorry. Habit."

I need to play the part. With that comes acting as powerful as everyone around here expects. If I have to be an asshole doing it, so be it. But I also need certain people to trust me.

And this kid is one of them. Plus, I like him. It pisses me off he's here. He's too young and has too much potential.

I shake my head at the eighteen-year-old biker wannabe. "My position might've changed, Ricky, but when we're alone, you can still call me Boz."

"Thanks, man. You called for me?" The tension rolls off his shoulders as he exhales. Everyone is used to Damian's volatility. No one knew when he'd go off or what it would be about, and this kid has heard the tales. Ricky Monroe has only been working at the house for a few weeks. It was my idea to bring him in as a direct line of communication to the Jackals.

"Sit."

Ricky closes the door and moves to a leather chair. His boss, Logan Pritchett, has been a member of The Violet Jackals for years, working his way to the top. Logan recruited Ricky into the club recently. Dennis Alba isn't the only organized crime group who wants a piece of the Marino pie. Contracting with outside organizations allowed Damian to keep his hands clean. He spread his work far and wide to make sure all his stones were spread thin. The fact that so many crime rings are tied to Damian, makes this case one of a kind. Not only will I get the revenge I want, I'll take down organizations like the Albas and the Jackals too. They'll drop like dominos, one after the other.

I'm banking on the fact each one will do what they can to rat out the other when the time comes.

I'm not there yet. But having complete access to Damian's business, I'm a hell of a lot closer than I was yesterday.

"Heard you married Mr. Marino's fiancée," Ricky says, as he pushes a lock of his dirty blond hair from his forehead.

I minimize the spreadsheets I was studying and lean back in my chair. "I did."

He hikes a brow and I can't tell if he's shocked or impressed, but his answer says it all. "Badass. Even if it is kind of whacked."

I tip my head to one side and glance around the office. "Señor Marino knows I'm his best bet at running the business right now. No one was closer to Damian than I was. It's my way to honor him."

"Still, it's whacked."

My lips tip up on one side. I can't argue with that. "I didn't ask you to come in here to talk about my current life changes. I asked you here because you're getting a new assignment."

"Did I do something wrong?" Every muscle in his body goes taut as his knuckles whiten when they fist the arms of his chair. I guess I need to get used to that. "I can fix it. Swear, boss. I need to prove to Logan and the Jackals I can handle this—"

I put a hand up. "Chill out. I said you had a new assignment, not that you were fired."

He barely relaxes. "What do I have to do? I don't mind running back and forth between here and the club. It's what they sent me here for."

"Don't worry about the club. They sent you here to work, they don't get to dictate what you do for the family. You're done cleaning pools and mowing the yard. From now on, you work for me."

He frowns. "For you?"

"I need an assistant, and I want someone who has a direct line of communication to the Jackals. If you work directly for me and happen to pass Logan on the street and say hello, we all win. I'm working from Damian's playbook—keep my hands clean at all costs."

"But not get dead," he adds.

"I do not plan to get dead."

He pulls his sleeve up and glances at the unfinished tattoo on the inside of his forearm. It's the mark of their club, but only half of it. Half of a skull that's fading off into the night. The mark is only a month old. He's a prospect and a high school dropout despite being one of the top wide receivers in southern California.

I had Carson pull his background. His mom is dead, and his father is in prison. The kid bounced around in foster care and is now on his own.

I know more about every person who comes into contact with the Marino family better than they know themselves. Ricky should be finishing his senior year and picking from a slew of scholarship offers. Instead, he was recruited to this path—a head dive straight to hell.

At initiation, he'll get the rest of the tat. Initiation is no joke.

And it pisses me off that the kid sitting across from me is about to fall down that dark hole. He'll never claw his way out.

"I'm not sure what the Jackals will think," Ricky mutters.

"You don't need to be sure. It's done." Ricky's gaze jumps to me through narrowed eyes. I go on. "Consider it an order. This is your assignment."

A muscle jumps in his cheek.

"It could be worse. Much worse," I go on before he has the chance to argue. "Get with Spencer and tell him your sizes. He'll make sure you're presentable. I have business meetings you'll attend. We'll both get kicked out if you look like that."

He glares at me. "I don't want to wear a fucking tie."

"You'll wear a tie if I have to wear one." I glare back because I need him to realize he can't fuck around. "And pack a bag. You're moving into the house."

His light-brown eyes widen, and his eyes dart around the room. "I'm moving in? Here?"

I'm about to turn back to the computer and send him on his way, when one of the French doors to the bedroom opens. Ricky and I forget each other and look across the room.

Her messy blond-haired head peaks through the cracked door before she pushes it far enough to step inside Damian's office. She wraps her arms around her middle, and if I'm not mistaken, she's not wearing a bra. She's rumpled, messy, and looks like she just slept for a decade.

She might be hotter this way than she was walking down the aisle. I can't take my eyes off her. "You're up."

She looks around the office and hugs herself tighter when she looks from Ricky to me. "The, uh, bedroom door is locked. Why is that?"

I don't answer and motion to my new assistant who'd better clean up and play the part. "This is Ricky, my new assistant. Ricky, my wife, Mrs. Torres."

"Rocco," Ricky amends and clears his throat. He sits up straight in his chair as he takes in my wife. "You can call me Rocco. It's my given name."

She lifts a slim shoulder. "You can call me Landyn."

"He'll call you Mrs. Torres." I swivel my chair forty-five degrees so I can get a better look at her. Without tearing my eyes away, I give Rocco one last order. "Go find Spencer about your new wardrobe and think about a haircut. You'll start this week after the funeral. We'll talk later. I want time with my wife."

My new assistant stands and moves toward the door. He

doesn't want to be here anymore than the rest of us. "Yeah, got it. Ah, see you around."

Landyn watches him leave, and when the door shuts behind him, her eyes snap back to me. They're alert, and her tone proves how irritated she is. "Why am I locked inside the bedroom?"

I lift my hand to motion around us. "You're hardly locked in the bedroom. You came in here freely, didn't you?"

"You know what I mean," she snaps.

I ignore that too. "How did you sleep?"

She pulls in a big breath. "I have no idea what time it is, so okay, I guess."

"Since it's late afternoon, I guess you did."

"You didn't answer me," she presses.

I'm not about to tell her she won't be far from me as long as we're in this fucking house together. "We have things we need to discuss. I told June we would eat dinner downstairs tonight. You need to be ready in an hour."

Her eyes narrow. "I'm not hungry."

I stand and make my way across the office until I'm almost toe to toe with my wife who needs to learn to act like it for both our sakes while we're in this house. I take her hand and hold tight—despite the fact she does everything she can to pull hers from mine. I drag her through the bedroom and straight to the bathroom. I slam the doors and turn to her. "Dinner isn't an option. Damian's funeral is in the works, and we're hosting a couple members of the family who live in the States. You need to be there, and you need to be a grieving yet blissful new bride."

Her blue eyes aren't only fully alert, they're horrified. "You want me to grieve the man who bought me while chipper to have been forced into marrying ... you?"

I stuff my hands in my pockets as I take her in. "That's exactly what I want. And failing isn't an option. You can throw your attitude when it's the two of us, but if you think about doing it in front of family, we're going to have issues. And just when you think you might know what those issues might be, I promise, you're wrong. Dead fucking wrong."

She mulls this over for two seconds, but her only comeback is lame. "You're crazy."

Most days, she'd be right.

But especially today.

"Seeing as how we skipped the courtship, I have no clue how long it takes you to get ready. While you do that, I'll rip the cameras out of the bedroom. I can't sleep more than one night knowing they're watching me."

I step to the side to move around her, but she catches my wrist. I turn back and raise a brow in question. "You slept in the room with me?"

"We're married. Where else would I sleep?" She crosses her arms and looks like she's trying to kill me with a glare that's about as menacing as a puppy. My mind is on getting those damn cameras out of the bedroom, when I turn back. "One more thing."

She drops her arms and exclaims, "As if I haven't done enough."

"Wear black."

She rolls her eyes. "A blissful bride in black. That's the first logical thing anyone has said since this whole nightmare started."

Touché, my new wife.

Tou-fucking-ché.

Then I do what I've been itching to do since we got back—rip these fucking cameras down. If I could rip every memory of Damian from this place, I would. I told the guards it would happen today. Once I get them down, I can remove the listening devices I planted months ago that go straight to DEA headquarters and the CIA.

I'm aching for a tiny bit of privacy. This bedroom will be it.

7

DISRESPECT

Landyn

I wonder if Damian Marino imagined I'd be wearing the black dress he ordered his personal shoppers to buy for me to mourn his own death?

It's actually stunning, and I know it's not off the rack. This little black number is couture. And since I've hardly eaten in the last day, it fits like a glove.

I've never felt better about myself while planning a funeral.

Okay, fine. I've never planned a funeral before today. I can't imagine many twenty-three-year-olds think about funerals. I've been to a couple but never planned one.

And it's not like Damian made a good impression for the few moments we spent together at the church. He was intimidating and mean and downright violent.

And he needed to brush his teeth.

So sitting in Damian's ostentatious house, eating a glamorous meal his cook prepared, and drinking his expensive wine while listening to details about how the world will say its final *fuck you* to the man who choked me in a church, I'm shocked at my new level of chill.

Maybe it has something to do with my new husband. Besides our wedding kiss and pushing me into the shower to tell me about how my dead fiancé was into voyeurism, he hasn't touched me the way a wife would expect a husband to touch her.

But, really, I think it's just the wine.

"More wine, Mrs. Torres?" Spencer asks. Besides keeping my glass full, I'm not sure what Spencer's official role is. He answered the door for our guests, served the salad and dessert but not the main course, and has played bartender to our weird foursome. The table can seat sixteen, but since there are only four of us, we're in the center. Boz is at my side and an older couple sits across from us.

My smile is probably too big for the topic of death, but when your wedding is shot up, your fiancé is murdered, you're kidnapped, and then end up marrying another man all within twenty-four hours, you just don't care. "Keep it coming, Spencer. Thank you."

"No." My dear, broody-hot husband snatches the crystal from my hand. "She's had enough."

I frown. I'm sure it's the fermented grapes, but I'm feeling fine and brave. "You know, *Brian*, some of us deal with death differently. And, kidnapping, for that matter. I want another glass of wine."

Boz's dark glare doesn't move from me when he hands over the glass to the man I thought was my only friend here. "My wife has had enough. You can leave us to talk, Spencer. Thank you."

"Sir." Spencer gives Boz a teensy bow and runs away with my wine.

Damn you, Spencer.

I start to roll my eyes, but Boz's hand catches my chin and forces me to look at him. He hikes a brow as his thumb drags its way across my bottom lip. "We'll talk about that later, baby. You can have all the wine you want in our bed, but not now."

I gape at him. He hasn't looked at me this way since our

nuptials. He's not irritated like he usually is. He looks like he wants to devour me.

Like make-our-consumption-one-for-the-record-books devour me.

Shit. I really need to keep my mouth shut like he told me to.

"She's a fucking disgrace. Damian would never have allowed that. And Nic wouldn't have it either. You have no business being in this house, running Damian's business, or being the one who got her."

I jerk my chin from Boz's hand and gape across the table at the man who hasn't spoken two words to me since he walked through the door, but he doesn't need to. I can tell he's about as happy with me as he is to be planning his nephew's funeral.

Ed and Eliza Decker are Damian's aunt and uncle. Two minutes before the doorbell chimed, Boz told me they were tasked with planning the funeral. They live in Santa Barbara, and Eliza is Alamandos' much younger sister. I have no idea if they have anything to do with the Marino business, but I did find out during the main course that their son is Nic—the angry one who was dragged away because he wanted to marry me.

That little tidbit causes the salmon to turn in my stomach, no matter how delicious it was.

But I'm thrown for another loop when Boz wraps a hand around the bottom of my dining chair and yanks it so I'm pressed to his side. His arm circles my shoulders right before he leans in to press his warm lips to my temple. He holds me tight to him when he settles back into his chair. "I'm not Damian or Nic, and I can handle my wife just fine, Edward. I answer to Alamandos, not you. You're here because he can't come across the border, and he wanted his sister's input in the funeral. Landyn is mine now. You'll never talk about my wife that way again."

"She's nothing but a pawn." Ed turns red in the face and does not heed my husband's warning as he turns to me. "They say it was the Lazadas who attacked the church, but no one knows for sure. Your father should've been taken down instead of Damian.

He started this shit show. The rest of us are left to pick up the pieces and deal with you."

Boz's glare across the table turns ominous. "You've been warned, Decker. I won't say it again. You disrespect my wife, you disrespect me. You got your directions from Alamandos, and your son is lucky to still be around. I'm in charge, and you fucking know it."

Ed has been on edge all night, but the mention of his son makes him look like his head might explode. Eliza looks like she wants to crawl under the table in case bullets start flying again.

Ed turns his attention to Boz. "You're too young—hell, you're not even a Marino. Alamandos' an idiot, and so was Damian. You took one bullet for him, and they think you're the Second fucking Coming."

"That's exactly what I was. It's the reason I'm sitting here instead of your son or a Marino," Boz replies. He's calm and cool compared to Ed. Cocky even. I have no idea what this *taking a bullet* is about, but the man protecting me just agreed to being compared to the Second Coming and owned it like a badass.

Yikes.

Big dick energy to the power of Jesus.

It doesn't get any bigger than that.

With the back and forth between the men at the table and through my tipsy state, all of a sudden, I can't take my eyes off Eliza.

I didn't see it before.

Until now, the talk has been about Damian. Between the brewing war between the Marinos and Lazadas, and the wedding fiasco, the Marino family is afraid to congregate again so soon. It's been decided that the funeral will be in San Diego. Damian was, after all, a prominent businessman here.

Albeit an asshole, but he's known to most of the world who doesn't play in the dark shadows as a successful man who broke away from his father's drug dealings. No one has been able to prove otherwise. My father talked about it all the time.

He was even jealous of how Damian managed to do it.

But Eliza Decker hasn't said a word other than when we were introduced or to thank our servers. She's not just submissive. This is different.

She's downright fearful.

I shouldn't care about Eliza Decker. It's the wine. I know it is. I have enough on my plate to worry about her, but right now I do.

I can't help but wonder if this is my future. I have a feeling it would have been had Damian lived, and I don't know Boz at all. He could go off half-cocked at a moment's notice.

I look into her sad brown eyes. "Are you okay?"

Boz immediately pulls me tighter to his side.

Ed tenses, and Eliza's eyes flare as she whispers, "What?"

Ed does not whisper. He growls. "She's fine."

I don't take my eyes off Eliza. "You haven't looked fine all night."

Eliza gives her head small, quick shakes. "No, I'm fine—"

"Is her pussy that sweet that you're afraid to control your own wife? If you want to do this job, be a fucking man, Boz," Ed thunders.

Boz doesn't try to shut me up or control me. He gives me the tiniest hope that, if this is the life I'm stuck in, I lucked out with a husband who is nothing like Damian or the man sitting across the table from us who won't allow his wife to speak.

My husband shifts in his seat, but never lets me go when he produces a handgun from inside his sport coat.

Eliza gasps when it hits the table. I tense, but Boz's arm constricts around me even more, gluing my back into the crook of his arm and chest.

Boz palms the gun nonchalantly, but there's nothing casual about his index finger that flirts with the trigger.

And the barrel is pointed across the table straight at Ed.

Ed tries to move quickly, but he's older, rounder, and not at all spry.

I wonder if he ever was.

The butt of his own weapon stuffed inside his jacket peeks out, but before he can draw to match Boz, three men enter the room in a rush—two from the kitchen and one from the entryway.

All with guns.

And all are drawn on Ed.

"What's the meaning of this?" Ed balks.

Boz's tone is low and deep. I feel every word rumble through my body. "Say one more fucking thing about my wife, I'll take you out into the Pacific myself, but only one of us will return. I gave you a warning, and you still ran your mouth. Try me again and you're dead. I don't want to know what goes down in your bedroom, so stay the hell out of mine. While I'm running the family business in the U.S., Landyn is the queen of this house, and you'll fucking treat her like one."

I don't dare move. My heart races as I take in the older couple across from us. Eliza is trembling, and I'm worried Ed might suffer an aneurysm right here in the dining room given the protruding vein on his forehead.

The room is silent other than the rhythmic gong in my chest.

Boz never takes his eyes off Ed. "What do you say?"

Ed says nothing. His frown deepens.

"You just talked about my wife's pussy as if she's not sitting here next to me. That's on top of your lack of respect for me since she's mine." Boz picks up his gun and trains it across the table over our dirty dessert plates. "For the final time, what do you say to my queen for disrespecting her?"

Eliza whimpers. A tear falls to her lap, but she never looks up.

"I..." Ed croaks as his beady eyes shift between Boz's gun and me.

Boz's finger hovers over the trigger. "You know I'll do it."

Ed looks like he's in physical pain. "I-I'm sorry for disrespecting you."

Boz doesn't lower his gun nor does he miss a beat. "The funeral will be small—invitation only. I'll take care of security and make arrangements for Damian's body to be taken back to Tijuana to be buried with his family. If you even think of glancing in my wife's general vicinity again, you'll pay. Feel free to spread the word. You'll grant her every ounce of respect I expect you to give me. I'm not Damian or your fucking son—I don't share, and I don't fuck around with what's mine. Got it?"

"Got it," Ed says, but it comes out on a grunt.

Boz continues to stare at Ed through the sight of his gun. "Get the fuck out of my house."

Ed proves he can move faster than I gave him credit for. He might not look at me, but he does stand so abruptly, his chair crashes to the floor behind him, echoing harshly through the silent space. He grabs Eliza by her upper arm and yanks her to her feet. I lean into Boz and have to look the other way when she cries out in pain as he drags her out of the house while muttering curse words under his breath.

The door rumbles through the big house when it's slammed. The guards lower their guns as I try to even my breaths. Whatever buzz I was enjoying through dinner burned off in a snap.

Boz's gun hits the table with a thud, but he doesn't let me go. "Leave us."

I wonder how those men knew to come in when they did. It has to be the cameras Boz told me about. They're watching us all the time.

"Landyn."

I jerk against his chest when he calls for me, but I say nothing.

"Chica." He's called me that before, but this time it feels softer, more familiar.

Or so I thought. But then he takes familiarity to a new level.

He snakes his hand up my middle and between my breasts without ever touching them. Up my chest and neck, finally landing on my chin, where he forces me to tip my face to his.

His beautiful dark eyes bore into mine. "You okay?"

I shake my head immediately and realize I'm trembling. "That was my fault. What she's going through right now ... it's my fault. I didn't know that would happen—I swear."

His voice is even and controlled. "You didn't turn him into a wife beater. The way she was acting, I'm sure he's always been that way. He was an asshole before he got here, and he'll be one long after today. That's not on you."

I shake my head and tears fall down my cheeks. "No, but I made it worse for her. And you had to do the whole gun thing and magically bring others in to back you up. I'm not used to this. I'm sorry."

"I'm not. He knows not to fuck with you, and his son had better not fuck with you either. Word will get out. If it doesn't, I'll spread it myself. I need you to trust that I'll take care of you."

I nod. Until now, he's given me no reason not to trust him. I've also seen the horrible paths I've avoided, some thanks to him.

We haven't budged. His arm is still bent up my body between my breasts, his big hand slides down and wraps around my neck. After what just happened, there's something comforting about sitting here in his arms after he stood up for me.

"Boz?"

His voice is low and close to my ear. "Yeah?"

I turn my head a fraction to look up at him. "Can I ask you something?"

His hand around my neck tightens a touch. I expect him to say no, change the subject, or ignore me altogether.

Instead, he tips my head to the side and a shiver runs down my spine when he drags his tongue up the side of my neck. My eyes fall shut, and I let out a little moan when his taste turns into a suck right below my ear.

The wine.

The fear.

And now this...

My body can't take the mood swings.

My panties go instantly wet.

This cannot be happening. I didn't even want to get married. What is he doing to me?

He trails kisses across my jaw until his lips land on my ear. There, he whispers, "No. You cannot ask me questions here or anywhere else in the house. Later, in our bedroom. I ripped out the cameras today."

Shit.

I was right. They are watching. I need to get used to that.

I exhale and try to catch my breath.

"And chica?"

"Yeah?" I squeak.

He forces me to look up at him. This time he's not warm or comforting. His words are firm and come out as a warning. "Don't ever call me Brian again."

Shit.

My teeth sink into my lip.

I nod.

Note to self: do not be a smartass with my new husband.

8

BEAUTY QUEEN

Landyn

I roll over on the sofa I've slept on two days in a row. The king-sized bed is messy and unmade, but my new husband is nowhere in sight.

After Boz put his lips and tongue on me and warned me never to call him Brian, he took me by the hand and led me to our bedroom.

I followed on shaky knees. My nerves were frazzled from the rollercoaster I'd been riding for days. When Boz locked us in our room, he told me to take the bathroom first. After I changed and washed my face, he was nowhere to be found.

I was so tired, I grabbed a pillow and blanket and claimed the sofa again. There's not room on it for both of us. If he wants anything more from me, he'll have to physically drag me to the bed.

But, for the second night in a row, he didn't. He didn't touch me. And it wasn't because there were people watching. The cameras are gone.

Thank goodness for that.

I pull on a robe on my way to the bathroom, when I hear voices. One of the double doors to the connecting office is cracked. I move that way to peek through.

Boz is sitting behind the desk again, glaring at whoever is talking to him.

Or, talking at him.

He's in his usual dress of business casual, sans the sport coat. His steel-blue dress shirt fits him to a T, and the top two buttons are loose. It's paired with crisp trousers the color of a stormy night. If I didn't know he was running the North American side of a drug cartel and that he threatens dinner guests with a drawn gun, I'd think he stepped off the cover of GQ.

And then there's the fresh scar that's hidden beneath his expensive dress clothes. I really want to know what that's about.

His dark eyes flit to me. He holds a finger up to silence the angry voice that's escalating by the second as he takes me in slowly from head to toe. He glances across the desk and back to me. "Come here."

A demand.

I glance down at myself before shaking my head.

He swivels in his chair and widens his legs as he holds out a hand. "Baby. Come here."

The air whooshes from my lungs. It's the second time he's used that term of affection.

Yes, I'm keeping track.

Aside from *chica*, which rarely feels affectionate, my name has been bitten out in irritation, but that's it.

I pull my robe tighter around me and step into his office.

But I stop in my tracks when the man on the other side of the desk comes into view.

Holy shit. It's Nic.

Nic from our wedding.

Or should I say, Nic, the man who was dragged from our wedding because he threw a fit he wasn't the one marrying me.

Nic Decker looks like he could be the same age as Boz. But unlike my husband who is scary in the way he's willing to pull a gun at dinner because someone was crass about his new wife, Nic is menacing in a whole other way.

His lecherous eyes make me feel more exposed than I already am. I'm wearing a matching silk shorts and cami set beneath the thin robe. My arms tighten around my chest as I shuffle back a step toward our bedroom.

Nic's head tips an inch, and I don't miss his hand balling into a tight fist on the arm of his chair.

"Landyn."

My gaze darts to my husband.

"Come."

All of a sudden, I want nothing more than to be close to Boz with this guy around. I don't hesitate and move across the large room on bare feet to him. When my hand finds his, he pulls me between his open thighs.

But he doesn't stop there.

He pulls me to him until my ass is perched on his thick thigh. One arm rounds me as the other clamps down on the outside of my thigh.

My eyes widen, and my hands come to his chest when he gives me a good yank.

I'm pressed to him.

Everywhere.

From the bulge between his legs to his hand that slides down to my ass, finding a home there where he cups me and holds me tight.

His warm eyes roam my features before they settle back on mine. "How did you sleep?"

Even after clearing my throat, my words come out strangled. "Fine. Good. I mean ... I slept."

We're face to face, our noses a breath from one another. So he doesn't have to move far to brush the end of mine with his before his lips land on my jaw.

My eyes fall shut when he pulls me tighter, and the bulge between his legs thickens against my thigh.

Holy shit.

Breathe, Landyn.

When he gives my ass a good squeeze, I open my eyes to his lustful expression focused on me. "I didn't want to leave you, but I had this meeting. I'll have June bring us some breakfast. Then we can shower."

"Oh." The tips of my fingers press into his chest, and all I can think about is being back in the shower with Boz, but I'm sure he's not planning for us to be fully clothed again. Not if his cock has anything to say about it. Consummating our marriage has to be on his mind. "Um—"

"I see you're settling into my cousin's house a little too much, aren't you? Running his business. Ordering his staff around. Fucking his wife."

Boz doesn't let go of me when he swivels back to face Nic, but his words surprise me. "The only wife I'm fucking is mine. If you didn't get the message from your father after last night, I'll warn you only once—don't talk about her. You might've wanted her, but she's mine. No one disrespects what's mine."

All thoughts of Boz lying about fucking his wife and our impending shower escape my brain when Nic bites, "She was never meant to be your wife. You're an imposter, not a Marino. Alamandos' a fool who's proven to have lost his mind when he gave her to you. Why Damian put so much trust in you, I'll never know."

Since I'm wrapped up in Boz, it's easy to feel his energy. It's controlled yet hyper aware, all at the same time. "I took your meeting request this morning out of respect for Damian. But if you act like you did the other night, I won't let you into this compound again. I'm not the one who's fucked up time after time. You're not good for business, Nic. Don't blame me for your shitty venture that lost Marino revenue. Shit isn't easily forgotten when it's attached to money, especially when you're in the red instead of black. You think you can fuck up like that and expect Alamandos to hand over a jewel like *her*?"

At the mention of *me*, Boz slides his hand inside my robe, high on the bare skin of my thigh. He's flirting with my ass encased in silk so luxurious, I've never slept so good on a sofa. Not even the night before when I was exhausted.

I don't want to be here, but I really don't want to be *here*—anywhere near Nic, or the business Boz is carrying out for the Marino family. This might be an extension of the life I grew up in, but that doesn't mean I have to be a part of it. At least my father pretended to run a legitimate business for the sake of our family. And he certainly never wielded a gun at a dinner party.

Marrying into the Marino family—whether my husband is a true Marino or not—is nothing like the life I led just a short drive down the coast in San Diego.

I give Boz's dress shirt a little tug and try to move out of his arms. "I'll just go get dressed and let you finish your business."

"Yeah, do that," Nic seethes. "You haven't earned the right to know shit about my family."

Boz doesn't let me go, and his glare never wavers from Nic. "Landyn will be anywhere I am. If I want her in my lap while I fix your incompetence, that's where she'll be."

"We've been over this. It wasn't my fault," Nic grits.

Boz's hand lets go of my ass, and the tips of his fingers draw circles on the small of my back, turning his attention to me. "See, baby, Nic was trying to make a move on Damian by going over his head to pitch an idea to Alamandos about taking control of shipments from the border. He begged and begged until Alamandos finally gave him a shot. Right after your dad's truck was taken down, Nic got his chance. His delivery went through, but the load was light when it arrived."

I have no idea why he's telling me this. I don't want to know the ins and outs of the drug business, let alone transporting loads across the border.

"I didn't fucking skim," Nic growls.

My eyes shoot to the man across the table. It looks like he's doing everything in his power not to fly across the desk and tackle Boz.

"Someone did," Boz states. "And since it was your load, it falls on you. Which is why I'm sitting here and you're not."

My ass is all of a sudden encased in Boz's big hand once again. I have a feeling he's not just talking about a job.

Nic doesn't miss the move either, and his knuckles turn the color of powdered cocaine.

"Fuck you, Torres," Nic growls before dragging his gaze up and down the length of my body. "And your new piece of ass. I don't know how you managed to snow the entire Marino organization, but I'm going to make sure Alamandos kicks you out if it's the last thing I do."

A treacherous smirk tugs at Boz's lips. "I'd like to see that since you're not even capable of a simple delivery. If you came here for another chance, you're not getting it from me."

"I was a horse holder for Damian before you pushed your way in. I want back in the fold. Fuck, I deserve the seat you're sitting in. The one you stole from me."

Boz contemplates the man across the desk as the air in the room goes stale from the visual standoff. I have no idea what a horse holder does, but I hope Boz's answer is a big fat no. I have no desire for Nic to be lurking around the house I now live in.

Nic is about to open his mouth, but Boz stops him. "You want to work for Alamandos, that's up to him. I don't need you here."

"But—"

"It's done, Nic. Take it up with Alamandos. I'm sure he has a safehouse you can pretend to guard." Boz keeps poking at him. "Maybe a nightclub if you're lucky. Traumatizing women is your favorite pastime, after all."

Nic's expression turns to stone, but it doesn't faze Boz. He lets go of my thigh, picks up the phone and speaks into it. "Nic is done. And when I say done, I mean don't let him back in after you show him out. Tell June that Landyn and I are ready for breakfast."

The next thing I know, two men in suits enter the office from the hall.

But Nic doesn't move.

Neither does Boz.

Just when I think we're going to have a repeat of dinner last night with guns flying, Nic juts to his feet. But he doesn't leave before delivering my husband one last warning as he points at us from across the desk. "You might've fooled Damian and my uncle, but not me. Watch your back, Torres. I've got eyes on you. The first misstep you take, I'll ruin you in a way that'll make you an example to anyone else who tries to dig their way into our family."

"I might not have Marino blood running in my veins, but at least I'm not an incapable asshat and a thief." Boz nods to the men at the door. "Show him out—for the last time."

Nic shrugs off one of the guards and storms out of the room. The last guard shuts the door, but not before Nic yells at them one last time to keep their hands off him.

Boz's hand slides from my ass to my waist. I feel him exhale as he drags a hand down his face.

I should move off his lap, but I can't. My palms are clammy, and my heart is racing.

I clinch the silk robe at my breasts and hold it tight. "Is your business always this intense? I mean, at least there weren't any guns today, I guess."

Boz turns to me, and the only thing I see is his chiseled jaw, full lips, and impossibly dark eyes. "Nic is a fuckwad, and everyone here knows it. He was patted down before he was allowed in the house, not that I trust him even without a gun. I wasn't worried. He and his father are trying to make a play on Alamandos now that Damian is out of the picture. They need me out of the way."

I lick my dry lips and swallow over the lump in my throat. "But Alamandos trusts you?"

"Damian trusted me, and Alamandos knows it. He also knows I'm capable of handling things here." Boz puts his hands to my waist and sets me on my feet. "June will be up soon with coffee and breakfast. I need to make a phone call, then I'll join you. We need to talk."

Talk.

I wonder if talk is cartel code for getting naked. I don't know how much longer he'll let me avoid consummating our marriage.

A chill runs down my spine, and I have to hug myself again to cover my nipples from poking through the thin layers of silk.

"I'm not hungry," I lie. I'm starving. The wine last night burned a hole in my stomach. I need coffee and food in the worst way.

Boz turns to his computer and mutters, "Then you can sit and listen. Give me five minutes. Shut the door behind you."

His words are cold, and his order is clear. I don't have to be told twice. I turn on my bare foot and move to the double doors that lead to our bedroom with my messy hair flowing behind me.

I don't give a shit if talk does mean get naked.

I'm not talking, getting naked, or listening.

If my groom wants me, he's going to have to damn well bust through the bathroom doors to get to me. I don't care how hot Boz is or how my body reacts to him, I'm not showering with anyone.

I might not be able to hold him off forever, but it's not happening today.

I ignore the knock on our bedroom door that's no doubt June. If dinner last night is any indication of how good breakfast will be, it's not easy to ignore.

I move across the room before Boz wants to join me for any type of talking—literal or metaphorical. He might like to boss me around in front of other people, but not when it's the two of us.

He can kiss my ass.

Brax

Fuck me.

Rhetorically, that is.

I adjust my rock-hard cock that's unhappy and trapped in my trousers. I lean my head back on the leather chair and try to think of anything but my fake wife, who I have no business thinking about in any way other than keeping both of us alive to see the other side of this operation.

It's been a long time since I've had a woman in my arms. Let alone a barely dressed one pressed against my dick.

It's like he's forgotten what we're here to accomplish and has a literal fucking head of his own.

A head that's hogging all my blood at the moment and wants nothing more than the woman in the next room.

I grip my raging hard on through my pants and try to calm down. I thought Damian was the road block I needed out of the way, but pretending I'm fucking the beauty queen that every man in the Marino cartel wants might be the thing that actually does me in.

Protecting her might be harder than taking down the Marinos. And in this world, protecting her is no joke. She has no clue that her life would have already been a living hell had I not convinced Alamandos to give her to me.

I might be closer to my end goal with Damian out of the way, but dealing with Landyn Alba makes me feel like I'm starting this marathon all over again.

9

SIX FEET UNDER AND CHIPPER AS FUCK

Landyn

I'd like to know who prepared for my arrival.

Not one thing in this house is my own. I haven't seen my cell phone since the day the Marino family took me and my parents from our home. Not my clothes, my makeup, or my hair products. I wonder if I'll see my car again, let alone be allowed to drive myself.

I might've been handed the keys to my Rover by my dear old, human-trafficking-asshole of a father, but I love that car.

I've not only been treated like a flight risk since my world turned to hell, but I'm a prisoner locked in luxury.

This may be romanticized on Netflix or in the most outlandish fictional tale, but in real life, it's beyond disturbing.

I escaped from Boz's office and locked myself in the bathroom. He hasn't broken the door down, so I'm calling that a win for married life.

At least for today.

Small victories and all.

Even though nothing on my side of the bathroom or my closet

are my own, it doesn't mean I hate any of it. Even if I am continually creeped out as to how perfect everything fits.

Down to the bras and panties.

Yes, creepy-as-fuck, top-of-the-line lingerie. It's a shitload of lace and none of it is itchy. After I dropped out of college, I went full time as a personal stylist at Nordstrom. I know quality when I see it.

I try not to think about it as I pull a sundress over my head and turn to look into the full-length mirror. It flows from below my breasts and hits my knees. But it's cut so low, I might as well be wearing a bikini.

I have a feeling my dead fiancé might've made some demands when it came to my new wardrobe.

Whatever. It's not anything I haven't worn before, even though I probably wouldn't pick it for breakfast on any random Tuesday.

I run my fingers through my damp hair and turn on a bare foot. I'm starving and need coffee if I'm going to make it through the next dramatic guest who visits Boz.

I open the door to the bedroom and find him sitting on the sofa that has become my bed. He's leaned back with one expensive loafer hiked on the low table in front of him that's littered with empty plates and others that are still covered. He's holding a cup of coffee in one hand and a cellphone in the other.

His eyes rake over me right before he pulls in a big breath and taps the screen a few more times before tossing it beside him. "That was not fast."

I shrug a shoulder. "I never claimed it would be. I haven't even done my hair or makeup yet. If you want a low-maintenance wife, we should talk about an annulment—I'll happily be on my way."

"I bet you would. And don't speak of an annulment again unless you want to cause a stir in the family." He lifts his mug and motions around the expansive space. "They might not be watching and listening in here anymore, but to everyone around us, you and I are husband and wife in every sense of the word. Got it?"

As if the aroma of coffee draws me in, I move across the room, but stand behind a chair positioned perpendicular to him. "Stir?"

"Nic wanted you. I'm sure he's not the only one, even if he was the only one who had the balls to say so. The first rule I need to make sure you understand is no one can know there's trouble in paradise."

"Paradise." I roll my eyes. "Right."

"Sit and eat, Landyn. I'm sure it's cold."

I don't like obeying his every word, but I'm starving. I choose the chair so we don't have to share the sofa, even if it is my bed. The first plate I uncover is a spinach omelet with cheese and a side of potatoes. I'm not usually a breakfast eater, but I also don't have meals like this delivered to my sofa either. I grab a roll of silverware and throw the napkin over my lap before I dig in.

"Coffee?" he asks.

I nod and speak with my mouth full. "With all the cream and sugar. Load me up."

"Load you up," Boz mutters. I wonder if this is him being sweet as I stuff my mouth while he spoons sugar into my steaming mug.

He sets it on the table in front of me and leans forward to rest his elbows to his knees. "I need to make sure you understand my expectations."

My jaw freezes mid-chew, and I'm caught in his intense stare. My mother would kill me for talking with my mouth full. "Expectations?"

"Yeah, about us."

I'm finally able to swallow. "What about us?"

He pulls in a deep breath.

I hold mine.

"This room is the only place we can be ourselves."

My fork falls to the plate with a clank. "You're going to have to expand on that, Boz."

He stares at me for a long moment before leaning closer and lowers his voice. "Outside of this suite, we're being watched. Every corner of this house is under surveillance twenty-four-seven."

I fist the material of my dress. "You, ah, hinted at that last night."

"Consider it more than a hint. The way you act and what you say outside of this room is your lifeline, Landyn. Don't trust anyone but me. Don't go anywhere with anyone if I'm not with you. And when we're out there," he lowers his voice another octave and tips his head to our bedroom doors, "you'd better act like you're so fucking into me, you can't see straight. It's the one thing that will keep you safe."

Just when I think I've gained some footing with him, he whips the rug out from under me all over again. My heart pounds in my chest. I can't help but raise my voice in desperation. "I thought marrying a Marino would keep my family safe—all of us. That's what my dad said."

His words aren't careful or measured. They're as blunt as an old rusty knife. "Your father made that agreement with Alamandos to save his ass. Alamandos was pissed about the load being taken down, but he never threatened you or your mom. I was in the room, Landyn. Your fucking father was quick to take the deal and hand you over as payment."

I feel like I've just been hit in the chest by a linebacker and am forced to lean back into my chair. The last week has been a tsunami. I've been going through the motions, pushing forward—moment by moment—doing everything I could to emotionally make it to the next day.

To stay alive and save both my father and my mother.

But when it comes down to it, I wasn't given a choice.

Learning that I'm only here so my father could save his own ass with no regard for me is...

I swallow over the lump in my throat.

This is more heart-crushing than anything I've had to deal with yet. And it's been a long week.

"I want to leave." The words spill from my lips for the first time. "Do what you want to my father. I'm not a part of his business. If he messed up, make him pay. But, please, let me go."

Boz drags a hand down his face before shaking his head at my plea. "That can't happen. Not now. The deal is done."

"But—"

Desperation bubbles under my skin when he interrupts. Boz scoots down the sofa closer to me, bleeding intensity. "Don't do that, Landyn. You're in this now, and if you try to go back, they'll come for you. It will not be pretty if that happens. Instead of begging me to let you go, you should be dropping to your knees grateful that you're my wife and no one else's. You might be living and breathing luxury in this house, but you're not free. You're nothing more than a possession."

Possession.

Holy shit.

"And now you're mine," he adds.

"I don't want to be anyone's," I utter in a broken voice.

"But you are. The sooner you deal with your reality, the better. And trust me, chica, being mine is like winning the fucking lottery."

My spine immediately straightens as I jut up in my seat to lean forward. "My father sold me to save his soul. My wedding was a bloodbath. I'm married to a stranger. I hardly feel like a winner, Boz. And for you to demand for me to act like I'm into you on top of all this," I throw my hand out motioning to my new environment which is nothing more than hell on earth when what I really want to do is slap him across the face, "is absurd."

Boz pinches the bridge of his nose before leveling his eyes back on me and delivers his words with a punch. "Are you going to cooperate or not? Because if the answer is no, I need to know what I'm dealing with. And if you feel like a prisoner now, then your reality is about to take a turn to a darker side than you're already living. The last thing I need is to worry about you running away. Alamandos' men will deal with you, and they won't sit you down over breakfast to explain that shit. They'll leave you with a lifetime of emotional scars and probably some physical ones too."

I pull in a breath. I need to get my shit together. "It feels like you're only giving me half the truth."

He gapes at me. "What more do you need to know that saving your ass would depend on?"

I take a chance and close the distance between us. We've been like this a few times since I was thrown into this tailspin of a life, but it's always him who's instigated it. And every single time, we always have an audience in one way or another.

Never when we've been alone.

My heart skips a beat when I look into his stormy eyes. There's so much swirling in their depths, I wonder what's going on in his mind.

His aftershave is fresh and crisp, masculine with an after-scent dripping in power and money. There's nothing basic about my new husband.

But there's something else about him...

He talks about this world. He fits in it while he's nothing like it.

"What do you need to know, chica?" he presses.

I shift in my seat and lower my voice. "If I have to fall head over heels for you out there, what am I expected to do in here?"

He glares at me.

"You've laid it all out, *hubbalicious*." His eyes narrow at my smartass, so I reach out and tap his knee twice with the tip of my index finger. "You announced that we were going to shower together this morning, that I could drink wine with you in our bed, and you've gone above and beyond defending my honor to the point of threatening to put a bullet through someone's head. I need to know what your expectations are everywhere, not just out there."

Boz finishes what I started and leans in closer. So close, I think this is going to be it.

That I pushed the line too far, and my marriage is about to be consummated.

He lowers his tone. "You want to know when I'm going to fuck you?"

I freeze in my spot. I hold steady, but it's hard when he talks about fucking me.

The silence must be enough of an answer, because his warm

hand engulfs my bare leg and slides up where he grips me. He gives me a yank, and his breath tickles my skin when his lips hover over my ear. "I don't care how much you might want it, Landyn. The last thing I'm going to do is fuck you. Get used to a life of celibacy, because unless we're putting on a show for the world, no one is going to touch you. Especially not me."

My breath catches in surprise.

This is not what I expected.

"A life of celibacy?" I ask.

He leans back far enough to gaze into my shocked eyes, but I don't get an answer. "Do you have any other questions?"

I pull my lip between my teeth and shake my head.

"I expect you to cooperate."

I exhale and throw his words back at him. "Yes. I'm so into you, I can't see straight. You're the love of my life. You know, all the normal fairytale stuff that happens when your father sells you off to a cartel leader's son but you end up married to his right-hand man. I only have eyes for you, my hot, broody husband."

One perfect, thick brow hikes a notch, and I lose his touch. He stands, leering over me. My view does not suck as I tip my head back to look up his body. My chin is claimed between his thumb and index finger, and his tone is gruffer than normal. "The stage is set, then. We both know what to expect."

"A marriage made in hell," I add.

"Indeed," he agrees.

He hasn't let go of my chin, and we're locked in this passive-aggressive conversation laced with tension.

If I'm honest—which I will not be with anyone but myself—sexual tension.

"How am I supposed to act head over heels in love with you when I know nothing about you?"

"It's called *improv*."

"I'm not a thespian," I argue.

My chin gets a little pinch, but where I feel it most is farther south when he follows it up with a thumb swipe across my bottom lip. "For your sake, you'd better be a quick study."

And with that, our dreaded conversation about not consummating our marriage is over.

"Wait," I call as he heads to our bathroom. "Where are you going? And what am I supposed to do now?"

He's got one foot inside the bathroom doors when he turns back to me with a tense expression. "I'm hitting the gym. Do what you want, but don't try to leave the house. It's not like you could if you tried."

I twist in my chair to fully face him. "But I don't have a phone or a computer. What am I supposed to do all day, every day?"

"Entertain yourself, but we have a dinner meeting tonight. You need to be by my side. Tomorrow is Damian's funeral. Prepare to be solemn as fuck."

And with that, he slams the bathroom door.

I turn back in my chair and stare at my cold omelet.

A life of celibacy was not what I expected. I should be happy.

It's a relief even if an entire lifetime with no sex is a little depressing to think about. But only if the sex is my choice. So many contingencies I never thought would be in play.

I relax back into my chair and pick up my coffee.

There's one thing I know for certain.

Pretending to be in love with Boz Torres is going to be much easier than acting like I'm not chipper as fuck about Damian being dropped into a grave six feet under.

That is something to celebrate.

10

BIKINI POLICE

Brax

I hit the weights and treadmill for over an hour. Damian either had good intentions or pretended to work out when he designed that wing of his house. The place is a small version of the most elite gym and outfitted with the top-of-the-line machines and weights.

Once I moved in, I was the only one to use it. Damian told me to help myself, but that's when I was recovering from a bullet wound.

One I took for him.

The GSW that wasn't supposed to happen.

Who knew that bullet would get me to where I am today. I rose through the ranks faster than the summer temps in the low desert. Thank God it didn't do worse damage.

Getting thrown into the line of fire that saved Damian's ass bought his everlasting trust. He thought I took the bullet for him, and I didn't let him think anything other than that. He fucking loved me, trusted me, and kicked his own family to the side to make room for me.

It also put a target on my back.

Shit has been hot because of it, and now sitting in the number two seat of the Marino family when I have zero Marino blood running through my veins, the flames are licking my ass on a daily basis.

> Carson – There's no way the Jackals are crossing above ground. They disappear in the night, and my asset spots them east of Tijuana. I want that tunnel before we wrap things up.

I can't exactly ask the President of the Violet Jackals to map out their underground system to Mexico over dinner tonight.

> Me – You want a lot of fucking things.

> Carson – It's not just me. Your home agency misses you. I'm surprised you haven't gotten a midnight booty call. They're jonesing to have you back. But before you make all their dreams come true, those tunnels are a high priority on both our lists. If we follow the drugs, there's a good chance there are bodies too. And since I'm the one funding your fun and games, I want the bodies.

> Me – You and your talk to text. It's not a baseball game. I don't need the color commentary. I want the tunnels shut down too.

> Carson – Don't question the talent of my thumbs. They can run with the wind. And notice, no errors. My perfection knows no bounds.

The man who made it possible for me to go this deep undercover is fucking chatty like we just finished an old man softball game. Some days I think he forgets I'm running this shit show and keeping things short would be beneficial to me not getting dead.

> Me – You know I'll find your tunnel. That starts tonight. I'm stepping things up, remember?

> Carson – Yeah, I can tell you're stepping things up with your fake wife. We need to talk about that.

Shit.

I've got bugs all over this house, and the feed goes straight to headquarters and the CIA. They're listening to every word but what's said in the bedroom.

> Me – I'm keeping her safe. No one is happy that I'm the one who ended up with her, especially Nic and Uncle Eddy.

> Carson – Yeah, I heard how he disrespected your "queen" last night.

> Me – Acting the part. What was I supposed to do?

> Carson – I've got a queen of my own. I would've done the same thing.

I'm done.

> Me – I've got to go. I'll hit you up tomorrow if I can. If I can get him to talk, you might get a hint about your tunnel.

> Carson – Fan-fucking-tastic. I'm jealous. Some days, I miss being in the action. Watch your back.

> Me – Always.

I delete the app. If anyone can create a secure line for me to communicate with the real world, it's the CIA. I didn't think I'd have that while I was under. I haven't talked to or seen my family in almost two years, but I've got a line to Carson who can get me in touch with my supervisor at the DEA.

I pull up the Marino surveillance cameras on my other phone. Landyn was gone after I got back from the gym. She was snooping and wandering around the house. She's learning her way around while peeking in every closet and opening every shut door that isn't locked. When she made it to the kitchen, she started chatting with June, who acted like she was being interviewed by Border Patrol rather than the new mistress of the house.

And Miranda refused to speak a word to her. She's meek and cautious to a fault. Hell, she's not just cautious—she's a mouse in a lion's den, afraid the pride is going to make her a mid-afternoon snack.

She wants nothing to do with anyone in this house but June, and Landyn was no different.

I showered and have a call in ten minutes with the funeral home, but my wife is nowhere to be found.

I flip through the camera feeds one more time, but backtrack when I get to the lanai overlooking the pool and the Pacific crashing against the rocks.

What the hell?

Landyn

Cassidy Hooper was my best friend in elementary school. We lived one block from each other and were inseparable. But her family was nothing like mine.

Her mom was a nurse, her father worked in construction, and her grandmother lived with them.

My father's parents died when I was little, and my mother's parents never wanted anything to do with us. Having a grandmother around was a novelty I wasn't used to.

Cassidy's grandmother cooked, made sure she did her homework, and baked us cookies after school.

My mother has never made a cookie in her life, and since her parents want nothing to do with us, it's safe to say my grandmother wasn't picking up the slack while my mom cocktailed her way through long lunches. Being tipsy at four in the afternoon didn't exactly scream homemade snickerdoodles.

Needless to say, we spent way more time at Cassidy's house than mine. No one was tipsy or working their way up the chain of a third-class mafia organization. Her family actually cared where she was.

I was in the fourth grade when my father really leveled up. I'll never forget the day when my mother announced we were *moving to a respectable part of town* and that she could *finally entertain her friends without being embarrassed.*

I don't ever remember my mother being happier than that moment.

I was heartbroken.

There would be no more bike rides a block over. No more homemade cookies. No more long afternoons with my best friend.

I'd have a new school, a new house, and as per my mother, new friends who would be more like us.

Like us.

I lost track of Cassidy after that. My mom refused to drive across San Diego—away from the coast and toward the desert—just for me to have a playdate. And after begging and begging Cassidy to come to our house, she finally admitted that her parents didn't want her to visit.

Looking back, I realize her parents saw what was normal life for me and didn't want their daughter in that environment. Who can blame them?

Hell, look where it got me.

Time did its thing and healed my fourth-grade broken heart. I looked up my best friend on social media years later. She and her family moved to Nevada to another humble home similar to the one I spent countless hours in. It had most of the same furniture we used to build blanket forts.

Her grandmother still lived with them. I never knew her grandmother's name. I only remember her as *Grandma*.

When I walked into the kitchen earlier to bring our dirty dishes downstairs, June reminded me of that beautiful woman. She was hustling around the kitchen, talking to Miranda, who is probably around my age, and cooking up a storm. She was animated and sounded like she had as much vinegar as she does sugar.

That was until she turned and saw me.

My presence put an end to any and all authentic conversation. She was stilted, formal, and only spoke to answer my questions.

Miranda was worse and tightened up like a clam.

I guess it's better to know what I'm dealing with if this is where I'll be forced to live.

The whole situation was awkward. Especially when she told me not to bother returning our tray, and they would take care of it when they tidied up our room. It was actually more of an order.

I guess being married to Boz means the staff can boss me around.

We'll see about that. I'll tidy up our room tomorrow all by myself. If I have to scrub a toilet to make a stand, I will.

The only women in this house besides me want nothing to do with me. My new husband made it very clear that we're fake. And I have no communication with the outside world.

This is going to be a lonely life.

I push off the wall and make it halfway across the pool before I have to come up for air. I can swim, but I'm no athlete. My form is shit and I zig-zag across the pool, but I'm antsy, and there's nothing else to do to pass the time.

When I reach the other side in a path that looks like Lombard Street, I grip the wall while I catch my breath.

"I see you found a way to entertain yourself."

I twist when the deep voice hits me from behind me and swipe my hair away. Boz is standing at the edge of the pool with his arms crossed and a scowl on his face.

I do not appreciate his tone.

"You told me to find something to do." I look around to see if we're alone, though I'm not sure that matters. He said we're never alone. "You told me not to leave. You never said I couldn't swim."

He exhales a dramatic breath and turns to glare toward the wall that lines the property.

"What is your problem?" I demand.

He drops his arms and looks down at me. "Come here."

My gaze darts around to try to figure out what he was looking at as I whisper, "Why?"

He squats at the edge and points to the spot in front of him, but says nothing. His man sign language is loud and clear.

Or maybe I read it loud and clear, because I let go of the edge and swim through the deep end where he's waiting for me. And not patiently if his glare is any indication.

I get to the edge in front of him and hold on from an arms-length while I continue to tread water. "What?"

He crooks a finger at me. "Closer, baby."

It's not lost on me that I'm barely dressed, and he's completely dressed. But just like when we're alone yet being watched, he always finds a way to make sure we're close.

Like *close*.

I pull myself to the wall.

He reaches into the water and dips a finger beneath the thin tie that is solely keeping me from being topless. One tug and my breasts will be floating bare between us.

I hold steady, but suck in a breath to prepare.

Goosebumps cover my body when his index finger runs hot across my skin. "Where did you get this?"

I try not to gape, because until now, he's seemed like a pretty bright guy. I have no clue what his business skills are like, but he's gotten me out of one tight jam after another. If nothing else, he's street smart, but it seems I have to remind him of my less-than-ideal situation. "Did you forget that you brought me here with nothing to my name but a bloody wedding dress? This was in my closet. Which, by the way, if you think you can swing it, I'd like to know who shopped for me. Not only do they have impeccable taste, but they are incredibly skilled at fitting strangers. I'd like to thank them."

My bikini top cinches up on one side when he wraps his thick finger around the tie and pulls me closer to him. "If I find out who picked this out for you, I'll make sure they never work for the Marinos again."

I reach up and grab his hand to push it away, but I'm afraid he'll rip off my top since he's essentially tied himself to me. "What is your problem?"

"Baby, do you know how many men are watching you right now? I'm not saying it's not fine, but your ass is as bare as a full moon."

I roll my eyes. "It's called a thong, Boz. You're either from the dark ages or the bikini police. How old are you, anyway, grandpa?"

The tie to my bikini top tightens further. "They're watching you. Or, I should say, they're watching your ass."

"Have you been to the beach in the last decade, dear husband? This is what everyone my age wears. I'm not naked."

His tone is low and rough. "You might as well be."

I try to relax my expression as my hand tightens around his. "They'll get even more of an eyeful if you don't let go of my top, Boz."

He lets me go immediately and stands, stalking to the lounge to grab my towel. He holds it out in front of him and growls, "Get out."

After the last week, I'm not sure why this is the battle I'm willing to fight. It's probably because I know I would never win any other one. "No."

He flicks the towel he's holding between us and narrows his

eyes. "Get the fuck out. I have a call that I'm already late for. I don't want you out here by yourself."

"I'm no Olympian, but I can swim, Boz. You told me to find something to do, and I did. I don't need a lifeguard," I snap.

He lowers his voice to a menacing growl. "That's exactly what you need, chica. Get out of the fucking pool, or I'll pull you out myself."

My eyes widen. "You wouldn't."

"Try me. See how happy I'll be then."

"Wait. You're serious?"

"We don't know each other well yet, but you need to get it through your head that you're married to a serious fucking guy. I'm also lacking patience as of late. Don't make me tell you again."

I stare up at the man who claims to not be a bucket of fun.

He holds my gaze, and I try not to think about how the afternoon California sun makes his skin even more beautiful than it normally is.

Instead of arguing further, I put my hands flat to the edge of the pool and push myself up. Boz's eyes drag down my body as I stand in front of him still holding out the towel.

I don't reach for it and feel confident in my very skimpy bikini. It's one I would have chosen had I been granted the choice. I wore things like this all the time in my previous life.

You know, like last week.

"Just so you know, I was about to get out anyway. I need to get ready for our dinner. I wouldn't dream of being late."

He shakes his head once, and before I know it, I'm wrapped in an enormous towel and the thick arms of my husband. He pulls me flush to his chest—I'm sure his pristine outfit will be wet, but that's on him. My arms are pinned, and I'm held hostage in a whole other way.

Strangely, it doesn't feel horrible.

He lays down the law ... again. "No more swimming by yourself."

Water drips from my face, but I don't blink away from his gaze. "Who am I supposed to swim with? June and Miranda want nothing to do with me. Trust me, I tried to talk to them. I doubt the old butler guy wants to take a dip. That leaves all your men who pop out of the woodwork with guns. I don't want to hang out with them."

"You're not to speak to them," he bosses.

"So that leaves me with no options."

"That leaves you with me," he pops back.

I try to shift in his arms, but he holds tight. "Right. Between planning funerals, hosting drug lords for dinner, and being the grumpiest husband on the planet, when will you have time for me?"

"Torres."

Boz shifts us, and we both look to the side. It's one of the men who like to pop out of the woodwork during stressful situations. He's probably always watching.

"Yeah?" Boz answers.

"Your call with the funeral home is waiting."

He gives him a chin lift before turning back to me. This time, his hand comes up to frame the side of my face as I feel him fist the towel at my back, causing it to tighten further.

Then he takes my breath away.

He doesn't taste the skin below my ear.

He doesn't whisper secrets that no one can hear but me.

He takes my mouth with such ferocity, it's like he actually wants to kiss me and can't wait another moment to thrust his tongue in my mouth.

This kiss isn't chaste, nor is it gentle. It reminds me of the way he consumed me after I was forced to say *I do* in front of God and drug lords.

I'm pressed to his every muscled plane through my wet towel as his hand on my face tightens to tip my head for better access. His tongue presses through my lips as I gasp for air.

He tastes like mint and danger.

I'm bound tight where he has me confined. I shouldn't want him to kiss me. The man makes my head spin.

And not in the flowery, romantic way that makes a woman's

knees go weak and causes her to view life through rose-colored glasses.

No.

Boz Torres makes my head spin in frustration and anger and confusion.

Just this morning he told me to expect a celibate marriage. That the last thing he wants to do is fuck me, let alone do other things to me. That for my own safety, I'd better act like I'm gagging for him.

But evidence proves otherwise. I feel it—long and hard—pressed into my stomach through his trousers and my wet towel.

And if this kiss doesn't affect him the way it does me—because I'm very much wet, and it has nothing to do with my abysmal attempt at swimming laps—then the man deserves an Oscar, because he sure has me fooled.

His tongue gives mine one last swipe, and his lips are still on me like they're begging for just one more moment. My body is overheated, but it has nothing to do with the warm afternoon sun.

It has everything to do with Boz Torres.

And then just like before, those skilled lips find my ear. "Give me a break, chica. I'm doing the best I can. But the thought of these men jacking off to security feeds of you wearing scraps of material is something I can't deal with on top of everything else."

I tip my head back far enough to look at him through the bright rays. If his lips are any indication of what mine look like after that kiss, I can't imagine the expression on my face right now. His tone is frustrated with a hint of desperation.

"You're serious?" I mutter.

He nods.

I know he's serious about the guys. Guys are like that.

I lick my swollen lips. "No. I mean about it making you crazy."

His lips purse into a line before answering. "Baby, I'm not sure how I can put it any more bluntly for you—I'm always fucking serious. No more parading around in bikinis by yourself."

I narrow my eyes. "So my ass can hang out as long as I'm with you? What's the difference?"

"There's a huge difference. For one, I'll be with you. No one will jack off to the sight of you if I'm around."

"How do you know?"

"Because I'm a hot-blooded man and know anyone like me would jack off to the sight of you. But not if I'm here."

I let that sink in. I should keep my mouth shut, but I am me. He might have me bound in this towel, but I press my stomach into his long erection. "Do *you* jack off at the sight of me?"

One side of his full lips tip to the sun. "I'm your husband."

"That's evasive and not at all romantic."

"I'm the least romantic man you'll ever meet, Landyn. The funeral home is on hold for me, and we're standing in the hot ass sun talking about me jacking off. This conversation is over."

"This conversation is on hold, my dear, complicated husband. I can't exactly move while you have me tied up in a straightjacket."

I lose his touch in an instant. He shifts the towel around my body and shoves the edges into my hands. "Go straight to our room and get ready for dinner."

He puts a hand to the small of my back, but the tips of his fingers graze the swell of my ass.

The man is unnerving. He's made it clear everything he does is for show.

But every time he touches me, it feels very, very real.

11

ANNIHILATED BOUNDARIES

Brax

June is barely out of the dining room with the dirty plates when Logan Pritchett changes the subject to his newest prospect. "We need to have a conversation about Ricky."

I stretch my arm out across the back of Landyn's chair. So far, the night has been a bust as far as gaining information. Who knew you could actually have small talk over dinner with the president of a one-percenter organization.

I wondered when this was going to come up. I've been waiting for his lead to talk business. "What about him?"

Logan leans forward and rests his forearms on the table. "He's a Jackals prospect. He was sent here to cut your fucking grass or pick up dog shit so we could exchange information without communicating daily. Now he's living in your guest room and wearing Dockers. This was not part of the fucking plan."

"We don't have a dog," Landyn pipes in like she's done all night. Then, just to torment me, her hand lands high on my thigh and her big blue eyes shine bright. "I want a puppy. And not some alpha guard dog. I want a lap dog. But not too small. It can't be breakable when we start having babies. And it has to be a girl. I'll name her Cherry."

I toss my napkin on the table in front of me and reach under Landyn's chair to yank it closer to mine. Her eyes flare as she settles into the side of my chest. My wife has embraced her part tonight, even if she has laid it on thick. "We'll talk about it later, but we're never-fucking-ever naming anything Cherry."

The skin between her brows crease as she turns to one of the most-wanted men in America. "What do you think of the name Cherry?"

Logan downs the last of his whiskey and the crystal lands on the table with a thud. "Sorry, lady. No fucking way would I be seen yelling for a dog named Cherry."

My fake wife's hand tightens around my thigh when she mutters, "I can already see naming our children will be an issue."

This is not what I had in mind when I told her to act like she's into me. The only time she really does that is when I touch her or kiss her. But that doesn't feel like an act. It feels like a whole lot more.

My dick is red-hot proof.

Landyn looks like the wife of a politician, not one who was just sold to a drug lord having dinner with the president of a violent motorcycle club.

She might look the part, but I have no fucking idea what's going to pop out of her mouth at any given moment. We need to have a talk about that when I get her back to our room.

She's made small talk her bitch from the get go. If I touch her, she reciprocates. Sometimes she touches me first.

In fact, she touches me a lot.

So much, I've had to have a dozen silent conversations with my cock to calm him the fuck down. He hasn't gotten the memo that my wife is fake and that she's a part of the job.

Basically, she's driving me mad. I find myself thinking of reasons to be in public with her, just so I can have a reason to touch her.

I've faked this life with precision for two years. Besides taking a bullet for Damian—that I did not mean to do—I haven't made one misstep and have convinced everyone around me that I'm one hundred percent someone I'm not. I've worked my way to the top, and if all goes as planned, I'll take down three organizations, not just one, while I get the revenge I've wanted for years.

So if the twenty-three-year-old daughter of a mobster is the thing that finally does me in, I might cut off the hand that I use to jack off with.

I'll deserve the torture.

The first thing I'm going to do when we get back to our room is to educate the woman beside me to dial it down when people talk business.

Then I'll lock myself in the bathroom to take a long shower. If I want to survive another day here, I need to jack off to be able to focus.

Logan breaks into my thoughts. "This doesn't look good for you or the club. My brothers at the table are not happy. We made this arrangement with the prospect to transfer information, that's it."

"I disagree. What doesn't look good is a high school dropout who was a top-ranked football prospect sporting a cut with your club's patch on the back. You've got enough attention from the law as it is. Do you really want that kind of scrutiny? If he's with me, he's an intern. I can tell everyone he's the son of a friend who's come to stay with me to learn the ropes." I motion to the fortress where I'm now the one calling the shots. "Look around. No one will find him here, and he'll still be our main line of communication. Let some time go by, people will forget about him, then he can return to you for the rest of his tat. He'll learn a hell of a lot with me that will benefit you later on."

Logan reclines into his chair and takes me in as he mulls it over.

Landyn shifts next to me, like she's about to jump into the middle of negotiations on behalf of me and Rocco, so I bring a hand up and give the end of one of her perfect waves a tug.

"Look," I say, purely to cut off Landyn. "I already told you I see the Jackals becoming a more integral part of the Marino business structure. I'm changing the landscape, and I see you in it."

Logan's gaze shifts to Landyn before settling back on me. "You mean your new father-in-law is out of the picture, and you need legs to get your product over the border."

Landyn stiffens at my side at the mention of her father. I turn to her and press my lips to her temple.

She's not loose or relaxed any longer. Not like she has been since we sat down for dinner. At the mention of her father, her expression blanks.

I turn back to Logan. "My father-in-law is still a sensitive subject."

"Yeah," he mutters. "I can imagine."

"My business with others is confidential. I hope you can appreciate that. I'm not going to flap my gums about you to anyone else either. My offer to you is fifteen percent of the sale when the load is safely delivered, and Rocco will remain here. He'll work for me as cover while this arrangement is in place."

Logan hikes a brow. "Rocco?"

I shrug. "It's his name. He can finish out his tattoo and live on with the Jackals later. Do you want the deal or not?"

He shakes his head once, but responds immediately. "Forty percent and you can have the kid for as long as you want."

"Fuck that," I bite. "You just ate at the Marino table and drank our whiskey. We've been getting along just fine until now. Do not come into this house and straight up insult me. No one gets forty in this business, and you know it."

He nods toward Landyn when he argues, "I can provide security her old man couldn't. With me, your product will be delivered just fine."

I narrow my eyes and challenge, "You still have to get from A to B. Do you have your own set of submarines that I don't know about? It still has to come over the border."

His expression turns smug, and he lifts his chin. "Not over—under. Unlike the mob, the Jackals don't mind getting their hands dirty—literally."

And this is what I've been waiting for.

It's like Landyn knows something is coming and anticipates it as much as I do. Her slim fingers press into my thigh just inches from my cock where she hasn't let me go.

"You've got tunnels," I state.

"All I'm going to say is we're not the navy."

I give him a slow nod. "I suspected but didn't know for sure."

"No one knows the Jackals business."

"Yet you just shared your lack of submerged warships," I counter. "I see a long-term relationship in our future."

"Only if the terms are right." He looks again from me to Landyn and this time addresses my wife. "No offense, lady, but your daddy played old school and almost got dead because of it. At least you look like you're still in one piece after he sold you to save his ass." Landyn stiffens against my chest. Logan shakes his head and turns back to me. "I thought we've had some rumbles in the past. Nothing beats the Marino wedding that never was. News traveled far and wide. That's a tale that won't soon be forgotten."

"Which explains my changes. Twenty-five percent and Rocco. If you have tunnels, we can move more product—as long as you're up for the work."

"Thirty," he demands. "And you can have *Rocco* as long as you want while this business deal is in play. If shit hits the fan, he's a Jackal again."

If my ass.

When shit hits the fan. The way things are going, I'm going to blow the fucking fan up sooner than later. And there will be no Jackals for Rocco to go back to.

I shift Landyn in my arm to extend my right one over the table, offering my hand to close this deal. "Thirty and Rocco. It'll be a pleasure doing business with the Jackals."

He takes my hand. "Fuck yeah, it's a pleasure."

I raise my voice a touch and call, "Spencer."

The older man appears at the threshold to the dining room. "Sir?"

"Mrs. Torres and I are ready to get on with our evening. See

Mr. Pritchett out." I turn back to Logan. "Your weapon will be returned to you when our car leaves you at a different drop-off spot. You can call someone for a ride when you get there. The next time we meet, it'll be because shit went south. No offense, but I hope to never see you again. I have a reputation to uphold, and yours doesn't jive with mine."

Logan looks around at the opulence surrounding us. "No offense, Torres, but you don't jive with the club either."

I turn to Spencer and motion to the door. We get one more chin lift from the club president who's dancing near the top of the FBI's most wanted list.

They can check him off soon right after they thank me for laying him at their feet. I've got so many balls in the air right now, if I drop one, they'll all detonate the moment they hit the ground.

And I'm alone with my wife again, even though alone is a relative term.

I turn to Landyn who hasn't relaxed since the mention of her father. "You okay?"

Unlike the last dinner we hosted, she barely sipped her wine all night. She's stone-cold sober, alert, and soaking everything up like a sponge.

She shakes her head before shifting her icy blue eyes to me. Her gaze isn't playful or challenging or even scared.

They're guarded.

"Chica, what's wrong?"

Her gaze darts around the room, but she doesn't hesitate. "Are my parents really safe, or is all of this for nothing?"

I allow my hand to feel its way down her back to palm her hip and ass that's encased in another dress that leaves nothing to the imagination. This one isn't black—it's stark white and reminds me of the moment I saw her for the first time wearing the wedding dress she wore when she married me.

Or the me she thinks she married.

I don't worry about the cameras because this is known. "Baby, your father sold you to pay off his debt. Why are you worried about him?"

She tries to push away from me, but my hand on her ass holds tight. I can't deny, I like it there.

She sighs and gives in. "I know this life, Boz. I grew up in it. People make promises all the time that they have no intention of keeping. I'm so angry at my father for putting me in this position. I hate him. I never knew I could hate someone this much. No one has literally put a gun to my head since the day we were taken from our home by Damian, but the figurative one that has been pointed at my skull ever since is very real. The longer I'm here, the longer I sit through meetings like this, and the more I learn, I know I'll never get out. No one will allow it. But they're still my parents, and my mom didn't do anything wrong other than choose my father. So I need to know—are they safe or was that a lie?"

"You shouldn't give a shit after what he did."

"Do you have a family, Boz?" She fists my dress shirt and leans in closer. "The only thing I know about you is by day you play the part of a legitimate business man, but you're not who everyone thinks you are—these meetings prove it. You don't know me, just like I don't know you. I can't change who my parents are or what they've done. But I need to believe that *this*," she stresses, "isn't for nothing."

Fuck.

Even if her meaning behind it is different, she doesn't know how close to the fire she's flying when it comes to me.

I decide not to feed her any bullshit and tell the truth, because *this isn't for nothing* has become my mantra for the last two years. There are times I have to chant that shit in my head over and over just to make it through another day.

As I try to figure out what to do or say to make her feel better without straight up lying, I realize her eyes aren't guarded.

Not anymore.

They're desperate.

I've been so busy trying to make sure I don't drop any of the balls that are circling my head since the day of the wedding, for the first time, guilt washes over me.

I'm used to the life I've invented in order to survive.

She doesn't know the difference between reality and lies.

But the worst of it is, I'm the reason she's here.

It was my tip that led the authorities to the load her father lost, which led to him bartering his only daughter. I'm the one who dragged her into this, I'm the one playing with her emotions, and as the days click on, it's getting harder and harder to focus on the end goal and not her.

It's hard—really fucking hard.

Especially when she looks at me like this. She's not only mine now, but it's also my responsibility to get her out of this safely and intact, so she can move on and live the rest of her life when I'm done.

Knowing full well the cameras are on us for whoever wants to watch, and that includes Alamandos should he be so inclined, I grab her hips and pull her ass across my lap.

I think she's getting used to my hands on her because she doesn't argue. Her fingertips return to my shirt as she peeks up at me through her thick lashes.

"This isn't for nothing." I repeat her words and my number one slogan that should be tattooed on my body by now. I hold her tight to me and my voice is low, not that it matters who hears. I have to tell her the truth. "Your father was desperate to get into the mix. He's an asshole for what he did to you. I can't speak for anyone else, I have a lot of power here, but not over everyone. If it makes you feel better, I promise not to touch your father. *This*," I wrap my arms around her tighter and give her a squeeze, "means something."

Her blue eyes turn glassy. Through everything she's been through, she rarely shows this kind of emotion. She looks like she's doing everything to keep her tears at bay and swallows hard over the lump in her throat.

"You give me whiplash," she whispers.

"I get that. I'm sorry, but I doubt that's going to change anytime soon."

"It's a lot to deal with." She looks back down to her fingers and pulls in a deep breath before rolling her eyes and settling them back on me. "You know, until death do us part, and all that jazz."

The tears that never spilled have almost dried up, and I realize I lucked out to fake-marry a woman full of snark rather than drama. If she can make it through this, she'll be just fine when it's all over and I set her free.

"'Til death do us part," I repeat, but in my head add, *until I exact revenge and wrap up this damn case.* But she can't know that. "No harm will come to you. I'll make sure of it."

Her gaze jumps to me, and her eyes flare. Her tits rise and fall practically in my face in another tight-ass dress. Her tongue sneaks out to wet the crease of her lips, and I can see it written all over her.

All I have to do is make a move. A real one—not like today by the pool for show. But when we're like this, nose to nose, breath to breath, it's different. By the look in her eyes, I can tell she feels it too.

I can't step over the line, no matter how easy it would be with the air crackling between us like two haywire currents that are about to erupt into flames.

Fuck, her hand slides up my chest and lands warm on my skin at the open neck of my dress shirt.

It feels fucking good. So good, my cock decides to dive into whatever utopia he thinks he's living in as he thickens in my pants. And since it's pressed to her thigh, I bet she feels it too.

She shifts against me.

Yeah, she feels it.

That does not help the situation.

"Boz—" she starts, but I interrupt her.

And I do it with my lips.

She melts into me. Dips her fingers into my hair. And becomes an active participant.

I'm afraid of what she was about to say, but really, as one day bleeds into the next, it's harder and harder to stop myself.

She moans against my lips and instantly opens for me. I grip the back of her bare thigh in one hand and press into the middle of her back with the other.

She should push me the hell away for good, but she does the opposite. Instead, she presses her perfect tits to my chest.

My dick thinks he's in heaven.

That this is it.

The big shebang.

I don't blame him. There's been no shebang in two years. If I offer him a handful of body wash in the shower again, he'd slap me across the face if he could.

He only wants her.

I slide my hand farther up her dress only to find her ass bare and beautiful.

My roots sting when she fists my hair. When I deepen the kiss, she holds on tighter.

Fuck, this woman. She doesn't know what she's doing to me. It doesn't matter which way I spin it, this isn't good.

I mean, it is.

It's fucking great.

But it's so, so bad.

She shifts her legs, and I move my hand just enough to find a strip of material. Her thong.

But beyond that, she's wet.

So wet.

She lets go of my mouth and gasps. I look into her blue eyes and am about to apologize for my hand wandering between her legs, but let's be real, I'm not sorry at all.

Landyn jerks in my arms when June yelps from the side of the room. I rip my hand from under her dress, and wrap her up in my arms. She stuffs her face in my neck and fights for a breath.

"I'm sorry, Mr. Torres," June squeaks and stares at the floor in front of her. "I ... I didn't hear anything and was just coming in to clean up from dinner. I'll leave you be."

"No," I demand and clear my throat. "I have some calls to make about the funeral tomorrow, and then we're going to bed."

Landyn pulls back long enough to look up at me where she

still sits in my lap. Her eyes flare. I'm not sure if she's embarrassed or pissed I didn't send June away so I could fuck her next to the dirty dishes.

The pull is real, and it's not just me. This proves it.

I put my hands to her hips and steady her on her feet before taking her hand. We're on our way from the dining room when Landyn gives me a little tug to slow down. "Thank you for dinner, June. It was delicious, just like always."

June nods. "Ma'am."

We make our way silently through the house and up the stairs. I've got the door open to our bedroom when she tugs on my arm harder this time. I turn to look down at her where she's stopped outside our door.

"What?" I snap.

"Are you really going to your office to work?" She pulls her hand from mine and folds her arms across her chest. "After that?"

I pull in a big breath. My need to adjust my junk is greater than the need for world peace.

"I am," I grunt. "The funeral is tomorrow. I'm in charge of security and seeing as your wedding day turned into a massacre, every detail needs to be thought through."

"But—"

I shake my head. "Go to bed. I'll be late."

Her expression pinches, and a blush warms her beautiful face. She drops her arms and points behind her when she hisses, "That was real, and don't try to tell me it wasn't."

I close the distance and wrap my arm around her lower back. I'm not gentle when I pull her to me and put my lips on hers for the sole purpose of shutting her up. I keep this kiss firm but quick before dragging my lips to her ear. "Not sure what I need to do to impress upon you, these halls are monitored, chica."

I look down at her and put my finger over her lips when she tries to talk again.

"Go to bed, baby, and don't wait up. I'll be late."

I don't wait for her to say anything else. I leave her in the hall, turn to the office doors, and shut her out.

Fuck the cameras. I'm so damn sick of the remnants of Damian's irrational paranoia. I've spent two years working my way up in this organization, knowing I'm being watched every single moment unless I'm on the shitter. In fact, that used to be the only place I could text Carson.

I'm surprised he gave us privacy in there.

I open the laptop and pretend to focus on market futures. I need to get to Manhattan and check on the east coast business that Damian ran for Alamandos. But now I have the added stress of keeping tabs on Landyn, on top of watching my own back.

There are people who hate me. And now that I'm sitting in this chair, they hate me more. Hell, the target on my back is probably bigger because I was the one who landed the Alba girl.

Landyn Torres.

She's pissed.

And I deserve it. There is a reason for boundaries.

If you annihilate them, they blow up in your face.

12

FUNERAL

Landyn

I don't have a lot of skills.

I dropped out of college because I finally decided that I would rather have my toenails plucked out, one by one, than sit in statistics for one more excruciating minute.

Horrid.

My major was marketing, only because I couldn't decide on one, and I loved my job as a stylist. I figured it tied in somewhere, right?

Wrong.

Probability and data distributions have nothing to do with understanding that pairing black and navy can be stunning when done right. Or to say fuck it to the rules your mother crammed down your throat about white pants after Labor Day. Or avoiding a style you love because society says it's a no-go for the body God gave you. Or, the biggie, that thrifting a pair of perfect jeans that have already been washed a million times, letting someone else do the work to break them in, is like finding gold on the side of a mountain.

So satisfying.

Not like orgasm-level satisfaction, but it ranks right up there with a girls' trip to Napa.

An orgasm is always at the top of the list.

Which gets me back to my short list of hard skills in life. Nearing the top of my *Things I'm So Good At, I Dare You to Come at Me* list is my delivery of the silent treatment.

I can rock a silent treatment with the best of them. Just ask my parents. My last marathon of silence started when my father informed me I was to marry a drug lord because Dennis Alba is an idiot.

If anything has ever deserved the silent treatment in the history of the world, it's that.

From the time we were delivered to the Marino resort in Tijuana to the moment I was made into a reluctant—and I use that term loosely—bride, I spoke not a word.

Not one fucking word.

He deserved it. My mother ... not so much. But I was going through some shit, having to save their lives by giving up my own and all. I wasn't worried about anyone's feelings at the time but my own.

Which gets me back to orgasms and the silent treatment.

My husband is hot. Like, hands down one of the most beautiful men I've ever witnessed in real life. I mean, hot is hot when someone looks like him, but his looks are only fifty percent of it.

In the short time we've been together, Boz Torres rescued me, protected me, defended my honor, and became so possessive, I'm sure most therapists would consider it unhealthy.

And he touches me.

Lord, does he touch me.

But never when we're alone.

When we're alone, he's a straight up asshole and wants nothing to do with me. At least that's what he says.

It feels a whole lot different.

I know when a guy wants to use me, and I know when he's into me.

And my husband is into me.

When he touches me, kisses me, devours me ... there's a smoldering vigor waiting to ignite. I've never felt anything like it.

I know nothing about him other than he's taken over the operations of a drug cartel and isn't afraid of whipping out his weapon at any given moment.

Though, not the weapon I'd prefer. Especially in the dining room last night.

When he left me at our bedroom door hot, bothered, and needing an orgasm in the worst way—but given my current life circumstances, who wouldn't need a shot of dopamine to calm their nerves—I decided I was done.

I will not allow him to play with my emotions any longer.

Fuck that.

I'll do what I do best—Brian "Boz" Torres is getting the silent treatment.

"Landyn." Boz bites out my name like he's chewing on an overcooked piece of cheap steak for the millionth time today. No more *baby* or *chica*. He tried those before we left the prison he calls a house. I wouldn't be surprised if he starts growling *Mrs. Brian Torres* to remind me to whom I belong. "We're almost to the church. All eyes will be on you. If you get out of this car and act like you're anything less than heartbroken over the man who was supposed to be your husband and think that people won't notice, you're crazy."

The number one rule when breaking a silent treatment is to dish it up with a dash of snide.

I continue to stare out the window. "Heartbroken while so into you, I'm gagging for it. I'm on it."

"Fuck," he hisses before mumbling to himself. "What did I do to fucking deserve this?"

The number two rule when it comes to silent treatments: it's okay to speak as long as you're throwing words back in their face.

My head whips around to him for the first time since he insisted on opening my car door when we left the prison. "If you don't know what you did to deserve this, then *you're* crazy."

He turns into the full parking lot of the church and goes straight to the front row where a man is standing in the only open spot holding it for us. I recognize him from the standoff in the dining room when he gives Boz a low wave.

I feel my seatbelt unclick but refuse to look at him until I feel his touch on my chin. It's a different kind of commanding than it is when he's about to kiss me.

He says nothing, but his stare is irritated while almost pleading. "This is about last night. I get it. I don't know what came over me, but it won't happen again. Are you happy?"

Am I happy?

No.

Not even a little.

But I can't deny the fact I was happy last night when his fingers worked their way between my legs.

I have no choice but to lie. "Thrilled."

"Please." He lowers his voice to utter a word that I'm surprised he comprehends the meaning, let alone has a place in his vocabulary. "I can't walk in there without knowing you'll cooperate. If you insist on going silent, can you at least pretend it's because you're mourning your dead fiancé?"

"Since my only memory of him is jamming a gun into my side while choking me right before his brains were splattered all over me, that's going to be hard."

"Now is not the time, Landyn. We're going to be front and center and need to act the part."

I throw rules for a successful cold shoulder out the window and turn to him fully. "You know, for someone who was so close to Damian, you don't seem very broken up about his new status."

There's a tick in his muscled jaw before he turns forward and slams his hand into the steering wheel. "Fuck!"

I jerk at his outburst that causes our luxury SUV to rock.

Maybe I was wrong, and he really is upset about Damian. I hardly know him. How am I supposed to know how he reacts to his boss and friend dying a violent death?

He doesn't give me another glance and pushes his door open. I don't move and watch him stalk around to my door. He opens it and silently holds a hand out for me as he stands there in the bright morning San Diego sun. He's in all black other than his tie that's a beautiful gold silk with a touch of gray woven through. I can't see his eyes behind his opaque shades, but I can only imagine what they're silently screaming right now.

"You're angry," I state.

His voice is low and controlled, and I don't like the sound of it. "I'm a lot of things, baby, but anger is one thing I don't have time for. Let's go."

Mourners file into the church. I can't exactly put this off any longer. If my father taught me anything growing up, if you want people to think you're normal, you should at least act like it.

I'll do my best to blend in, which in this case means faking how upset I am about not being married to Damian.

I grab my cream-colored clutch and put my hand in Boz's. He helps me down and doesn't let go of me as we head to the front doors of the church.

Guards are everywhere, making no effort to blend in. They don't have their weapons drawn, but everyone gives them a wide berth.

My heels click double time to keep up with Boz when I hear my name called right before we get to the front doors.

"Landyn. Sweetheart, wait!"

Boz stops before I do and steps in front of me to block my view and mutters, "You've got to be fucking kidding me."

I put my hand to his arm and peek around him.

Shit.

"What are you doing here?" Boz grits in a tone that isn't at all inviting. "This is a closed service and you weren't invited."

"You're not answering my calls." Dad's eyes land on me. "I want to check on my daughter."

Wait, he's checked up on me?

"That's interesting," Boz drawls and holds me behind him. "Your voicemails said nothing about Landyn and everything about wanting another shot at running Marino products. You have a lot of gall showing up here after what you did to your daughter and getting our load taken down by the feds."

"But I've done business with the Marinos for years." Desperation bleeds through my father's voice before his blue eyes shift back to me in a frenzy. "Don't listen to him, Landyn. I've been so worried about you. I've called every day—they won't let me talk to you."

I grip Boz's arm tighter and look up to him. "Is that true?"

Boz doesn't look away from my father but wraps a thick arm around me. "I still have his voicemails, baby. I'll let you listen when we get back. He begged for another chance, but not once did he ask about you."

My eyes dart to my father. I have no reason to believe Boz. Not one.

Other than the fact my father handed me over without a second thought solely to save himself.

Even without trusting Boz, the expression that settles on my father's tired face says it all.

It's a lie.

Which means Boz is telling the truth.

And for the first time since the Marinos took me from my home and forced me into this life, I'm not scared about what will happen next.

I'm completely and utterly devastated by what my father did to me. He had a choice. He could have done anything not to make that deal, but he didn't. He took the easy way out and saved himself. A parent should protect their child above all else, not offer them up on a platter to be devoured by the enemy.

But Boz is different.

In his own way, he's done nothing but protect me. I know I'd be married to Damian at this moment instead of attending his funeral had my wedding not turned into a bloodbath. That thought makes me shudder.

Boz pulls me tighter to his warm, hard chest. It's the only thing holding me up as tears threaten to ruin my makeup.

"Get out of my fucking sight," Boz growls. Two guards from the house have moved in to flank us. "Damian's funeral is not open to the public. I don't need another bloody ceremony on my hands. If Landyn wants to see her mom, I'll make that happen. But not you. She's mine now, and there's no way I'm going to let anyone near her who's willing to auction her off like a cow."

A single tear betrays me, but I don't have time to collect myself because Boz turns to one of the guards. "Get Alba out of here, and make sure he stays gone. We need to get inside."

With the side of my face tucked to his chest, Boz turns and leads me into the church. I catch a glimpse of Ed and Nic Decker glaring at us. Poor Eliza sits next to her husband staring at the pew in front of her. I turn my eyes to the marble floor to avoid everyone else as we walk the long, somber aisle. It's not lost on me that this feels very similar to the ceremony where we almost died.

So much black.

But this time, it's for a real funeral, not my figurative one.

We move to the front pew. Boz stuffs a handkerchief into my fingers and forces me to sit. When his lips touch the top of my head, he whispers for only me to hear, "Get through the next hour, baby, and you can put that man behind you once and for all."

Well.

The ironic part is, I have no idea if he's talking about Damian or my father.

I guess it doesn't matter. Even though I have no clue what my future holds, at least I can put them both behind me.

I dab my eyes.

If anything good came from that ugly exchange with my father, it's that everyone in this church will think I'm crying over the loss of Damian.

Nothing could be farther from the truth.

But Boz will get what he wants ... once again. I'll act the part, just as he demanded.

I'm lost. So damn lost. Even if Boz would let me go and I could have this damn marriage annulled, I don't know where I'd go. If he's right, and Mr. Marino would come after me, I'd never make it on my own.

The casket is wheeled down the aisle. I don't want to see it or think about that horrid day.

The organ starts to play a different piece than it did at my wedding, but it brings back memories all the same.

I tremble.

"Please rise," the priest orders.

Boz's lips touch my ear. "Don't move, baby. Just sit here. I've got you. We'll make it through the next hour together."

I nod against the lapel of his jacket. I'm sure my makeup is a mess, but I don't care. Between thoughts of that day and knowing my father doesn't give a shit what happens to me, I'm going to lean on Boz.

I'll figure out how to deal with the rest of my life after this damn funeral.

13

MY HEART

Landyn

The tide rolls in and out, lapping the sand and rocks. It's white noise for the soul after another day in hell.

I've lived here all my life, but I've never been to this spot. There's hardly anyone here.

We left the church as fast as we arrived. Boz put me into his big SUV and headed west. He went through a drive thru and ordered so many tacos, I wondered if we were going to an after-funeral party. Then he stopped at a gas station and told me to "not get out of the fucking car under any circumstance".

He was back in a flash with a six pack of beer.

That's when he drove straight to the shore. He ripped his jacket and tie off and tossed them in the back seat.

That was over an hour ago. Maybe more. I've lost track of time. We're sitting hip to hip on a bench at the edge of the sand. We're on our second beer, and I lost count how many tacos Boz inhaled.

I dig my toes into the sand and let the sun heal my frazzled nerves.

"How old are you?" I ask.

There's a pause, and I realize he's not going to answer me.

I turn and squint into the sun as I look up at him. "We're married. I think I should get to know how old my husband is."

The only reason I know he throws me a glance is from the turn of his head. His beautiful dark eyes are hidden behind his wayfarers. "Twenty-nine."

"Huh."

"*Huh* what?"

I look back at him and shrug. "Nothing. Just *huh*. I thought you were older."

He puts his beer to his lips as he mutters, "I've aged beyond my years. Good to know."

"You seem older," I amend. "You've got that whole *fuck with me and I'll kill you vibe* that doesn't scream twenty-nine."

"Yeah? How old does my vibe make me?"

I take a sip of my beer and study him from the side. His short-clipped beard frames his strong, square jaw. The longer I'm around him, the less he scares me. Don't get me wrong, he's scary. But as the days pass, he's scary in a way that makes me feel safe.

And I never thought I'd feel safe in this world.

He finally turns to me again when I don't say anything. He hikes a brow, demanding an answer.

"I'm not sure your vibe has to do with age. It's about experiences. Most twenty-nine-year-olds these days are barely figuring out life. You've been elevated to run the Marino business, and you're not even one of them. That takes a certain level of…"

"Of what?" he presses.

I'm not about to talk about the big dick energy that rivals the Almighty. I'm also not going to call him cocky to his face. I'm exhausted. Funerals and silent treatments can really take it out of you.

I settle on something more positive. "Confidence."

He turns back to the ocean. "I guess that's better than looking ten years older than I am."

I can't help the smile that tugs at my lips for the first time today. "My husband has a touch of vanity in him. I never would have guessed, Boz."

He sighs, and I feel like we're finally having a real conversation. "I feel like I've aged decades, chica."

I swing my foot and nudge his calf. "That's what happens when you work every waking minute of the day."

"I have a lot of shit to do. I don't have the luxury of down time."

"Trust me, I know. Technically, we're in what most marriages consider the honeymoon phase. But for us it's been a lot of death, threats of death, the weirdest dinner meetings I've ever experienced, and a funeral. You've been a barrel of fun, hubbalicious." I look back to the shore and sigh. "Until now. Thank you for this. Thank you for not taking me right back to the house."

"Thought you could use a break."

"How long have you worked for the Marinos?"

He takes a long pull from his bottle. So long, he drains it. He leans forward and drops it back into the six pack and picks up another barely cold beer. After he cracks it open, he finally answers. "Two years. Two long years."

He sounds different than he normally does. Tired. I realize I've never seen him sleep, even though I know he sleeps because the bed is always rumpled when I wake up on the sofa. But he comes in after I pass out and is gone before I wake.

"That's not very long," I say. He turns and hikes a brow. I go on. "I mean, for being in charge. Mr. Marino—Damian's father—trusts you."

"He should. I saved Damian's life once. Not twice, obviously."

I shift on the bench. "You did?"

"I took a bullet for him the second month I worked for the family."

I rest my beer on my bare knee and shift to him. "What happened?"

I wish I could see his eyes when he speaks. "I was new to the organization. If you think there's a lot of guards around now, you should've seen it then. At first, I just thought he had a big head, but then I realized he thought someone was out to kill him everywhere we went. He got that from Alamandos. Here in the States, he could've gone about his business, but he was paranoid."

"Did it happen here?"

Boz shakes his head. "Mexico. We were coming back from a meeting and were ambushed. I was Damian's bodyguard that day."

My eyes widen. "You threw yourself in front of him?"

He tips his head and looks back out to the waves. "Does it matter? I caught the bullet and saved his life."

"That's horrible." I can't stand the thought of him getting shot for anyone, least of all Damian.

His full lips tip on one side. "It wasn't the level of shitshow as your wedding, but bullets were still flying. I had to recover at Alamandos' estate and was treated by his doctors. We didn't want it on record."

"You didn't even go to a hospital?"

"Nope," he mutters and takes another drink. "That was all it took. I guess Damian never had anyone in his life loyal enough to do shit like that. He elevated me to be his right-hand man. Don't get me wrong, I was still his bodyguard. But he also brought me into the business in a way that shuffled everyone else down that ladder. People like Nic and Ed Decker. Even though Ed isn't a Marino by blood, he's been in the business since he married Alamandos' sister. He hates me and wants Nic to take over."

I raise the bottle to my lips and take a sip. "Nic and his father. So charming."

"You haven't seen the worst of it, chica."

"You spared me from that." It's a statement that gets his attention. He shifts to me and drapes an arm across the back of the bench. He stays silent, so I keep pressing. "That doesn't make any of this less confusing for me. I want to understand."

I flinch as he brings a hand up. The tips of his fingers brush the hair from my face that's blowing in the light, ocean breeze. He doesn't try to make me feel better or help me understand anything about my new life. Instead, his words come out of left field. "I didn't lie to you about your dad. He left three messages in the last couple days, all about business. If you want to see your mom, I can make that happen."

For the second time today, emotion washes over me. "You'd do that?"

His fingertips tease the side of my face. "I will, if it's what you want. But there's no fucking way I'm going to allow your father to see you. He's not getting near you again."

"You're different," I whisper. I'm almost afraid to say it even though we're in a wide-open space, safe from cameras and security and eavesdroppers.

He pulls in a breath as he studies me. I've never wanted to look into his eyes more than right now. "Yeah? What makes me different, baby?"

"Everything," I explain. "You say I'm a possession, but you don't treat me like one. Not like everyone else has."

His jaw goes tight, but he doesn't confirm or deny my assumption.

"I still can't believe I'm here," I go on and motion around us. "I'm living in the same city I grew up in. My parents are here. My friends are here. But it feels like I've been picked up and plopped into an alternate universe. I've been forced into a marriage I didn't want, nor one I understand. But it's easy to see, Boz. You're not like the rest of them."

He shakes his head once, and this time, his tone is low and rough. "You don't know who I am, baby."

"Maybe." I can't take it anymore and reach up to pull his shades away from his face. He doesn't flinch when the big ball of fire in the sky hits his beautiful eyes. It's like this is the first time I've looked into them. They're deeper, less black, and there's something smoldering behind them that piques my curiosity even further about my new husband. "Do you know how strange it is to be married to someone who you know nothing about? If this is forever and ever, until death do us part, I want to know everything about you."

"Trust me, baby. What you see is what you get. You drew the short stick."

I shake my head and reach up to touch his hand where his fingers twist a lock of my hair. "I doubt that."

His dark eyes narrow. "Be careful, Landyn. You have no fucking idea what you've waded into."

"No, I don't." I press his palm to the side of my face and relish in his touch. As much as I don't want it to affect me, it does. Every time he lays a hand on me, even if it is for show—no matter how much I wish it weren't for show—it wakes a place deep inside me that's new and exciting. I can't stop thinking about that place. "Please, Boz. Help me understand."

Brax

She's the distraction I do not need.

And she just won't stop.

Every word, every touch, every time she looks into my eyes—she claws deeper and deeper below the surface. She's about to break into a place I forgot existed.

It's something I can't let happen. Not only can I not afford the distraction, I absolutely cannot allow anyone to want more from me. It doesn't matter how much I like it.

And I can't deny that I like it.

I don't pull away from her, because touching her is something I've become obsessed with. And to touch her while we're alone is new. "Helping you understand is one thing I cannot do."

She continues to torture me and leans into my hand farther. "Yet I have to trust you and do what you say? I'm not okay with that, Boz."

"You don't have a choice, *Landyn*."

"Oh, I know I don't. That was made clear when I was taken from my home at gunpoint." She pulls her lip between her teeth to chew on that thought. "Is that the reason for a celibate marriage?"

She just won't stop, and I can't keep the bite out of my tone. "Any other woman who was forced into marriage and told she didn't have to consummate it would not look that gift horse in the mouth. Accept it for what it is. I'm not into non-con, Landyn, and I'm no rapist. Drop it."

She doesn't heed my warning. Instead, a smile settles on her lips that looks like it was dipped in the finest sugar.

I want to kiss it off her face.

She scoots closer to me, and we were already really damn close. She doesn't let go of my hand when she leans up and presses those sweet lips to the underside of my jaw.

My blood rushes south even though her smile dissolves into an expression so serious, I forget about my cock. "And that right there is why I know you're different. You can deny it all you want, but I'll stand my ground when it's just us—when it's you and me, and no one is watching or listening or studying us. You might work for a drug cartel, but you're not like them. You're not even like my dad who considers himself swanky in the world of crime."

I need to change the subject. There hasn't been a time in the last two years that I was afraid of being made. If I'm made, I'm as good as dead.

When Landyn entered the fray, I knew I needed to wrap this up fast. Now I really need to crank up the heat to get the fuck out of this hellhole and away from the temptation of the woman who's a fake everything to me.

No. That's all wrong.

I'm the fake.

She's as real and as genuine as they come.

Then it flashes before my eyes like a damn strobe light. What I didn't see, or hell, what I buried deep because if I admitted what I was truly feeling, it would be real.

Anger.

I'm pissed she doesn't know the real me. That my name isn't the one sliding across her lips when I touch her.

I'm pissed this is fake.

And I'm even more pissed that there's no way this will ever be anything more than a sham.

When this is done, I'll be the liar.

There's no doubt she'll hate me. And I'll deserve it.

"Thank you for today, Boz."

I shake my head, more to clear it and to wipe those regrets from my brain. There's no room in my life for regrets. I need a clear head to focus on the goal. "You're thanking me for forcing you to go to a funeral?"

She lifts a shoulder. "Thank you for standing up to my father and making the funeral you forced me to go to bearable."

"I do what I can," I deadpan—dead being the operative word.

"Can I ask for a favor?"

Finally, something I can be truthful about. "I can't make any promises."

"Don't play with my heart."

I pull in a deep breath to control myself so I don't fall to my knees in front of her and beg for forgiveness before she even knows who I really am.

She just won't stop. Her words might as well be a knife to my gut. "On top of everything else, I won't survive that."

She doesn't give me the chance to answer. She shoves her beer at me, steals my sunglasses, and stands.

"What are you doing?" I ask as she moves away from me.

Her blond hair flips over her shoulder as I watch her walk toward the Pacific. "I'm taking advantage of my freedom while I have the chance. Don't worry, *darling*." I'm not sure if any other word could sound so unnatural falling from her lips as that one being thrown at me when she just keeps pushing my buttons. "I'm not an idiot. You could tackle me to the ground in a nanosecond. I think being kidnapped and forced into marriage is messing with my head, because I'm afraid I might enjoy being tackled by you. But that's just one more thing my heart can't take."

She turns from me and heads straight to the water. Reaching down, she yanks the bottom of her dress that barely hit her knees and pulls it up under her ass as she wades in. I set both bottles down and lean forward to study her. I have no clue what to expect from this woman. If I have to run in and save her, I will. The fact she just told me she'd enjoy me tackling her to the ground makes me want to do just that.

She's careful as her bare feet navigate the rocky sand. This stretch of the shore is quiet for a reason—it's not a wide-open beach. There are never swimmers, surfers, or tourists. I fucking love it. If I can ever steal a moment to myself, I come here.

After the funeral, I told the guards to stay with Damian's body as they took him to Mexico for the burial, that my wife couldn't take any more today. I lied about a meeting with our investors on the east coast.

Really, I just needed to get the fuck out of there and didn't want to make Landyn have to sit through the burial too. Alamandos can't hold it against me if it's for work.

She turns back when she's knee deep in the Pacific. Her dress is bunched right below her pussy that I really need to stop thinking about. It's all my cock wants after our time in the dining room last night.

I just want all of her.

As she wades deeper, she bends to pick up shells from the ocean floor. I watch her do this over and over again, tossing them back to the water before searching for another.

I finally get up to walk to the edge of the ocean and stuff my hands in my pockets. If she's going to push my buttons, I'm damn well going to push back. "Why aren't you angrier about this?"

"You mean this?" She motions between the two of us.

I stare at her through the bright sun. "Because if I were forced into the situation you're in, I'd be angry as hell."

The waves lap at her bare thighs, soaking her dress where she has it bunched. Since she stole my shades, it's all I can do not to look at her legs. The same ones that were wrapped around my waist last night.

"Do I have a choice but to be in this situation?" she asks with a bit of a bite that I'd expect. Hell, who am I kidding? I need her to be pissed. Her anger will make it easier for me to not want her.

All of her.

"No," I answer honestly. "Not unless you want the Marinos to hunt you down."

"You promised to protect me," she states. "Were you lying?"

She's making it harder and harder for me to be frustrated with her, and easier and easier to want her more.

"Haven't I protected you so far?"

"You have. And that's why I'm not angry. Anger gives me anxiety. I don't need that bad energy. There's enough swirling around us as it is."

She's got me there. I've had nothing but bad energy since I went undercover. But this would be a whole lot easier in the end if she hated me along the way.

"You grew up as a mobster's daughter. You know there's not much good energy in this business."

At the mention of her father, she studies the shell in her hand before leaning down to rinse it off. Then she dries it on her black dress, not at all caring about the mess it makes. Without looking away from her hand, she asks, "Do you know the legend of the sand dollar?"

I'm from Queens, and we rarely went to the shore. But these are things I can't tell her. "Can't say that I do."

She turns the shell over in her fingers and inspects it as she talks. "There are lots of legends. Some say they're coins lost by mermaids or from the mythical city of Atlantis. Some even think it represents the story of Christ. The Birth, Crucifixion, and Resurrection."

"I've never given any thought to a sand dollar before, baby, let alone that much."

"I think they have a different meaning." She looks up at me through my own sunglasses. "I think they represent freedom, strength, and even choosing your own path."

What in the hell was I thinking bringing her here for tacos and beer? I assumed we'd sit in the sun and escape reality for thirty minutes, but all she's done is mesmerize me. And that's dangerous. "How's that?"

"Strength because the creature who lives in this shell has protection from predators. They have the freedom to go wherever they want. Sometimes it's together and other times alone."

She studies the shell one more time before flipping it across the water at me. I catch it in midair before it falls for some other deep thinker to find. I turn it over in my hand. It's dead and not even twice the size of a quarter. It's not at all special and I bet there are tons just like it on this stretch of beach alone.

"They're known for choosing their own paths, Boz. They represent freedom and the ability to walk away from environments that are no longer working for them. Doesn't that sound like the perfect life?"

"That is a legend," I say and slide the fossil into my pocket. The cynical side in me doesn't have a hard time shining on any day. "Hardly possible in real life."

She lifts a foot and kicks saltwater my way. "So negative, Boz. We need to work on that."

I need to change the subject fast. I do not need to get in deep with Landyn *Torres*. What I really need to do is push her away while keeping her alive and safe. "I need your help with something."

She tucks her hair behind her ear. "More scary dinner guests to entertain? I'm getting good at that, if I do say so myself."

I shake my head. "Rocco. He's moving into the house and will work with me as an intern. I want him to get his GED, and I want you to tutor him."

"Want, want, want," she mocks. "You do remember I dropped out of college, right? I'm no teacher."

"Not asking you to help him pass the MCAT, chica. I want you to help him get his high school diploma."

She swishes her foot around in the water. "I'm trying to figure out what it means when you call me chica or baby or just plain Landyn."

I ignore her and keep talking. "He needs his GED, and you need something to do. Problem solved."

"So I'm your problem now too?"

"You're a lot of things, baby. A problem is at the bottom of a long list."

"You're way sweeter at funerals. I like sweet Boz, but I don't like funerals. Though Damian's was nice."

I don't try to bite back my smirk. "Be careful who you say that around."

I can almost see her roll her eyes behind my shades. "You don't have to worry about that."

I lift my chin. "Let's go. We need to get back before they come looking for us."

She carefully makes her way over the rocky ocean floor until she's standing in front of me with her black dress still hitched around her upper thighs. "You don't seem like a picnic kind of guy. Thank you for today."

Even though I know I shouldn't, I can't help but touch her when she's this close. I lift my hand and tap the end of her nose with the tip of my index finger before claiming her hand. "Time to get back to reality."

"Reality," she drawls. "You're a real downer. You're forcing me to be the optimist in our marriage."

I shake my head, but agree. "Baby, you are not wrong."

14

BONDING

Landyn

"This is giving me a headache," Rocco complains.

I toss the papers onto the floor where we're sitting in the great room overlooking the pool and ocean. I'd much rather be swimming, but after the fit Boz threw the other day, I don't dare ask Rocco if he wants to take a dip with me. My husband might just lose it.

I look across the room to the man child I'm supposed to be tutoring. "How do you think I feel? I barely passed this class the first time and dropped out of college so I didn't have to take geometry again."

"I don't know why the fuck I have to do this. I was sent here to cut the grass and clean the pool so I could chat with your old man. Now I'm living here, had to cut my hair, and look like I work at a fucking department store. Do you know who shops at department stores? Old people."

I gape at the guy who looks nothing like he did when I first met him in the office adjacent to our bedroom. "Seriously? I love department stores. I worked at one before I got married. You know, like, a couple weeks ago."

"People like me don't shop at department stores," he continues to complain.

I wonder how Boz would feel about this. As much as I'd rather pluck out my own eyelashes one by one than relearn how to find the slope of anything, I really don't think Rocco has anything to complain about. Other than the fact Spencer made him get a trim. He didn't even make him cut his hair short. It actually looks great. It's still charmingly shaggy, just without the split ends.

When Boz and I returned from the funeral last night, I learned what a quiet night as newlyweds looked like.

I showered off the makeup, tears, and saltwater. Boz decided we would have dinner in our room, but unlike our picnic, the conversation wasn't meaningful or deep. Then he disappeared into his office to work the rest of the night. But before he disappeared, he told me more about what he *wanted* when it came to his new employee Rocco.

Honestly, the way Boz talks about Rocco, he sounds more like a project than an employee. But what do I know? I'm just here to pretend to know geometry. And shoot me, tomorrow we're moving onto parts of speech.

I lived through my own wedding massacre only to be tortured with high school homework all over again.

"This is the dumbest shit ever," Rocco keeps on.

If I didn't feel loyal to Boz out of sheer will to survive, I'd warn my new young friend that someone is always watching in this place.

Rocco rolls to his back where he's stretched out on the floor, his new business-casual attire in a mess of wrinkles. He's playing catch by himself with an apple—up, down, up, down, up, down—as he continues to talk about anything besides geometry. "Are you and boss man going to live here forever? This place is the shit. I've only seen houses like this on TV."

We studied for almost two hours. Rocco is a talker, which I

didn't expect from a biker club prospect. Unless he's chatty just to get out of geometry. Who could blame him for that?

Not me.

"I'm not sure how long we'll live here. We haven't had that conversation. I'll add it to the long list of things we need to discuss. I'm actually curious about that, too, but it's been a little busy. Can I ask you something?"

"I guess." The apple continues to spin in the air as he catches it perfectly every time. "Doesn't mean I'm going to answer."

"Why did you drop out of high school?"

"Why did you drop out of college?"

He's got me there. I shouldn't have told him that, but I had to warn him at the beginning of our tutoring session that my "tutoring" could be sketchy at best.

"That's different," I clip and do my best to sound like an adult. "Boz told me you played football, and you were good. Why give that up when they have real teachers to make sure you pass these ridiculous classes."

He says nothing.

"Rocco?" I call one more time.

The apple finally stops, and he stares at the ceiling. "Wasn't going to go anywhere anyway. Why waste one more year when I could get a head start working for the Jackals. At least that was my plan. But now I've got a closet full of fucking ties, working for the cartel, and studying geometry." He looks over at me. "Don't get me wrong, you're hot and you seem cool. But this isn't what I signed up for."

What I want to say is *touché, young man*. I didn't sign up for this either.

He and I have a lot in common. Neither of us are here by choice. Instead of expressing that, I find the need to defend my husband. "I'm sure Boz has his reasons for wanting you to get your diploma. It can't hurt, right?"

He looks over at me. There's something smoldering behind his honey-brown eyes. It feels like anger laced with a hint of resentment. "You think the club is going to toss me my patch and give me the second half of my tat because I have a diploma? No way. They don't give a flying fuck. If they knew I was wasting my time on this, I'd eat shit for the rest of my days."

If there's one thing I understand in life, it's the need to fit in. And it wasn't society or peer pressure that drilled that into my core like it was an integral piece of religion we needed to make it through in life.

It was my parents.

I pick up the review packet Boz left for me this morning and don't look Rocco in the eyes when I add, "Then what they don't know won't hurt them, right? Let's get back to it before I forget everything I just learned. At this point, we're in this together. Maybe at the end, I'll get another diploma. It's always good to be a little extra in life."

"You're extra enough without the bonus diploma," he mutters.

"Be careful how you talk to my wife."

Rocco shifts to a sitting position, and I turn toward the deep voice. The same voice I'm becoming more and more in tune with, especially the closer it is.

Like when his lips touch me. That deep timbre feels good on my skin.

I haven't seen him today. I'm not necessarily a light sleeper, but the man's ability to steal in and out of our bedroom while I'm snoozing every single night and morning is weird. And I got up early this morning to be ready for my time with Rocco. When I came down for coffee, June told me he left early for meetings.

What kind of meetings could he possibly have at that time of day?

"Where have you been?" I ask with an underlying hint of irritation.

Boz's intense gaze turns to me as he makes his way to the back of the sofa where I'm sitting. In one fluid motion, his hand slides into the back of my hair, and his lips land on mine.

This isn't a *honey, I'm home* peck. This kiss is demanding, involves tongues, and causes me to stop breathing. Other chemical reactions he's causing my body to experience definitely piss me off. When he finally lets me catch my breath, he reminds me what it's like for that deep voice to rumble close to my skin. "You missed me. It's good to know the honeymoon phase is still going strong."

Our marriage gives new meaning to the term *honeymoon phase*. I wonder if that means someone died this morning.

But him throwing that term out in front of Rocco when everyone around us assumes we're banging like bunnies since that's the impression Boz is determined to make with his public displays of affection, is...

Well, I'm not sure I'm ready to admit what it is.

I look up into his dark eyes and frown.

He drags a heavy thumb across my angry lower lip. "How is geometry?"

"Just as bad as it was when I was in high school," I snap and try to pull my head back, but he won't let go of me. "You didn't answer me. Where were you this morning, and why do you leave so early every day?"

"I have a good deal of work that can't come to the house, and I'm an early riser. If you want me to wake you before l leave from now on, I'll be more than happy to do that."

I don't answer because I want him to do that. And not just for the reason he's insinuating to everyone watching us.

Boz Torres has become a security blanket. He found me when I was kidnapped. He saved me from having to marry Nic Decker. And he stood up to my father, which I didn't have the nerve to do.

Then he fed me tacos.

Tacos should not be the thing that nails my coffin shut when it comes to this man, but it might be. If he would've added warm churros to our drive-thru order, I'd be a goner.

Thank God he didn't. I need some form of defense against this man.

But it really comes down to the fact I don't like being in this house without him. Even though he claims to run the legitimate side of the Marino business, it all comes back to drugs in the end, and the Marino family owns this house. The same family who took me and forced me into a marriage against my will.

So far, Rocco is the only one who has pretended to like me, and he doesn't want to be here either.

"You didn't tell me you'd be gone this morning. We might need marriage counseling when it comes to communication, *Boz*."

A low whistle sounds next to us.

Boz looks at Rocco. "What?"

"Nothing, other than your old lady popping your name at the end of that sentence," Rocco mutters.

Boz narrows his eyes. "Don't bust my ass for something like that and try to tell me you don't understand the parts of speech when it comes time to take that test." Boz looks back and speaks to me in the same tone. "We'll *communicate* about that later."

There's no way I'll admit to the fact it makes me nervous to be here without him. I don't need him to know I'm clingy on top of everything else.

"I'm hungry," Rocco announces.

Saved by the starving teenager.

Boz stands and moves for the door. "Eat and get back to studying. Come and see me later this afternoon, Rocco. I need to get a message to Logan about next week. Landyn, I want you to come and see me first."

I stand and decide I'm done being bossed around. I'll help Rocco study because I like him, and I'm bored. But just because Boz wants something, doesn't mean he's going to get it. I'm completely prepared to not give him what he *wants* any longer. "I'm busy the rest of the day."

He stops at the edge of the room and demands, "Busy with what?"

"Besides geometry and earth science, I found a book. I'm going to read it." That's a lie. I haven't seen a book since I got here. Surely there's one around here somewhere.

"You can't fit me into your afternoon because you found a book?"

"Maybe tomorrow, Boz."

"There she goes again," Rocco mutters.

"Landyn," Boz demands.

I say nothing, but I do hike a brow.

He stares me down, but I don't give in and stand my ground. I'm proud of myself.

He looks between Rocco and me.

Finally, he shakes his head. "Dinner tonight in the dining room."

"In the dining room?" Rocco gapes.

Boz nods. "The three of us. I don't care how enthralling your book is, Landyn. Be there."

"The dining room," I echo and hold my head high. "I wouldn't miss it. All the good stuff happens in the dining room."

I don't wait for him to answer and turn for the kitchen, and I don't care what June says. Today I'm going to make my own lunch, and then I'm going to load my own damn dishes into the dishwasher by myself.

I'm done with people telling me what to do. I might not be able to leave, but if I have to live here against my will, then I'll damn well do it on my own terms.

Rocco follows me into the kitchen. June has barely warmed up to me, and Miranda will hardly glance in my direction. Both of their heads pop up when we enter their domain. I stop across the island and Rocco stands to my side, probably waiting for my lead.

"Ma'am," June starts. "I haven't started lunch yet, but I'll get on that right away. Are you hungry for anything special? Where would you like it served?"

"Since you're asking, I want a burger—" Rocco starts, but I elbow him in the side to shut him up.

"Please, don't bother today. We can manage lunch on our own."

Rocco frowns at me. "But she offered."

"It's our jobs, ma'am," June insists as she motions to Miranda.

"Not today, it's not." I round the island and head to the refrigerator. "We'll figure it out on our own. Take a load off."

Miranda's young eyes flare when she gapes at June.

I open the industrial size refrigerator. Wow. It's like a small grocery store. Rocco, on the other hand, opens the freezer and isn't nearly as impressed as I am, and mutters, "No pizza. Or corn dogs."

"Grilled cheese," I announce. I reach in and grab butter and a package of sharp cheddar before turning to Rocco. "You can have as many as you want. Cut up some fruit and see if there are chips in the pantry."

June hops off the barstool she was perched on and tries to steal my cheese. "I'll make it for you."

I yank it back. "I don't cook, but I can make a mean grilled cheese. Don't steal my thunder, June. In fact, I'll make you and Miranda one too. We'll all eat lunch together, right here in the kitchen like normal people. How does that sound?"

"I don't think—" June starts while Miranda shakes her head in silence. Neither one likes the sound of anything I just said.

I ignore them both, find a skillet, and crank on the burner. "Find the bread, Rocco."

"Got it." Rocco dumps an armful of food he collected from the pantry. Bread, two bags of chips, some crackers, and three candy bars. He tears the wrapper of one of the chocolate-covered candies and bites off a hunk.

Whatever. I'm only supposed to help him study, not make sure he eats a balanced diet.

"I don't think Mr. Torres will be happy about this." June is standing at my side with her hands on her hips. Miranda is chewing on the tip of her thumb with anxiety.

"Boz told us to eat lunch. Why would he be unhappy?" I ask as I butter the bread.

"This is our job, Mrs. Torres. We're here to serve the family. It's not customary for you to even be in the kitchen."

I stick the knife in the butter and turn to her. "Seriously?"

"Yes," she snaps and throws a glance at Miranda to yank her hand away from her mouth, and whispers, "Wash your hands."

Miranda rushes to the sink, and I look back at June. This time I really look at her. I don't think she's old and stuffy and set in her ways any longer.

No.

She might be snappy with me, but I think it's because she's nervous. Or, more like stressed.

Miranda finishes at the sink and scurries back to June's side.

Since I've been here, all Boz has to do is pick up a phone and food magically appears. Or the car is waiting outside the front door. Or an entire wardrobe appears. It happened for Rocco, and I bet the same thing happened for me before I got here.

I cross my arms and speak to both of them at the same time. "Help me understand this. Do you two get in trouble if someone in this house isn't served by you?"

Miranda stares at the floor in front of her, but June just stares back at me, steadfast in her silence.

"Answer me. Please," I prod.

I swear a touch of pink touches Miranda's face.

I hike a brow at June.

Nothing.

I lift a finger and point back and forth between the two of them. "Don't move, and whatever you do, do not make a grilled cheese sandwich. I'll be right back."

June finally breaks her silence, and calls after me, "Ma'am!"

I ignore her. My feet carry me up the stairs and down the hall before I know it. I don't knock, barging right into the office off our bedroom.

"No, that won't do," Boz speaks into the phone, but his gaze comes straight to me. "Make it happen this week. I need the inspector to sign off or the entire project will be late. I've got cash to move and can't afford to sit on it much longer."

I make my way in long strides to the front of his desk and cross my arms.

"Let me know when it's done." Boz looks me up and down, and hangs up. "What?"

"Why are June and Miranda so skittish?" I demand.

He leans back in his chair, but says nothing.

I keep going. "Every time I go into the kitchen, June freaks and Miranda turns ghost white. Miranda won't say a word to me, let alone make eye contact. June acts like someone will chop her hand off if I make my own sandwich. And I'm not allowed to put my dirty dishes in the dishwasher."

Boz tips his head. "It's what they're used to."

My arms drop to my sides. "They look scared. Like, really scared."

He leans forward and puts his forearms to the desk and lowers his voice. "I'm only going to say this one more time, it's what they're used to."

My expression falls. "That's all you're going to tell me?"

His full lips clamp shut, and his eyes narrow. He wants to say more, but he can't.

Well then.

I cross my arms. "I want to make lunch, but June said you wouldn't be happy. Is that true?"

The muscles around his eyes relax a tad. "Baby, I don't care what you do as long as you don't leave this house or swim in that fucking bikini."

"Okay. That's what I thought, but I wanted to make sure." I exhale and try not to think of our time at the pool the other day when he turned into a walking-growling-possessive monster with an erection I'll never forget. "I was going to be mad at you if that were the case."

He leans back in his chair again and looks more like he did yesterday at the beach when a smirk tugs at his lips. "I can't have you being mad at me."

I bite the skin inside my cheek to keep from smiling. "Are you hungry?"

"Are you going to make me lunch?" His smirk swells with the playful touch of his words.

"Only because I'm not mad at you."

"I can't wait."

I put a hand out. "I'm no June. Temper your expectations."

He lowers his voice, and it doesn't matter that he's a whole desk width away from me, a tingle spreads across my skin when he says, "I'm not going to lie, I can't wait ... to eat it."

I exhale and speak in a rush as I take a step backward toward the door. "Great. I mean, it's a grilled cheese. I'm not fancy—hope you had a big breakfast before you left before the crack of dawn this morning."

His eyes darken. "Chica, I'll take anything you want to give me. I'm fucking starving."

"Um..." I swallow hard. "I'll ... make you two. Do you want anything else?"

He doesn't take his eyes off me, even when his cell vibrates on his desk in front of him. "If there's something else, I'm here for it."

My back hits the door. "No, that's it. I'll send Rocco up when it's done."

"I'd rather you deliver it."

I shake my head. "Sorry. I'm bonding with the kitchen staff on top of quizzing your intern. My day is full."

"Then I guess I'll see you at dinner."

I step out of the office and grab the handle to put some much-needed distance between me and my groom. "Yeah. In the dining room."

The last thing I see is a smile tugging at the lips that I wish would kiss me more often than they do.

Hell, I wish they'd kiss me in private, and not just when people are watching us.

"Baby?"

I stop and turn back to him, warm in all the right spots. "Yeah?"

"I invited your mother to the house."

I forget all about kisses or being warm and wet, even though I'm both. "You did?"

He nods. "She'll be here tomorrow afternoon."

I'm overcome. "Thank you."

He shrugs like it's not the big deal that it is.

"Really, Boz. It means so much to me."

"Your father isn't welcome here."

I shake my head. "No. I don't want him here. I don't want anything to do with him."

His rough voice softens a touch. "Good, baby."

Baby.

It's a gentle one too.

Damn. I shouldn't like that. "I'll make you a sandwich."

"I can't wait."

I close the office door and head for the kitchen. I have cheese sandwiches to grill, and a kitchen staff to charm.

15

A REGENCY ROMANCE GONE WRONG

Brax

It's been a day.
Followed by a week.
Hell, it's been two long fucking years.
I rarely meet Cole Carson and Tim Coleman in person. I can count on one hand how many times before the wedding and since I went under, so two times in one week is a lot. It's a chance none of us can afford to take—namely me—since I'm the one buried so deep it's getting harder and harder to keep a grasp on reality.

But with Damian out of the way, it's time to get on with shit.

When I got an alert on the phone I'm never away from unless I'm in the shower—and even then, I hardly take my eyes off it—I knew it was important.

I dragged my ass out of bed hours before dawn. My wife was sound asleep on the sofa where she's been every night since we got here. She was on her stomach, and the blanket was pulled away just enough to show a bare leg, and a peek of her ass cheek that taunted me from inside a small pair of silk shorts.

If I were a gentleman, I'd give her the bed.

If I were half a gentleman, I'd invite her to sleep on the other side of the bed.

But I'm me, trying to keep my focus and both of us alive, so I haven't done either.

The way I'm drawn to her when I'm alert and awake, I'm afraid of what would happen when I'm not. And since I've touched a good deal of her body with the only intention of keeping her safe, I've proven I'm no gentleman. If she enters that bed, my last two years working within the Marino organization will look like child's play compared to the challenge of not touching her when no one is watching.

So I slipped out of our bedroom quietly and decided she can stay on that damn sofa forever.

I told the guards I had business to take care of with a customer who was trying to back out of our arrangement since Damian isn't at the helm any longer. That was enough for no one to think twice about why I was leaving before dawn on my own. I was out of town in no time, driving the very car that will turn into our eyes and ears.

At least, that's the plan.

While Carson's tech crew worked on the car, I had to stand there and take shit from my CIA Officer and DEA supervisor about Landyn. And since they do have ears on every single thing that goes on in that house other than the bedroom, they know everything.

It was not a fun meeting.

Eating their shit and being their punching bag for thirty long minutes was an experience I could have done without. I took every jab and choked down every taunt about how, from the sounds of it in the control room, there's nothing fake about my *wife*.

They also commended me on my dedication to the job.

How I'm really giving it my all.

Fuck me.

What I am giving my all to is my pure unadulterated willpower when it comes to Landyn *Torres*.

And that resolve is shaky at best.

When Damian told me he was going to marry the bombshell daughter of a dried-up mobster, I assumed she'd be spoiled and self-absorbed. At the very least, I thought she'd be a pain in my ass once I realized I had no choice but to step up and take care of her. There was no way I could allow Nic Decker to put his dirty hands on anyone. My conscience couldn't take it.

Her mob father sold her to the devil. He knew exactly what he was doing and what her fate would be marrying into the Marino family. Dennis Alba deserves to rot in hell for what he did to Landyn.

That cocksucker's name is now scribbled in Sharpie at the top of my list of people to take down. Not only will he be charged with trafficking cocaine, but a human too.

The very human my brain and cock are completely obsessed with.

Then I assign Landyn to my Rocco-needs-a-GED project for the sole reason to give her something to do. They spent one day lamenting over geometry, making sandwiches, and bonding with the kitchen staff. Within twenty-four hours, June is talking Landyn's ear off, Miranda doesn't look like a terrified mouse, and Rocco is actually acting his age instead of a one-percenter wannabe.

In fact, you'd think he and Landyn were new-found siblings who had just discovered each other through some mail-your-spit-to-find-your-long-lost-family website and are now making up for lost time.

The three of us ate in the dining room last night. Landyn was by my side like she has been for every other shit-show meal we've hosted since she got here, but this meal was different. It was unlike anything I've experienced since I first stepped foot in this house.

It was normal.

No business was conducted.

It was nonstop chatter, laughing, and joking. Landyn even threw a roll across the table at our new houseguest when he teased her for being an old married woman when she announced she wasn't allowed to swim without me.

That was when I ended dinner and announced I was ready to have my bride to myself. I forced her to tell the staff and Rocco goodnight and I told them not to interrupt us until morning. With Landyn's hand in mine, I dragged her back to our room.

I have no fucking idea what Rocco did after that. I don't care. I locked us away and watched Landyn glare at me before escaping to the bathroom. I heard bathwater and pretended to study bank account deposits while thinking nonstop about her naked on the other side of the door. The rest of the house assumed we were busy being newlyweds, even though there was only silence coming from our room.

I don't know why the hell Damian didn't have a TV in here. If I don't have something else to focus on soon, I might lose it.

I'll remedy that tomorrow. I need a distraction more than I need federal search warrants.

I filed another day behind me as a frustrated, blue-balled married man. But it's time to get back to business.

I'm sending Rocco to meet with Logan in the car that's equipped with ears and a GPS. Logan basically came right out and said they've got tunnels. I want to know where they are and what else they're running through them.

And my mother-in-law is scheduled to visit for the first time. I'm anxious about this for many reasons. I'm curious to see how Nellie Alba acts after the deal that landed her daughter in the middle of Marino territory. It will be telling how ingrained she is in her husband's business.

Obtaining a federal warrant for Dennis Alba got easier after he made the deal for his daughter. But I want more. I want to know where every dime he makes comes from. He got off clean when we took down the load because he puts enough space between him and his mules and employs a crafty accountant.

I want to take him down and make sure he stays there. Timing is everything and inviting Landyn's mom here will kill two birds with one stone.

There's a knock on the office door.

I exit out of the screen I'm working in. "Come in."

Rocco takes up most of the doorway. "You called for me, boss?"

I motion him in. "I need you to get a message to the Jackals. I have a shipment that will be ready to come across soon. I'm counting on you to set that up."

He hesitates a beat, and I wonder if he's having second thoughts about the club.

He finally lifts his chin. "I can do that."

I pick up the keys that are sitting in front of me and toss them across the desk. "Take one of our cars. This will be available to you while you're running messages for me. Tell him I've got a load going to Vegas. After he gets it across the border, I want to know how he's transporting it. The last guy I contracted with lost the entire fucking thing, which cost us millions."

"Yeah, but you got Landyn out of it," he points out.

"Mrs. Torres," I correct, because I have no desire to talk to him about anything besides the Jackals. Especially Landyn.

"Sorry, but the way I see it, you lucked out. She's cool. And she doesn't seem to hate you, which is good if you've gotta be married to someone."

I tip my head and wonder why he thinks Landyn doesn't hate me. Because she should, and she sure seemed like it last night when I ended the fun at dinner.

Rocco proves he's as chatty as my wife. "She's not busting your balls or some shit. I've seen it. It's why my dad was always drunk. The longer it went on, the drunker he got, which only made shit worse. But that's all my mom did—bust his balls. Who wants to stick around for that?"

The kid is a talker. Every conversation or meal we share, the more he opens up. It's too bad he had to go and find a family in the Jackals instead of a Division 1 team.

I glance at the clock and get back to the subject at hand. Landyn's mom will be here soon, and that's a show I don't want to miss. "You think you can do this? I want details, Rocco. I want to know where it's happening, what my product will be transported in, and how they're going to secure it. Logan cut a high-stakes deal with me, and I expect details in return. Since I'm paying out the ass, I deserve to know everything."

Rocco stands and stuffs the keys into his pants pocket. He looks nothing like he did when he got here. He's cleaned up, his dress shirt covers his tat, and he looks more like a frat boy from generations of money than he does a one-percenter. He pulls out his cell and starts to tap at the screen as he mutters, "I got you, boss. Logan will come through, and so will I."

"Come straight to me when you get back. Do not tell anyone else anything. Got it?"

He reads something that comes through on the screen before looking up at me. "Got it."

My gut wants to tell him to be careful and watch his back.

Damn. Who am I?

I've become my dad.

Or worse, my mom.

I pick up my phone when it rings. It's Spencer. "Yeah?"

"Mrs. Alba is here, Mr. Torres. She just entered the gate and is about to park in the circle drive. Will you be joining them? Mrs. Torres has been pacing the front door for almost twenty minutes."

I wake my computer and log into the surveillance system. Nellie Alba pulls her BMW up to the front doors and puts it in park. I've done everything I can to avoid Landyn today, so now is not the time to butt into her time. "Maybe later. Show her in and put them in the great room. Do not allow my mother-in-law farther into the house. I don't trust her."

I hang up immediately and sit back and watch.

Also known as investigate.

Landyn

I haven't seen Boz all day. He was gone when I woke up this morning.

Again.

Shocker.

I had a lot of fears when the Marinos took me from my home.

I feared for myself physically and emotionally. Thank God I didn't end up at the hands of Damian or Nic. I have a feeling my worst nightmares would not come close to what my reality would have been.

Being ignored by the man I ended up marrying should make me happy. Being ignored in my current situation is a gift—one I should not take for granted.

But instead of embracing it for the peace of mind it should be, it pisses me off.

I had one not-so-horrible day, even if I did have to dig into the recesses of my brain and take a trip back to geometry in my sophomore year of high school.

Once Rocco got over trying to be something he isn't, he gave me hints he's lived a hard life and has half the tattoo to prove it. He's funny with an innocence about him, even though I have a feeling there's not one thing innocent about him.

Then I spun magic with grilled cheese sandwiches. I thought my husband was softening up to me.

But dinner last night changed all that.

It was fun and real, without a gun in sight. Honestly, it was refreshing, and the best day I've had since the Marinos kidnapped my family.

But apparently living in a happy house is not in Boz's wheelhouse. He didn't utter a word through dinner, until he not so vaguely insinuated he was ready to fuck me through the night.

That's when I decided I was done trying. If he demands that I be by his side for appearances, I guess I have no choice. But, from now on when it's the two of us, he can kiss my ass.

I have once again engaged the cold shoulder, and this time I'm determined that it's here to stay.

Me and my chilly shoulder will adjust to our new life just fine, sans the geometry. I could do without that. But since Rocco is my only friend, I'll continue to attempt to calculate slope for his sake.

Literally the most useless skill for ninety-nine percent of the population of the entire universe. I have no clue what the other one percent does with it.

This is all too much for anyone to deal with.

But today, I get to see my mom. I have no idea why I'm nervous, but I am.

We're not close and never have been. She was incensed about what my father did, but that was more about what her country club friends thought instead of my safety or happiness.

Even so, a glimmer of hope flickers inside me that maybe she'll do something to get me out of this arrangement, and I can go back to my normal life. Should I ever get that chance, I've promised myself not to take anything for granted ever again.

Like my freedom.

"Ma'am," Spencer breaks into my thoughts. "Your mother has arrived."

I wipe my sweaty palms down the linen dress that hangs perfectly on me without looking like a gunny sack. "Thank you."

"Mr. Torres said you may visit with her in the great room. If you wait there, I'll bring her to you."

"You know, Spencer, you don't need to be so formal with me. This isn't some regency romance book. I can answer the door."

He grimaces, as if I'm trying to swipe his job security out from under him by lifting a finger for myself. "I'll bring her to you. June will serve beverages."

This is a regency romance gone wrong, but there are no regular rakes.

Just cartel members.

Lucky me.

I'm pacing back and forth in the opulent cartel great room, when I hear her voice. "Landyn!"

I spin on my espadrille wedge and meet her in the middle of the room. She shocks me when she wraps her arms around me in an embrace. I return it and say, "I can't believe you're here."

She lets me go and holds me at arms-length, looking me up and down. "I was so worried after the bloodbath at the church. We barely got out of there and had no idea where you were. The next day your father got word Damian was dead and you were okay but married to another man."

I lift a shoulder and decide to spare her the part where I was kidnapped and almost had to marry Damian's cousin instead of Boz. "That's basically right."

She takes in her surroundings for the first time and hikes a brow. "What an impressive estate."

I narrow my eyes but say nothing. Is she really focused on the soaring ceilings and window treatments after everything I've been through?

"Not at all what I expected from Damian Marino. You could have it a lot worse, I guess." She gives her head a shake. "I still can't believe you're here. Had you just considered one of the many young men from the club that I tried to set you up with, you wouldn't have been single, and this would not have happened."

I take a step back as her words deliver a different kind of sting than they used to. Her I-told-you-so comments over the years have been irritating at best. But not today. Today, her victim shaming is a slap across the face. "You're blaming me for being in this position because I was single?"

Her expression turns conciliatory, and her tone sounds like she's trying to reason with an overly-tired toddler. "That's not what I meant. All I'm saying is that had you already been married, they would not have wanted you."

"Or, had Dad not pawned me off to save his own life, I also would not be in this situation."

Her lips press into a thin line—at least as thin as they can go with her filler injections. "I'm not blaming you. I had a feeling when he started working with the Marinos a few years ago it was bad news. He saw it as a way to diversify and provide for us. He never saw this coming."

I cross my arms. "Well, I guess if he didn't plan this, it makes it all better. He made it clear he only cares about himself. I'm not here because there was no other choice. He didn't have to take the deal and hand me over to the Cartel."

She shakes her head and reaches out to run a hand from my shoulder to elbow. Her touch is as tender as it is fake. "That's not the way it happened, sweetheart. They threatened all of us. Anything else you've been told is them feeding you lies about your father. They're going to do everything they can to poison you against us. They cut your father out, and it's taken a toll on the business."

My eyes flare, and I jerk from her touch. I don't give a shit who's listening and throw my hand out. "Look at where I am, Mom. Do you think I give a shit about his business?"

"Ah-hem."

Our gazes shoot to our sides where June is standing at the entrance to the room holding a tray.

"Excuse me, Mrs. Torres. Tea and cookies for you and your mother."

My mother smiles and nods like she's at Buckingham Palace instead of a mansion funded by cartel money. "That sounds lovely. Thank you."

June moves to the coffee table and turns back to me. "Do you need anything else, ma'am?"

I shake my head and wonder if June and Miranda ever get time off. They've been here daily for every meal. I need to ask Boz about that. "No, thank you."

The woman knows her role and plays it well. She exits the room as quietly and as quickly as a mouse.

My mother moves to the sofa and proceeds to pour two cups of tea. "Come here and tell me about everything that has happened."

I stand frozen in my spot. She's speaking to me like she's catching up with her sorority sisters instead of her daughter who was traded to pay off a debt. "You know what happened."

She picks up a cup of tea and pats the sofa next to her. "Sit and talk to me. When we learned that Damian was killed, I knew things were going to change for the better."

I move to her but not to sit and chat. I stand across the coffee table and glare at her. "I'm glad you feel better about things. Meanwhile, I'm still here."

She takes a sip of her tea and pauses before lowering her voice—little does she know it'll take a lot more than that to keep a secret in this house. "Tell me about this Boz Torres you married. I want to know everything about him. Has he been..." Her blue eyes, the color of mine, dart around the room before she whispers, "rough with you?"

"What? No." I cross my arms to hug myself. "He's fine. I mean, for the most part, he's been fine. But I can't live like this. I'm a prisoner."

Her teacup clinks when it hits the saucer. "That's a relief. Your father said you looked fine when he saw you at the funeral."

I lower my tone, and it has nothing to do with who's listening. "He thought I looked fine?"

"Yes." She actually sounds relieved, as if my dad who barely gave me a glance that day thought I looked *fine*. "I was happy to hear it."

"I might be making the best of a horrible situation, but I am not fine, Mom. Not at all. Though, I can't say I want my old life back, because this is where my old life got me. I wouldn't feel safe going home after what Dad did."

She extends a hand over the coffee table. "That's what I want to talk to you about."

I reluctantly go to her and sit.

"Landyn," she starts. "This whole debacle started when your father *lost* the Marinos product. However, the more he's looked into it, he thinks he was set up."

I sit back and lower my voice. "By whom?"

She lowers hers even more and leans in close. "By the Marinos."

16

GOOD ONE

Brax

I lean back in my desk chair and crank up the audio.

This is interesting.

"You think the Marinos tipped off the feds and took down their own load?"

Nellie tips her head and shoots her daughter a smug look. "That's what your father thinks. He thinks he was set up."

Well, fuck me. I do not hate this scenario.

"Why would they do that?" Landyn bites back. "And it's not like Dad got caught. The driver took the fall, and he's already out on bail. Dad proved he knew nothing about it."

"Damian probably knew your father couldn't repay the retail price of that load. It was big—bigger than normal—worth over fifty million dollars on the street."

I can see my wife's blue eyes widen from here. "Fifty?"

"Personally?" Nellie takes another sip. "I think Damian had his sights set on you the whole time. That horrid man. You know, now that he's dead, people are talking."

Landyn sits back and bites her lip. Good girl, chica. Keep your mouth shut. "I have no clue."

Nellie scoots on the sofa and closes the distance between herself and my wife. I have to turn the audio up as high as it will go to pick up her words. "Well, you're in the perfect position to find out. You can poke around, listen to conversations. See what you can find out."

Landyn's expression turns hard, and her glare is like a laser. "Why would I do that? Why would I help Dad after what he did to me?"

"Because he's your father, and you're an Alba." Nellie's words are razor sharp. I can see from here, they slice through Landyn and cut her deep. All of a sudden, Nellie's expression takes a turn to the dark side. "Your father's business is falling apart. When he lost that load, his reputation went down with it. No one will do business with him, and we all know the legitimate side of things is not enough to support our family."

Landyn nods once. It's slow and methodical, and I can see the shade of her fair skin turn with emotion over the camera. Her words are choked when she whispers, "Well, then it's good you don't have to worry about me ever again."

That's it.

I'm out of my chair and down the stairs.

By the time I hit the main level, I don't need the surveillance to hear every word they're saying. Voices are elevated, and Spencer is about to round the corner when he sees me.

I put my hand up to him. "I've got this."

He nods and backs away but doesn't disappear completely.

"I refuse to be anyone's spy," Landyn hisses.

When I round the corner, both women are standing, and Nellie has her daughter's forearm tight in her grip.

I barely recognize my own voice. "Get your fucking hands off my wife."

They both turn to me—mother and daughter. They share the same eyes, the same build, the same complexion. If it weren't for the selfish bitch that Nellie Alba carries in her soul, I'd say whoever ends up with Landyn for life is a lucky man.

But Landyn is nothing like her mother.

There's a shit ton going on in this room, but all I see are the tears streaking Landyn's face.

The moment her blue eyes hit me, her tears flow faster. It feels like an anvil landed on my chest.

I don't hesitate and reach for her. I pull her to me, but I also pull her away from the woman who calls herself a parent.

Nellie Alba is no mother.

I know. I have the best there is.

And despite ignoring my wife most of last night and all day today, she falls into my arms. My shirt is fisted in her hands and her face is planted in my chest.

I dip my hand in her hair and put my lips to the top of her head. "You okay?"

Her tremble says it all, and hell if it doesn't touch a place deep within me.

I look over her head and glare at the woman who did this to her.

Nellie takes us in, wide-eyed. "Boz Torres?"

"I invited you here to give Landyn a piece of her family after what she's been through. You're just as fucking selfish as your husband. Dennis Alba might have made a deal with the devil to hand her over, but for you to use Landyn so the Alba's can weasel their way back into the Marino business is just as bad."

Nellie shakes her head quickly and takes two steps toward us, doing just as shitty of a job pleading her case as her husband. "No. I'd never try to use Landyn. We were just talking and catching up. She's upset about what she's been through. Tell him, Landyn."

"You'll stand here in a Marino home and lie to me? I don't offer second chances. This was your one and only opportunity to salvage a relationship with your daughter. You blew it."

Nellie's expression falls. "No, please. Boz—"

"Mr. Torres," I demand.

Nellie takes a step back and grips her own hands in a tangle of desperation as she tries to climb out of her pile of shit. "Of course, I'm sorry. Mr. Torres, Landyn and I were only talking—catching up on what she's been through since she…" she pauses before choosing her words carefully. "Since the two of you were married."

"You're checking in on married life while asking your daughter to spy on me, my business, and this family? You've been deep in this world since you married your husband twenty-six years ago, Nellie. You should know that waltzing in here with the assumption you can make demands of anyone—especially *my* wife—is a mistake you'll only make once."

"No!" Her desperation climbs to a new pathetic level reserved for the most selfish of humans. "I would never disrespect you or the Marinos. Please, let me explain. Dennis wants another chance—he'll beg you for another chance. That's all I was trying to do. No one will do business with his company since the Marino family blackballed him. Our lives are falling apart."

"You asked your daughter to cross her husband."

"No." She continues to backpedal. "We're family now. You're my son-in-law—"

"I'm not your anything," I growl. "Your daughter is mine. Word must not have traveled fast enough. I'll have to do something about that sooner rather than later. If you disrespect my wife, you disrespect me."

"I'd never disrespect you—I swear," she cries. "We're family. That has to mean something, right?"

I drag my fingers through Landyn's hair far enough to wrap it around my fist and give it a tug. For the second time in a matter of days, her own fucking parents have reduced her to tears. "Do you want me to protect you from your family?"

She swallows over her tears as her blue eyes sear me, warming me, bringing life to a place that's been dead for years.

"What does that mean?" Nellie screeches.

Landyn and I don't move a muscle. We stare into each other's eyes, and it doesn't feel like anyone's watching. It feels like we're alone.

I lean down to take her mouth in a deep, hard kiss. Her salty tears feed me and ignite me in a way I'm worried about my own personal resolve.

This does not fit into my plan. She doesn't fit into my life—or lack of—since I'm living and breathing one lie after another. When I let her mouth go and tip my forehead to hers, she looks like she's at her own crossroad to hell, and like me, once she crosses, there's no going back.

I don't waste any time. "All you have to do is say the word, baby. Before you even blink, it'll be a done deal. They'll never hurt you again."

"Landyn," Nellie cries out, begging her not to do to them what they did to her.

"Chica," I coax. "You need to choose. Them or me."

Them or me. It echoes in my head like a gong.

Fuck, if she chooses me, this web will be so tangled, I may never find my way out of it unscathed. Still, I find myself praying she chooses me.

Her sweet body sinks deeper into mine. Even with her mother standing in the same room, I feel my cock swell. I haven't had her in my arms like this since her asshole father upset her at Damian's funeral.

Her voice is small, but that doesn't mean there isn't power behind it. She makes a choice.

"I choose you."

Fuck. My hand slides down to the swell of her ass where I hold her to me and let my imagination run free.

I give her a small nod.

"Landyn, no!" her mother exclaims.

I don't look away from the woman who has no idea what she just signed up for as I say, "Spencer."

"Sir?" His voice hits me from behind where I know he was lurking. There's always someone in the shadows.

"Remove my mother-in-law from the house." I don't look away from Landyn. The resolve and weight of my words vibrate through me with every demand I make. "Make sure she never returns."

There's commotion and drama, but I don't wait to watch it play out. Spencer might be three decades older than me, but he's no slouch. He can handle Nellie Alba on his own.

Instead, I claim Landyn's hand and head to the stairs.

"Boz, wait," Landyn calls, but I keep going. The need to be alone with her is overwhelming. I'm so fucking sick of being the star of the show in this house.

As Nellie is dragged out the front door like yesterday's trash, I don't give a second thought to the Albas. Little do they know their days of freedom are limited to the amount of time I need to tie the Jackals to the Marinos, right before I make sure my personal business is taken care of with a finality that does not include prison.

More like six feet under.

Which means I just put myself on another clock.

The make-my-fake-wife-not-hate-me clock.

We're almost to our bedroom when Landyn won't move another step. "Boz, what are you doing?"

I turn back to her and frown at the woman who's turning my world on end. I wonder what I'm doing every fucking day. If this is even worth it. The price to pay for revenge is higher than I ever imagined.

But whenever I can tell this woman the truth, I take advantage of the opportunity. "I'm pissed that you're crying again."

She sniffs and wipes at the black smudges under her eyes. "I'm sorry."

I press her to the wall outside of our bedroom door and lower my voice. "No, baby. I'm pissed your parents have made you cry twice this week. The one thing I can promise is that you chose well. You will not take shit from your parents ever again. Not as long as I'm here to stand in the way."

Her tears have faded but her eyes are still glassy as they stare up at me. "I was already in a bad mood before she got here."

"Yeah?" I drag my thumb across her bottom lip before sliding my hand down to circle her neck. I don't have to hold tight to feel her pulse race beneath my touch. Her eyes flare, but other than that, she doesn't flinch at my hold. "I feel like I've been in a bad mood for a lifetime."

Her tits rise and fall where my forearm rests. I press my hips into her stomach, needing to feel her.

Needing her to feel what she does to me.

This time when she swallows, I feel every microscopic movement through her shallow breaths. "Why are you the way you are?"

I shake my head. "You can't know that. Not right now."

There. More truths.

"But I don't understand any of this." She throws her arms out to the side. "I at least need to understand you."

"I'm the last thing you'll understand, baby."

She brings her hand up to mine on her neck and squeezes. "You've protected me from everyone and everything."

I tip her face to mine with my hold. "And I'll continue to do that."

"Everyone but you."

My eyes narrow.

"We're married." She breathes lies she doesn't even know she's telling. "You've made it clear I'm not going anywhere. That I'm a possession to the Marino family."

My grip on her neck tightens at the thought of her belonging to anyone but me. "You'll never be that kind of possession, chica. Not the kind you were intended to be. I promise you that."

She grips my shirt with her other hand and pulls me in closer. Her tone is so low, I'm not sure the audio will pick it up, but I sure do. I feel her words on my lips when she asks, "What was I intended to be?"

I shake my head and say nothing.

"Please," she begs. "I deserve to understand—"

My lips land on hers, to shut her up, and because it's impossible to be this close and not claim her.

Her grip on me tightens as she opens her mouth. I take full advantage and press her into the wall, my hand falls from her neck to her tit and down to cup her ass.

When I squeeze the tender flesh there, she hikes a leg up my side, making it easier than it should be to reach under and cup her pussy through the thin material.

Fuck.

I want to touch her again.

All it takes is one swift move, and her legs are wrapped around my waist. My cock is wedged between her legs where it's begging to be buried deep.

Her hands come to my face and I rip at her dress, needing to touch her. Wanting nothing between us.

Skin to skin.

She moans into my mouth when I finally fist bare skin encased in lace.

Wet lace.

Just like the other night, I slip my finger beneath the thin fabric.

She moans, and not quietly at all. I know everyone in the control room heard that, dammit. The thought of those men watching her, knowing what she looks like and sounds like when she comes…

I'll go rabid.

"Fuck," I mutter against her lips. "What am I going to do with you?"

She runs one hand around my neck and holds me as tightly as I am her. "Don't stop."

That's the last thing I want to do.

But it's not happening here.

My hand stays planted between her legs—warm, wet, and mine—as I angle my other arm up her back and move for the door.

Her eyes fly open, and panic takes over her beautiful face. "No!"

I freeze. "What?"

"Don't take me in there," she breathes, desperate and needy.

"We're not staying out here." I cup her tighter, and for the first time, slide a finger into her tight pussy. I might never be the same. I lean in and put my lips to her ear when I give her a second pump.

"This is mine, Landyn. No one's going to watch you come but me. Do you understand?"

She exhales against my face as she presses down onto my hand. "Just ... I don't want to go in there."

"Why?"

"Once we're shut in that room, you ignore me. I can't handle that, Boz. Especially today. Please," she begs. Her lust-filled gaze hits me as hard as her words. "Don't push me away. And don't stop."

Landyn

Boz puts a heavy foot to the door. Its slam echoes off the high ceilings and through the vast space.

I grip him tighter. I meant what I said. If he lets me go, I might fall apart for good.

My back hits another wall before my head does, because he finally gives me what I want.

Him.

And another finger.

My mouth falls open, and I'm pretty sure my eyes roll back in my head when his strong thumb circles my clit.

I forget about being used as a payment for my father's debt. I forget about being married into a cartel. And I forget about my mom victim-shaming me.

I don't think about anyone but my husband. The man who's protected me and defended me.

His lips hit the skin on my collarbone where he sucks. "I've ignored you for my own sanity, chica."

Oh, and there's that. My husband who ignores me when we're alone.

But he's not ignoring me now. He's everywhere. My panties cut into my skin. It should hurt, but nothing hurts in a bad way. My body is ablaze. Ever since Boz said I do, and he kissed me for the first time, he's been nothing but pure kindling.

"This wasn't supposed to happen." His words rumble against my skin as I can't stop grinding down on his fingers. His thumb circles my clit. What he's saying is so very opposite of what he's doing. "This is wrong. Trust me, baby. I did everything I could not to touch you. It was for your own good."

I should have let him ignore me. Accepted it as the gift it was. Gone about my life in a marriage I was forced into.

But every time he's touched me, looked at me, and especially protected me...

Well...

The first two might have been for show, but not the last.

I might be a possession in this world, but he makes me feel safe in it. When I'm with him, I know nothing will hurt me.

And it's time I tell him.

"You're the only good thing that's happened to me since I was taken. Everything is wrong, Boz. Everything but you."

His hand stills between my legs, but he doesn't let me go. He holds tight, like he's as afraid to let go as I am to lose his touch.

He lifts his head far enough that all I see are his moody dark eyes. "Everything is wrong, baby. Every-fucking-thing. I thought this world was fucked up, but since the day they threw you into the cauldron, I don't know which way is up. You've got me spinning, and I can't afford to lose my sight."

I draw my knees higher, and my arms constrict around him. "The moment I was taken, I was afraid of everything. Is it crazy that the only thing I'm scared of now is being away from you?"

His breath blankets my face on one heavy exhale. Most men in his position, with a hand between my legs and fingers filling me—quite literally owning me inside and out—would spout bullshit to make me feel better.

Tell me what I want to hear ... that he'll take me to bed, make love to me, and promise that everything will be okay.

But not Boz. Not my husband.

"You should be scared. You'd be crazy not to be."

That realization hangs between us like a cold, dead body.

And it only makes me want him more.

I can't hide the desperation in my voice. Not when he's my only protector. "Please, Boz. Don't ignore me. I can't handle that on top of everything else."

His eyes fall shut. I only thought his grip on me was possessive. When he opens his eyes, his gaze sears me right before his lips devour mine. When his fingers move, we might as well become one.

I dissolve into him when he works my clit. I'm in knots. Tension builds through my core. Every ounce of stress and anxiety since this nightmare started comes to a head as he brings me closer and closer.

He lets go of my mouth. I can barely focus on him when I see stars.

I moan and gasp and fight for air. When I come for the first time at the hands of my husband, my body trembles around him. He holds me close as his lips trail kisses up the side of my face ... his tongue tasting my skin ... his teeth nipping the lobe of my ear.

"Fuck," he mutters into the side of my face. "I didn't even come with you and I can't catch my breath."

I lick my lips as I recover. "It's your turn, then."

He shakes his head. "No, baby. We'll get to me, but not now. Not yet."

My lungs and heart are forced to work double time to recover. I cup his jaw in my hands and plead, "We can't go back to the way we were before. Promise not to make me feel more alone than I already do."

He removes his hand from my panties and sets me on my feet before taking my face in his hands. "You're going to kill me, chica. I have a feeling I'll die a slow, painful death before this is over. But other than working, because I have a project that is more important than you know, you'll have my undivided attention."

A small smile plays on my lips. "And I'm tired of sleeping on the sofa."

He pulls in a big breath. "Then my slow painful death will be a quick one if I can't wrap up my project even faster."

I reach up and press my lips to his. "You're a good one, hubba-licious. I knew it from the first moment I laid eyes on you. You're different. And the good ones don't die."

His expression changes. It turns ominous and heated and completely intimidating. I try to take a step back, but he doesn't allow it. "The good ones do die, Landyn. Every-fucking-day. It's why I made you mine in the beginning. You're the good one, baby, and I'm not going to let anything happen to you."

He pulls me in for another kiss, one that feels different. It's laced with desperation and a tinge of guilt.

I don't dare ask what it means.

Because I finally have something to be happy about.

17

INITIATION

Brax

"You've been grieving your only son. The next load is taken care of. I contracted with the Jackals. It's happening next week."

With Damian out of the way and my promotion within the family secured, I have direct access to the leader and founder of the Marino Cartel.

No boundaries.

No barriers.

"The Jackals?" he bites. "Did they come through and finally prove themselves? Damian had been working on them for months, but they refused to pull the trigger—the actual fucking trigger."

I grip the phone and pause for two beats, because I have no idea what he's talking about. And I can't let on that I'm sitting here clueless on the other end of the line, so I do what I always do—fake it. "They came through. Finally."

"When?" he bites, causing my insides to twist with adrenaline. "I follow the news. I haven't seen anything."

The news? What the hell?

There's nothing like flying into the pitch-black abyss with no clue how to get out. "Trust me, we're good."

"I want to know when and where." His old voice, which is usually raspy and shallow, turns sharp. It has an edge to it that gives me a hint as to who he used to be ... the evil, sadistic leader that did anything and everything to claw his way to the top of the worldwide drug trade. "I want proof. I want to know how it was done. Then we can move forward."

I stand and stride to the window, as if the answer will crash against the cliffs of the rocky Pacific shore so I can get myself out of this pinch that really feels like the damn walls are closing in on me.

Wishful thinking.

"Tell me what you want, Alamandos. I'll make sure you get it. You know I'll do anything for you."

"I want to know when and where it happened. I want a name. I want to know the family they left behind. I want to know how they died." Evil bleeds through the phone with each and every sinful demand. "I want the fucking picture of the dead cop. If it's a Fed, even better. It'll go straight to the top of my collection."

All of a sudden, I can't see anything. Not the ocean, not the cliffs, not the ground or the pool or the armed guards that are on point at every corner of the estate.

My vision hollows.

Dead cop.

Shit.

It's an initiation?

"Boz?"

A fucking initiation?

"Here," I grunt and do everything I can to keep my composure. I squeeze my eyes shut, force myself to speak, and steady my voice. "Tell me what kind of proof you want. I'll get it."

"I want links to the news story. Details on how it was done. And I want a fucking background on the pig they took down. Pictures. I want it all."

"Done," I snap, even though I have no fucking clue how I'm going to come through with anything on that list. All I know is I need to end this fucking call. "My schedule is back-to-back the rest of the day with the other side of the business. I'll have it to you by tomorrow."

I have no fucking idea what I'm going to do, but I'll figure it out right after I throw up and plan his demise, step by fucking painful step.

I also need to salvage this deal with the Jackals. No one else is delivering this load other than them.

"Impressed with you, mijo. I've been hazy with grief. You mean more to me than my own blood remaining in this world. Knowing I can trust you means something, Brian."

Brian.

Fuck.

I can almost taste the bile bubbling in my gut. "Appreciate that, Alamandos."

"I look forward to your report." My report. I look forward to seeing what I can pull out of my ass too. "One to add to my collection."

That's it.

I'll kill the man myself before this is all said and done.

"You'll hear from me tomorrow," I promise.

I don't wait for him to express how much he looks forward to adding to his collection of dead cops. I hang up and put a hand to the wall to support my weight.

I need to get a fucking grip.

I knew it had happened in the past—that they killed cops. But I thought it was only as a defensive move. Who wants that kind of attention?

In my worst nightmares, I didn't think it would be for some sick initiation.

My phone vibrates in my pocket. The real phone, my only connection to reality.

Before I dare look at it, I go straight to our connecting bedroom and bathroom. Landyn is with Rocco in the dining room studying biology. She told me the only reason she's doing this is because she's bored to tears, and if she can't be with me, she might as well hang out with Rocco.

I lock the door—safe from surveillance cameras and my fake wife—pull out my cell, and sit on the closed toilet.

> Carson – What the fuck. Is that what I think it was?

> Me – Your guess is as good as mine, which is really fucking good, so I think yes. That's exactly what it is.

> Carson – Get the hell out of there and call me. We need to figure this out.

> Me – I can't. I have a meeting with New York, and Alamandos could find out if I miss it.

> Me – They're killing cops, Carson. Randomly putting a target on their back just for the pleasure of getting to work with the Marinos. You know what this means.

> Carson – I know, man. I fucking know.

> Carson – But I also need to know that you're steady. I'll pull you from this if I have to.

The thought of that happening before I finish makes me want to rip this fucking mansion down with my bare hands.

> Me – You do that and you'll have more problems than you know what to do with.

> Carson – Then do what you need to do and finish this shit.

> Me – You heard what he wants. As much as it turns my stomach, I need a fictional dead cop. How the hell you're going to do that is beyond me.

> Carson – I think I can make it happen. I've got a guy—Ozzy Graves. He dabbles in the dark web. This is sick as hell, but he should be able to come up with something. He can create bogus links, devise the lie from the ground up.

> Me – I need it by tomorrow.

> Carson – You act like I wasn't there for the actual conversation and have a recording of it for memorabilia and federal warrants. I know what you need. Chill the fuck out so I don't have to raid the place and personally drag you out of it. I don't fuck around when it comes to my assets, Brax. Do not go cowboy on me.

> Me – Like you weren't playing in the wild, wild west when we met.

> Carson – Right back atcha, my handsome friend. But I've gone to bat for you more times than I can count since this shit started. I'm kind of attached to you at this point. You'd better not get made on my watch. I need to call Tim and update him. He'll kill me if anything happens to you.

Carson has gone to bat for me, probably more than I know. But it's my neck on the line.

> Carson – A fucking initiation. You okay?

I drag a hand down my face and am about to answer that, no, I'm the farthest thing from okay right now, when I hear her.

"Boz? Are you in here?" Landyn calls for me.

Shit.

I stand and flush the toilet so I don't look like a freak.

> Me – I'm good. Gotta go.

I slip my phone in my pocket and open the door.

Her smile, which hits me right in the gut, is different. For once, the woman I pretended to marry doesn't look miserable or afraid.

She actually looks happy.

She's so fucking clueless.

I'm jealous.

"Hey." She moves across the marble to me. "I've been looking for you. You weren't in your office."

That twists in my gut. It was easy to justify lying to her in the beginning. My lies saved her from a living hell that no human should have to endure.

I go straight to the sink, and she follows. I focus on washing my hands so I don't have to look her in the eyes. "I've had back-to-back meetings and another call scheduled in a few minutes."

I turn off the water and grab a towel. When I turn to her, it's all I can do not to think about the very illicit orgasm I gave her when I should not have touched her to begin with. I should've kept my hands to myself and my eye on the prize. If I were stronger, I would've ignored my own desires and the hurt in her eyes.

But both got the better of me.

I need to get this wrapped before I can think about telling anyone the truth about anything.

Her arms are crossed and she's leaning a hip to the counter looking up at me. She's still wearing the same dress I had bunched around her waist when I damn near ripped her panties off.

Not only did I want to shred them because I wanted nothing between her and me, but also because Damian provided them for her.

My mind is in too many places right now. They're underwear—sexy as fuck underwear, but just underwear. I should not be jealous of the dead man who bought them for her.

"Spencer told me they're putting a TV in our room," she says.

Shit. The TV that was supposed to distract me from my new wife. I reach up to pinch the bridge of my nose before pulling in a deep breath. "We're in there a lot. I figured it's better than the silence we were sitting through."

She nibbles on her bottom lip, probably trying to decode my words versus my actions.

Well, same, baby. Same. If someone could help me figure out how to get to the finish line, I'd appreciate that too.

"But that was before. Right?" she confirms.

I exhale and decide to focus on her instead of the sick revelation I just learned. I close the distance between us and for once, choose the easy way out, and use the woman standing in front of me as the distraction I need, probably more than I've needed anything since I got here.

I pull her to me, bury one hand in her soft, blond hair, and plant the other on her back so low, my fingertips press into the curve of her ass. "Yeah, chica. That was before."

She's about to open her mouth to say something else, but I beat her to it.

"After my call, I have a meeting north of the city. I won't be here to have dinner with you, but I'll be back after."

Her lip goes slack and her eyes widen. "Is it something I can tag along for?"

I shake my head. "It's not that kind of meeting. This is legit work and the Marinos don't want you anywhere near that side of the business. I shouldn't be late."

She fingers a button on my shirt before looking up to focus her deep blues on me. "I was going to see if you wanted to put the new TV to use ... watch a movie or something?"

I hold her to me tighter. There's nothing I need more right now than self-preservation. If the only place for me to find that is with Landyn, I'm selfish enough to take it.

And I'll apologize to her later.

I pull her face to mine and press my lips to hers. Her grip on my shirt tightens, and she presses her sweet body into mine, holding herself to me.

Desperation.

It's bleeding from her. It's different than it's ever been. I recognize it because I feel it too.

Determined, sure.

Driven, absolutely.

But not desperate.

The wedding—that's when it all changed.

In some ways, Landyn and I are searching for the same thing ... a resolution. But for much different reasons.

Her tongue moves with mine, and my hand slides south on her ass. I can't make myself pull away from her. She's the only real and good thing I've touched in two years. The longer I allow myself this reprieve from the hell I've been submerged in, the more I want her.

My obsession is becoming so strong, I can no longer deny it's a problem. I can't afford to focus on anything else other than the end goal.

And Landyn Alba *Torres* is not a part of that.

Fuck.

When I force myself to tear my lips from hers, I breathe in her exhale as if my heart needs it to keep beating. But I don't let her go.

"Boz," she murmurs. "Is something wrong?"

I open my eyes to find her staring up at me, trying to figure out the man she thinks is her husband. I shake my head. "It's been a day. When I get back, we'll watch whatever you want."

A smile touches her lips. "You won't be too late?"

"I won't now," I tell her the truth and go on, probably saying too much. "Not with you waiting on me."

Her smile swells. "Thank you."

I pull her to me one more time and press my lips to her forehead. And this time, I don't lie when I say, "Baby, you're the one who was torn from your life and forced to marry a stranger. Never thank me for anything."

She gives my shirt a tug to get my attention. "I have a feeling I have more to be thankful for than I realize, and all of it has to do with you."

I shake my head, but don't say anything else. If I keep talking, I'm afraid of what will fall from my lips. Instead, I force myself to let her go. "I'll see you tonight."

18

TRINKET

Landyn

June tries to clear our dirty plates from the dining room, but I put my hand out to stop her. "Nope. Not tonight. I'm making a new rule: when Boz isn't here, Rocco and I will help clean up."

I have a feeling Boz wouldn't allow it. I might not be able to leave the house by myself, but when he's gone, I'll do what I want. Nothing feels more normal than loading the dishwasher with my own dirty dishes.

And this all surprises me. I didn't realize just how small of a small player my father is until I experienced everything Marino.

I thought we were wealthy. I thought my father was actually someone in SoCal. I had no idea he was a pawn in this dark underworld of drugs, trafficking, and every other illegal activity that crosses his hands.

Now that I'm here, I realize he's the one who made me believe these things. He built himself up to be the biggest and best and the most powerful.

I'm sure it made him feel bigger and more important than he is.

Because I didn't grow up with live-in servants or cooks or butlers. Looking back, if I had grown up with this opulence, I'd probably eat it up.

But I want no part of it. Allowing June and Miranda to cook and Spencer to wait on me hand and foot feels like I'm buying into this life I was sold into.

Cleaning up after myself or insisting on making my own lunch might not be much of a stand, but it's my own way to keep a hold on reality. Even if that hold is weak and by the tips of my very blunt fingernails, it's all I have left.

I push my chair out to stand and look across the table at my new, young friend. "I'll get this, Rocco. You were gone for most of the afternoon and didn't finish the geometry review."

He pushes his dark blond hair from his forehead. "I'd rather do dishes."

"Please, ma'am," June tries one more time. "Mr. Torres would want you to help Rocco. I'll get this."

I shake my head and put my foot down once and for all. "Rocco is smarter than he lets on. It took one day of him diving back into it, and all the miserable theorems and equations came back to him. At this point, my job is to make sure he stays on track—he doesn't need me looking over his shoulder. I'd rather do the dishes."

Rocco rolls his eyes and hands me his plate. "I never thought I'd look forward to a test, but I can't wait for this shit to be done."

"You have to stay on track. If you finish, we can hang out before Boz gets back."

Rocco stuffs his hands in his pockets. I'm not sure he'll ever be used to wearing business casual. Just like always at the end of the day, he's rumpled and wrinkled. "Gotta admit, this is a weird-ass family I never thought I'd have. When they told me I'd have to work here for the Marino family, I never thought I'd be sent back to fucking high school."

I stack the plates higher. "The sooner you pass the test, the sooner you can get back to doing ... whatever you used to do."

"I can't wait," he mutters. "I've only been at this for a couple days, and I'm sick of it already."

I turn my back on him and head to the kitchen, but call over my shoulder, "Don't make me check your work."

He yells back at me, but I can tell he's teasing, "You're barely older than me, Landyn. Quit trying to be my mom."

I smile to myself and ignore him. Despite the four to five years that separate us, Rocco isn't wrong. This is the weirdest family dynamic ever. And being Rocco's mom is the last thing on earth I want.

What am I even saying...

I was forced to marry a man I didn't know, but being Rocco's mom is the last thing I'd want?

That thought is wrong on so many levels. Even so, I can't wipe the smile from my face.

It's been a good day.

An orgasm and a promise.

Both from my husband.

When I get to the kitchen, Miranda is scrubbing pots and pans at the sink and June is still complaining because I want to help. "I can't get over you being in here, Mrs. Torres. I've worked here for years and this never would've happened under Mr. Marino."

Thank goodness that's not the case, but I don't dare say that out loud. I think it will be ingrained in me forever that I'm being watched.

Instead of celebrating aloud, I mutter, "God rest his soul."

June crosses herself, and Miranda mutters something in Spanish so quietly, I doubt the cameras are able to pick it up.

I'm rinsing plates in the second sink at the island when long, intricate chimes ring through the house. I flip the water off and turn to the two women, who also stop what they're doing.

"Are we expecting someone?" I ask.

Miranda's eyes widen, and June shrugs. "I don't know. Spencer is off tonight. The guards at the gate always call him when someone is here."

"Do people show up unannounced often?" I ask.

"We cook and clean. We have nothing else to do with the business." June glances at Miranda and back to me. "I'll call the guards."

The bell chimes again, and it's not lost on me how deep and creepy they are. As many visitors as we've had since I got here, this is the first time I've heard the doorbell.

"It's okay. I'll get it. The guards wouldn't let them through if it weren't okay, right?"

June wipes her hands on a towel as she thinks it over. "I guess that's true."

"I'll be right back," I mutter as the bell chimes again.

Holy shit, they're impatient. If I had access to the security system, I could look to see who was standing on the other side. I need to ask Boz about that. He did say this was my house too.

When I unlock and open the big heavy door, it's all I can do to even my expression and straighten my spine.

"Well, look who was allowed to answer the door by herself. Not sure I've ever seen anything like it at Damian's house."

Nic Decker.

Of course he decides to stop by when Boz is gone and Spencer is off.

I grip the handle and fight the urge to slam the door in his face. I have a feeling that wouldn't be good for the strained family relations I've experienced since I've been here. "What can I do for you?"

Nic ignores me and takes a step forward. I couldn't slam the door if I wanted to. He moves inside and looks around before turning to glare down at me.

He's nothing like his dead cousin. The man is fit, though not quite as tall as my husband. He would even be considered handsome by those who don't know him.

But to me, he's ugly in the worst way.

Nic's ugly has nothing to do with the way he looks. As far as

I've seen, the young Decker is just like his father and nothing like his mother—that poor woman. I haven't stopped thinking about her since our dinner when her husband manhandled her out of the house.

It's not like I'm married to a saint. Boz might run the legitimate side of the business for the Marino family, but he's still knee deep in moving drugs. But I didn't hold back the other day when I told him he was a good one.

I feel it. I might not have a college degree or a career or even a solid part time job at the moment, but I do have my intuition. And when it comes to things like this, I've never been wrong.

Take me to a bar, and I'll not only point out every sleaze bucket in the place, but I can also pick the trustworthy one you want to walk you to your car at the end of the night.

It's a gift.

But no one needs super powers to see that Nic Decker is an asshole. He shines that beacon for all to see.

He crosses his arms and drags his eyes up and down my body. The hair on my arms stands straight, but I don't budge. I refuse to give him the satisfaction of knowing how uncomfortable I am.

Nic finally looks from me and scans the house. "Where's Boz?"

"In his office." My lie is crisp and clean, and I'm mighty proud of my quick thinking.

His wicked stare jumps back to me. "Bullshit. The boys at the gate said he's been gone for hours."

Shit.

The boys at the gate are not on my side.

I cross my arms, but add a hitched foot for effect. "Do you have an appointment with my husband?"

"Fuck no. This was Damian's house. Boz is an intruder. He's not a Marino and neither are you. I don't need an appointment to show up here. I'm family, and no matter how many changes Boz thinks he can make, I can be here whenever I want."

I pull in a big breath. It's everything I can do not to run to the kitchen to hide out with June and Miranda or jump headfirst into geometry with Rocco. I'd take anything at the moment other than standing here talking to Nic.

I need him to leave, but his father already doesn't like me, and I know both these men have a direct line to Alamandos. I don't want to do anything that will be bad for Boz.

I swallow over the lump in my throat, but can't force myself to smile, no matter how hard I try. "If you tell me why you're here, maybe I can help you until Boz gets back."

"Maybe you can." His brows rise as he motions to the side. "Shall we talk in Damian's office—I mean, *Boz's* office?"

I shake my head. "Just tell me why you're here. Or if you'd rather wait for Boz, feel free to relax, and I'll have June bring you something to drink. But I need to get back to what I was doing."

He tips his head and contemplates me. "You're Dennis Alba's daughter. Come to think of it, I'd rather talk to you."

"I know nothing about my father's business," I insist and motion to the room we're standing in. "I'm here, which is proof that he's not even good at what he does. Really, let me have June bring you a drink. I can call Boz and let him know you're here."

"That's cute you still think they'd give you a phone."

Shit.

"Why wouldn't I have a phone?" I lie.

"You were payment, Landyn. A trinket that Damian wanted to play with. A sexy-as-fuck one, but nothing more. I know what you're here for, and there's a reason you haven't been given direct communication to the outside world."

All the air in my lungs leaves my body in a whoosh. He might as well have punched me in the gut.

A smile takes over his full lips. Sleazeball. Goosebumps race up my body at the same time my palms go sweaty.

He moves.

I take a step back.

"Chill out," he drawls in a low voice. I can't step away fast enough when his hand grips the back of my arm and squeezes. I try not to call out in pain, but I have a feeling that will leave a mark. He dips his head, and his voice slithers through my messy hair, causing a tremble to vibrate down my spine. "I just want to talk to you."

"No," I bite and try to pull away. This reminds me of how his father dragged his mother out of the house that night. I struggle and pull, but he's moved us the short distance to the office off the front of the house. "Nic, stop. You're hurting me."

And just like that, he lets me go. He pushes me into the room and I stumble forward, forced to right myself on the desk as he slams the door behind us. I look around the space for the first time. It might as well be in a furniture store showroom. No computer, no papers, no pencils. And there's definitely no letter opener, which I could really use at the moment.

I spin around and hold onto the desk behind me. "What are you doing?"

He reaches behind him, and I hear the click of the lock.

It might as well be the last tick of my heart. I can barely catch my breath.

He moves forward, one foot in front of the other until I have to tip my head back to look up at him. His fingers grab the ends of my hair, but on the way, the backs of his fingers brush the underside of my breast.

No.

This is not happening.

This cannot be happening.

He leers down at me.

"I feel like you haven't gotten to know the Marino family. Your husband..." His lip twists into a sneer as he focuses on curling my hair around his fingers. "Boz Torres is not a Marino. He poisoned Damian against me. Had Damian not been killed, this would have happened, and Damian would have allowed it."

My chest heaves, and there's no staying calm anymore. "What?"

He leans in closer, and his words are like a slap. "Didn't Boz tell you? Damian wasn't jealous or possessive. Controlling, sure. But he didn't plan to actually keep you to himself. You think he gave a shit about you enough to do that?"

"Stop it," I bite and reach up to slap him away, but he's fast.

My wrist is caught in his big hand and twisted behind my back in no time. I cry out in pain.

"I came here to tell your fucking husband he'd better not disrespect my father again. But seeing as he's not here, I'm going to take this opportunity to sample what should've been mine to play with had Damian not bit it. And even then, you should've been mine, bitch. I was next in line, but Torres has his nose so far up my uncle's ass, I had no chance."

"Please," I beg. Between the pain and fear, tears prick my eyes. "Don't do this. There are cameras. They're everywhere. If you hurt me, they'll know. Boz will know."

"Boz can't do shit to me," he bites as anger radiates through his voice. "And I know about the cameras, Landyn. I know everything, and no one will stop me. You think the guards aren't used to this?"

No.

My brain and every reflex in my body shifts to pure self-preservation. He's so close, his dark, malevolent eyes bore into mine as instinct takes over.

I spit in his face.

Twist my body in his hold.

And scream.

I scream bloody murder.

I don't think he's going to actually murder me, but if my worst nightmares come true, I might wish for death.

And I'm not going down without a fight.

"Bitch!" His growl echoes off the dark-paneled walls as his hold on me tightens and twists even harder.

And I thought the pain was bad before.

My scream for help turns to one that expresses sheer agony. I'm twisted, my back to his front, when his other hand wraps around my neck and suppresses my cry to a desperate gag for air.

"Fight me, bitch. The harder you fight, the harder I'll get off. You have no clue how much I want this."

I gasp when he releases my neck and drags a hand down my chest, his nails score my skin on the way to my dress.

Cotton rips as his teeth bite into my earlobe. My dress hangs open from the front, and my bra is askew.

It's all I can do to jab him with my elbow, but it doesn't do anything. He shifts enough that I manage to reach over my head to claw at his face. The moment I find a grip and catch skin, he shoves me to the side.

I crash into the side of a chair.

All oxygen leaves my body in a whoosh when the wood frame connects with my ribs.

I grasp at the torn material of my dress as I roll to the side. On my hands and knees, I try to put the chair between us, but when I look back, he's standing over me.

He's too big. Too strong. I'll never get away. All I can do is roll into myself...

And pray.

"Come here," he grits at the moment I scream out in pain again from my head being yanked back. My hair is pulled at the roots, his face is close to mine when he twists me around to spit in my face. "I was so fucking pissed when Alamandos gave you to him. I fucking hate Boz. I'll make sure he gets what's coming to him right after you do."

He flips me to my back and wedges a knee between my legs.

"Please," I beg through ravaged tears. "I'll talk to Boz. What do you want? Just, please, stop."

"Landyn!" My name bellows from the other side of the door followed by a bang that has to be a fist. So much banging. "What's happening? Open the fucking door!"

Rocco.

I can't string coherent words together, but I scream at the top of my lungs, crying out. I can't form words through pain and fear.

"Landyn?!" Rocco calls again.

"Who's that?" Nic seethes. My dress is yanked to my waist, my wrists bound in one of his hands.

"Hel—" I start to scream, and barely get the word out before his other hand clamps down on my face.

Nic's eyes are wide and wild and terrifying. "Who the fuck is that?"

Another bang hits the door, but this one isn't a fist.

It's bigger.

Harder.

The hand over my mouth tightens and bites into my jaw. "You stupid bitch. Everything went south the moment your fucking husband entered my world. I was next in line. It was supposed to be me. I'm going to make sure he pays, and it starts with making you mine."

That last word slithers over me in a way nothing ever has.

Boz told me ... he warned me. And even after experiencing Nic's parents at dinner, I didn't realize.

I had no idea how bad my life would've been had he not stepped in. My time with Boz has been pure bliss in comparison.

And to think I complained about being bored or him ignoring me.

Tears stream down the sides of my face as I struggle against his shackles.

Another bang.

His hand slides away from my mouth.

I barely pull in a gasp of air to scream when his fingers wrap around my throat.

I was afraid of him raping me.

But he'll kill me first.

Another bang.

And another.

I see stars and hear a gurgle as my hearing tunnels.

Then...

A crash.

Nic is gone.

I gasp and roll to the side. I cough and sputter, my hands fly to my neck and mouth as my lungs fight for air.

Vital, life-saving oxygen.

"Motherfucker," Rocco growls. "What did you do to her?"

Fists connect with flesh, over and over again. I don't dare look.

If I could slither away to another universe, where I was more than merely a possession, I would.

"I'll kill you," Nic grunts.

I jerk when bodies crash to the desk behind me. It hurts to move—it hurts so bad—but adrenaline takes over. I push to my bottom, wrap what's left of my dress around me, and watch the boy who's barely a man take a fist to the face.

My chest heaves desperately as I watch my new friend bleed...

For me.

But that's when it happens.

Rocco is blind to it. Nic reaches under his shirt, and grabs a gun tucked in his pants.

"Rocco!" I scream. "He's got a gun!"

Rocco's back is to the desk, but as soon as the word *gun* is spit from my lips, his eyes flare.

I scream when Rocco grabs Nic by the ears and pulls him in so hard, I hear skulls crash.

He headbutted him.

Nic's gun clanks to the wood floor, but Rocco doesn't stop. He pushes Nic back far enough to put a boot to his chest.

Nic stumbles, and Rocco follows.

The brawl continues. Fists fly, and grunts and profanities follow. I scramble and grab the gun in a shaky grip. The weapon clanks and scratches on the floor as I crawl back to the wall.

Rocco has maneuvered himself between Nic and me. He's bigger, but Nic is sadistic.

I can't sit here and see my friend get hurt. Not over me.

I've never held a gun, let alone shot one, but I don't have a choice.

I squeeze the trigger.

Or try to.

It's stiff in my trembling hands.

Then, it happens.

I fire a gun for the first time, and the two men fighting in front of me freeze.

The room is silent aside from my heart pounding in my chest

and their heavy pants. I move the gun from where I just put a bullet through the ceiling and point it straight at Nic.

"Get out," I whisper. "If you touch him again, I'll kill you."

Nic turns his head and spits blood on the floor right before dragging the back of his forearm across his cut mouth. "You couldn't hit a target if you wanted to."

Rocco moves. The next thing I know, he swipes the gun from my hand and points it at Nic.

"I can hit a target as small as the spot between your beady fucking eyes," he rumbles. "Feel free to stand there and test my skills. I'm happy to play target practice with your fucking head."

Nic turns his stare from Rocco to me and seethes, "I'm not done with you, bitch. You'd better hope Boz doesn't leave you by yourself again. I've got eyes everywhere. I'll know when you're alone."

Then, he's gone.

When I hear the front door slam, my eyes fall shut, but that doesn't stop my tears. Silent tears of relief.

"Is she okay?" I open my eyes, beyond Rocco, who stands over me with Nic's gun dangling from his hand, June is in the doorway that's now splintered wood from Rocco breaking through it. Panic with a mix of relief is etched in her old features as she takes me in. "There was nothing I could do when I realized what was happening. I locked Miranda in her room and ran to get Rocco. What did he do to you?"

I can't answer. I can't even utter a word.

But June does. She's not panicked any longer. She acts like men attacking women and gunshots through the ceiling are things she's accustomed to dealing with, because she takes charge. "The door is locked. I called Spencer. He's calling Mr. Torres." Her old, wise eyes focus on Rocco. "Give me the gun and get her upstairs to their bedroom. If I need to call the doctor, I will."

"No," I whisper, and realize my top lip is swelling. Hell, I don't even know how that happened. "Please, don't call anyone."

June takes the gun and slips it into the pocket of her apron like it's her own personal holster. "We'll let Mr. Torres make that decision when he gets home. Get her up. I'll get her changed and comfortable."

Rocco bends at the knees. Beyond his bloodied face, all I see is disheveled hair and tortured eyes.

He saved me.

My vision blurs as my tears flow again, but with regret and guilt this time. "He hurt you. I'm sorry. I'm so sorry."

Rocco shakes his head, and his tone isn't light or friendly like normal. "He can't hurt me. That's nothing I'm not used to."

I don't have a chance to ask or think about what that means.

Rocco doesn't help me to my feet. As I cling to the torn material of my dress, he slides an arm behind my back and the other under my knees. I wince when he stands straight and pulls me to his chest. We're out of the office, up the stairs, and to the bedroom I share with Boz before my brain can start to process how this happened.

My new husband will be back eventually.

And I have no idea how he'll react.

19

BRIAN

Brax

We located the entry point for the tunnel.
It's two hours east, far into the desert in the middle of nowhere. I'm not sure if it's classified as a farm or a ranch. It's a shit piece of land, too barren to harvest, let alone have any resources to keep an animal alive.

Finding it was a little luck and a lot of strategy. I sent Rocco to communicate with the Jackals about the upcoming load. This isn't just a tunnel to Mexico, it's their safe house. I heard enough on the transcripts from the wire that we planted in the car I gave Rocco.

The kid is easy to be around and hard to hate. He's also easy to be jealous of since he gets to spend most of his time at the house with Landyn, even if it was my idiotic-slash-brilliant idea for him to get his GED and for her to tutor him. I didn't plan to have a fake wife or a live-in MC prospect who shouldn't be in the club to begin with.

Ask me if I feel bad about using Rocco to get to the MC.
The answer to that is fuck no.

I'm documenting everything he does and doesn't do to make sure he's in a position to plea out. Maybe if he gets his shit together before he digs in too deep, he won't ruin his life completely.

My dinner meeting was of the legitimate variety. It's been on the calendar for two months, and there was no way I could cancel. I had to go so they could see Damian's company still has its shit together with him six feet under.

Part of Damian's responsibility to the Marino family was managing their real estate ventures in southern California. Surprisingly, he wasn't shit at it, even if it was hard for him to rein in his vile spirit if things didn't go his way. He had to force himself not to pop off and cap someone's ass when he didn't win a deal the legitimate way. This part of the business is integral to the drug trade. They can clean drug money by taking the highest bids and arrange for kickbacks under the table. Cash has to get in the bank somehow, and this is their system.

I graduated with a finance degree and even worked on Wall Street right out of college for two years. Working as a junior analyst was a grind, but that's what I wanted from the time I was little and we'd go into the city for the day.

I had goals and dreams and ambitions. I wanted to wear expensive suits and look like I was meant to be there. I thought working in lower Manhattan meant that you'd made it. That you were important.

I wanted it all, and I thought that would be my life.

Never did I want to spend two years living among the biggest and most dangerous cartel in the western hemisphere and pretend to be one of them.

This was not a part of my well-planned life.

Until we lost Brian.

That's when everything changed.

Then we found out what happened—*how* it happened.

I was changed forever.

As we traveled down that dark road, there were no answers. No closure. And no charges.

That's when my goals changed. I had new ambitions, ones I never dreamed of before.

They fueled me in a way I've never experienced.

It hasn't been fast. And as of this morning, I still had no resolution.

Until my conversation with Alamandos.

Finally, a clue.

The initiation.

Focus has been a bitch since the wedding fiasco. Throwing Landyn into the mix has made everything harder.

I claimed her. She's my responsibility. I need to make sure she comes out of this unscathed.

That should've been easy. I planned to lock her up and make sure no one could touch her. I shouldn't care if she's bored or doesn't like to be ignored. She'll get over it in the end when she realizes I saved her from what a true Marino marriage would've been and what undoubtedly would have happened had I just let her run.

The family would have hunted her down and killed her.

Locking her up for safe keeping, throwing away the key, and ignoring the blue-eyed beauty should've been the easiest thing I've ever done.

But this obsession...

I'm so close. I've got to get a grip.

I cannot afford the distraction. If I stray from my one true objective in this operation, I'll get made. And I won't be able to protect Landyn.

It is not lost on me that all the things that are fucking with my focus are directly related to my very fake wife.

She's fucking with my head.

I'd like her to be fucking with other things, but I will not cross that line. No matter how much I want it—want her. She might hate me for the lies in the end, but she'll get over it when she realizes she's still single and free to carry on a normal life, with a normal man, by her own choice. Not because she ended up with me after being traded for a debt.

I cannot deviate from the end game. I'm close. I feel it.

But everything is harder than it should be.

In the beginning, this job was easy to fall into and work my way up the chain given my background. Damian might've been an asshole, but he wasn't a stupid one. When he realized the value of my very real knowledge, my fake resume spoke for itself.

Fake resume.

Fake identity.

And my very fake marriage to my very fake wife.

I'm so sick of fake. If I could torture myself for thinking this was possible, I would. Only a few people in this world know where I am and why I'm here.

Carson. He was an easy sell. He's a crazy fuck who went off the rails for his own personal reasons at one time.

Micah. He was my roommate in the academy. His background makes mine look like the *Game of Life* compared to his *Game of Thrones*.

Tim. He only knows because of our mutual love for bourbon that encouraged me to share one night over a bottle of Willett.

And ... my mom.

When I told her what I was doing, she stared into my eyes like she was looking at a ghost.

Then she fell to her knees and cried.

I held her and promised I'd return. She told me she was scared. She was afraid I wouldn't come back. And that she loved me.

She, of all people, didn't need to tell me that. My mother's love for everyone in her life runs as deep as the ocean and shines brighter than the sun.

The harder you love, the harder you break. My mom can't break any more than she already has.

There will be nothing left of her if she does.

Which makes my focus more important than anything. It also makes the line I crossed today with my *wife* very, very dangerous.

It doesn't matter how much I want her. Anything more with Landyn is a hard no.

She'll hate me for touching her when all this is over. It won't matter how hard I try to convince her that when I had her against the wall today—when the moment was private and only ours—it meant something to me.

I get on the highway to head south from Oceanside when my phone rings over the Bluetooth. I look at the screen and frown when I answer. "Spencer. I thought I gave you the night off."

"You did." His tone is rushed and not at all professional like usual. "I'm on my way back to the house. June called. Something happened—there's been an ... incident."

I grip the steering wheel, change lanes to pass the car in front of me, and hit the gas. "Incident?"

"Mr. Decker came by the house tonight."

"Ed?" I clip. "He knows better than to come to the house uninvited after the way he left last time. What the hell did he want?"

"No." His tone goes tight. I've never heard him sound like this before. "Not Ed. It was Nic."

"Fuck."

"Sir, are you close?"

"Not close enough. Dammit!" I bellow, hitting the steering wheel. "What the fuck did he do? Tell me."

And just like he's been trained to do in the Marino house, he does exactly what I order.

He tells me in acute detail what went down.

What I allowed to happen, because I left her.

I wasn't fucking there.

20

INFERNO

Brax

Figuring out why the guards let Nic in instead of following my orders to keep him out should be my first concern. I know they were watching the security feed and did nothing to stop Nic from what he gets off on—rape. Just like most of the men in this fucking family.

There's no other way around it. I heard Damian was almost as bad as his cousin back in the day.

Almost.

It's why I couldn't leave her to him.

But this means I'm working among men I can't trust. I need to get them the fuck off this property and away from me.

That should be my first priority.

Instead, one of the iron gates scrapes down the side of the Cadillac as I barrel through, gun it up the drive, and don't bother with the garage. Nothing else matters right now.

I can't trust anyone in the Marino world. The only reason anyone was loyal to me was because Damian elevated me to work by his side. Any respect that was thrown my way came out of fear of Damian, and now, Alamandos.

That doesn't mean everyone I work around is like Damian or Nic. My gut has always told me that Spencer is a good man. I've run backgrounds on everyone in this house. Spencer is not a U.S. citizen nor does he have a visa. He also has no prior records here or in Mexico, and he works his ass off to support his family.

Tonight proves my gut instinct was right about him. He's at the door waiting for me when I run up the steps. He greets me with a grave expression and a gun tucked into the front of his jeans.

"Where is she?" I demand.

"In your room. June and Rocco are with her." He slams the door and turns the lock, following me up the stairs. "The boy won't leave Mrs. Torres. No matter how many times June has ordered him out so she can help her clean up, he won't budge. I tried, but he won't listen to me either."

I'm about to burst through the bedroom door when he calls for me. "Wait."

I turn to him before I go in. "What?"

He stares at me through his tired, old eyes. "The boy saved her."

I lower my voice so no one but him can hear me. "You're telling me the guards let Decker through, saw what was going on, sat on their asses, and allowed it to happen after I made it fucking clear that if anyone touched my wife, they'd be dead?"

Spencer pulls in a deep breath before confirming what I just said with a nod. "I'll find out what I can. I'll pull the surveillance."

I drag a hand down my face. "I want names—everyone who was on duty tonight. I want their background and their connection to the Deckers. I want it before anyone sleeps tonight, got it?"

Spencer's jaw goes hard. "I shouldn't have taken the night off."

I shake my head. "This isn't on you. It's my burden. But from now on, if I leave this house, you're here. Got it?"

He nods once.

"Get me that information. Once I find out who can't follow an order, we'll take care of them."

For the first time since I've met him, Spencer answers in a way that's not professional or subservient the way Damian expected those who worked for him to act and speak. "Fuck, yeah, we will."

There it is.

My gut is right. Spencer doesn't belong in this world any more than I do.

I can't think about that right now. I need to get to Landyn.

I push the door open, but stop at the threshold.

Fuck.

My heart.

I didn't know the organ that kept me alive could seize and beat simultaneously. Only the sight of her in this state could defy science.

Her petrified blues hit me with force. In all she's been through, they've never looked like this. She's huddled in the corner of her sofa, white knuckling a blanket at her chest, and tears stain her face.

She's trembling.

She might as well be stuck in a blizzard instead of sitting in a bedroom suite of a posh estate.

June is standing in the middle of the room, arms crossed, in a standoff with Rocco. The kid has planted himself between the two women, as if June is a threat.

The tension in the room is off the charts.

"He won't let me tend to her, let alone take a step closer," June bites. Her arms fall to her side as she points across the room. "I know what to do. I need to get her cleaned up and those cuts on her face need to be treated."

I can't tear my gaze from Landyn, but with Rocco standing in front of her, it's easy to see his bloody fist constrict and loosen.

June keeps talking, every word escalating. I wonder what happened in this very room before I got here. "Make him get out of the way."

Another tear falls from Landyn's blue eyes.

I can't take it.

Unlike June, I have no fucking idea what to do. What I do

know is I can't let her sit here balled up like a broken doll. And I can't take another moment being this far from her.

I shrug my jacket down my arms and pull at my tie. They land somewhere behind me on the floor as I move across the room.

Landyn's eyes close, and she turns her head from me, but I don't stop. Rocco chooses well and steps to the side to let me pass. If he tried to keep me from her, I'd have to throw him across the room.

My gut clenches when I get close. I don't know what I'll do if she pushes me away. I bend to gather her in my arms. She folds into herself tighter as I bring her to my chest.

But then she turns to press her face into my neck.

Her tears melt into my skin, and a wrath sparks in me that I've never felt, which says a lot since my life has been fueled by rage since the day we got news about Brian. Even I can recognize this is different.

What happened to Brian started with grief and turned into an inferno.

But as Landyn's trembles rock through my chest, they send an electric charge to my heart.

It wakes something inside me.

I hold her tight, turn to June and Rocco, and barely recognize my voice. My words sound like they've traveled a long, cratered road when I growl, "Get out."

"No," June argues. "Put her down so I can clean her wounds."

Rocco does the opposite of my orders and takes a step toward us.

For the first time since I walked into the room, I take him in. His face is bloodied and battered. He's already swelling between his eye and temple, and his expression...

It's haunted.

Fuck.

The evidence proving what Spencer said is right in front of me. He saved her.

My hold on Landyn tightens when I speak to him. "Do not leave the house. Let June clean you up and try to get some sleep.

You and I will talk first thing in the morning. I need to be with her, so you'll have to be good until then."

His stare is intense when it moves from the woman in my arms to me. He answers with a simple lift of his chin, but remains silent.

I turn to June. "Take care of him. I'll take care of my wife."

Finally, the old woman's shoulders drop just enough to let me know she might finally follow orders. She proves she's more business than maternal and walks to the door but stops. "Come, Rocco. I have a medical kit in the kitchen. Let's get you cleaned up."

The kid hesitates as his stare hangs on Landyn.

Given the fact I was jealous of him just yesterday for the easy relationship he's developed with the woman in my arms, right now I have nothing but gratitude, even though I'll kick him out if I have to. "Grateful for what you did tonight. We'll talk about it in the morning, but right now I need to be alone with her."

His eyes fall shut before he turns to leave. June shuts the door behind both of them.

The minute the latch clicks, a single sob bleeds from Landyn.

"Shhh, baby. Let me tend to you." I move to the bathroom.

She groans when I set her on the counter between the two sinks. It kills me to let her go. Fuck, her beautiful skin is marred. Her bright eyes are stormy. And her spirit is broken.

By him.

The need to kill Nic Decker with my own hands is overwhelming.

She calls for me as I start to dig through cabinets and drawers. "Boz?"

All of a sudden, there's little I hate in this world more than Nic Decker and her calling me Boz.

I dump everything I can find to clean a cut on the counter and flip the water so it will warm and toss a rag in the sink. She's still shaking. "Right here, baby."

"Is that what would've happened to me if Damian wouldn't have died?"

My jaw goes hard. I've hinted that her life would have been

much different, but to come right out and tell her seemed useless. After all, I married her for the sole reason to save her from that.

And it almost happened to her anyway.

Turns out, the guilt is heavier than any burden I've shouldered so far.

I don't answer. We can talk about that later. I need to make her feel safe.

I flip off the water and ring out the cloth before turning to her. I kiss her forehead before pressing the wet rag to the drying blood on her face. "I'm so sorry. Should've brought you with me. I won't make that mistake again, baby. I thought you'd be fine as long as you were here. Consider yourself glued to my side from now on. No one will ever touch you again. I'll make sure of it."

"You didn't answer me." She lets go of the blanket she was fisting and reaches for my shirt. The moment the blanket slips from her small frame, I see the evidence of the horror she went through. Her dress is ripped and her bra is mangled. Scratches down her chest disappear into torn lace.

The sight in front of me burns into my brain like a wound that will never heal.

With the evidence sitting right in front of me, I decide that Nic is as good as dead. I can make it happen in a heartbeat. Fuck my job and the code of ethics that makes me different from them.

Nic Decker will pay for what he's done. It'll happen my way and before I'm done with this assignment.

She jerks when I press an alcohol swab to a cut at her hairline. But the burn doesn't distract her from what she wants. If anything, it makes her more insistent.

Her fingers wrap around my wrist and her blue eyes are as demanding as her words. "Answer me, Boz. Did my father sell me into this family to become some sort of toy for them to sadistically pass around?"

I toss the cotton to the counter and place my hands on either side of her. Boxing her in after what she just went through might not be my best move, but she proves she trusts me by closing the space between us even more.

Her hands land on my jaw. "Tell me."

I pull in a deep breath. "Yes. That was Damian's plan."

We're so close, her quick breaths blanket my face. "Did my father know this?"

I lift a shoulder and tell her the truth. "Damian's reputation didn't come close to his reality. He was worse—much worse. I have no idea what your father knew, but Damian's antics are known far and wide in this world. Passing women around, sharing, doing shit that Nic did tonight is the norm in the Marino family. He wanted people scared of him, and he got off on pushing boundaries to feed his reputation."

Her hands drop to her lap, but her gaze doesn't break from mine. "Just when I thought it couldn't get any worse, it does. My father knew."

I place a hand on the side of her neck. "What happened tonight will never happen again. Nic will pay for what he did."

Her eyes well with tears once again.

"Promise you, chica."

I wish I could tell her everything. That I'm not one of them. That I'll move mountains to keep her safe. And beg her to forgive me when she learns this is all a lie.

A lot of shit floated to the surface tonight. The fact I have people around me I cannot trust. Others proved their loyalty.

And the biggest....

I'm not willing to drown my feelings for my fake wife. Not anymore.

"This will never happen again," I stress. "I'll earn your trust. If anyone touches you, they will die."

She licks her dry, cracked lips and swallows hard. "Thank you."

I lean in and press my lips to her forehead and leave them there when I whisper. "Let's get you to bed."

Landyn

If anyone touches you, they will die.

Those words cycle in my mind like a news ticker.

Over and over and over.

I don't know what to think of them. I shouldn't love it. Such simple words when used individually, but strung together...

They're menacing.

And spoken by a man who I don't find at all scary.

I mean, he is when he's defending me. But not when we're like this.

He cleaned every cut. Inspected every bruise. Touched every spot on my body and somehow declared that I don't have any broken bones. Then gave me enough over the counter painkillers to ease every ache Nic inflicted on my body.

"Let's get this off you," he mutters.

He doesn't ask if it's okay. He grips my dress below my breasts and rips it the rest of the way down the front. When he pushes it over my shoulders, it falls to the counter behind me, leaving me barely covered in my panties and torn bra. Then he disappears into his closet and returns with a T-shirt.

This whole time, he doesn't look at me like he has before. Certainly not like a man who had me pressed to the wall with his hand between my legs. Focused only on his task, he reaches around me and flicks the clasp to my bra. I'm sitting in front of him in my panties when he gathers the T-shirt and pulls it gently over my head.

It hurts to raise my arms, but I manage to slip them through, one after the other.

The shirt is huge and soft on my skin. I look down to see the worn logo for the Buffalo Bills and realize that despite the fact I trust this man, I know nothing about Boz Torres.

I look up. "I assumed you were from California or Mexico since you work for the Marinos."

He starts to unbutton his dress shirt but doesn't take his eyes off me. "There are days I have no clue where I'm from." He tosses the shirt with my bra and toes out of his shoes. "Do you need anything else?"

Only for my life to be normal.

I shake my head.

He picks me up and pulls me to his chest. Like a bride.

His bride.

Which I guess I am.

I wrap my arm around his neck to hold on. "I can walk."

He strides straight to the bedroom, puts a knee to the mattress, and pulls the covers down. "You can walk tomorrow. Tonight, you're sleeping in this bed next to me. I wasn't shitting you, chica, when I said you'd be glued to my side. Consider us a unit from here on out."

He sets me in the middle of the bed and I groan as I lean back into the pillows. My side hurts and my head starts to throb.

"Those meds should kick in soon. You can have more in six hours. If you feel like you need something stronger, I can make that happen."

"I'm sure I'll feel better by tomorrow." I watch him unload his pockets onto the nightstand. Keys, wallet, a money clip, and two cell phones. I'm surprised that's it. My father usually has three or four cells at any given time.

His intense stare leaves me only to rip his undershirt off. His belt, slacks, and socks join them on the floor, leaving him standing before me almost naked in a pair of boxers that leave little to my imagination. I haven't seen this much of him since our wedding night when he dragged me into the shower when we were covered in Damian's blood.

Tonight, it was my blood he was cleaning up.

Boz flips off the lamp. His skin is smooth, his thick muscles move fluidly when he climbs in bed next to me, and his body is warm when he pulls me into his arms. He puts a hand to the back of my head and presses my face to his chest where I can hear and feel his words rumble through me. "Never again, baby. They'll have to kill me before they can get to you again."

"Don't say that," I whisper. "I wouldn't be able to live with that mark on my soul, Boz."

He presses his lips to the top of my head. "I won't let that happen. There's no way my soul can bear the brunt of this again."

I allow myself to sink into my husband in bed for the first time. A bed we've never shared or consummated our marriage in.

That thought used to haunt me.

It doesn't haunt me any longer. I'm intrigued, nervous, and even anxious.

This is new. I'm not used to my husband's affection in private.

I could get used to this. I like it. I like it a lot.

Especially after what happened today. Since the whole thing started, I've only felt safe when I'm with him. This gives me hope that if this really ends up being my life forever—a life I didn't choose—it might not suck.

In fact, it might be a whole lot better than not sucking.

I drag my leg up his, because the need to be close to him is overwhelming.

"Boz?"

He sighs, and for a second, I wonder if he's angry. But when he answers, his tone is low and as gentle as his touch on my hip where his fingers are methodically strumming against my skin. "Yeah, baby?"

"Thank you." I pull my head out of his hold and look into his eyes through the darkened room. "For taking care of me."

"I don't deserve your thanks." His tone abruptly turns hard. "I'm the one who left you. I wasn't here to keep Nic from touching you. Now is not the time to thank me. This is my fault, and I know it."

I start to argue and shake my head, but his finger touches my lips to keep me from talking.

"I need you to know one more thing before you shut your eyes to end this day from hell."

I frown.

His wide chest expands as he pulls in a deep breath. "What I told you about Damian and the Marinos? About his plans for you, and his history of doing that with other women?"

I tense, which causes his embrace to hold me tighter. "What about it?

He pulls me up his body until we're almost nose to nose. "I never took part in that. I worked for Damian, helped manage his business, and even took a bullet to save his life. But that shit was fucked up. No matter how much he tried to push that part of his life on me, that's where I drew the line. You don't know me, baby. Not really. I've done a lot of shit working for this family, but that's a line I'd never cross."

I let that sink in. His words warm me as much as his body. I tip my head and press my cut lips to his. His fingers press into my back and it feels like he's doing everything he can to control himself.

When he finally ends the kiss that I started, I look into his eyes. "I knew you were a good one."

His dark eyes fall shut and he exhales, returning me to his chest. "I hope you always believe that, baby."

"You are," I whisper against his skin. "I feel it."

"Landyn, please. Go to sleep." His voice is rough, and his plea feels desperate.

I press my lips to his pec before relaxing into his body. I know what happened tonight will never happen again.

Because I married a good one.

21

CROSS THE LINE

Brax

She sleeps.
Finally.
I had to make her stop talking. I gave her too much information as it is. My job is to blend in, pretend I'm one of them, do everything I can to *be* one of them.

But she had to know that's a line I'd never cross. I can deal with her thinking I run a cartel and do all the dirty shit her father does or worse, but there was no way I could go one moment longer without making it clear that I didn't participate in the same shit that got Damian off.

Hell, Damian asked me once if I was gay when I refused to join his fuckfest for the tenth time. He even offered to find me, and I quote, *some nice dick*, so I could join in on the fun.

I told him it didn't matter if I preferred pussy or dick—groups, sharing, and non-con weren't my kink.

That was enough to keep him off my back. I stuck to business —stealing his secrets and setting up wires that went straight to

Cole Carson. Damian was stupid enough to focus on whatever flavor of fetish he was in the mood for that day while I carried on.

And I didn't lie to Landyn when I told her if anyone touched her, they'd die. Which is why my life goals are out of whack and finding Nic Decker is at the top of my list.

> Spencer – I watched the surveillance three times. Nic talked his way in. Convinced them he just spoke to you and he was ordered to wait here until you returned. I emailed you the cut of the video. Nic was convincing.

> Me – They still did nothing to stop him.

> Spencer – Nic's last name might be Decker, but he's still a Marino. These men respect the name, and they're scared of him. They know they fucked up.

> Me – I want them gone. Where's Nic?

> Spencer – I don't know. I thought he'd go to his parents' home in Santa Barbara, but he hasn't shown up.

I focus on Landyn's steady breath against my chest so I don't throw my fucking phone across the room.

> Me – How do you know?

> Spencer – I have contacts too. Don't make me tell you how I know, because I won't.

Interesting. I guess the hired help talk. But it makes sense Nic would run to his parents. He knows he's in deep shit.

For me to get close to Damian, I needed Nic out of the way. I had a feeling Nic was skimming product off the top. All I had to do is exaggerate the numbers when I brought it to Damian. Paranoia took over, and the rest is history.

Blood is not thicker than money in this world. Nic was cut out by Damian and Alamandos. The only reason he's still breathing is because he is a Marino.

> Spencer – The guards are freaking out about what you're going to do.

I let my hand slip down to rest on Landyn's ass.

> Me – They should. I'll deal with them in the morning. Nic can't hide forever. If he shows at his parents', let me know.

My next call should be to Cole Carson.

Should be.

But that would put this on the record, and for the first time since I stepped foot into the Marino world, I need something to be off the record.

> Spencer – Of course. And, sir, I just want to let you know, everyone in this house has your back. After tonight, I think you can safely add the boy to that list.

I let out a deep breath.

> Me – Appreciate that.

I flip over to a text thread that's new.

> Me – You okay?

Bubbles appear and disappear over and over before I get an answer.

> Rocco – Only if Landyn is.

> Me – She will be, thanks to you. Be in my office at nine. We need to talk.

This time I get an immediate answer.

> Rocco – As long as our conversation is about torturing that motherfucker.

> Me – Settle down. You work for me, and you don't make a move without my orders. He'll pay. I'll make sure of it.

> Rocco – I want to kill him.

Stand in line, buddy.

> Me – Nine o'clock. My office.

> Rocco – I'll be there with a shit-eating grin on my fucked-up face if we're planning his murder.

Shit. The kid is intense. I like it. But if he only knew I'm trying to keep him out of prison instead of putting him in it, he'd tone it down.

> Me – Enough. We'll talk tomorrow.

> Rocco – I can't fucking wait.

I put the phone down because he's not going to stop. I roll and stare down at the woman in my arms.

Just a few hours ago, I made myself swear off her, and now we're glued to each other with hardly any clothes on.

No matter how much I know this is crossing the line, I've wanted nothing more than to be right here. At first, I thought it was because she's the closest thing I've had to normal for two years.

But as the days click on, I realize it's just her. Especially after today. Touching her, making her come, and knowing she wants me as much as I want her.

Knowing that someone else touched her. Hurt her. Fuck. That changes everything.

I can't stand the marks on her fair skin. The scrapes, the scratches, the bruises.

I lean in and kiss the top of her head and whisper, "No one will hurt you again, baby. Ever."

22

NOTHING AND EVERYTHING

Brax

"Five minutes is a long time to be away from my wife after last night, Rocco. Are you going to answer my question?"

He does the same thing he's done since I sat him down. He stares at me—unmoving and intense.

I thread the pen through my fingers, staring right back.

Finally, he gives me one shake of his head.

I toss the pen to my desk and lean forward. He looks like he got hit in the eye with a wrecking ball. His lip is twice the size it was yesterday at this time, and he might've tried to hide it, but I could tell it hurt when he sat down across from me.

"You were an open book last night when you were talking about vengeance and murder. But now, when I want to know something about you, you clam up."

"You don't need to know anything about me."

"That's where you're wrong. You saved my wife last night. I want to know everything about you."

His face contorts, and his brows tense when he spits, "Why?"

"Do you know how many people I trust after last night?" I

spear him with an intense stare. "Not a lot. My wife is one of them, two men who you don't know, and I'm thinking about adding you to my list. I want to make sure I'm making the right decision."

"My parents have nothing to do with who I am," he growls. "My mom is dead. The last time I saw my old man, he was so strung out, he didn't recognize me. There's nothing more to know."

I lower my tone the way my dad used to when he was sick of my dumbass attitude. "Something haunted you last night."

His jaw tightens.

"See?" I hike a brow. "I'm right."

He stands and points to the double doors leading to my room where Landyn is still sleeping. "You say all you care about is her. Why are you interrogating me?"

"Sit down and cool off."

I don't have to wait long. His hot-headed asshole that comes with age and whatever hell he's lived through shows when he throws himself in the chair. His glare on me intensifies, and it's clear he's not going to tell me on his own.

I want to hear it from him.

I want him to trust me.

"There's something in you..." I let my words trail off and think about what Landyn has said to me more than once. I can say the same about Rocco—he's a good one, but I don't dare. He's doing everything he can to sabotage his own life. "You fought for Landyn when she couldn't fight for herself. You're going to pass the GED with flying colors. And in the short time you've been here, you fit in like a little brother or a mascot."

"I'm no mascot," he bites.

"No, you proved last night you're no joke." I point to him across the desk. "You're the real thing."

He shakes his head.

"You don't know me, but I might be the most powerful man you'll ever meet. I can get my hands on any information I want. I know you, Rocco. I was trying to give you the chance to tell me something I already know." I let that sink in and watch his expression fall with every word that drips from my lips. "Your dad killed your mom when you were eleven. You saw the whole thing."

He starts to move from his chair, but all I have to do is put a finger up to stop him.

"He beat her to death, but if I had to make a calculated guess, it wasn't the first time he put his hands to her."

Rocco simply stares at me, and I wonder if he'll try to jump me from across the desk. I knew this was a risk, but given the look on his face after he threw down for Landyn, I need to pull him in closer.

This will either work brilliantly, or he'll run, and I'll never see him again.

"Saw it in your eyes when you were standing in front of my wife and wouldn't let anyone touch her. I *saw* it."

"You didn't see shit," he whispers.

I don't stop. "You stepped up and saved her. So when I asked if you were okay last night, it was not some off-handed comment. I want to know if you're okay."

"Why do you care?" He's found his voice, and his words come at me like venom. "You're not my counselor. I had enough of them in my day. You're only a fucking drug dealer."

Just like when I do it with Landyn, speaking the truth feels good. Like I'm clinging to who I am with bloodied fingers. "I'm a lot of things, Rocco. If you stick around long enough, you'll figure that out. If you're smart, you'll use it to your advantage."

He stands from his chair again, and this time I mirror his action, because he doesn't stop. He might actually come across the desk at me.

But we both freeze when her voice breaks through the tense room. "Your face."

Landyn stands in the double doorway to the bedroom in the shirt I slipped over her battered body last night. It hangs on her small frame. I'm grateful she at least put on a pair of loose pants. It's clear she didn't take the time to put on a bra, because the shirt hangs on her nipples.

Before I have the chance to tell her to turn around to put some real clothes on, she's across the room and wraps her arms around Rocco. "Thank you."

He stands there, holding his arms out, not knowing what to do. His eyes widen, and he stares at me from over her head where she's face planted into his chest.

The only reason I'm not completely overcome with jealousy is because she slept in my arms last night with my hand firmly planted on her ass.

Landyn keeps on, not knowing what she just interrupted or giving a shit that I'm standing right here. She looks up at Rocco. "Are you okay? I'll never forgive myself for answering the door. You were hurt because of me."

Rocco doesn't know what to do with his hands and looks from me to her. "Umm ... it's no big deal."

Landyn pushes back and waves to her face. "Are you serious? You saved me from him. It's a huge deal, Rocco. I'll never forget it." She turns to me, and a pang hits my chest when her eyes well. "Tell him—tell him what a huge deal it is."

I can't take it another second. I round the desk and go to her. I stayed in bed with her as long as I could and haven't showered yet. I threw on a pair of joggers and a tee, but I'm the only one in the room who isn't sporting bruises and cuts.

I grab her hand and pull her into my arms, but I don't take my eyes off Rocco. "Don't worry, baby. He knows what a big deal it is."

When she gives my shirt a yank, I look down at her as she begs, "Don't let him go back. Make him an offer he can't refuse so he can work for you and stay here with us."

As long as I've been here, lying has been a life-saving skill and something I did gladly. But with her, it drives me mad. "It's complicated, baby."

Landyn presses her good cheek to my chest, and turns back to Rocco. "I'll never forget what you did for me. You need to stick with Boz. Please, think about it."

I put my fingers to her chin and tip her face to me. "Look at my wife, making business deals for me."

She's not at all apologetic. "He's like you. I can tell. A younger you, but he's good."

"Ah, I'm gonna go," Rocco mutters.

"We're not done talking," I say.

"We're done," Rocco amends and moves to the door that leads to the hall.

"Wait," I call. He turns around and sighs. "The Deckers are not a powerful family, but we don't know what Nic will do. Don't leave the house. You have a meeting with Logan today—cancel it. Tell him I need you on a special project. But don't say a word about what happened last night. The Jackals don't need to know that you might have a target on your back."

"Even more of a reason for you to work with Boz," Landyn clips. "I doubt your club has your back like this."

I keep talking. "Stay here today. You've got your test next week. Study, and we'll have dinner together tonight. I owe my wife a day of shit TV."

Landyn looks up at me. "Really? You're not going to work all day?"

I pull in a big breath. "I can't promise I won't work, but I'll do it in front of the TV with you."

Her body melts into mine and makes me think of all the ways I cannot have her. Not when she thinks I'm someone I'm not.

Her smile is small and swollen and sweet and I can't wait for her wounds to heal. Keeping myself from the things I want with her is going to be fucking torture.

"Thank you," she says.

"I'm really out of here this time," Rocco mutters.

"We'll see you at dinner," Landyn calls as he slams the door. She looks up at me. "A whole day together. Nothing could make me happier after last night."

"Chica." I pull her to me to take her mouth but keep it light and short so I don't hurt her. "You need to up your expectations."

Landyn

I'M LULLED into a blissful state of veg.

This is what happens when trash TV and Boz team up on me.

Shockingly, after last night, I had the best night's sleep since I got here. I picked at my breakfast, Boz made me take more pain meds, and forced me to use an ice pack on my face.

But then we came straight back to bed.

Lunch has come and gone. Dirty dishes litter the bedside tables, and I have subjected my husband to the most mind-numbing shows on cable TV.

And he's sat through it all.

Aside from working on one of his phones now and then, he's been content and hasn't complained once. I had no idea what today would bring.

The answer to that is positively nothing and absolutely everything.

Boz sits shoulders to the headboard, leaning against a mountain of pillows. His abs are the only cushion I need as he drags his fingers through my hair with one hand and the other plastered so low on my hip, it teases my ass from time to time.

We've gone from watching the drama of teens being moms, to house flipping, and now employees on a yacht hooking up. It's mindless and shallow and a beautiful thing to focus on something so gratuitous after what happened last night.

"Baby, this is the most stupid shit I've ever watched."

This is the first time he's complained since he turned on the TV and handed me the remote.

I roll to find him gazing down at me, rumpled and delicious, with a different look on his face that I've never seen. "I haven't watched this stuff in forever, but it reminds me of a time when I had nothing to worry about."

He brushes the hair from my face. "I haven't complained because I know you need the distraction. But watching the hired help on a boat hooking up might be my limit, chica."

I lick the cut at my lip so I can smile. "What do you like to watch?"

"I can't remember the last time I watched anything on my own. My job is..." He shakes his head and sighs. "A lot."

"Then why did you have a TV moved in here?"

"To distract me from you."

I lace my fingers with his. "But that was before."

He hikes a brow. "Before?"

I hike mine right back and widen my eyes. "Before yesterday."

"Do you mean before the orgasmic event or before Nic?"

"Either," I say before correcting myself. "Both."

"I can't lie, baby, I had myself talked into ignoring you again after one and before the other."

I let go of his hand and twist to my hip. My tone goes hard and demanding. "Why?"

His tone, on the other hand, is equally steady and unapologetic. "It was my way of protecting you."

"What about yesterday when we were together before you left? You were going to come back after that and ignore me all over again? I don't understand you." I put some space between us and tell him the truth. "I don't know what I expected when Damian's people took us other than dread. Maybe it was my brain's way of protecting me. I just knew my life wouldn't be the same, but I didn't expect this." I motion between him and me. "I never expected a connection or trust or ... whatever this is."

He pushes to his ass and reaches for my hips. He drags me over his lap in no time and holds me close. "You are the last thing I expected, baby. The timing could not be worse. I wish I could make you understand. I just have to hope that someday, when you look back on this moment, you will."

I give my head a tiny shake. "I never dreamed that your way of protecting me would be so maddening."

Framing my face with his big hands, intensity radiates off him.

"Trust me, chica, everything in my life is maddening right now, but nothing as much as this thing between you and me."

My heart skips a beat and not in a good way. The fact that a marriage I was forced into might be maddening to him twists my insides. "You mean our marriage?"

"Yes," he bites. "Our fucking marriage and everything else."

Shit.

I didn't know anything could hurt more than what Nic did to my body and spirit last night, but that does.

I blink my emotions away and try to pull out of his hold, but he doesn't let me.

He pulls my mouth to his.

It's the first time he's really kissed me since last night. It's not like yesterday when he had his hand between my legs and made my body sing. That felt like he was doing everything in his power to hold back and not consummate the very marriage that is so exasperating to him.

This kiss is gentle and slow and feels the exact opposite of his words.

I slept in his arms last night. The only times we've been apart are for quick trips to the bathroom. He's given me his complete attention and time.

I hate myself because I like it.

Hell, I hate myself that it actually makes me happy.

He puts a hand to the middle of my back and another to my head when he twists me on the messy bed. He doesn't give me his weight and hovers over me. I fist his tee in my fingers and drop my knees to the side and open for him.

An invitation.

And pure desperation.

I should be desperate for a lot of things.

My old life.

Choices.

Freedom.

Maybe I'm the one mad, because all I want is him. I'm

desperate for him—the man who finds our marriage and everything about me frustrating.

He does the exact opposite of accepting my invitation. He breaks our kiss and drops to his forearms on either side of my head. His body never touches mine. I relish in his fingertips dancing over the cuts and bruises at the side of my face. Even that feels good.

When he speaks, his words surprise me. "Trust me, baby. I'm doing everything I can to make sure you don't hate me."

"Why would I hate you? You've proven everything you've done is to protect me."

He pulls in a big breath and says on an exhale, "You'd be surprised."

It's official.

I'm losing my mind. The more he talks, and the longer we're together in this forced marriage, the more I want him.

I've even wondered if this is Stockholm syndrome. But it's not like he planned this. There's no way. Not how this played out. My own father sold me off, and my mom knows everything. If they cared about me more than their own protection or supporting their life through illegal business, they'd call the police.

Which brings me back to me. It's not like I can't actually pick up a phone and dial 911.

I could.

But I haven't.

And it's all because of the man staring down at me and our very unconsummated marriage.

"I don't hate easily," I say. "But I hate my father, and I really hate Nic. I don't know what you could do to make me hate you, Boz."

His eyes fall shut, and it feels like something is brewing within him. Like he's warring with himself.

I keep talking. "You don't want me?"

His eyes fly open, and he spears me with his red-hot gaze. "That's something you should never question."

"Why wouldn't I question it?" I press. "Your actions and words never line up. One way or the other, you're hot or cold."

"I'm never cold, baby. Not with you or us." He shakes his head, and his gaze is heavy, studying my features intently. "The man you married is a drug dealer. If the world were different and your dad wasn't a flaming asshole, would you have chosen me? This life?"

My answer comes quickly. "That's not fair."

"Why? Any man would be crazy not to want you. But for you to want me because you have no choice?" He shakes his head. "I want you, but I don't want that. I'll never want that."

I untangle my fingers from his tee and smooth the material for the sole purpose of running my hands down his chest. Confusion does not begin to describe my brain that's in a constant battle with my heart.

I stare at my fingers as I speak, because I'm afraid to look into his eyes. "I think had we met in a bar, or at a party, or even in the ethnic foods aisle at the grocery store, I would've given you my number. I mean, if you asked for it and didn't have some creepy pick-up line." When I peek up, his expression isn't as intense as it was before. He's amused. "I guess I shouldn't assume that you'd ask. If we were in the grocery store, there's a good chance I'd come straight from the gym or rolled out of bed. Then I wouldn't blame you for not giving me a second glance."

He fingers the hair on top of my head and lowers his voice. "Married you while you were covered in another man's blood, and you were still fucking gorgeous. I would've given you more than a second glance."

"What I'm saying is, in a parallel universe where my father isn't an asshole and you weren't forced to marry me after a bloodbath of a wedding, it's possible this could have happened."

He presses lips to mine. "This absolutely would've happened in a normal world, chica. No way would I let you walk past the pasta or the tortillas or the wasabi without stopping you. I don't give a shit if you were in sweaty gym clothes or your pajamas."

I roll my eyes. "Stop it. Now you're making fun of me."

He shakes his head. "No way. I would've insisted you give me your number. If you refused, I would've forced mine on you and dropped to my knees right there in front of the chipotle peppers and begged you to call me, because I wouldn't be able to live in a world without your blue eyes."

I give his chest a small push. "Boz—"

Even though he looked serious before, he's even more so now. "Baby, do me a favor and give me a nickname. I'll take *B* or even *hey you*. Hell, call me *asshole* if you want."

My brows rise. "Are you serious?"

His one word tells me how serious he is. "Deadly."

I hesitate and let my thumb run under the band on my left ring finger. "Only if you'll do something for me."

"I wish you could see that I'll do anything for you."

My heart speeds, but I decide to go for it. "Show me that you want me."

He studies me for a moment.

But that moment is short.

He doesn't give me his weight, but he does give me something else.

His cock.

Right where I want it, even though it is through two layers of thin material.

He's long, thick, and so hard.

"Is this what you want, baby? Does this show you how much I want you?"

I suck in a breath, and my eyes fall shut. Lord, he feels good.

He grinds into me again—harder and deeper. Up and down on my sex. Even through our thin clothes, the friction on my clit is everything I need.

"I want more of you. I want every inch of your body to touch mine."

I grip his sides and pull, but he doesn't come to me and shakes his head. "No way. Not with your bruises. You wanted me to show you how much I want you—this is it. No matter what happens or what force tries to wedge its way between us, I want you, Landyn. I've wanted a lot of things in life, but nothing more than you."

I'm lost in his words and his touch, but neither is enough. I lift my hips to meet him for more. "The more you talk, and the longer I'm here, the less I understand."

"You'll understand in time," he says on a growl and thrust.

"In time? Some days it feels like the clock stands still and others like we're racing against a ticking time bomb." I drag my hand down his chest and his abs but don't stop. I almost reach my target, his cock that's worked me into a frenzy, when he pulls away from me. My eyes fly to his. "No, don't stop."

I might lose his cock, but I gain his lips, and not gently this time. His tongue spears my mouth and his kiss sears us together in ways that leave me wanting everything until the end of time.

Being seared to him in every way is the only thing I want. Regret courses through his groan when he breaks our connection and moves. The next thing I know, I'm in his arms with my back plastered to his front. One hand slides up my shirt to my bare breast and the other dips south, straight into my pants and cups my bare sex.

I moan.

His lips hit my ear. "Baby, you make it really hard for me to be good."

I press my ass into his long, hard cock that I barely got to touch before he ripped my hand away. "Why do you get to touch me, but I don't get to touch you?"

"I want you so fucking bad. If I let you touch me, there's no way I'll be able to stop. I'm leading this, baby. If you don't like that, then I'll have to go back to ignoring you, and that's the last thing I want to do."

I whimper in protest.

His tongue outlines the curve of my ear.

He's holding me in the most basic and carnal way. I'm impossibly wet when I try to move against his hand, but his every muscle constricts around me. "Tell me what you want, chica."

I try to turn my head to him. "I feel crazy. I shouldn't want you, but I do. I'm desperate enough I'll take anything you want to give me."

He runs his nose up the side of my neck and inhales. "You don't know what desperation is. I can hardly see straight after last night. If you could see inside my brain right now, you'd understand desperation. I'm worried about my focus."

I wiggle my ass back and forth against his erection. "Maybe you'd focus better if we were naked."

He finally moves. His fingers dance between my legs, playing with me, circling and touching me everywhere but my clit. "If you tease me, I'll give it right back to you, baby. If you want to get down to business, you've got to tell me what you want."

I arch and bring my hand up to hold his to my breast. "Please, Boz."

He twists my nipple. "What did I say about calling me Boz?"

"How can you expect me to remember anything right now?"

I suck in a quick breath when he finally gives my clit some attention.

"Tell me," he demands.

I turn my head to catch his gaze. "I want you to make me forget about last night. I only want to think about you and us. Please ... *hubbalicious*."

That wins me a smirk.

And attention exactly where I want it.

He presses a thick thigh between my legs and forces me to open for him. "Can't wait to get my mouth between your legs. You can beg all you want, but I plan to take my time. Open for me, chica. Wide."

My eyes fall shut, and I spread my legs farther for him. "What did I do to deserve you?"

His lips hit my collarbone where he gives me a suck. "It's the other way around." He spears me with two thick fingers. "You deserve so much more than this life." I almost lose my breath when those fingers circle and press in on my clit. "In time, I'm going to make sure you have everything you want."

This is like yesterday against the wall but better. He's given the word edging new meaning with the way he strings me along. He lifts his knees between my legs and spreads them, opening me wider, touching me everywhere. I don't know how much more I can take when he finally gets down to business.

I gasp and moan, and not at all quietly. He teases my nipple and circles my clit, winding me into knots. When I fall, I don't feel anything but him. Not a bruise, not a cut, and not one ounce of pain.

My husband holds me tight—all I feel is him.

All I can think about is him.

Whatever syndrome this is, I'm here for it and never want to be cured.

As I float back to earth, he cups me tight between my legs, never breaking our connection. He's still hard as a rock, his cock pressed between my ass cheeks. I don't begin to understand why he's keeping himself from me. If it weren't for the very hard evidence, I'd wonder if he had a problem.

But from everything I can tell, my husband is as healthy as a horse ... a stallion. And a premium one at that.

I settle into his arms, and my words are breathy. "I wish I understood why you're the way you are. But even more, I wish you'd trust me enough to tell me."

His arms constrict around me, but he doesn't answer. We lie here in silence until his poor, ignored cock settles down.

He finally presses his lips to the side of my head. "We need to get ready for dinner or Rocco will be eating alone."

He shifts me to climb out of bed, and I watch him adjust himself as he strides to the bathroom, shutting himself in. I stare at the ceiling as I listen to the water turn on and wish I were with him.

23

FAKE

Brax

"I knew I could count on you. No one works with the Marinos until they've proved themselves. If they ever get caught and try to flip on us, we can fuck them up with our own proof."

I want to hurl the dinner I just ate. I stare out at the sunset shutting down another day.

Another day of my life that I've given to this fucking case.

I'm so close, I can taste it. I thought finality to the hell my family has been through would be sweet. I thought I'd relish and celebrate it.

Instead, all I taste is bile.

I force myself to steady my tone and lie through my teeth. "Pleased you're happy, Alamandos."

Carson's man, Ozzy Graves, came through in a big way. A fake cop, his fake family, a fake death, and even fake news reports.

What's not fake is my new level of disgust, and that's saying a lot. I didn't think it could rise to a higher level after bartering for Landyn only to keep her as a toy.

The only reason this is possible is because Graves knows how to play on the dark web and has access to his own satellite system. Those links look as legit as the real thing.

I turn when I hear Landyn laugh, a sound I only hear when she's with Rocco. If I weren't in a constant watch-my-back situation twenty-four-seven, I'd be jealous I wasn't the one making her that happy.

Not that I haven't made her happy in other ways. I'll take orgasms over humor any day of the week.

Landyn and Rocco are a pair. They're sitting straight across from one another at the middle of the dining table where I left them to take Alamandos' call. They're wearing matching bruises, cuts, and scrapes. Landyn didn't bother getting ready for dinner and her hair is still wet. She's constantly late when she does herself up, so tonight was a nice change.

I lower my voice. "There's something else I need to talk to you about."

I hear Alamandos shuffling around. His age and failing health bleeds through the line. "What?"

"Nic. I had a meeting last night with the real estate developer. He talked the guards into letting him in without me here. There was a..." I hesitate because I can't make this about Landyn. Alamandos won't give a shit. "Scuffle with the staff. The man shows no respect to me, Damian's legacy, or your decision for me to carry on your son's work. It was a slap in the fucking face to me and to you, Alamandos. I'm done."

He sighs. "My fucking nephew. He needs to be taught a lesson."

This is stepping over the line, even for me. I've looked the other way a lot since I started this gig—you have to when you're undercover. What I've never done is instigated this shit on my own.

But the bruises all over Landyn are making me willing to cross lines.

The CIA and DEA are listening, and as much as Carson is

willing to push boundaries, I still need to be careful. What I can do is bait Alamandos so it's his idea.

"He already skimmed once and stole from you. I'm looking out for the family. But he is your nephew."

"Bring him in," he bites. "Nephew or not, no one steals from me or questions my orders. Put a bounty on his head if you need to."

A smile creeps over my face, and I have to do my best to keep it out of my voice. This is the easiest order I've carried out for Alamandos. "I'll see if we can find him before I offer the bounty. I'll keep you up to date on the load this week. Working with the Jackals will be a good move. Your product will be transported underground. We'll be good."

"The bikers have tunnels," Alamandos mutters. "Who knew?"

Me. That's who, asshole.

Instead, I offer, "I'll update you later in the week about that and the new project I had a meeting about last night. If I can close that deal, it'll be the biggest venture yet. We can increase our cash flow by over thirty percent."

"This is why I keep you close, mijo. Good work."

Alamandos knows the cartel side. He's an idiot when it comes to legitimate business. The man is easy to impress.

"Anything for you, Alamandos." Fuck him. It's all for me. And as soon as I find out who added Brian to Alamandos' sick list of initiations, I'll take everyone down at once.

I hang up, return to the table, and take my seat next to Landyn.

She turns to me with wide eyes. "Did you know Rocco had multiple offers to play in college?"

I look across the table and lift my chin. "I heard."

"From all over the country," Landyn adds before turning her eyes back to Rocco. "Why did you quit?"

Rocco's expression is similar to what it was in my office this morning when I was interrogating him. He's uncomfortable, irritated, and doesn't like this kind of attention.

He pushes his dirty plates away and crosses his arms. "What's the point? School is a pain in my ass. Even if I would've played, I'd still be stuck in a classroom for another four years. Football is cool, I guess, but not if it means dying a slow death in a lecture hall."

Landyn proves she's lost her filter when it comes to her new friend. "So you'd rather chance dying a quick death and work in the underworld of society for the Jackals?"

Rocco narrows his eyes and glares at the woman he saved just twenty-four hours ago. "Heard about your wedding. And do I have to remind you that you're still married into the cartel?"

Landyn shakes her head. I put my arm around her and pull her close as she looks up at me with imploring eyes. "Would you talk to him? Explain to him that he has choices."

Rocco doesn't give me a glance, yanks up his sleeve, and points to his half-tat. "I made my choice."

I give her a squeeze. "Baby, give him a break."

She ignores me and keeps talking. "But you're here now. You have us. And you're going to get your GED next week. You can still make different choices."

Rocco's stare turns to me, and he's pissed. "Did you put her up to this?"

The conversation has taken a sharp turn from whatever they were laughing about two minutes ago to this.

I shake my head. "She's spearheading this all on her own."

What I don't say is since he saved her from Nic last night, I have a feeling she wants to save him in return.

"We're a unit," Landyn presses. "Let us help you."

Rocco picks up his drink and takes a big gulp before his empty glass hits the table with a thud. "You're whacked in the head, Landyn. You want me to go back to school when you just told me you dropped out after two years?"

Landyn is committed to the task. "That's different. I wasn't a superstar."

"Fuck," Rocco mutters and glances back at me. "Do something about your wife."

"Whoa—" I start.

But I'm interrupted by my *wife's* gasp. "You did not just say that!"

I put a hand up to stop the conversation. "Let's get past the GED. I'm going to start taking you to meetings with me after that. We can debate superstar status later."

"You can't be mad at me," Landyn demands. "I'm only trying to look out for you."

Rocco sighs and proves he has more patience than he pretends to for the woman who's taking over both our lives. "I'm eighteen. I don't need a mom."

Landyn's hand lands high on my thigh and slides north. When I look down to see what the hell she's doing, I'm awarded with a beautiful smile, proving that a day of rest, trash TV, and an orgasm might've helped just a little.

"Do I look old enough to be his mom?" she teases.

I don't know what the hell is wrong with me, but talk of her being a mom causes the blood to rush to my dick. I can't help it. I lean down and claim her mouth for a quick kiss. "No, chica. An annoying older sister maybe. We'll talk about you being a mom privately."

A chair scrapes across the wood. Rocco's plates clank against one another as he stacks them high and stands. "I'm going to let my food settle and hit the gym."

"You should study," Landyn quips. Rocco rolls his eyes. "Do you want me to quiz you?"

"No." Rocco heads straight to the kitchen and mutters, "Carry on with the honeymoon. I'll be just fine on my own."

When he's out of earshot, I drag my hand up her back and turn her makeup-free face to mine. "You're laying it on a little thick, baby."

She's not smiling or teasing anymore. She's serious when she shakes her head. "No way. I'll never quit. I'm determined to save him like he saved me." She pokes me in the chest. "And you need to help me."

I lean in and kiss her again, but this time it isn't quick. I don't give a shit about the cameras or convincing anyone this is real. My obsession and desperation are rapidly escalating at equal rates when it comes to my fake wife. As much as it kills me why I need to keep her close to me wherever I go, it was the slap in the face I needed to realize that I want her. I don't know what we will look like when this operation is over, but I'm determined to make her understand and pray she doesn't hate me when I tell her the truth.

The first might be easier to do than the latter, though neither will be fun. I'm not looking forward to it even though I can't wait to get us the hell out of here.

"Baby, I'll help you do anything. I'm pushing him to get his diploma, but he's a man. He's got to want it."

She leans into my chest and slides a hand up, wrapping it around my neck. "You have to do everything in your power. Promise me, B."

B.

Fuck.

That's a step in the right direction. She has no idea the effect that has on me.

I nod and wonder if there's anything I won't do for her. "I promise."

A small smile settles on her lips. "Thank you."

I nod. "It's been a good day, chica. I hate to end it this way, but I need to work and make some calls."

"I know you said you wouldn't leave me, but I can entertain myself while you work."

After I showered, I threw on a pair of jeans and a clean tee.

I'm never casual. It's small, but it's claiming a piece of my old self.

But when Landyn threw on a pair of short shorts with a tank that really just made me want to rip them off her, there was something about its normalcy that made me not give a shit about looking the part.

For one night, I'm giving myself normal.

That is until I get her settled and make my next call. I can't fucking wait to do that.

I watch her walk back and forth to the kitchen on bare feet as I send a text to set up a meeting.

For the next fifteen minutes, I check my emails and watch the surveillance cameras while Landyn does what she wants to do in the kitchen and talks to June and Miranda.

The table is clear and ready for a new day when I take her hand and lead her upstairs.

She yawns. "How can I be so tired when all we did was laze around all day?"

I lock us in the bedroom and breathe a sigh of relief like I have every time I walk into this room since I ripped out the cameras. I lean down and press my lips to her forehead. "Go to bed. I don't know how long I'll be, but I'll be right through those doors if you need me."

She proves she's not only resilient after last night, but she trusts me. "I know. I'll be fine."

"I'll make sure you'll be more than fine." I put my hand to the side of her face and tip it to mine. What I really want to add is that I'm willing to make that commitment for the rest of my days, but since she assumes we're really married, that would not be my best move.

She starts to push up on her bare toes, but I get to her first and take her mouth.

This is new.

A new level of trust and passion and need.

My hand slides down to cup her ass and she presses her body to mine. I have to fight to get my dick under control as it thickens in my jeans with only a mind for her.

I'm not far behind him.

Now that I've given into this—this very real relationship that's playing out inside of a lie—I wonder how I'm going to be able to put her off much longer.

Because I want her more than anything. I'm too close to the end to fuck it up.

But my need for this lie to be real is overwhelming. It's taking over my motivations and my actions.

I think about what's waiting for me in the office next door and break our kiss. We're both breathless, and I'm halfway to hard, which I do not need right now.

I tip my forehead to hers. "I'll meet you in bed."

She licks her lips and nods.

I brush my thumb lightly over her cheek. As the swelling goes down, her skin is turning a tint of blue that feeds my rage. It's about the only thing that will drag me away from her right now.

"I'll be in soon," I promise, giving her a nudge toward the bathroom. I wait until she closes herself inside before turning to the double doors.

He jumps to his feet as soon as I open the door. "Boss. I came right away."

I move to my chair across from him and settle in. He's nervous, which he fucking should be.

"Sit," I demand.

He falls to his ass immediately.

There's a hierarchy in this organization, and Don has worked his way to the top of the middle. He has enough power that what happened under this roof last night falls on his shoulders.

But he's also far enough down the chain, he should be scared as hell sitting in front of me, because it's his fucking responsibility that Nic got through.

I don't have to ask him anything because he starts to beg. "It won't happen again, boss. Nic talked them into letting him in. They were afraid to stand against him because of who he is."

I narrow my eyes. "They were afraid of a man they don't report to?"

He shakes his head and continues to spew bullshit that does not matter right now. "Sir, they were about to break in and stop him. I swear—"

"But they didn't. It doesn't fucking matter what they were about to do. My wife has the bruises to prove it." I recline back in my chair and level my eyes on him. "I put this order out once, and I'm only going to do it one more time before someone pays for their fuck up. No one touches my wife. You can open a door for her or carry her shit, but that's it. If she so much as offers you a hand to shake, you'd better run the other fucking way, and that includes every man connected to the Marinos."

His chest rises and falls quicker than it should. "Yes, sir."

"Not one fucking finger, you got it?"

Beads of sweat dot his forehead as he nods. "Got it. Run the other way. Not a finger. I'll make sure everyone knows."

I sit up straight and pick up a pen. Then I scribble two short sentences that light a fire in me.

I fold the paper and slide it across the desk.

Don stares at it.

When I lift my chin, he slowly leans forward to pick it up. I watch him as he reads my order. His gaze jumps to me, and his eyes widen.

I tip my head.

He nods.

I send him on his way. "Go."

He proves he doesn't want to be here anymore than I want him here. He tosses the paper to my desk and is out of my office in record time.

I pick up the paper and read it one more time.

Find Nic.
I want him in the garage.

I'm in the business of collecting information. I document every fucking thing I come across, whether it's legit business or that run by the Marino Cartel.

But not this.

I swivel in my chair and feed the paper into the shredder that's never gotten any use by me since I got here. Alamandos put out the order, but I don't need it on official record with the federal government that I aided him.

Nic is going to pay for every mark he put on Landyn.

Then he's going to pay again for doing the same to Rocco.
And I'm going to be the one to deliver the message.
If he lives through it, he'll understand.
If he doesn't, even better.

24

REVERSE SEXUAL PSYCHOLOGY

Landyn

I stare at myself in the mirror.

The cuts on my lip and face are almost healed. My dark bruises have faded to a lovely yellowish-green. I've gone from looking like a punching bag to a crumpled paper bag.

Better ... ish.

It's been a full week since Nic pushed his way into the house. A week of settling into a new norm that has included constant attention from my husband and a new dynamic with everyone else under this roof.

Spencer actually smiles at me.

June is less businesslike. When she bosses me around, it's surprisingly affectionate rather than intimidating.

And Miranda has gone from silent to actually carrying on short conversations.

Those conversations are focused on food, but it's a step in the right direction.

I'll take it.

And I haven't let up on Rocco. I don't care how irritated he pretends to be with my constant pestering about his life choices, I refuse to stop. He's gone from irritated to annoyed to amused.

Though, only slightly amused. I know this because I straight up asked him.

I can't help it.

He's at a fork in the road. I've made it my mission to make sure he doesn't mess up his life. I might have been forced to marry into a drug cartel, but that doesn't mean I'm going to sit by and watch my new friend travel a road he doesn't have to.

I wasn't given a choice. I'm just lucky I ended up a Torres and not a Marino. Or a Decker for that matter.

A Torres...

Landyn Torres.

Married in name only. B wasn't kidding when he said he wouldn't fuck me. Not that he hasn't touched me. He has.

Lord, has he touched me.

He keeps telling me to trust him, to be patient, and that, in the end, I'll thank him. That only creates more questions.

What does he mean by *the end*?

But unlike my constant pushing with Rocco, I have not pressed B for more answers. I'm not sure if there's anything I wouldn't do for him, so I've gone against every natural inclination of who I am.

I'm being patient.

And I'm trusting him.

It's easier since I got my period five days ago.

But my period has come and gone. My cuts are practically healed. And my bruises are fading.

I feel like a new woman. I woke up this morning refreshed, energized, and...

Wanting everything with the man I was terrified to marry. There are times I wonder if he's playing mind games with me. Because the longer he holds out, the more I want him. If he walked into this bathroom, I might jump his bones.

I have no clue how he's so self-disciplined.

I'd be worried that it says more about me than him—that he might not want me the way I crave him. But when I wake up every morning with his hard cock pressed into my back or my thigh, the evidence is there.

And who needs evidence when he tells me he can't wait until the day he can make me his.

Reverse sexual psychology.

I wonder if this is a secret weapon only the most cunning and smart men use on women.

Because it's working.

This morning I woke up alone, missing my husband. The office door was cracked and a low light was shining through. I could hear the faint tappity-tap-tap on his keyboard.

I have no idea how long he'd been up, but I missed him.

I wanted him.

And now that I'm officially done with my period, I can do what I've been contemplating for days.

I'm feeling good. And that I don't look like a prize fighter who lost the biggest match of the year helps too.

I got out of bed, took a shower, and am actually putting some extra effort into getting ready for the first time in a week.

Blinking into the mirror, I make the last swipe on my lashes. I twist the tube shut and toss the mascara in the drawer and fluff my hair.

I go straight to the closet full of clothes that I've made mine and rip the tank over my head. B is still in his office. His deep voice has been carrying on conversations all morning about real estate and investments, followed by less legitimate conversations about the load the Jackals are delivering soon.

I yank another loose dress off the hanger and tear the tag off it. I turn to my reflection in the floor-length mirror. The thin material hangs on my breasts, my very hard nipples front and center since I'm not wearing a bra.

It's loose, ties at the shoulders, and hits me at the middle of my thighs. There's nothing fancy or sexy about it. This is nerve-wracking enough as it is. If he turns me down, at least I'm not walking in there in lingerie or a dress that screams sex.

I can play this off as I got dressed for the day. And since I haven't bothered with a bra for most of the last week, this isn't a stretch.

I'll put one on before I find Rocco. His test is tomorrow, and I promised to quiz him all day, even though he insisted he didn't need the help.

What else am I going to do?

Besides seduce my husband.

I turn on a bare foot and head straight to his office. "First, he stole from Alamandos, and then he pushed his way into this house. The word is out—Alamandos wants him brought in. He has to know we're looking for him—he can't hide forever."

I hesitate before tapping on the door lightly as I push it open. His eyes jump to me as he speaks, and they're heated in a way I'm not used to. He's angry, but he always is when the subject of Nic is on the table.

He must have gotten up earlier than I thought. He's also ready for the day, though I bet he's probably wearing underwear. He's in black trousers with a crisp cadet blue dress shirt.

His cell is plastered to his ear, and every muscle in his body is tense.

Seeing him this way shouldn't turn me on.

But it does.

I mean, more than I already am.

I've been barging in on his work all week, and he's welcomed me. This isn't the first phone call I've walked in on about Nic Decker.

When I take my first step toward him, he swivels and spreads his thighs. Like a magnet, I walk straight between his legs, and he pulls me onto his lap.

A place I'm getting very comfortable.

His stare is intense as it makes its way up and down my body, hesitating on my breasts and nipples that are now close to his face as he keeps barking orders. "He's not hiding at his parents' house.

Don't ask me how I know that, but I'm certain. It's been a week, and I have my orders from Alamandos. Fifty grand on his head to whomever can deliver him alive and healthy. Put the word out. Someone will give him up."

I have no idea who's on the other end of the line, but B doesn't give them a chance to respond or say goodbye. He hangs up and tosses the cell on the desk next to us.

My index finger trails down his skin where his dress shirt is open at the neck. "Good morning."

His hand lands on my bare thigh and moves north to my also bare ass. "Good morning."

"You were gone when I woke up."

"I wanted to let you sleep." He squeezes my ass. "Did you miss me?"

"You're always close. I rarely have the chance to miss you." I bite my lip. "But I did this morning."

He slides his hand farther until he catches the strap of my thong, as if he was curious if anything was there at all. He hooks an index finger beneath it and drags that finger around my hip and down to my sex, never shifting his gaze from mine. "You're ready for the day."

"I am..." My tongue wets my lips. "Ready."

His eyes narrow. "Chica."

"Darling."

His finger stops between my legs where he's traced my thong to my very wet core, and a smirk touches his lips. "*Darling*?"

I shift my legs open for him a tad. "I'm trying out new nicknames. You said I could call you anything I wanted."

Gone is the anger that was rolling off him in spades just moments ago. His intensity has shifted from ire to lust.

For me.

His lips tip up at the corners, and his dark eyes warm. "I did. And lucky me, you haven't gotten to *asshole* yet."

I bop the tip of his nose with my index finger. "Not yet."

He puts a hand to the middle of my back and presses in,

forcing me to arch, which juts my breasts closer to him. "I'm not looking forward to the day when you try that one out."

"All married couples fight," I point out. His gaze lifts to my eyes. "I'm sure it will come. You know, after the honeymoon phase is over."

"The honeymoon phase," he deadpans.

I feel his cock harden beneath me. I shift in his lap just enough to rub against it. "I'm still waiting for the honeymoon phase to begin."

He drags a finger through me, slow and measured. So slow, I'm tempted to move against his hand to create the friction I want.

But I want something else more.

"You're wearing very little," he notes, as his eyes drop to my nipples, awake and alert through the thin material.

"You're wearing too much," I counter.

He looks back up at me and leans in. When his lips brush the skin of my ear, he whispers, "Baby, if there weren't cameras in here, I'd lay you out across this desk, strip you bare, and put my mouth between your legs. You'd come so hard, your screams would wake the sea creatures off the coast."

With that, he slides a finger inside me, and this thick thumb circles my clit.

My head starts to fall back, but his hand slides into my hair, and he stuffs my face in his neck.

I want more, but I'm breathless as he continues to whisper into my ear. "Do not come, Landyn. Do you hear me? The guards are watching. You walked in here practically naked under this slip of material to tease me. Now, I get to tease you."

My eyes fly open. I try to pull back to look at him, but he doesn't let me move. He holds me tight, his fingers working me between my legs as he rolls his chair closer to the desk, and continues to murmur in my ear. "There's no fucking way I'm going to allow anyone to see you come."

"I've never seen you come," I whisper back. "There's a power imbalance in our marriage. I don't like it."

His hand grips my hair. "Baby, don't kid yourself. There's definitely a power imbalance in our marriage."

I get another delicious swirl around my clit without him touching it. My face puckers with a frown. "That's not fair."

"I agree. That's what I'm trying to protect you from. From me and everyone else who wants to hurt you for no other reason than to make a power play." He pumps me with two fingers and shakes his head. "Hell, at this point, I'm doing everything I can to protect you from yourself."

"I know what I want ... *honey*." I watch him hike a brow and even I can't bite back my wince. "Okay, that one's a no-go. But seriously, I know what I want. I'm not some naïve virgin."

It's the truth. I'm not well traveled around the block, but I have made a couple trips. Enough that when I say I'm experienced, it's not a lie.

"When I'm right here, chica." A shiver runs down my spine when he finally touches me where I want, and it makes me and my clit very happy. "I don't want to hear about anyone else."

I shift my legs open for him and suck in a shaky breath. "Got it."

He leans in and traces my ear with the tip of his tongue. "Do I need to take you to our bedroom?"

I straighten my spine—metaphorically speaking, since I'm twisted into a sexual frenzy—and retort, "Depends on what you're going to do there."

His words continue to hit me in a low rumble when he puts his lips to my ear. "What do you think? I'm going to make you come. I'm sure as hell not going to do it here."

I squeeze my thighs around his hand, force him back far enough to look at him, and try to muster the courage to do what I came in here to do. "I can do that by myself."

His teasing touch on my sex turns into a firm grip. "I don't like that."

I try to cross my legs, but he only holds me tighter. "Sorry, sweetheart."

Wow. And just when I didn't think his grip could be more

possessive. He's not trying out pet names like I am, but this time mine is growled in a very different tone. "Chica."

"Sss...snookums." I blame the impending orgasm for my foggy brain. "Stud muffin. Nutter butter. Sugar plum."

He pulls in a deep breath that blankets me in a frustrated exhale.

"Do you not like baked goods?" I ask through shallow breaths.

Now it's his turn to bite back a smirk, because he ignores my clit but doesn't move his hand.

"I can switch to superheroes. Hulk. Black Panther. Captain America." I grip his shirt and pull myself closer to him. "And my personal favorite—Thor."

He manages to move his thumb between my thighs, and I get another shiver. "If you call me Thor, we're going to have more problems than we've ever had. And that's saying something, baby."

I'm about to move onto a different themed list of pet names, but one of the cells on his desk vibrates. His eyes dart to the screen before I lose his hand. He at least wipes his fingers on his pants before picking it up and tapping the screen a million times to unlock it.

A frown mars his handsome face. And not one that tells me he doesn't like Marvel.

"Hey," I call for him, but he continues to stare at the screen. I put my fingertips to his chin and tilt his face to mine. "What's wrong?"

"I don't know," he mutters. He's looking straight into my eyes, but it's like he's in another world. Then, with a blink, he's back, and my face is framed in his big hands. "Baby, as much fun as this is, I need to make a call. Swear on my life, I would not push you away if it weren't important."

"It's okay." His tone is unsettling and sobering. "Can I bring you a cup of coffee?"

He pulls me to him and presses his mouth to mine. This kiss is different.

It's not sensual ... it's desperate.

When he finally lets me go, he tips his forehead to mine.

There's not a trace of banter in his tone. "No shit, baby, put on a bra before you go downstairs. Give me five minutes to make this call."

I place my hand on his freshly shaved face. "Okay. I'll be back in five minutes."

And this time, I do exactly as my husband asks. I have a feeling the next five minutes will feel like an eternity.

25

GROUNDED

Brax
Two years ago

"I'm begging you, Braxton. Don't do this. I can't go through it again. It'll kill me."

"You won't." I bite and try to reach for her hand. She pulls away from me, stands, and stalks to the other side of the room. "I know what I'm doing. This is different."

"You're right. This is different. So damn different, Brax." She shakes her head, dragging her fingers violently through her hair as she stares out the window. "You're marching into the lion's den willingly. One wrong move and—"

"I won't make a wrong move. I've got the DEA and the CIA at my back. This is different. Brian was hunted. I'll be on the offense the whole time. My contact at the CIA will make sure I'm one step ahead."

When she turns to face me, her expression might as well be a dagger to my chest. Pained tears streak her face.

And just like that, it all comes back to me with a force.

The day we got the call. In the days after we found out Brian died,

I unofficially moved home, and I hadn't lived here since before I left for college. But I was here with her, day and night. Reporters camped in front of my childhood home for days. It was impossible to come and go without someone wanting a piece of us.

My mom. My sisters. Me. There was no way I could leave them here alone.

"Don't do it," she begs. "You can change your mind. It doesn't matter what you promised anyone. They can't make you do this."

I take the three steps that separate us and pull her into my arms. With everything life has thrown at her—first losing Dad and then Brian—Mom seems like she's a fraction of herself, and it has nothing to do with her naturally small frame.

I keep talking. "No one is making me do anything. I need to do this. I need to find out who and why. It's time to uncover the truth. It affected all of us differently, but that doesn't mean we're not all paralyzed in some way. I want to put an end to that."

She shakes her head against my chest. "I'm afraid."

I put my hands to her shoulders, push her back, and look into her green eyes. The girls and I took after dad. Dark hair, eyes, and skin. You'd never know by looking at our family that our Hispanic father, who moved to Queens when he was ten, met and married an Irish beauty when he was still in high school. Brian, on the other hand, looked just like mom. Had he not been built like a brick shit house, just like Dad, you'd never know we were related.

I lean far enough to look into her eyes, the ones that remind me of my older brother every single time I look into them. "I'm not afraid. This is why I changed careers. The opportunity presented itself, and the time is right. This was meant to happen."

She shakes her head. "No. Don't say that."

I lower my voice. "I'm going to find out who did it. Swear to you. And you'll be able to sleep at night knowing that the people who took your son from you paid the price."

"And what price is that?" she bites.

"You know the price, Mom. An eye for an eye."

She cradles her face. "I already lost your father and Brian. This is too dangerous. Let it go. I can't lose you too."

I shake my head and pull her to my chest again. "Not a chance. I'll be back. It'll be like I wasn't even gone. I'll get in, do what they want me to do, poke around, and get out. I'll be back before Christmas."

"Promise me, Brax. Promise you'll come back to me."

"Do you think I want to get popped on the side of the head with a wooden spoon for lying to you? I learned my lesson a long time ago."

"You were always the cunning one—naughty and sneaky," she snaps. "Which worries me more."

I try for the grin that usually wins her over, even though I can tell she's not in the mood. "You have my word. I'll get in and get out. My goal is to fly under the radar. It's not like I'm going to report to the head of the Marino family. They'll barely give me a glance."

She finally realizes that there's no way she'll win this battle and wraps her arms around my chest. "If you're not back for Christmas, consider yourself grounded."

Shit.

That hurts more than telling her about the operation. I have a feeling there's no way I'll be back by next Christmas, let alone this one.

But she can't know that.

She can't know anything.

"I'll be here."

Her arms tighten around me in a way I'll have to pry her off to catch my flight.

Fuck.

I'll make it up to her. Because I'm not coming home until I know who killed my childhood idol.

My brother.

"It's a risk," Carson says. "One we rarely take. In fact, none of my assets have ever done this."

"He's my agent," Tim growls right before barking the order. "Get on a damn plane, Brax. I know you can come up with something. We'll figure it out from there."

I stare at the marble under my feet where I shut myself in the bathroom. I've got more problems right now than I know what to do with and none of them have anything to do with the Marino Cartel.

That's a first since I got here.

I need to get to New York. Tim is right—that part is nonnegotiable.

But there's no way I'm leaving Landyn here.

The men on the phone, who have had my back this whole time, have no clue my fake marriage has turned into a very real relationship that I cannot turn my back on.

And Landyn…

Well.

This is going to be a conversation I didn't plan on having until this whole thing was over.

"You there?" Tim bites.

I have no choice. I have to go.

"Yeah. I'll arrange meetings in Manhattan."

The door to the bathroom pushes open, and my head pops up.

Landyn is standing there holding a steaming mug of coffee. She moves silently across the room where I'm ass to the vanity. She's still barefoot, but at least she put on a bra. She sets the coffee on the counter between us and doesn't move.

I continue talking and watch her expression change with every word I say. "I'll be on the first flight out. I'll let you know where I'm staying once my arrangements are made."

Landyn's expression falls, and she tries to take a step back, but I wrap an arm around her and pull her front to my side.

"I don't like this, but I get it," Carson gives in. "I'll agree to this as long as you allow me to make the arrangements when you get here. I can make sure you're safe."

"Done," I agree without looking away from Landyn.

"Watch your back, Cruz," Tim says. "You leaving by yourself will throw up every red flag in the cartel handbook."

He's never been more right.

"I've got to go. See you soon."

No one bothers to say goodbye, and the line goes dead. I slide my cell in my pocket and pull Landyn to my front.

"You're leaving?" she exclaims, without giving me a chance to explain

"What did I say to you?" I put my hand to the side of her face. "Glued at the hip, right?"

"But you just said—"

"I've got a meeting I need to be at in person in Manhattan. Pack a bag, baby. You're coming with me."

A look of joy fills her eyes. "Really? I get to come with you?"

I nod and wonder if that's the last time I'll see that expression in her bottomless blues.

"Yeah, but I need you to do something for me."

The sweetest smile spreads across her face. "Anything. I'll do anything for you."

Shit.

The feeling that she's about to slip through my fingers strangles me. I shove that thought away and frame her face in my hands. "Some shit came up. I can't explain now. I need to buy plane tickets and book a room. But I want you to promise—no, I need you to promise—that you'll keep an open mind."

She wraps her hands around my wrists. "My father spent his life pretending he doesn't work in organized crime, but he does. We're married, I know what you do, and I'm shockingly okay with it only because it's you. I never, ever thought I'd be okay with being right here. I'm not sure what else there is for me to have an open mind about."

Shit.

I press my mouth to hers for the simple fact I have no fucking idea what to say.

When I finally let her go, I decide to keep it simple and deal with the truth later. "Get packed."

Her smile lights from within as a dark storm brews within me. "I'm so excited. I've only left the house for a funeral since you brought me here. This will be like a honeymoon."

She gives me one more peck on the lips and heads straight to her closet.

Honeymoon.

If only.

26

ASSHOLE

Landyn

Something else hubbalicious needs to learn about me is that I am not a fast packer. It goes hand in hand with being late. When I go on a trip, it requires forethought, lists, and plenty of options, not to mention time to change my mind.

Basically, I'm a high-maintenance traveler.

But that wasn't an option today. I had approximately forty-three minutes to pack. I didn't have time to check the weather in the Big Apple or figure out what our plans were when we got there so I'd have the appropriate choices. Hell, my groom didn't even tell me how long we'd be there.

I honestly can't remember what's in my suitcase, but there's a one-hundred-percent chance I'm going to need to go shopping when we get there.

I overheard B explain to Spencer that something came up and he had to be at meetings in Manhattan. I spent those two minutes hugging Rocco and wishing him good luck on his test tomorrow.

Then we were gone.

We barely got through security and had to run to our gate. We were the last ones on the plane, the door hit us in the ass, and by the time we were settled in our first-class seats, I could barely breathe and was making promises to myself to hit the fancy home gym when we got back.

Once we were settled, I asked about our trip. B just gave me a peck on the lips and told me we'd talk about it when we were alone.

I watched a movie, napped, ate every snack they gave me and one of B's, drank two glasses of wine, and silently complained to myself about being stiff. What I did not do is play games or scroll on my phone.

Because, I still don't have one.

My husband spent the five-hour flight alternating between working on spreadsheets and pinching the bridge of his nose.

I have no idea what happened that caused us to jump on the first flight out of San Diego, but it can't be good.

No matter the reason, I'm here. B hasn't broken his promise, and he's been glued to my side. He might pretend to run the legit business for the Marinos, but I know what he really does. My healing bruises are proof of how women are treated within the cartel, so dragging me along for the ride is probably not standard procedure in the organization.

He doesn't complain about the weight of my suitcase when he tosses it into the trunk of the cab like it's a pillow packed with feathers. The sun has set on New York City as we sit in rush-hour traffic.

I'm no idiot and can take a hint. My husband doesn't feel like talking. I'm also not sure what it says that nothing has made me this uncomfortable since the first few days of our marriage. It's also not like me to sit back and not demand answers. But the thing is, I don't really care why we're here.

All I want to know is why my husband has turned into a ball of ice-cold nerves.

I watch him stare out his cab window at the people, the traffic, and the hustle and bustle of life in the city. I've only been here a few times, but I love New York City. It's different than living on the

West Coast. Especially the way I grew up. There's an energy that's unmatched.

Much like the unparalleled energy emanating from the man who has consumed every part of me.

I reach over to grip his hand in mine. He turns, and his dark eyes mirror his body language.

Tense and agitated.

I can't help it. I don't care where we are or who we're around. I've been patient all day.

"When are you going to tell me why we're here?" I demand.

He pulls my hand to his lips where he presses them to my knuckles. "Trust me, sooner than I want to."

The frustration I've tried my best to manage all day bubbles over. "What does that mean?"

He pulls in a breath but shakes his head as our cab turns into a circle drive of one of the poshest hotels in Manhattan. He lets go of my hand and tags me around the neck. When he kisses me, it's unlike ever before. It's desperate and fraught with anxiety that is not at all like the man I've experienced since my wedding day. My husband isn't afraid of anything—not even guns being drawn at the dinner table.

I'm breathless when he finally lets me go and tips his forehead to mine as the car comes to a halt at the entrance. I don't look away from his stormy, dark eyes as he baits me with more promises. "Let's check into our room. I'll make time to explain."

"Make time?" I echo, but my door is opened behind me.

The concierge calls for me and offers a hand. "Ma'am."

B is out of the cab and slips a wad of cash to the driver.

If the hotel is posh outside, opulence clings to every surface on the inside. The bellhop follows us with our bags, and we check in as Mr. and Mrs. Torres. When we got to the airport, B had my old passport. I didn't think about it until today, but I haven't had anything updated. Not my driver's license, passport, or my favorite magazines. I don't even know Damian's address.

Not that I go anywhere. But I certainly can't live the rest of my life locked away in the cliff-side estate that really belongs to the dead man my father sold me to.

More information to demand by the time we get home.

Home.

Wow. It's the first time I've thought about that place as home.

B grips my hand as the elevator zips to the sky. It's been a long day, and all I've eaten is airplane food. First class might be a nice step up while flying, but I need a real meal.

The bellhop moves our luggage into our room and is grateful for his fat tip.

Finally. For the first time since this morning in our bathroom, I'm alone with my husband.

I toss my purse on the king-size bed and am about to demand to know everything, but when I turn, B is standing in the middle of the room staring at me with a cell plastered to his ear. "Yeah. I'm here. What's the status? Okay, I need to take care of something. Give me twenty minutes. I'll be ready."

Ready?

Ready for what?

He's barely disconnected his call when I decide that I've had enough. "Who was that? And what will you be ready for?"

He drags a violent hand through his thick hair before looking at his watch, confirming he really is on the clock. Then he moves.

But not to me.

What he does next sends a shiver down my back and puts me on edge. He positions himself between me and the door. His stance is wide and looks like he's prepared for the worst.

"Boz, what's going on?" I demand.

He shakes his head and his stare is heavy, lasered in only on me. His next words sound more like a warning than a wish. "I told you not to call me that."

I cross my arms and take a step back. For the first time, I wonder if I've made a mistake trusting the man I was forced to marry. "What's happening?"

His jaw tenses, and his words are forced. "We're not here on business. We're here because there's an emergency."

"I'm not an idiot. You gave me approximately three minutes to pack for a trip across the country. I assumed we're here for you to manage some type of crisis. I want to know what it is. I *deserve* to know what's making you act this way."

"I'm not here to manage anything. I'm here on a prayer that I'm not too late."

My arms fall to my sides in frustration, and my voice rises. "How long are you going to speak in code before you tell me what's going on?"

He drops his gaze to the floor in front of him for long, agonizing moments. I'm about to scream in frustration, but he looks up just in time. "The call I got this morning when we were in my office was from a friend ... a co-worker."

"Okay." I shrug. "What did they want?"

His words feel crafted and chosen with precision. I don't like any of it. "My co-worker ... he's more like a partner."

I frown. Partner can have so many meanings. "What do you mean?"

"I mean, we've worked together since the beginning."

"Just spit it out," I bite. "The beginning of what?"

"The beginning of my career." He hesitates. I'm about to say I've never heard anyone talk about their work in organized crime as a career, but I don't get the chance because he rocks my world. "My career ... with the government."

My face falls, and a one-word question slips out on a breath. "What?"

He takes a step toward me.

I immediately take one back.

He puts a hand out low to stop me. "It's okay. Let me explain.

"Explain?" I demand and take another step back. "Holy shit. What is there to explain?"

"I'm not who you think I am."

My heart speeds, and my lungs fight for oxygen. "Wh-who are you?"

He shakes his head. "Baby, I need you to calm down."

Fuck that. The last time someone told me to calm down, the

Marino guards were at my family's door, and I was sold to pay off a debt.

I lose it and scream, "Don't tell me to calm down, dammit!"

He takes another step and this time doesn't stop when I retreat. Each of his eat up two of mine, and I panic, before stumbling when I hit the corner of the bed. He grabs my arm to keep me upright, but at the same time, I'm twisted.

My back is plastered to his front.

My wrists are bound in one of his big hands.

And the other wraps itself around my neck and jaw.

His touch is firm and controlling. His hold is impossibly stout. There's no way I'll escape.

These hands that have touched me everywhere. They've been firm with me, cared for me, and even controlled me in the most private and carnal ways possible.

Stockholm syndrome floats through my mind again, because I've loved most of it.

But I don't love this.

His lips brush my ear, and his words hit me in a whisper, not unlike when we're at home and he doesn't want the cameras to pick up what he's saying. "Baby, I need you to listen. Let me explain. Trust me, this is not something I wanted to do right now. I wanted to wait until the time was right."

"The time was right?" I echo, not at all in a whisper. "You work for the Marino Cartel. You report to Alamandos. How did you have a career with the government?"

"Not past, baby." His body tenses around mine. "Present."

I can barely form words, and my mind tries to make sense of what he's saying. "I don't understand."

"Chica." That word has come to hold many meanings. Sometimes it's informal, sarcastic, or even laced with frustration. This time it's none of those. That word is completely and totally reverent—laced with something more than it ever has been. He inhales, dragging his lips across my temple. "You don't know how many times I've had you in my arms thinking of this moment.

Dreading it and wanting it at the same time. I'm not scared of anything, Landyn, but this fucking terrifies me."

Tears well in my eyes, and my words tremble. "You're scaring me."

"I'll tell you, but you have to trust me. Swear to God, Landyn, every single thing I've done since I laid eyes on you has been for you. To protect you. I didn't mean for this," his hand on my neck falls to my chest and presses in over my heart, "to happen. I did every single thing I could to stay away from you and still keep you safe. It was so fucking hard. In the end, it was impossible." His hand comes back to my chin to tip my face to his. Only genuine honesty bleeds from his eyes. I realize this look on him is new. And that scares me more than anything. "This was not supposed to happen."

I say nothing.

There's nothing left to say, at least not from me.

"I'm a special agent, baby. I work for the Drug Enforcement Administration."

My eyes fall shut. "Oh my God."

"Yeah," he agrees. "And the fact I'm telling you this right now puts my life at risk. But this trip was not optional, and there was no way I'd leave you behind. If this gets out—if I get made in any way—I'm dead. And my guess is, it won't be quick or painless. Your life has been in my hands this long, baby, but right now I'm putting mine in yours. You trusted me to take care of you. Tell me I'm doing the right thing. I need to trust you too."

Brax

I'M NOT LYING.

Well, not anymore.

But I'm really not shitting her about the trust. I don't know what I'll do if she turns me away. I don't even want to think about the possibility that she'll run after learning the truth. If she doesn't accept me for who I am, then I'm going to have more heartache than just figuring out how to keep her safe.

"So, um." Her erratic heart races against my chest. "You're not a drug dealer?"

"I'm the very opposite of a drug dealer, baby. I've got many goals in this undercover operation. Taking down the Marino family is just one of them."

"You lied this whole time." The tears that race down her face might as well be a knife to my gut. "You pretended to be someone you're not."

"No." I let go of her wrists to turn her in my arms. She doesn't dodge me to escape. I think it's pure shock from what I've told her, but I'll take it. I cup her face in my hands and look into her confused, hurt blues. "I'm the same man who's been right here with you the whole time. I have a different job than you thought. It's the only lie I've told you."

Her lower lip trembles as I swipe the tears from her cheeks with my thumbs. It kills me that of all the things she should be afraid of, her fear is focused on me. "What do you mean taking down the Marinos is only one of your goals?"

I pull in a deep breath and shake my head. "It's a long story, and we're going to have to leave in a few minutes."

She pulls out of my hold and takes two steps back. "I'm not going anywhere until you tell me everything."

I take a step toward her, because I need to make her understand. "Chica—"

She puts a hand up to stop me. If tears could turn from hurt to anger in a heartbeat, she just proved it could happen. "Don't fucking *chica* me. And don't you dare tell me to trust you again. I didn't think I could trust anyone, but I trusted you."

I pull a hand through my hair and glance at my watch.

Shit.

She swipes her face with the back of her hand. "Swear to God, Boz, I will scream this hotel down and you won't be able to stop me. Either tell me the truth or deal with the attention I'm sure you don't want, seeing as you're not who you say you are."

"About that..." I start.

Her eyes widen. "About what?"

"I might've told you two lies. My name isn't Boz."

Her face falls before her eyes shut. "Holy shit."

"And it's not Brian either. Going by Brian was ... symbolic," I add. I don't say anything else and wait for her to look at me. I've come this far with her. She needs to know everything. If she's the person I think she is, only the truth will win her over. "But my brother's name was Brian."

Her frown deepens. "What does your brother have to do with anything? And what do you mean *was*?"

"He died years ago—killed in the line of duty."

That softens her frown, but only by a touch.

As much as I don't want to get into this right now, I spit it out. "It wasn't by some freak accident or a stray bullet. He was targeted, Landyn. Ambushed and taken. He was missing for a week. When his body was found, he'd been tortured. It was so bad the autopsy report was a fucking novel."

Her eyes well all over again as her fury melts away.

But mine is back, and it's bleeding from me with every word I spew.

This time it's her turn to take a step toward me but she stops mid-step when I keep talking, describing the nightmare that put me on a path that brought me right here.

"All evidence pointed to the Marino Cartel, but they didn't have anything solid. His body was dumped at the border near Tijuana. The feds were brought in to investigate, but there's not much they can do outside the U.S."

I watch the woman who turned my life right-side up in an upside-down world take in everything I say. I can't blame her for being confused or angry. I certainly can't blame her if she wants nothing to do with me after this.

But she says nothing.

Not one fucking thing.

And I'm running out of time, so I keep talking. "I was a different person when it happened. Just out of college and starting my life. I was a peon on Wall Street, working sixty hours a week trying to prove myself. This," I hold my arms out, "was never my plan."

"Then why are you here?" she whispers.

"Our dad died when I was twelve. Brian was eighteen. Young enough that he didn't need to step into any role, but he did. He was more than a brother. I always idolized him, but he was the man I needed in my life at the time. He stepped up when he didn't have to. He didn't go away to college the way he planned to. We grew up in Queens. He stayed local when he could have gone anywhere, and he did it for me. He finally moved to the West Coast when I went to college. His dream was to leave, but he waited until I was out of high school. He was selfless and loved his family to a fault, but he always wanted to be a cop. When we found out how he died, that simmered under my skin until it got so hot, I knew I had to do something about it. I'm bilingual, so when I applied to the DEA, I was a shoo-in. I never thought I'd end up here, but when the opportunity presented itself, I had to take it."

She gives her head a little shake and starts to say something, but I keep going.

"I never thought this would happen. This." I stop to motion between her and me. "Has been the distraction I did not need. But every single thing I've done since I laid eyes on you has been to keep you safe. In the beginning, it was an act to make sure everyone else knew to keep their hands off you."

"An act," she whispers.

"Yes," I confirm. "It was. But not anymore. You got under my skin, and what was fake turned very fucking real, Landyn. I've pushed you away because there was no way I was going to fuck you when you thought I was someone else, even though I know I could've."

She blinks in slow motion before crossing her arms. "That's presumptuous."

I close the distance between us, cup her cheek in my hand, and tilt her face to mine. "I know it's true and so do you. The sexual tension between us is so thick and heavy, I'm surprised it hasn't combusted in our faces. You don't know how hard it's been for me to push you away, or focus on my job, when all I want is you."

She leans her cheek into my hand, and I realize I was about her age when Brian was killed. At too young of an age, we were both thrown into a world neither of us wanted or planned for—all because of the Marinos.

I'm ready to wipe them from the face of the earth forever.

"You still haven't told me why we're here," she pushes.

I exhale and shake my head. "My mother had a heart attack last night. They had to do a bypass this morning. Leaving her to go undercover was one of the hardest things I've ever done. She begged me not to do it. And now this has happened. I need to see her, but I couldn't leave you. Swear, baby, I was going to tell you all this. I just didn't plan for it to be now."

She puts her hand to my wrist, and it's a punch to the gut when she pulls away from my touch. "I don't know what to think."

I'm about to yank her into my arms and make her listen to reason. Force her to accept me—the real me—for who I am, what I've done, and the lies I've told.

But three strong raps interrupt us. Her gaze jumps to the door. "Who is that?"

I don't move to answer it and keep my eyes on her. "My partner. The Marinos know we're here, and I have actual meetings set up for tomorrow night as a legitimate reason to get to Manhattan. I can't just waltz around New York without the risk of being followed or seen. They're going to make sure we get to the hospital safely."

Her eyes widen. "We?"

"Baby, I'm not sure what more I need to say to get this through your head, but you're not leaving my sight after what happened to you last week. And now you know the truth. If you thought we were inseparable before, get used to a whole new level of me invading your personal space. Because until further notice, you're stuck with me."

I go to the door, because he's not patient on a good day, but she calls for me. "Boz—I mean..."

I turn back to her and hike a brow.

Her tears are dry and she crosses her arms, a stance that shows she means business again. "After everything we've done, I think I deserve to know your real name."

"That depends," I say.

"On what?"

"Can I trust you, baby? With my life?"

She pulls in deep breath and drops her arms on an exhale. "I think I have a reason not to trust anyone. But I'm certainly not going to rat you out to the Marinos."

I ignore the door when Micah bangs twice from the other side and calls for me. "You in there?"

"What about your father?" I push. "What's your allegiance to him?"

She shakes her head and hurt is laced in her tone. "You know how I feel about my father. And my mother, for that matter. It's not lost on me how alone I am. If you say you're the same person you were, then tell me your name."

I pause, because I haven't uttered my own name in what feels like a lifetime. "Braxton Cruz, but everyone calls me Brax."

"B," she whispers. "Brax."

Fuck.

I like the sound of my name on her lips. It's the sweetest sound I've heard in two years.

But I have no time to relish in it or beg her to chant it to me while I bury myself inside her. I'm officially out of time. My burner phone—the one I use for Carson, Tim, and Micah—vibrates in my pocket.

I ignore the phone and turn for the door. When I swing it open, the man who's been my closest friend since we went through the academy together, pushes through. "What the fuck took you so long? Were you taking a shi—"

But he stops in the middle of the room when he realizes we're not alone.

He turns to glare at me.

Then back to Landyn.

Then back to me. "What the fuck?"

I shake my head and shrug because I have no explanation for my lack of self-discipline or rationale for bringing Dennis Alba's daughter here and telling her my real identity and what I really do.

I have no excuse other than I'm pussy whipped.

And I haven't even had her.

Yet.

"Did you forget to tell us something?" Micah demands.

I glare back at him. "I couldn't leave her."

Micah's eyes widen, and he asks the same question again he's asked two other times since he entered the room. "What in the actual fuck, man?"

"Don't give me shit," I bite back. "Can we get moving? I want to get to the hospital and see my sisters before visiting hours are over."

"You have sisters?" Landyn asks.

I lift my chin. "Two."

"This is messed up, you know that, right? Carson is going to have your head, right after he gives the rest of us an *I told you so*, because he can't keep his fucking mouth shut about you and your *bride*." Micah looks from Landyn to me. "Is she going to run?"

"I don't know." I look at the woman who I'll chase to the ends of the earth if she does. "Are you going to run?"

She stares at me, and I wish I knew where her mind is at. "I'd like to know where you think I'm going to run to in a city where I know no one. It's not like I can go to the cops, since you are the cops. And you took my phone."

I tip my head in agreement, but refute, "They took your phone, not me."

She narrows her eyes. "Well, you could at least get it back for me."

"For fuck's sake," Micah mutters and turns for the door but on his way out, he jabs me in the chest with an index finger. "Good to see you, shithead. You'd better not get dead over a mobster's daughter."

I hear Micah yank the door open behind me because I don't look away from the woman who holds a hell of a lot of power over me right now. "Yeah, I hope I don't get dead too."

Landyn's eyes fall shut as she shakes her head. Then she marches past me, grabbing her purse on the way. When her shoulder brushes my chest, she mutters, "Asshole."

Well then.

A new pet name for me to add to my collection.

Micah shoots me another *what the fuck* glare.

I shake my head.

I'm exhausted.

But Landyn isn't running away or screaming down the hotel.

And I'm going to see my mom and sisters.

It could be worse.

I just hope I'm not too late.

27

TONGUE-TWISTER FAMILY

Landyn

My husband isn't who I thought he was.
Not Boz. Not Brian. And he's definitely not a Torres.
Braxton Cruz.
Everyone calls me Brax.
Give me a nickname. I'll take B or even hey you. Hell, call me asshole if you want.

I'm tired. Tired of being confused and played and not given a choice in the way my life is playing out.

And I'm pissed. So fucking angry.

But really, I'm hurt. The man I was falling hard for lied to me ... about everything.

Between my father, the Marinos, and now *Braxton-call-me-Brax-Cruz*, I'm proof that a woman can lose her identity and her will to be who she wants to be. To be told who she'll spend the rest of her life with and be forced to live with it.

They can be turned into just a possession, tossed around, bartered, and used.

I don't need to find myself. I know who I am. It doesn't matter how hard I was falling for the man I was forced to marry. Hell, it was just hours ago that I was doing everything I could to throw myself at him. Seduce him.

When I woke up this morning, there wasn't anything I wanted more than to consummate our marriage. The marriage I did not want.

I was gagging for it.

I thought by making that choice, I was actually taking my life by the reins—regaining the control everyone had stolen from me. It might have been within the confines of what I was given, but this morning I knew what I wanted.

Or I thought I did.

Telling myself that I could actually be happy with my husband in Marino land was stupid.

At least I know I don't have Stockholm syndrome. If that were the case, I'd still be falling all over him, professing my love no matter what his name is. I'd be desperate for him. But more importantly, he wouldn't have begged me to forgive him.

It's not like our time together has been a walk through a field of wildflowers, but I am in one piece because of him. I've even got the fading bruises to prove what my life would've been like had he not claimed me. There's no doubt he made me feel safe in a very unsafe place.

So as we ride through the streets of the city that never sleeps, it's not lost on me I just climbed into a creepy white van with no windows, the very kind you were told to look out for as a kid because it's what kidnappers drive around with buckets full of candy to lure their prey.

But there's no candy here. Only tech equipment and a lingering stench of old, fried food.

I'm not sure what it says about me, because no one had to lure me anywhere. I could've screamed and begged for help. We walked by an entire team from housekeeping, through a bustling kitchen that looked like it was in the throes of serving an event for hundreds, and four delivery trucks in the process of unloading crates of wine.

Note taken: when living your life undercover, you have to sneak back into reality.

Still, my opportunities were plentiful, and I chose to keep my big, fat mouth shut.

I have no idea where we're going or how long we've sat in the back of this creepy, windowless van. The air is musty besides the lingering scents of onion rings and the cologne I was obsessed with just earlier today. It's an aroma that has become comforting, especially after the last week.

I'm doing everything I can to white knuckle my anger and not let it go. Just like the last week since Nic attacked me, my husband is not giving me personal space. Not that there's much of it with all the equipment. Brax's large frame is pressed to mine, our sides glued together just as he promised.

Literally.

Figuratively.

Frustratingly.

He's ever present and doing exactly as he promised.

You know, besides all the lies.

"Talked to Bristol before I got to the hotel. Patty's been moved to the ICU. She's stable, but she'll be there for at least a day or two. It's actually safer for you there. I got security clearance for us to stay overnight. Not sure how I'm going to talk them into your plus-one that wasn't on the invite list."

Brax glances at me. "She's my wife. I'm sure it won't be an issue. You don't have to stay. We'll be fine."

"Yeah, your wife," Micah mutters. "I'm not leaving. You're stepping into the real world for the first time in two years, and your mind is on your mom. I've got your back."

Special Agent Micah Emmett is rough around the edges compared to Brax. His arms are covered in sleeves of intricate tattoos, though I haven't been close enough to him to make out what they are. He looks like he hasn't shaved in days and doesn't care that he's overdo for a haircut. If I were comparing these two to football players, Brax would be the tall, lithe quarterback and Micah would be the brick wall who doesn't allow anyone to lay a finger on him. He's the kind of man you give a wide berth to while passing on the street, but still take a second look because his kind of scary is still hot.

Menacingly hot, but hot all the same.

If I could pick one man in this van who looks like they'd work undercover, it would not be the one who's lied to me since the moment we met. Micah looks like the men my father would hire to do his dirty work. Brax looks like he works on Wall Street.

Which he apparently did.

My mind reels with the new developments.

But what really gets me is the anxiety rolling off him. I feel it where our bodies are pressed to one another. It's etched in his face and pouring off his taut muscles.

"This is us." Micah brings the van to an abrupt halt, and Brax wraps his arm around me to keep me from flying off the narrow bench seat we're sharing. "Tim is inside those doors and will take you to the ICU. I'll park and meet you there. You'd better hurry so you can see your sisters before they're forced out. I couldn't swing it to get that many people approved for the night."

When Micah throws it in park, Brax doesn't let me go. Instead, he brings his other hand to my face and forces me to look into his eyes through the dark van. "Baby, I'm sorry. I knew this day would come, but I had no idea it would look like this."

"Carson was right," Micah interrupts our moment. Brax's gaze drags over my face before he exhales, and we both turn to Micah who's shifted in his seat and is staring at us. "I lost a bet, you know. I had money on the fact you could focus and keep your eye on the prize. The moment we found out you demanded to be the one to marry her to keep her from Nic, Carson said you were a goner, but he's like Jason Bourne thrown into a sappy Hallmark movie who will stop in the middle of a car chase for a martini and cupcakes. The man is whacked."

"Only his kind of whacked would agree to this kind of operation. I'm just lucky our cases crossed when they did." Brax digs into his pocket and pulls out a one-hundred-dollar bill. "Landyn hasn't eaten. Pick up some dinner on your way in."

Micah frowns at the money. "I'll bring you food, but I'm not touching Marino drug money."

Brax turns back to me and must have only one thing on his mind—his family. "You ready?"

No. No, I'm not at all ready to meet his sisters or visit his mother who just had open-heart surgery.

But I tip my head and shrug.

"Let's go, chica. We'll talk more later."

I don't think I have the energy for more talking.

He claims my hand and reaches for the door.

It strangely feels familiar, yet all new.

Brax

I couldn't not touch her for another moment.

All I want to do is lock her away in our hotel room where cartel members aren't lurking and we aren't being surveilled twenty-four-seven. I want to focus on her and only her. I want to beg her to be mine—now and after and forever.

Lucky for me, I have the ultimate reason to force her to stay. I plan to use that to my advantage. Until I take down every Marino, Decker, Jackal, and her fucking father for selling her, she won't leave my sight.

But when this is done, it'll be up to her. That will be the true test on how bad I fucked this up.

I just need her to keep my secret. I can't think about what I'll have to do if she doesn't. I don't have the luxury of time to worry about that right now.

Tim Coleman was about as happy to see Landyn as Micah was,

but he didn't throw a fit or ask me *what the fuck* ten million times. He only asked me once and then rolled his eyes.

Micah eats, sleeps, and shits the job. He was actually jealous of my case with the CIA. He offered to take my spot when he found out my mom begged me not to go, but there was no way I was going to allow anyone to do this but me.

Tim is chill for the most part. He's been around long enough that nothing surprises him. It was my decision to bring Landyn back after they kidnapped her. If telling her the truth is the only way for me to keep her safe from worse shit than what Nic did to her, then I'll take that chance every day for the rest of my life.

The stench hits me hard. The scent of life and death masked by antiseptic and hand sanitizer hangs in the air so thick, I could cut through it with a rusty scalpel. It's quiet but not. The eerie background music is set by beeps and tones from machines coming from rows of ICU rooms while nurses and doctors and visitors talk and discuss and plan.

Tim points to the left. "Here."

My chest seizes, and I pull Landyn to a stop next to me.

She looks back at me and whispers, "What is it?"

Damn. I didn't expect coming back to be as hard as it was to leave.

Tim slaps me on the shoulder. "No one can get in here without an ID. Micah will be back soon to stay with you tonight. I need to get back to the wire room to monitor what's going on without you there. You good?"

I turn to him. "I appreciate everything you've done to get me here. I know this isn't easy."

He gives me a chin lift and glances at Landyn. "Let me know what you need. I'll check back with you tomorrow before your meetings."

"Brax?"

I look back through the glass, and Bristol's gaze meets mine. She moves, saying something to Brittney on her way out the door.

"You're here." Bristol throws herself at me, wrapping her arms around my neck. "I can't believe you're really here."

Landyn is forced to take a step back.

I wrap up my oldest sister in one arm because Brittney has pushed her way in and I'm forced to catch her with the other.

"You look like a different person." Brittney's eyes are glassy. "Mom would die if she could see you right now."

Bristol leans back and shoves my other sister. "I can't believe you just said that."

Brittney rolls her eyes as she wipes a tear. "You know what I mean."

I hold them back far enough to get a good look at them. "I can't believe I'm here either."

"I might not let you go back," Bristol says. "I don't care what Micah says."

Bristol is the oldest, then Brian, followed by Brittney, and then me. What I don't say to my older sisters is that they look like shit. I'm sure they've been here since they found out about mom yesterday. Anyone would look like shit after spending twenty-four hours straight at the hospital.

Bristol slaps me on the chest but looks straight at Landyn. "Who is this?"

"This is gonna be fun," Tim mutters.

Bristol puts on a frown, and Brittney's eyes widen. I turn to their focus and find Landyn nibbling on her bottom lip while hugging her middle.

Since I'm pretty sure she won't come to me, I close the distance and do what's become natural when she knew me by another name—put my arm around her. "This is Landyn. Chica, my sisters. Hellion one and two, also known as Bristol and Brittney. Our parents did everything they could to confuse teachers and grandparents when naming us. We're like the tongue-twister family."

When I give her a squeeze, the word "Hi" pops out like a squeaky toy.

Brittney's expression grows into a huge smile. "Holy shit."

Bristol's does not. The oldest Cruz kid deepens her frown. "Yeah. Holy shit. Is she a party favor from the cartel?"

"Bristol," I bite.

Landyn stiffens further in my arms.

"Don't be a bitch when mom just had heart surgery." Brittney smacks our obnoxious sister in the shoulder and turns to Landyn. "Don't pay attention to her. She's been this way since Brax's high school girlfriend broke his heart their freshman year of college."

"Oh ... kay," Landyn mutters

I'm shocked that she's shocked into silence by the Cruz sisters. She handled herself just fine with the president of the Jackals. This shit should not faze her.

I lean down and put my lips to her ear. "Ignore them."

"Holy shit," Bristol repeats. "Braxton León Cruz. She knows what you do for a living, right?"

"I do now," Landyn mutters. "That's literally a new development. As in, the last hour."

Brittney shakes her head and glares at me. "You're such a punk."

"I'm not thirteen, and I didn't come here for this shit. I want to see Mom."

The girls cut their shit out immediately and glance at each other.

"What?" I demand.

Bristol's expression turns solemn in a snap. "It wasn't one bypass, Brax. It was three. They just got her settled—she's still unconscious."

Brittney glances at the clock. "Micah told us he got approval for you to stay all night. We insisted on staying until you got here, but it's past visiting hours, even for family. He said he'd call if she took a turn for the worse before morning."

I stare through the glass where I can only see the foot of the bed. "I'll be here until morning. I've got a meeting with the CIA tomorrow and then other meetings I can't talk about."

"And she'll be with you?" Bristol asks, her tone less of a razor than it was before.

I glare at my sister and tighten my arm around Landyn. "Yes, dammit. There are things you don't know. Things I can't tell you right now. It's not safe for us to be here as it is, so I'd appreciate it if you drop the attitude. My guilt is heavy, Bristol. I know I contributed to Mom's stress that landed her in that room. Give me a break."

"She doesn't mean anything by it." Brittney reaches for my forearm to give me a squeeze and turns to the woman in my arms. "I'm sorry. It's been a long day."

Landyn shakes her head. "It's okay. I'm sorry about your mom."

I'm about to push my sisters out of the way when a nurse walks up to us. "I'm sorry, but our patients need to rest without the commotion. Visiting hours were over an hour ago. If you don't have permission to stay, I'm going to have to ask you to leave."

We all shut our mouths, and I follow my sisters to the room where they collect their things. Landyn holds onto my hand like a lifeline, and I let her. My sisters kiss Mom's forehead, and say goodbye.

Before I know it, I'm standing at the foot of the bed, Landyn is still tight to my side, and we're both staring at the woman who begged me not to leave two years ago.

She lost me for two years, after she lost Brian forever.

I can't lie. There are days I've regretted my decision to take on this case.

But today is the worst.

Landyn's voice cuts through the beeps and stale air. "I'm so sorry ... Brax."

I exhale. "I'm the one who should be begging you for forgiveness, baby."

She gives her shoulder a small shrug, but doesn't let me off the hook. "You can do that later."

I look down and put my fingers to her chin to force her to look at me. Her bruises are peeking through her makeup that's been cried through—tears shed because of me. They're an in-your-face reminder of why I put everything at stake and brought her with me. Of why I lied to her since I met her.

"I will. Until then, get comfortable. We'll be here all night."

She doesn't complain, but she doesn't move either.

She pulls her chin from my fingers to rest her cheek against my pec and stares at the woman who's a stranger to her.

28

KILL

Landyn

I've never sat in the hospital with anyone, and I've never been in an intensive care unit.

My legs are tucked beneath me in an armchair that's straight and hard. I did not come prepared to camp out at the hospital, let alone for hours on end. When I shivered over an hour ago, the man I'm learning to call Brax shrugged off his sport coat and draped it over me.

It was sweet and thoughtful and totally something Boz would've done.

I try to push that out of my mind.

Brax looks more uncomfortable than I am. He's perched on a round, rolling stool sitting vigil at his mother's side. The nurse is in and out on a constant rotation, checking Patty Cruz's vitals and other things that I have no clue what they are. Brax has asked more times than I can count if his mother should have regained consciousness by now, but apparently this is normal.

Micah returned with bags of burgers and fries. Even though I was starving when we landed in New York, there's something about learning your husband has lied about his identity—not to mention that his mother is on her deathbed—to swipe the appetite right out from under you.

I picked at my burger and ate half of my fries. I have no idea where they came from, but they were delicious.

Brax, on the other hand, did not eat, and Micah finished off the enormous bag of food for all of us. He's been in and out of the room as much as the nurse—pacing and stalking the halls as if the Marino Cartel or my father will burst through the locked doors of the ICU at any moment. He's more of a presence than Brax's sisters, because no one has asked him to leave or get out of their way.

The federal badge sitting on the waistband of his jeans might have something to do with that.

Micah has an energy about him that makes me want to slither up next to my husband and stay there, even if I should be mad at him right now.

He claims he's the same person I knew him to be just this morning when I tried to seduce him. Hell, I was desperate for him.

But I have so many questions. I should start a list, because I forget them as soon as they cross my brain. It's impossible to focus on anything as I sit here and watch Brax agonize over his mother.

I need to stretch, and I really need a bathroom.

I stand to fold his jacket over the arm of my very stiff chair. He looks at me over his shoulder when he hears me. "You okay?"

"I'm just going to run to the restroom?" I'm not sure why that came out as a question other than the fact I haven't been in public by myself since before the Marinos forced me from my home.

Brax starts to stand. "I'll take you—"

I put my hand up. "No, no. I'm fine. I'll be right back. Stay here in case she wakes up. She needs to see you."

"I'll take her."

My gaze whips to Micah who's standing in the doorway.

I shake my head and turn back to Brax. "I'm not an idiot. I'm not going to run—I have nowhere to go."

Brax looks over my head at his partner. "Stay with her. This place should be safe, but I'm not taking the chance."

Whatever. Follow me. Don't follow me. It feels like everyone in Brax's life hates me just for being here. And since being here wasn't my choice to begin with, it's beyond frustrating.

Micah can follow me. It doesn't mean I have to talk to him.

I grab my purse and mutter, "I'll be right back."

Micah shifts to the side when I push through the door. His boots clomp behind me. I do my best to hold my head high and pretend I'm a normal human who can make a trip to the bathroom by herself.

I hurry until I get to the sink to wash my hands and get a glimpse of myself.

Ugh.

I drag a hand down my face and mutter to no one, "I look like hell."

My clothes are wrinkled. My mascara is smudged from my tears. And my hair has never been more disheveled and lifeless. The fading bruise under my eye seems darker than it has been.

Everything ingrained in me simmers below the surface to freak out about this being my first impression.

I shouldn't care what anyone thinks of me. Not after what I've been through. Hell, Brax has seen me a million times worse and never blinked an eye.

I dump my purse on the counter and flip on the cold water. I'm not in a hurry anymore. I need a moment to myself. Just a second to process everything.

I rummage through my things until I find a comb and drag it through my hair before pulling it back into a clean pony. Then I cup the water in my hands and press it to my face over and over. The icy water is a balm to my swollen eyes. I do everything I can to wash away my day-old makeup.

When I stand to dry my face, I scream and spin on my heel.

"What the hell are you doing?"

Micah is leaning against a stall, staring at me, arms crossed, and hemorrhaging irritation. "I wanted to make sure you weren't trying to escape through the air vent."

Water drips from my face so I turn back to the sink and reach for a paper towel. "Do I look like someone who's going to crawl through an air vent?"

"That's the thing ... I don't know one fucking thing about you other than my partner is willing to put his life in the hands of a mobster's daughter. He trusts very few people, but I'm one of them. That makes it my job to make sure he's thinking with his brain and not his dick."

The paper towel is like cardboard when I drag it across the delicate skin under my eyes to rub away my stubborn mascara that's making me look like a raccoon. "That seems like a question for your partner. I'm obviously not a good judge of character since I thought he was a drug dealer only a few hours ago."

Micah continues to jump subjects on a whim. "That man cares more about his family than anyone I know. I'm not going to allow anyone—especially you—to get in the way of him finishing what he set out to do. He's lost too much time and given too much of himself. You don't know shit about him."

I toss my paper towel into the trash and turn to lean my ass on the counter. I glare at the man who's interrogating me in the ladies' room. "You're right—you don't know me. I haven't been a willing participant in any of this since I was thrown at the cartel and an undercover agent. And ever since your partner told me the truth after we got here, I'm more confused than ever."

"Which confirms that you know nothing about him," he spouts and shakes his head. "I'm here to warn you that Braxton Cruz has one goal, and it has nothing to do with you. When I walked into that hotel room tonight, I could tell he was distracted, and I don't like it. My only goal is to make sure he's alive at the end of this operation."

"Are you implying I might want the opposite of that? If you have something to say to me, just say it."

"I'm saying Brax trusting in you is a bad idea."

I try my best to keep my tone even, but it's hard. The last time I was alone with a man who hated me was Nic. "You don't know anything about me."

"You're right. And neither does Brax—"

"He does," I interrupt. "He knows me, maybe better than anyone ever has. He's the only reason I'm in one piece right now."

Micah drops his arms and lowers his voice. "Don't forget that. If he gets hurt because of you, I'll come after you myself."

I grab my purse and violently yank it up my shoulder. But before I leave, I take a step closer. I'm so pissed, my voice isn't shaky any longer. It's incensed. "You have no idea what's gone on between Brax and me. I don't give a shit who you are—I don't need your permission or your acceptance or your blessing to be whatever I want to him. I don't need to prove myself to anyone but my husband."

His expression goes from angry to shocked to almost amused. "Your husband?"

"Yes," I bite. "My husband."

He huffs one laugh as he rocks back on his heels as a smirk creeps over his face that doesn't have anything to do with humor. "You didn't marry Braxton Cruz, Alba. You married a man who doesn't exist."

My heart clinches.

Right before my stomach drops.

Holy shit.

"But..."

Micah hikes a brow. "Maybe I was wrong. Maybe you're into him as much as he's pussy whipped for you."

I can't listen to this. I need to get out of here.

I turn and yank the bathroom door open.

"Where are you going?" he calls for me.

I ignore him and pick up my pace. I need one thing right now and no one will be able to give it to me but Brax.

"Stop," he growls under his breath.

I don't. But when I get to Patty's room in the long wing of the ICU, I stutter to a stop in the doorway.

She's awake.

Tears stain her pale face as she stares up at her youngest son. She can't talk because of the breathing tube, but her expression says a thousand words. Brax is holding her hand, but his gaze jumps to me. His dark eyes are glassy with relief. Some of the guilt and stress that I've felt in him all day is gone.

And his lips tip up when he shoots me the smallest smile. "Chica, come here and meet my mom."

I don't hesitate. I push away the anger and confusion that's plagued me and move to the man who has had me tied up in knots since I met him.

In so many ways.

I go straight to his side, and he snakes an arm around my waist and pulls me flush to him. He looks down at his mother. "Mom, this is Landyn."

Patty Cruz looks horrible. She should. She just endured open-heart surgery. Who wouldn't look horrible?

She blinks her tears away and widens her eyes, her breaths come quicker through her tube.

"My wife," Brax adds.

I suck in a breath as my eyes jump from Patty to him.

His dark eyes are possessive and different than what I'm used to looking into.

His stare on me means so much more. It might as well set me on fire.

Brax

Two years is a long fucking time.

I didn't just take a new job across the country where I can call home anytime I want. I might not be dead like Brian, but I've been gone in every sense of the word. My family has had no communication and no updates.

It's a good thing my mom was in the ICU when she opened her eyes to see me. If she hadn't already had a heart attack, I'm afraid I would've given her one.

Surprise. Elation. Relief.

All while recovering from having her chest cracked open.

Maybe surprising her wasn't the best scenario, but being there when she woke up was what I needed.

She's been through hell. She lost Dad too early, and then Brian. I know I've contributed to her stress by leaving her for this long.

I talked to her for hours before they extubated her. When she could talk, she was exhausted from the pain meds. Before she fell asleep, I promised I'd be back once more before I had to get back to the world of cartels, mobsters, and one-percenters.

I didn't add that last part, but it's the truth.

The nurses assured me she's doing as well as can be expected and needs to rest, and since it will be visiting hours soon, our time was up.

This feels no different than anything else I've done the last two years. Slinking in the shadows when it has anything to do with real life.

When I said I was exhausted, it's not from lack of sleep.

I'm so fucking tired of pretending to be someone I'm not. My fake wife is the lifeline I needed to show me what I'm missing.

My wife...

There's nothing fake about Landyn. That's why I introduced her to my mom as my wife.

Introducing her as anything else, felt wrong.

Doing it felt right. It felt good.

Landyn looked shocked for about two beats, but after that, she fell into place.

By my side.

A place I want her to be when I'm me.

We leave the way we entered, and Micah looks up and down the hall as I pull out the keycard to unlock our hotel door. I hold

Landyn close when he enters the room first and does a sweep before I pull her inside.

Landyn tosses her purse on the desk and opens her big-ass suitcase. "I need to brush my teeth."

She doesn't look at me or Micah, but I grab her hand to stop her on the way to the bathroom holding an enormous bag of girl shit and pajamas.

"Thank you." I lean down and press my lips to her forehead.

She nods as a small, weary smile tugs at her lips. She glances at Micah giving my hand a squeeze and pulls away. The bathroom door clicks and locks.

Micah glares at me and lowers his voice. "Have you lost your mind and all sense of reality?"

I yank my shirt from my pants and start to unbutton it. "I just sat with my mom in the ICU for hours. I think I have a pretty good grasp on reality right now."

"That's not what I mean, and you know it."

I push past him as I get out of this damn shirt and rip my belt off. "I'm exhausted, Micah. You can pretend all you want that you're a machine and can work for days on end, but you need to get some sleep if we're going to do this all over again tomorrow night. And I have a dinner meeting with Alamandos' biggest distributor on the east coast tonight to justify this trip. I need to be on top of my game."

"Yeah, you do," he bites and eats up half the distance between us but points back to the bathroom. "And that is not the way to stay on top of your game. That is going to distract you. I can tell you're not seeing straight as it is."

I shrug my shirt down my arms and toss it on a chair in the corner of the room. "I've never been sharper. If anything, she's made me hone in to get this shit done. I'm close, Micah. So fucking close, I can taste it. Once I find out who killed Brian, I'm pulling the trigger."

He shakes his head. "You can't go back with her. She knows everything. Even if she is loyal to you—and that's a big fucking *if*, bro—she has no fucking clue how to work a case. How to pretend."

I can't lie, this is something I've thought about, but I'm not about to admit that to anyone. "She'll be fine."

"Everyone in that world is paranoid. They'd turn on their fucking dog if they thought it would snitch on them."

"She can handle it, and I can handle her," I assure him.

Micah drags a hand through his shaggy hair. I know I've been gone for two years, but he's pushing his I-don't-give-a-fuck mentality closer to the edge than I've ever seen.

"I don't like it," he bites.

I toss my belt on top of my shirt. "It's not yours to like. We've been up for almost twenty-four hours. Landyn needs sleep, and I'm positive she won't come out of that bathroom until you're gone."

Micah's long sigh is nothing but frustration mixed with exhaustion, proving he is human after all. "Call me when you wake up. We've got an agent sitting at the end of the hall in case you need anything. I'll get you back to the hospital tonight before you fly out tomorrow. Promise me you'll think about what I said."

Micah and I don't always see eye to eye, but he's always had my back. That still doesn't mean I have to promise him shit. "Thanks for being here for my family. You know what that means to me. I'll see you tonight."

"You're fucking frustrating," he mutters as he turns for the door.

He's gone, and I barely have a chance to flip the deadbolts when the bathroom door opens and blue eyes peer around it. She looks me up and down before asking, "Is he gone?"

I nod. "I swear, he's not always an asshole."

She doesn't take her eyes off me when she walks through the door. The rest of her smudged makeup is gone. Her hair is loose. She's wearing a nightgown that looks more like a tank. The straps are so thin I can barely see them since it's almost the color of her fair skin. It flirts with the top of her thighs and hangs on her nipples that are standing front and center, as if they're demanding me to wrap my lips around them.

This isn't unusual. Ever since Nic put his hands on her, I've all but seen her totally naked. And even though that's a line we've yet to cross, I've touched every inch of her in one way or another—caring for her or worshiping her.

Because she deserves nothing less than that.

Hell, she deserves more.

I force myself to focus on her eyes and do my best to ignore my swelling cock that very much wants to punch me in the gut. "It's been a long day, baby. When we left this room, you were pissed. I'm sure you have questions. Do you want to sleep or do you want to talk?"

Her tits rise and fall on a bated breath that leaves me hanging. "I was angry."

"Was?"

She lifts her slim shoulder a touch, like she's as confused as I am. "I have questions. They've popped in and out of my head all night."

I take a step closer but don't lay a finger on her. She seems smaller when she's like this. Wearing almost nothing. Not made up. Standing before me on bare feet.

I fucking love it.

Even though she just found out who I really am, when we're like this, there aren't any pretenses.

We are who we are.

And for me, there's nothing more satisfying or real than this.

The need to touch her is overwhelming. I have to fist my hands to keep myself from pulling her into my arms.

"Ask me anything. Nothing is off limits. I'll tell you anything you want, baby."

She rolls her lips in, pressing them into a thin line, but her first question is not what I expect. "Are you going to arrest Rocco?"

I tell her the truth. "It depends."

Her tone turns defensive. "On what?"

"I moved him into the house to keep an eye on him and to do

what I could to keep him clean. He hasn't done anything to implicate himself yet. My goal is to turn him after the takedown. It'll be up to him to cooperate or not. He'll have options, and it won't have anything to do with the damn GED."

"Why are you doing that for him?"

I tell her the truth. "Because he's young, his parents fucked up his life, and assholes like the Jackals are taking advantage of that."

That silences her.

"What else?" I press. I'm bursting at the seams to let loose and tell her every-fucking-thing.

She mulls that over for a second before she finally speaks. "Are you going to arrest my father?"

"Yes." My answer comes quickly, and when she doesn't respond, I add, "Even if you don't like the answers, I'm done lying to you."

She pulls in a deep breath. "I'm tired of people lying to me. I'm tired of them using me. I refuse to be a pawn any longer."

"I never treated you like a possession, Landyn. Not once."

"No, you haven't." She brings her hands up to her middle and twists her fingers. "I need to know one more thing tonight."

"Told you I'd tell you anything you want to know."

"A few days ago, I overheard Spencer talking to someone on the phone. He said you were looking for Nic. Then today in your office, you said the same thing."

I'm a controlled man, but the thought of Nic Decker makes me want to throw a chair through a window. "I am."

Her tone is low and hoarse. "Are you going to arrest him too?"

"No, baby."

"No?"

"No." I take another step so we're flush. Electric-charged air hangs between us, the only place we touch is where her nipples brush my chest. My cock is no longer swelling. I'm at full mast in a way that nothing is going to settle him down besides my fist, a cold shower, or the woman I'd give up everything for. I lift my index finger to wind the end of an unruly lock of blond hair around it. When I look into her icy blues, there's apprehension laced with hope. "I'm not going to arrest him. I'm going to fucking kill him."

All of a sudden, we're not only connected by her nipples. She presses her body to mine, and I gladly take her weight. I want it. Hell, I'm obsessed with it.

She has to tip her head back farther to look into my eyes. "You said you were the same person you were before."

"Baby, I am."

She shakes her head, and my insides tense. "No, you're not."

I brace. I'm about to drop to my knees to plead for her to believe me, but she doesn't give me the chance.

"You're better."

Fuck.

My hand drops from her hair, drags down her back, and lands on her ass. She's sandwiched between my hand and my cock. I'll fight, battle, and kill to keep her right here forever.

"Landyn..." Her name hangs between us.

She knows it's not a statement. It's a question. It's me begging for permission.

"Brax." She pushes up on her toes and drags her tongue along my stubbled jaw. "Yes."

The electric-charged air ignites.

I grip the material at her ass and pull. I barely have her nightgown over her head when she puts her thumbs to her hips and pushes her panties to the floor. Everything she was wearing now sits at our feet as I stare down at her.

Naked.

The way she was meant to be ... for me.

Only me.

Like magnets, my hands land on her ass before sliding down to her thighs when I lift. I pull her up my body and her legs part. "Baby, you don't know how much I want you—all of you. But I couldn't let this happen when you knew me as Boz. That was my best decision. Hearing my real name on your lips is the sweetest sound I've ever heard. When I bury myself inside you, it'll be me. And it'll be worth the wait."

Her nails drag across my scalp, and I don't waste another moment. I pull a nipple between my lips and suck. She fists my hair and presses herself to me. Her tit to my mouth. Her bare pussy to my abs.

I move until my legs hit the bed and bend at the waist. My hand lands between her legs, my fingers sliding easily through her. She moans beneath me.

"Fuck, chica, you're wet. Wet for me."

"Yes." The word comes out on a breath. I'm not sure if it's a confirmation or her wanting more, but I'll take either. "Please, don't make me wait any longer."

"No more waiting, baby. This is happening." I force her to look me in the eyes when I slide two fingers inside. "Nothing stands between us any longer. It's you, and it's me. If it ends up being us against the world, I'll take them all down. And I'll do it for you—I'll do anything to keep you by my side."

Her eyelids drop slowly as I circle her clit with my thumb. I've been here before—I know her body.

But this is different.

I'm not stopping until she's mine in every way.

I kiss up her chest and neck until our lips meet for a searing kiss. I press my tongue into her mouth and my hard on that's still confined in my trousers into her bare pussy. But this time I'm not going to stop to jack off to thoughts of her.

I can't take it any longer. I drag my lips from hers, and stand as I rip my pants open to free myself. She brings her knees together, her tongue sneaking out to wet her bottom lip when her gaze falls south.

Straight to my cock.

I fist myself and stare down at her bare body, wondering what I did to deserve her. Working myself with one hand I put a light finger on her knee and push.

"Open for me, chica. I've waited a long time for this."

She exhales a little moan and fists the bedding beneath her. Then she does exactly what I told her to do.

It's my turn to lick my lips.

Bare.

Wet.

And all mine.

I let go of my cock and drop to my knees. With my hands on the backs of her thighs, I push them up and out.

I take one lap from her pussy to her clit.

"Oh my," she moans.

She trembles beneath me as her hand lands on my head.

Fucking heaven.

29

BARE

Landyn

When I told Brax he was a good one, I meant it.
I knew he was different.
I thought I was a good judge of character. But, damn.
I'm really good.
There's no truer sign of a man's character than his love for his family. Not only is Brax's in abundance, but he's willing to put everything he's worked toward for two years at risk to be here for his mom.
And he trusts me when everyone around him is telling him not to.
But no one here knows the bond we've built. We've come so far from where we started, when I had no choice but to trust him.
And now he has no choice but to trust me.
The roles have shifted.
I'm helpless in this world, but to have the trust of Brax Cruz after everything I've learned today?

I've never felt more powerful, especially after I've been stripped of every freedom. I'll never take it for granted.

But I can't think about any of that right now.

My moan fills the room as he sucks my clit between his lips. My thighs might as well be held open in vise grips, his big hands hold me hostage to do whatever he wants.

Being held hostage by Brax is something I could live with for a very long time.

I think I might even love it.

"No," I complain on a breath when he lets go of my clit, only to bring his tongue down to my sex. "Oh, okay. Yes, please."

The word passes my lips to beg him not to stop. He gives me what I want, fucking me with his tongue, teasing me of bigger and better things I've been dreaming about my husband.

He loves this as much as I do. A groan vibrates against my sex when I lose his lips and tongue. "I could do this forever, chica, but can't fucking wait to bury myself inside you. Feels like I've waited an eternity."

Oh, yes. I'm ready for that too.

He moves back to my clit. It starts low in my belly before taking over my body, just like Brax has done since we met. This orgasm puts every one before it to shame—it's deep, earth shattering, and soul wrenching.

I arch and press my head into the bed. I'm not quiet when I come. My body quakes and stars fill my vision. But Brax doesn't let up. He devours me—lapping and sucking and tormenting me in the best way possible.

Just when I think my body is spent, I lose his mouth from between my legs.

His lips land on mine, and I think about all the kisses we've shared that have gotten us to this one.

They've built and grown, starting with the one after I was forced to say *I do*. Every one since has felt different and meant something new. Even when they were meant to be fake, they never felt that way. With each additional one, we became more and more real.

Just like my obsession that grew into desperation.

So when he slides inside me, my eyes fly open. "Brax."

He's got one forearm to the bed next to my head and the other hikes my knee high, as he sinks deep within me.

So big.

So full.

And so, so bare.

His dark eyes stare into mine when he pulls out only to fill me again, this time to the root. "Baby, there's nothing fake about this. This is as real as it gets. I'm not letting you go. You'll never be treated like a possession again. Even so, you're mine in every other sense of the word."

I run my fingers through his hair, down his neck, and my fingers bite into his wide shoulders to hang on. I lift my legs farther, and he takes advantage—pulling out and slamming into me, proving I'm his. "That's exactly how you make me feel."

"And I'm yours," he goes on while moving inside me. "I've never wanted to be anyone's, but fuck, baby. The thought of not being yours is worse than any bullet I could take."

Tears well instantly in my eyes as he becomes blurry. I nod, and my words feel weak as he takes me for the first time. "I've wanted you. Even when nothing felt right. And now that everything is different and new all over again, I know it's right. We're right."

He takes my mouth as he thrusts—his movements faster, harder, and without rhythm. There's a desperation about the way we've come together that's tangible. I feel it around me and within me.

"I'm desperate for you, and I'm desperate for this to be real and not end," I admit when he breaks our kiss. "Don't stop. Just, please, don't stop."

Every muscle in his body is taut under my touch. He presses in, filling me to the root and stops this time. He looks pained with every word when he admits, "I don't have a condom."

My heart sinks because I don't want this to end. "And I'm not on birth control."

His dark eyes blaze. "Baby."

My eyes fall shut, but I press my heels into his firm ass where his trousers are barely hanging on.

"Landyn," he calls for me and seals it with a kiss pressed to my forehead.

I open my eyes.

He pulls out and presses in.

I say nothing.

Another thrust—this one hits my clit.

I moan and feel the flesh of his shoulders become one with my finger nails.

He tips his forehead to mine and starts to move again. In and out—each time stronger, with more force than the one before.

It's like he's daring me. Playing Russian roulette with my emotions, or simply claiming me in every way he can.

In the biggest way.

It was only hours ago he introduced me as his wife to his own mother.

He claims my mouth again before muttering, "Chica, I can't hold off much longer. I'm barely hanging on."

He hits my clit again, and it feels so good, I put my feet to the bed for leverage. I press up, meeting his every thrust where I want it most. Every time we come together, it cements itself in my mind what I'm actually doing.

What we're doing.

Or what we're not doing. Because we're absolutely not being safe or cautious. Yet, at the same time, it doesn't feel irresponsible or reckless. It feels very different than that.

It feels so very deliberate ... like the intensity between us is an unspoken conversation that takes most couples years to get to.

"Don't stop." The words jump from my lips as I rise to meet him—my second orgasm within reach. I want it, and I want him. "Please, don't stop."

That's all he needs.

My husband ... he's unbridled.

And it's exactly what I want. I come hard and fast, loving every onslaught of his powerful body and his cock doing what they were created for—taking me and making me his.

My moans and his growls tangle in unison to create a beautiful harmony. It's my new favorite piece of music.

When Brax comes, it's dominant and beautiful...

And mine.

Because he comes inside me with nothing between us and with no discussion.

He gives me his weight and stays buried. I turn my face to his and press my lips to his jaw as he catches his breath. When he finally looks down at me, there's not one regret in his eyes.

"I'll give you normal as soon as I can, chica. Swear it."

Normal.

I had no idea something as mundane as that would be my love language, but it is.

I smile. Despite everything, I've never been happier.

He hasn't moved an inch, smothering my body with his.

"Brax?" I whisper. I love saying his name.

He presses his lips to the side of my head and inhales. "Right here, baby."

"I need to ask you something."

He presses into me one more time, like he's relishing in us after withholding himself for so long. "Told you I'd tell you anything."

I stare at his square jaw and hesitate.

He brings a hand up and forces me to look at his deep frown. "Do you regret this?"

"No," I answer too quickly, but it's true so I keep telling him the truth. "I've wanted this for ... a while."

"Good. I bet it's safe to say I wanted this longer than I care to admit." The corner of his full lips tip on one side with a smirk. "What do you want to ask me?"

I look into his dark eyes and hope they're mine to gaze into for the rest of my life. "Are we married? Like, you know," I lift a bare shoulder. "*Really* married?"

His thick arm tucks under my back, and he rolls taking me with him. I straddle his hips to keep our connection, like a desperate woman who may never get it back. He's still inside me, half-hard, and I vaguely wonder how that can be.

But I don't wonder for long because his words drag me back to reality. His expression is grave and intense. "I don't care where it happened, how it happened, or how we each felt during that moment. Our connection is real, chica. A connection I'll never feel with anyone else and never want to test it. Introduced you to my mom as my wife. Consummated it just now in the most ultimate way, and I don't regret it. I'd like to say *I do* again when you say my real name and we're not covered in blood. But that'll only be for pictures and memories. Because as far as I'm concerned, yes, we're married."

He becomes blurry through my tired eyes, and I immediately dip my face to hide in his neck.

One hand comes to my head and the other to my bare ass when he tenses beneath me. "Was that the wrong answer? Did I fuck that up?"

I shake my head. "No, Brax. That was definitely the right answer."

"Good." His exhale brushes my hair before he lifts my chin and once again forces me to look down at him. He brushes the tears from my cheek. "Looking forward to doing it again without the blood or the creepy priest."

A laugh bursts through my tears. "Right? He was so creepy."

"I'm going to need to fuck you again soon, baby. We have time to make up for. But we also need sleep."

I can't hide my smile. "This is the weirdest honeymoon ever. But I guess after our wedding, it fits."

He pulls my mouth to his, and if any kiss ever felt like a marriage, it's this one.

Brax

WHEN I TOLD my family I was leaving for an undisclosed amount of time with no communication to find the people who killed Brian, this was not the way I expected to return. Not once did I imagine I'd bring a woman home or have to leave again immediately.

Just when you think you know yourself, you fake marry a strange woman, and all of sudden you're really fucking happy about having unprotected sex.

So when I turn the corner to the bathroom to find that woman's ass peeking out from my T-shirt in a tiny pair of panties, bent at the waist with her hair flipped upside down, I reassure myself I'm not crazy.

I'm fucking lucky.

Lucky we've made it this far, and I'll do everything I can to keep her safe from the Marinos and her damn father.

Her father.

The look on her face when I told her I was going to arrest him said it all. I have no qualms about her loyalties.

I shrug my dress shirt up my shoulders and go straight to her. She jerks and stands straight when I cup each delicious globe of her ass in my hands. She's red in the face from being flipped upside down, but smiles at me through the mirror as she turns off the hairdryer. "You scared me."

I lean down and press my lips to her neck. "When I'm in the general vicinity of your ass and it's in the air, expect that I'm going to grab it every single time."

The only move she makes is to lean into my chest. "I'll keep that in mind."

I snake a hand around her waist and splay it under her tits. "We have a change of plans."

Her smile falters through the mirror. "Is everything okay?"

"We have a meeting before dinner with my boss at the DEA, my contact at the CIA, and Micah. It's the only time we can safely meet before we head back to California tomorrow."

Her face instantly falls the rest of the way into a frown.

I pull her to me tighter. "You okay?"

She sets the hairdryer on the counter and turns in my arms. Her touch on my bare chest where she fits herself in my open shirt is enough to make me cancel all plans.

Fuck the CIA, the DEA, and the cartel.

I want to lock her up in this room and throw away the key.

When I lift her chin to force her to look at me, I pull her lip from between her teeth. "If we're going to do this, I have to know what you're thinking all the time. What's wrong?"

"Your boss and this person at the CIA ... they know about us?"

"They know everything, baby."

"Do they feel the same way about me that Micah does?"

I narrow my eyes. "What do you mean?"

She looks away and focuses on her fingers that dance on my skin. "Micah doesn't trust me—I'm sure you see it too. It would be nice to know how the rest of them feel about me before this meeting."

I shake my head. "Micah is intense. I'm not sure he trusts anyone."

She flattens her hands on my abs and tries to push away. "Well, then he really doesn't trust me."

I pull her to me and force her to look at me. "Why do you think that?"

Her eyes flare. "Oh, hubbalicious. I don't think—I know. He said so in the bathroom last night."

My eyes narrow. "What the hell did he say to you?"

"I get it, given who my dad is. I mean, who can blame your partner for looking out for you?"

I can only imagine what Micah said. He has no chill and spouts what he feels without thought. I can't keep the irritation out of my tone. "What did he say to you?"

"It's not important right now. My last name is Alba. Like I said, I get—"

"No, you don't get it, and neither does he. Micah doesn't get to pick who I trust. He knows you on paper, that's it. I'll take care of him and the rest of the people I work with. Don't worry."

"I don't want to create a problem. Micah caught me off guard. I just want to know if the rest of them felt the same way so I can prepare."

I pull her mouth to mine, if for no other reason than to remind her how I feel. When I finally let her go, I keep her close. "Be honest. How do you feel about your father?"

My question surprises her, and her tone dips. "You know how I feel."

I shake my head. "I want to hear it."

"I hate him," she spits. "I hate him more as time goes on. I was numb in the beginning, but every day that I'm with you, even living in Damian's house, my revulsion for him grows. He knew exactly what would happen to me. Anyone willing to do that to their child deserves worse than arrest."

"He'll never hurt you in any way again. I'll make sure of it."

"No, he won't. I had no idea he was capable of that. I will never trust him."

"I'll take care of Micah, Carson, and Tim. I need to make sure you're prepared to handle this, the dinner tonight, and when we return to San Diego now that you know everything."

She's not hesitant any longer. Her response is quick and firm. "If it means helping you, I'll do anything. You deserve to know who killed your brother. I don't want to be like my father, and my mother is no better. I refuse to look the other way just to benefit from a cushy life supported by illegal activities."

I drag my thumb across her bottom lip. "Took you this morning when we woke up, followed by making you come again in the shower. If we didn't have this meeting, I'd strip you down and do it again. I didn't know I could want you even more now that I've had you, but I do."

She doesn't say anything, but her tongue sneaks out to swipe the pad of my thumb before pressing her lips to it.

I go on. "When we get to dinner tonight, don't do anything different than you've ever done. Take my lead, and you'll be fine."

She wraps her hand around my wrist and pulls my hand away. "How crazy is it that I'm more worried about our meeting with the agents than I am the east coast distributor for the Marino family?"

"Really fucking crazy. I'll take care of the agents. They're the last ones you need to worry about."

"If you say so."

"I say so." I lean down to kiss her as I grip her ass one more time. "You've been in here forever. Can you be ready to leave in fifteen?"

She drags a fingernail down my chest with a small smile. "One thing to know about me is I don't get ready fast. I apologize now for all the times you'll have to wait on me."

I smirk. "We'll work on that. You proved yesterday you're capable of traveling across the country at a moment's notice. You seemed to survive just fine. Be ready in fifteen."

"If you want me to get ready, you need to let go of my ass."

"Never." I give her a squeeze. "I could palm your ass for the rest of my life and die a happy man."

30

TWO DAYS

Landyn

"Torres. My wife and I are here for the private party."

My wife.

I don't care if it's real or not—it feels real. And it has everything to do with the way Brax treats me.

I wasn't ready in fifteen minutes. I was seven minutes late, which is a feat in and of itself. But Brax didn't seem to care. He sat at the foot of the bed and glanced between me and his phone while I changed clothes three times.

Even though my wardrobe was curated for a cartel wife, I questioned what would be best for dinner out at a Manhattan restaurant with an illegal drug distributor. I finally settled on a low-cut red slip dress and the most feminine trench coat I've ever seen. The soles of my shoes match the dress. I fit the part like it's always been mine as Brax leads me with a hand on the small of my back through the swanky establishment to the private party.

Three men stand in the middle of the room. It's Micah, Tim, and one other I've never seen. They're all dressed similar to Brax.

Even his partner is cleaned up compared to how he looked when he barged into the women's restroom to interrogate me.

Brax pulls me to a stop when the door closes behind us and looks down at me. "Baby, you've met Tim and my asshole partner. The one in the middle with the cocky grin is Officer Cole Carson. He's with the CIA."

Micah's glare shifts from me to Brax.

Tim Coleman rolls his eyes.

Cole Carson's grin swells.

I give them a small, awkward wave. "It's nice to meet you."

But I'm confused when Brax turns to face me and pushes me back a step before leaning down to peck my lips with his. He's not grinning or frowning. His expression is cool and composed. But then again, he's been that way since we first met on my dark, bloody wedding day.

The same one that turned out to be *our* wedding day.

Even when pulling a gun on dinner guests in the dining room, he's weirdly even tempered.

His dark eyes pierce mine, and he lowers his voice. "Don't move."

It's my turn to frown. "Wait ... what?"

He doesn't answer or give me a chance to ask further.

He leaves me rooted in my spot by the door and turns for the men. They look as confused as me, until the very last second when Brax loses his meticulous, unruffled composure.

From Micah's expression, I bet he doesn't think it will happen either. He barely lifts an arm.

And that's his first mistake.

The scene plays out in slow motion in my confused brain. That is, until Brax's fist connects with Micah's jaw. The sound echoes around the room.

"The fuck?" Micah growls as he stumbles back two steps holding his face.

"The fuck is right. What did you say to her?" Brax charges again, but this time Micah is ready. He blocks Brax's second punch and puts his hands to my husband's finely-pressed dress shirt to shove him back.

"No!" I scream.

Tim and Cole both take a step back to avoid getting hit by flying fists. Tim crosses his arms and shakes his head. Cole casually slips his hands into his trouser pockets while wearing the same grin he has since we arrived. He looks like he's taking in a comedy show—not two partners duking it out.

Over *me*.

Blood seeps from Micah's lip. "I didn't do anything you wouldn't do, asshole. You've turned into a pussy-whipped freak who can't see that she's only a cartel princess. She was a pawn to stir up shit between the organizations. Wake up, Cruz. She'll get you killed, and you won't even see it coming because you're too busy playing house in that fucking mansion."

"Brax, please stop," I call, but it's too late.

He's incensed.

Brax charges. Micah flies backward. Glasses teeter and tip on the dining table. A chair crashes to the ground. And Micah lands on his back.

"I did not see this coming," Cole notes.

"They're going to get us kicked out," Tim complains.

Finally, someone steps in, but it's not Cole.

Tim steps in front of Brax, planting a hand to his chest. "Is this the kind of attention you want to attract while you're in a room full of government agents?"

Brax doesn't answer. He reaches around Tim and points to his partner who's sprawled on the floor. "You had no fucking right. You don't know her or half the shit she's been through. You talk to her one more time without my permission, I'll hand you your balls after I rip them out through your throat."

Micah pulls himself to his feet and touches his thumb to his lip before squaring off with Brax again. "I'm doing what we do—what we've always done—have each other's back. You're in so deep, sometimes I wonder if you even know which way is up."

"I'm there every day, Micah. I'm fucking aware of my reality and hers."

"Don't go back," Micah grits. "It's time to wrap this shit up. We have enough to take down everyone."

Brax shakes his head. "I'm not done."

Cole finally says something. "And this, boys and girls, is what we came here to discuss."

I thought Brax was tense when he went after Micah, but that was nothing. He turns to the side and stares at Cole. "What?"

Cole points between Brax and Micah. "You two done?"

"No way," Micah bites at the same time Brax counters, "Landyn is none of his fucking business."

I can't stand here another moment and watch Brax fight with his friend on my account. I move from the spot he told me to stay in and take his hand in mine. I pry his fist open and force it to relax. "I'm fine. Micah was just looking out for you. It's okay."

"I'm glad you're fine, because you aren't going back," Micah spits as he glares straight at me. This time it's my turn to tense as he keeps talking. "It's been decided."

Brax looks between the three men in the room and pulls me to his side. "What the hell are you talking about?"

"We discussed it," Tim starts as he looks around the room to make sure no one is going to come after him too. "After what happened to her with Nic Decker, and the fact she doesn't know how to handle herself undercover, we've decided she should stay here. You go back alone and make an excuse as to why she stayed in New York, coordinate the delivery with the Jackals, and get out. That will give us more than enough for warrants for everyone and their dogs."

"You want me to walk back in there without the woman who was sold into the family to pay off a debt?" Brax demands.

"Tell them you left her at a spa. Isn't that what a cartel family would do who has hundreds of millions in the bank and even more in cash?" Micah barks.

Brax looks at him like he's lost his mind, which I do believe is possible. "Do you *want* me to get my head chopped off?"

"Please don't talk like that," I beg and look straight at Micah. "You don't understand what it's like there. If I don't go back with him, it will raise all sorts of red flags. Trust me, it's the last place in the world I want to be, but even I can see that."

"She doesn't know what she's doing." Micah bites, as I shrink into my husband, because he's not wrong.

"Have you heard one thing on the wires that makes you believe they question anything I do?" Brax challenges.

Micah presses his swelling lips together and his jaw goes taut.

Tim sighs.

It's Cole who speaks. "You've read every transcript we have. If anyone in that organization suspected you, we'd pull you out faster than an unwrapped dick on prom night."

"Exactly," Brax bites. "I came back here so my mother could see my face one last time in case she doesn't make it through this. If I thought I was close to being made, I wouldn't go back. I sure as hell wouldn't take Landyn back with me. Aside from the incident with Decker, which I'll never forgive myself for, she's been safe. We're down to days. *Days*," he stresses, the word vibrating through my body. I feel the agitation and tension bubble within him. "I'm going back, and Landyn is coming with me. She won't do anything different than she's done so far."

Tim shakes his head. "It's a bad idea."

"You might as well sign your own death certificate," Micah agrees.

I shudder at the thought.

But Cole says nothing. He simply contemplates Brax.

I fist the material at his abs, and he instantly pulls me closer.

When I look up, Brax shakes his head once and speaks directly to Cole. "Do not do this to me. I'm not done, and you know it. You of all people know that if you send me back there alone, you might as well put a bullet through my brain yourself. Let me manage this."

Cole isn't cocky any longer. He crosses his arms and settles back on his heels in a wide stance.

The energy in the room is jittery and tangible.

"Do not do this to me, Carson. I took a bullet for Damian. They dug the fucking thing out while I was conscious and stitched me up in the backroom of a market in Tijuana. I've proven I'll do anything to see this case to the end."

Holy shit, he didn't tell me that. I stiffen in his arms and stare up at his determined expression.

Micah looks like he's ready to explode.

Tim drags a hand down his face.

But Cole ... he's contemplating it.

"You've done this long enough to know that if I don't go back with her at my side, we might as well flush the whole operation down the shitter. We're close. I need days—two of them. That's it."

Silence blankets the room like a cold, wet towel.

"Okay."

I suck in a breath of air.

Brax exhales.

Cole points at Brax and then to me. "You'd better coach her. We hear every single conversation that goes down in that house. If I hear one slip up or nervous falter, I'll extract your asses so fast it'll make your heads spin. We're headed to San Diego right on your heels to be there for the takedown—you know I'll do it."

My nod is grave, and I wonder what in the hell I'm doing.

But I tell the truth and do my best to put on a brave face. "I can do this. I'd never do anything to put him in danger."

Cole's smirk isn't cocky this time. "I like that. Hell, it must be the romantic in me, because I believe it."

Micah looks like he wants to put a fist through a wall.

But Tim proves to be a team player. "We need an extraction plan. And then we need an emergency extraction plan. Hell, we might need a plan C extraction plan."

Brax looks at his watch. "We've wasted enough time—I have a meeting. Let's get this shit done."

And what happens next blows my mind.

The plotting.

The maneuvering.

The intricate details.

Brax leads it like he's been planning every aspect in his brain for years. Like these are the final pieces of his puzzle.

And he includes me in all of it with no hesitation.

The longer I sit here and listen, I become overwhelmed and scared.

The responsibility ... it's heavy.

But I take it all in. I study it. And I memorize it.

Because this is no game, and slipping up is not an option. I know what they'll do to him. If I had to guess, it will be worse than what happened to his brother.

I'll die before I let that happen.

Two days.

Hell, I lived through the bloodbath of a wedding and being attacked by Nic. Returning to San Diego and acting like nothing has changed should be a walk in the park.

I can do two days if it means living a normal life with Brax Cruz.

Brax

I DON'T DO anything without a plan.

Not one fucking thing.

But when I decided to bring Landyn to New York so I could see my mom, I had no idea how it would go. I was hopeful, but I knew there was a chance she'd freak and turn on me, and we'd have to put her into protective custody until I wrapped the case.

I'm cocky enough that I haven't been afraid of anything since I started this, but the thought of her rejecting the real me was terrifying.

It's not because I was worried about returning without her. She's right though—I might as well wave my own red flag in Alamandos' face. Landyn Alba is a prize made into a shrine that

Alamandos put on a pedestal to prove to the underworld what will happen when you play with the Marinos and fuck up.

No one is safe.

But she accepted the real me. Hell, I think she's happier now than she was. And we have a plan.

She can handle this. I'm confident in the woman who owns me in every way.

She proved last night during my bullshit meeting with the Marino's east coast dealer. In the process, he implicated himself and will have his own arrest warrant soon enough.

Then she sat at my side for hours and talked to my mom all night. We had one last visit before I promised the woman who gave me life that I'd be home soon.

For good.

Maybe before she gets out of the hospital.

We had two hours of sleep before we had to leave for the airport.

I'm dragging her back into the lion's den, and she hasn't once hesitated. She only wants to be by my side.

We're back in first class, flying thirty-thousand feet above earth, somewhere between wheat fields and the Rocky Mountains, when Landyn turns from staring blankly out the window and focuses her blue eyes on me.

And she proves she has no problem falling into this sham of a life while still being all her. "B?"

"Yeah, baby?"

She lowers her voice for only me to hear over the hum of the jet engines. "I need to ask you something. And I need you to tell me the truth."

I reach to claim her chin. "Not sure what more I can do to prove that I'll always tell you the truth, chica."

She nods but doesn't pull away. She leans in as close as she can until her lips brush the lobe of my ear. "Did you kill Damian?"

Shit. That was not what I expected.

I push her back far enough to frame the side of her face in my hand and look into her eyes. "Yes."

She looks like she has to force herself to swallow over a boulder in her throat, and her tone goes rough. "Was that the plan?"

I shake my head. "No, baby. That was the farthest thing from the plan. I actually fucked up all the plans that day."

"But you did it." She pauses and wets her dry lips with the tip of her tongue. "You did it for me."

"I did. I'd do anything for you."

Her eyes instantly glass over, and I swipe away a single tear with my thumb.

Then she moves—rips at her buckle and flips up the wide armrest that separates us. Before I know it, she's in my lap, and I'm cupping her ass in my hand to steady her as she throws herself at me. She claims my face in her hands and presses her lips to mine in a searing kiss.

I bury my hand in her hair and take over, claiming what's become mine. Her body is only the most recent addition to all the other ways I've claimed her—heart and soul.

She presses into me, and my thoughts go back to this morning when I pulled her panties down her legs and buried myself inside her. When I watched her come, I prayed I was doing the right thing by taking her back with me.

I feel her heart speed, and I break our kiss, because I can't go another moment. Looking into her blue eyes, I admit what's been on the tip of my tongue since I told her my real name. "I love you, chica."

Tears fall faster, and she nods, like she's known all along. "I love you too. I never thought I'd find love when my father sold me off. That's how I know this will all be okay. We've come too far to fail."

I'm about to tell her failure is never an option when it comes to her, but we're interrupted.

"Ah-hem." The flight attendant is standing there with her hands on her hips, glaring at us.

I only hold Landyn tighter and glare right back. "We're on our honeymoon."

"The seatbelt sign isn't on," Landyn points out as she looks back at me. "And I'll never get enough of my husband."

The attendant shakes her head and moves on, but we stay glued together. Landyn scoots down in my lap, and I tuck her face into my neck to hold her close.

We silently take in our last moments before we walk back into the Marino estate.

I have very little time left to find out who killed Brian, and then I need to get us out for good.

I'm ready to move on and start my life with Landyn.

31

MILF

Brax

"Mr. and Mrs. Torres, welcome home."

I nod to June as Spencer carries our suitcases upstairs and lie, "It's good to be back."

Landyn smiles at June and Miranda who greet us inside the front door. I shouldn't be surprised when the first thing out of her mouth is about her new BFF. "Is Rocco home?"

"He is," June says. "He's in the living room working on courses Mr. Torres left for him."

Landyn squeezes my hand. "He took the GED yesterday. What else does he have to work on?"

"He's taking online accounting classes." What I hope she realizes is that the classes are more to keep him out of trouble. If they stick, that'll be better than running drugs for a club.

She wrinkles her nose. "That sounds torturous. I think I'll say hello and rescue him from numbers and columns and formulas."

I pull her to me and kiss the side of her head. "You do that."

"I assume it will just be the three of you for dinner tonight?" June asks.

Landyn turns to look at me with a raised brow. So far, she's cool and calm. I knew she could handle this. As much as it would've killed me, I never would have brought her here had I thought she'd put either of us in danger.

She sat in my lap for the second half of the flight while we talked about details for the next two days. My goal is to keep our heads down, not meet with anyone in person, and take care of shit over the phone. Phone calls mean wiretaps and those can't be argued with in court.

I lift my chin and confirm, "Just the three of us."

Landyn has fallen back into our roles without a hitch. Her bright smile hits all of us. "Our happy little family."

I shake my head and watch her move through the long halls when Spencer meets me at the bottom of the steps. "Sir, we had a development while you were gone."

I freeze. "A development?"

He looks around. Other than Landyn and Rocco talking up a storm from across the house, there's no one but us.

"What is it?" I press.

"Sir, we found Nic Decker."

All of a sudden, my fingers are itchy. "Really."

"Yes. He's in the garage. He's been there since yesterday."

"Who knows that he's here?" I demand.

"Myself and the two guards who found him."

"Not Rocco?"

He shakes his head. "No, sir. The boy doesn't need to be tied up in that."

"No, he doesn't." I look back toward the family room. "I'll let Landyn know that I'm not far. Don't take your eyes off her or let her look for me."

"Absolutely."

"Oh, and Spencer?" The old man stops and turns back. "Landyn keeps asking about the boat. I promised her I'd make that happen soon. Make sure it's fueled and ready. We'll go as soon as we have some time."

"Of course. If you let me know when, I'll arrange for staff to accompany you."

I shake my head and give him a small smile. "I'm not Damian. I want privacy with my wife. I can handle the boat on my own."

Spencer nods as if I made him blush. "I'll make sure it's ready."

One thing done.

I go back to the family room where Rocco is stretched out on the floor with an empty bag of cookies next to him. Landyn is across from him curled in a chair with her shoes kicked on the floor in front of her.

"Chica," I interrupt.

Her gaze jumps to me, calm but alert.

Two days. We can make it two more days.

I lean down to kiss her. "I've got to talk to the guards. Hang out with Rocco but stay in the house. Spencer will be here if you need anything."

She relaxes into her chair and shoots me a relieved smile. "Twist my arm, hubbalicious. I'll make it my mission to distract Rocco from accounting for the rest of the day."

"You guys kind of make me want to throw up," Rocco mutters.

"Someday you'll be in love, Rocco," Landyn says. "I hope it's so huge that it knocks you on your ass, and you can't get up."

"That sounds like a geriatric commercial," Rocco spouts. "Am I going to need a call button for help? I don't have time for you women or your drama. Life was hard enough trying not to get dead in my slum-ass old neighborhood."

I ignore him and level my eyes on Landyn. "I'll be back soon."

"I'll be here."

I head straight for the soundproof garage. For the first time since I've walked into the Marino estate, I'm grateful for the way Damian built it.

Nic Decker is going to pay for what he did to Landyn, and it's not going to be a quiet experience.

Landyn

I HAVE no idea what Brax is doing, but since he's been doing this for two years, I'm not going to wonder. I'm going to hang out with Rocco while I can.

"When do you get your test results?" I ask.

He shrugs. "I don't know."

I frown. "They didn't tell you?"

"They might've. I can't remember."

"Rocco." I stand and walk to where he's sprawled on the floor. "There's no way you don't remember. Do they mail it or do you log in or what?"

He rolls his eyes. "Chill, mom."

My jaw drops. "You did not just *mom* me! We're of the same generation, jerk ... face."

"*Jerk face*? That's the best you can do? You *are* a mom."

I cross my arms and hitch a leg. "I'm an only child. I don't throw insults well. I'm not well practiced in things like that."

"You're not trying hard enough. I'll be your punching bag, Landyn. Lemme see what you've got."

I sit next to where he's lounged and nudge his shoulder with my bare foot. "You're the one who doesn't try hard enough. Now tell me, how long will it take to get your test results?"

He rubs his eyes with the heels of his hands. "You're so fucking annoying."

"Rocco." I kick him harder this time, not that I could hurt him. He's as solid as a tree trunk.

He exhales and looks up at me. "They said scores will be posted as soon as two hours—not more than twenty-four. I have to log in to get them."

"Then what are you waiting for?" I gape.

He stares at me, and for the first time, I don't see a bored teenager or someone too young trying to be a biker.

All I see is apprehension.

My insides squeeze in trepidation for him. Shit, what if he didn't pass? "Do you already know your results?"

"No. I've been putting it off. If I didn't pass, Boz is going to make me take it again. Taking it once was bad enough."

"I have a good feeling." I flip open the laptop that was sitting closed on the coffee table. "Let's rip off the bandage. It's the only way."

"You speak like you've had experience."

"Let's just say I've had to rip the bandage off a few times recently."

"Better than the duct tape." He makes no move for the computer. "That would suck."

"Give me your username," I demand and pull the laptop to my lap. When I wake it up, I search through the tabs on the top and find the site. "Are you sure you don't already know?"

"Landyn," he bites, but there's nothing fake or frustrated in his tone. It's anxiety ridden. "I didn't exactly thrive in school unless it came to fucking around or throwing a football. I'm already a drop out. If I didn't pass that test, I'll be the biggest failure ever."

I pull in a breath and lower my voice. "I might not have dropped out of high school, but I did drop out of college. And my dad sold me to save his own life. We might not have grown up across the street from each other, but that doesn't mean we don't have anything in common. We both landed here in this house together, and I think that means something. Let me do this for you. I'll look up your score. Whatever it is, we'll deal with it together."

He gives me his username and password, though I think it might be a defensive tactic to get me to leave him alone.

I don't care. I need to know, and so does he.

The page loads, painfully slow.

Numbers appear in front of me. I skim, but I have no clue what I'm looking for so I have to scroll to the top and start over.

This is probably why I sucked at test taking.

"Fuck," Rocco hisses. "Is it that bad?"

"Hang on. I'm trying to figure this out. You need smarter friends. I'm a slow reader."

"You're killing me," he mutters.

"Oh!" I sit up straight.

He pushes up from the floor. "Dammit, Landyn."

I look up at him. "You passed."

"I did?" His expression falls. "Wait, are you sure? You said you suck at comprehending shit."

"Yes. Your highest score was in math." I look up at him. "I'm totally taking credit for that, by the way. I quizzed you for days. Then Science."

"What about the other sections?" he presses.

"Do you want to see for yourself? You passed, Rocco. Every section." I look over the screen at his surprised eyes. "But there's more."

He frowns. "What do you mean more?"

"There are levels. Pass, college ready, and college ready plus. You're right on the line for college ready and college ready plus. And you're really high in math." I slam the laptop shut and lean forward. "You're so smart and have no clue what you're capable of. Maybe I should be your mom."

He stands and cracks his neck before doing the same to his knuckles. "No fucking way. I don't need my friends giving me shit about you being a MILF."

I look up at him. "I feel like a mom. At the very least, a big sister. I'm so proud of you."

"You know what this means, right?" Rocco bites.

I find it hard to swallow over the lump in my throat. I have no idea what will happen to Rocco in two days. I want to pack him up and take him with us. Brax assured me he's done everything he can to make sure Rocco would have options, but he's a man. It's on him, and he has to make the right choices.

I shake my head and clear my throat. "What does this mean?"

"It means Boz is going to make me keep taking these damn accounting classes."

Tears prick my eyes. I can only squeeze out one word while holding my emotions together. "Probably."

He flops on the sofa next to me. "At least I have three meals a day while I'm here, right?"

Shit.

Shit, shit, shit.

"Family dinner tonight." I try not to think about how it will be one of our last.

"Cool," he says, but doesn't ask what's for dinner. He doesn't care. Eating three meals a day is a luxury for him.

I want to give him something else to focus on. "You want to turn on a movie?"

He reaches forward and plucks the remote off the coffee table. "Yeah, but I get to pick. I'm the one who's college ready plus."

I shoot him a smile and do everything I can to control myself, so I try for a joke, but it comes out lame. "Anything but porn."

He gapes. "You think I'd watch porn with you?"

It's my turn to roll my eyes. "I was joking."

"First of all, no. Don't joke about that. And second of all, do I look like I have a death wish? Boz would literally kill me."

Well, after what I learned this afternoon, it wouldn't be the first time.

32

PLEASURE

Brax

Cartel members are simply refined drug dealers.
But not by a lot.
They might think they've leveled up, but they have no clue. They don't spend months running drills, or hours upon hours at the range, or train for tactical maneuvers.

It's why the bloody wedding was a shit show. There is no precision, accuracy, or finesse.

It was messy. I usually don't like messy, but I took advantage of it that day.

It's why I got away with killing Damian. No one will ever know.
Other than Landyn.
I've not once regretted that decision.
And I'm about to do it again.
The guards picked up Nic Decker north of L.A. He was hiding like a rat who only has the balls to come out at night. The guards told me they found him passed out with a hooker who was so doped up, she didn't even know they dragged his sorry ass out of his low-budget motel. The last we heard, he has no source of

income since the Marinos cut him off and he's been begging for cash from his parents.

They won't have to fund his pathetic life much longer.

Nicolás Decker is about to pay for touching my wife.

"You got a head start." My dress shoes click on the concrete of the garage floor as I circle the man who's about to die. It's the only sound other than the hum of the air conditioner and Nic's labored breaths.

It seems I'm not the only one who hates Nic. That's what you get when you're an asshole to those who rank below you on the cartel totem pole.

"We were told to bring him back. No one said we couldn't touch him."

I stop in front of Nic who's in bad shape. He's naked from the waist up, still wearing a pair of pants that are worn, filthy, and tattered. He's duct taped to a chair, and it's no coincidence it's situated right over the drain in the floor. His arms bound behind him and ankles taped to the legs. His face is bloody, eyes are swollen, and he smells like shit.

Literally, since he's been pissing himself and probably worse.

I turn to the guards. "I appreciate you finding him. I'll take it from here."

They look to each other and frown before turning their disappointment back on me. "Really? Damian used to sit back and watch while we did the rest."

I shake my head but don't confirm what I'm about to do. "Nic and I need to have a conversation."

"You're not going to kill him?"

I don't answer. "Go back to the gate. Like I said, I can handle it."

They look like I ate their birthday cake but do as I say. They weren't the ones on duty the night Nic pushed his way through security, into the house, and attacked my wife.

Those assholes were fired last week. I heard they were both arrested the next day on outstanding warrants.

Imagine that.

The side door to the garage slams behind me.

I'm alone with Nic.

Really alone.

No cameras. No wires. And no taps.

I know it since I'm solely responsible for the wires and coordinated the Marino surveillance myself.

"What are you going to do to me?" Nic rasps.

"I missed the fun stuff, even though it's not my style." I take a step back and enjoy the view in front of me. The bright fluorescents don't do him any favors. He looks like death, which isn't surprising since he's really close to it right now. "I'm not happy about that. I was looking forward to getting my hands dirty for once."

It seems to take all his energy to pull his head up and pry one eye open to look at me.

I stare back, unmoving. "I wanted to be the one to put every cut and bruise on your body. I wanted to do to you one-hundred-fold what you did to my wife."

His head falls. It's so quiet in the garage, I have no problem hearing him mutter, "Cunt."

I circle him as I speak. "I'd say you're not making a very good case for yourself. A smart man would beg for his life."

"I'm not begging for shit."

When I stop in front of him, he spits blood and phlegm on the floor between us.

I slide my hands into my pockets. "You know what your problem is?"

"You," he grunts. "You've been my fucking problem since you showed up. Damian practically had a hard-on for you since the day you took that fucking bullet."

I don't argue. "Damian was weak. If he didn't have an army surrounding him, he would've hidden under a rock. I was man enough to step up. You weren't. Look at us now."

He pulls in a labored breath and wheezes on an exhale. "No one is crazy enough to do what you did. That shit'll get you killed. Doesn't make you smart, asshole. Makes you crazy."

"Maybe so," I agree. I remember the day I was shot. I thought my mother would lose two sons to the Marino family. I thought I failed. "Proved I can't be killed. You'll never beat me, Nic. You tried, over and over. I'm always one step ahead of you. And you know what?"

His head bobs once.

I don't wait for him to guess or ask. I move the few steps toward the table decorated with every tool that can be used to torture a human. I don't need any of them. I shrug my sport coat down my arms and fold it before laying it across the back of a chair before I unbutton my cuffs and roll them up my forearms.

I lied when I said I missed out on the fun part. I have no desire to torture anyone. I don't get off on that—I'm no monster. I go straight for the medical supplies and pluck a pair of gloves from the box.

His head pops up when the latex snaps against my skin. "I was going to let you go down with the rest of them."

His battered and bloody expression is confused. If it didn't look painful for him to pull his brows together in a frown, I bet he would.

I take a step, lean down to look him in the eyes, and lower my voice. "Very soon, this is all going to go away. If I didn't hate you so much, I'd keep you around just for you to experience it. If you were here, I'd hit you with every-fucking-thing. Distributing. Trafficking. Money laundering. I'd even get you charged under the RICO act. But what I'd really get you for is rape."

His breathing speeds as he jerks in his chair even though he's trapped. "What the fuck?"

"That's right. I'm not who you think I am."

And just when I thought he was drained of life and energy, his body wracks. His chair almost tips backward, but I reach out to steady him. I snake my gloved fingers north and wrap them around his neck.

Then, I squeeze.

His eyes bulge and he croaks, "You're a—?"

I choke off his words with a tighter grip and continue to whisper. "You didn't stand a chance. I'm the man who's going to take down Alba, the Jackals, and the Marinos—including your fucking father. I can't wait for him to rot away for the rest of his life in federal prison."

If I thought he was freaking out before, it's nothing compared to now. And he can't utter a word since I've cut off his oxygen.

"You're going to escape the justice system and prison. I get to take care of you my own way because you tried to take something from me."

His eyes start to water, and he shakes under my hold.

"How does this feel?" I whisper, thinking back to the surveillance video when he did this exact thing to the woman I plan to spend the rest of my life with. "To not breathe? To have a hand wrapped around your neck? To have someone threaten you?"

He fights for air.

"I bet there's nothing more you want than oxygen. You should've thought about that before you laid a finger on my wife. You put bruises on her neck. Cuts on her face," I growl. "You actually fucking *touched* her and thought you'd get away with it."

Killing Damian was a knee-jerk decision. I didn't plan it or strategize or think it through.

Since I don't do anything that isn't completely deliberate and methodical, I'm not sure who to be grateful for to be the lucky man who ended up with Landyn.

I don't believe in fate or destiny or even pure, fucking chance.

The universe threw us together. I'm not going to let anything or anyone tear us apart.

Ever.

Which is why I don't have one remorseful bone in my body about the line I'm about to cross.

"You touched her," I repeat, because I'll never forget the images of her beaten and battered by the man I'm about to kill. "And you're going to pay for it with your pathetic life. You'll never touch her or any other woman ever again."

He sputters and spits, but I don't let go.

I lower my tone even more. "How does it feel? I'll be the last thing you see, asshole. There's a special place in hell for people like you. I hope you burn for eternity. The only person who deserves it more than you is Damian, and I already took care of him. When you join him, know I'm the one who sent you both straight to hell."

He can't respond, but can still comprehend. His evil eyes don't stray from mine as I squeeze the life out of him. The color drains from his face and his mouth falls open.

I wait.

I can be patient.

This is one of the easiest things I've ever done aside from falling in love with Landyn.

Finally, his eyes roll and his pulse weakens under my hold. As the life starts to seep from his body, I've never felt more powerful or at peace.

Landyn wasn't the first woman he ever attacked. It's the culture of the cartel. I knew it was bad, but didn't understand to what extent until I got here and had to pretend it didn't disgust me to look the other way.

It's why I didn't hesitate to kill Damian when bullets started to fly.

I'll take care of the rest of the organization the legal way.

Finally, Nic slumps. The only thing holding him up is duct tape.

I let him go and stand back to stare down at what I just did.

No regrets ... I've been planning this.

The only thing I feel is pure relief.

In two days, this will be over.

I'm about to find something to wrap him to dump him in the Pacific, when the door to the house opens.

I spin on my heel, and breathe a sigh of relief when I see who it is.

His eyes go from me to Nic for long, heavy moments before landing back on me.

He moves from the threshold to the house and closes the door behind him.

I brace. He's not at all new to this life, but in the time I've been here, I've never seen him involved in this part of the business.

He stares at Nic as his tired voice breaks through the quiet. "This is a good thing."

I don't take my eyes off him, but I also don't agree. I might be standing here with a dead body, but he didn't see me do anything. Not that the guards won't feel free to say there were two living and breathing humans when they left us.

Finally, Spencer's old eyes shift to me. "I don't know if you ever knew, but what he almost did to Mrs. Torres, he did to Miranda. More than once."

Every muscle in my body tenses. "Since I've been here?"

He shakes his head. "Before. He brought her across the border and promised her a life in America, but sold her to Damian. You know Damian—he grew tired of women quickly. That was before you moved in. June and I have done all we can to protect her."

"Fuck," I hiss. All of a sudden, I wish I could bring him back to life so I could torture him further and kill him all over again. "I didn't know about Miranda."

Every muscle in his expression is taut, angry, yet, relieved.

He spears me with a resolute stare. "Go to Mrs. Torres. I'll take care of this."

I shake my head. "This isn't something you do. You don't want to get involved—"

He gives me the palm of his hand to shut me up. "I've cleaned up worse than this. Getting rid of Nic Decker forever will be the best thing I've done since I started working for the Marinos. I wish I could have been a part of," he lifts his chin toward the dead body sitting limp between us, "that."

I contemplate the man who is nothing more than a glorified butler for a cartel leader's son. Despite where he works, Spencer is a good man.

But so am I.

Despite what I just did.

"Let me do this," he demands. "It will bring me a tremendous amount of pleasure to get rid of his body."

I nod. "Do you need help?"

"No. And I know how to clean up the garage. Mrs. Torres went to your room to unpack. June said she would do it, but your wife insisted on doing it herself."

I exhale but don't ask him any further questions. "Be careful."

I head for the door when he calls for me. "Mr. Torres?"

I turn back and hike a brow.

"I just want you to know, having you and Mrs. Torres as the head of the house has been..." he hesitates before finishing, "a pleasant change. June and Miranda agree."

I hope he feels the same in two days. "I appreciate that."

He says nothing else, snaps on his own gloves, and gets to work.

33

BLINDING

Landyn

There are two kinds of people in this world.
Those who unpack right away after a trip and those who live out of an exploded suitcase for days.
I'm the latter.
But there's no way I'm going to let anyone unpack for me. So, today, I'm the former.
June is that meticulous and organized. If I could be just ten percent her, I'd live a better life.
I toss the rest of my dirty clothes in the hamper and head straight for my makeup and toiletries, vowing to become a better person when it comes to unpacking.
Driving through the security gates to Damian's home was eerie. Everything is different. Knowing that the man I was "forced to marry" isn't who I thought is an emotional rollercoaster. Throw in meeting his sisters, his mom in the ICU, and federal agents, it's safe to say the recent turn of events is something from a dream.
I left San Diego with a man I thought I was falling in love with.

I returned with a man who's the same yet so much better. He saved me. From Damian. From the Marinos. From Nic.

And most importantly, from my father.

He's my protector and doesn't treat me like a possession, even though he could. Brax Cruz will forever own my heart. I never wanted to be a possession until I met him.

I'm his. And even being back in Damian Marino's home, I've never been happier.

I'm completely and utterly in love. When this is done, we'll move on to a different kind of forever.

We have a plan—one I'm very much a part of.

It makes me nervous, since it centers on acting normal. I never knew how difficult it would be to act normal.

Just ... *normal*.

Brax assured me he'd make the next few days as stress-free as possible.

No meetings.

No guests.

No drama.

He's going to coordinate the delivery with the Jackals and do everything he can to find out who killed his brother. Then, he'll take Rocco and me to dinner.

We'll leave this place and never return.

When the plan was set in the backroom of a Manhattan bar with the DEA and CIA, I might have flipped out about leaving Rocco.

He's young and made a bad choice in joining the Jackals, but he hasn't done anything wrong. Not yet.

He was born into a shitty situation, not unlike me. The only difference is my shitty situation was funded by organized crime. His wasn't funded at all.

Look where it got both of us...

Brax trying to save Rocco, just like he did me. The only difference is, I'm all in. Rocco hasn't been given the choice yet.

But he will.

In two days, Brax will offer him a deal.

I pray he takes it.

He has to take it.

Maybe it's whacked, but I'm not nervous for me. Brax has proven he'll do anything to keep me safe. He killed for me, and that's when he didn't even know me. In a couple of days, my life will look completely different.

I can't wait.

But Rocco has to buy into our plan. That means he has to actually sign and turn on the organization he dropped out of high school to join. He has to say goodbye to the only life he's ever known.

He'll have to do what I did—put all his trust in a man he thought was someone else.

If Rocco doesn't make the right choice...

I don't know what I'll do. I can't even think about it.

"Baby."

I jump and spin on my bare feet. "You scared me. How long have you been standing there?"

Brax's large frame fills the doorway to the bedroom, and that frame is not at all relaxed. His shoulders are tense, and his expression is extreme. My eyes flit to his right hand where his fingers flex in and out of a fist. I've never seen him like this. And since our time together has been intense, panic bubbles within me.

His silence is as heavy as his mood.

I grip the marble counter behind me thinking of all the things that could go wrong. Even though I know this is a safe place to talk, I whisper, "What's wrong?"

His eyes never leave me when he moves. One moment he's across the room, and the next, my face is engulfed in his hands. Every ounce of tense energy and emotion bleeds into me through his searing lips. I taste it on his tongue, feel it through his grip, and hear it in the rough growl that rumbles from deep in his chest. It vibrates through me where I'm pressed into the vanity.

One hand slides into my hair. He fists it and pulls my head back for him to deepen his kiss. His other feels its way down my neck and yanks.

The material bites into the back of my neck as buttons pop between us. I moan into his mouth when his hand slides around me to unhook my bra. His touch on my skin is searing and rough.

And confusing.

I love it, even though it scares me.

He tears his mouth from mine, and we're both breathing hard as he stares down at me.

My words are breathy and low when I repeat, "What's wrong?"

His gaze drops between us, to my breasts, barely contained in my loose bra, and he shakes his head. "Everything is wrong, chica."

He feels it when I start to panic.

His eyes jump to mine, but he's not quick to put me at ease. "In the middle of all the wrong, I somehow ended up with you. It doesn't make sense. I haven't figured out who killed Brian, and that's the only reason I'm here, but all I want to do is pick you up and run. Coming back here was fucking hard."

He yanks his dress shirt from his pants with one hand, while the other goes to the buttons at his chest.

"Did something happen?" I ask. "You're different than you were when you left me with Rocco."

His shirt lands on the floor before he reaches for my jeans and rips at the buttons. I'm left breathless when he dips his hand straight into my panties to cup me.

"Yeah, something happened." His gaze burns into me as hot as his hold on my sex as his fingers start to move in my tight jeans. His other hand comes to my face, his index finger traces the fading bruise below my eye. "You'll never wear a bruise or a cut again. I made sure of it." His finger trails down my skin, drags across my bottom lip, and falls to my shoulders where he pushes my torn shirt from my shoulders, followed by my bra. "No one will ever touch you but me. Do you understand what that means?"

I don't answer. I'm afraid to guess.

His dark eyes bleed with emotion. "I did what I promised. Nic is dead."

My heart speeds, and my breaths shallow as he fills me with

two fingers, hooking them inside me. I pull in a quick breath of air, but he doesn't let me talk.

He leans down and kisses the side of my parted lips. "Chica, get rid of the pants. Now. I've never needed you more."

I can't move. I grip the marble tighter.

He turns me without letting me go. I take in our reflection in the mirror. We're both bare from the waist up when his heated gaze meets mine through the reflection. His warm chest hits my back when he demands, "I'm not letting go, Landyn. No one will hurt you again. I'll make sure of it. You're going to watch as I make you come. Then I'm going to bury myself in you and pretend we're anywhere but here. I can't wait to get you out of here for good. I'm ready to shout to the world who I really am and that you're mine."

I'm overcome.

He said he would kill Nic. And just today he confirmed what I suspected more and more as I fall in love with him—that he was the one who killed Damian.

But this?

Now?

When we're so close to the end?

I assumed when he said he would kill Nic, it was figurative—that he would be on the long list of people with an arrest warrant.

But I'm relieved. I'm not sure what it says about me that the news fills me with joy.

And that it turns me on.

I lean into his chest and take in the sight of us. My messy blond hair against his smooth, dark skin. The contrast is beautiful and something I'm becoming more obsessed with every time we're together. It's impossible not to think about us as one, with all the unprotected sex. It makes me nervous and excited and ready for a new life.

A different life than I've ever known.

A better life ... with him.

He drags a finger over my clit and gives me a slow circle. When he crosses my body with his forearm, his fingers find my nipple.

A pinch.

A twist.

A pain that is so good, it shoots straight between my legs.

"Baby," he growls. "Jeans off. Now."

I tuck my thumbs into my waistband and struggle to push them down my hips and thighs while he holds me tight to his chest. I never take my eyes off him through the mirror.

His stare is heavy on my bare body as I struggle with my clothes. "There you go."

I kick my jeans to the side.

He takes advantage of me opening for him, and his hold on me gives possession new meaning.

I look into his dark eyes and tell him the truth. "I'm yours."

His tongue sneaks out and wets the crease of his lips. "Yeah, you are."

I keep talking because I need to finish what I started, and admit, "I never wanted to be anyone's. My entire life was dominated by my father. The only thing I ever wanted to do was be free of him. Now I only want to be yours."

His hands still on my body.

Even though there's nothing in my vision but me naked in the mirror, all I see is love in his eyes. "Baby, you are mine, but it'll never be like that. Ever. You'll never feel more free. I'll make sure of it."

I lift my hands to cover each of his, where his hold on me is lewd and loving and domineering. "I know. I've never felt freer than this."

His hands shift beneath mine. I feel every single movement as the tips of his fingers part my sex to tease me. His other massages my breast and milks my nipple into a hardened pebble.

My head falls to his pec, and his lips land on my ear. "I've got condoms, baby."

My eyes close, and I concentrate on his fingers and his words, thinking and dreaming of our future.

He presses his lips to the side of my head. "But I don't want to use them."

I open my eyes to find him staring at me through the mirror.

After being thrown together in the ugliest way possible, we somehow found this.

There's a beauty in us that's blinding.

His touch warms me from the inside out, and my chest heaves with labored breaths.

"We've given new meaning to tempting fate. I love what we're doing as much as I love you. I don't want to change a thing. If you want the condom, you're going to have to say the word."

All I see is lust and love in his hot gaze.

I tell him the truth with a tiny shake of my head.

"Say it, chica," he demands. "I want to hear it from your own lips. I want you to say that you want everything with me."

My words are breathy. "No condom. I don't want anything between us—ever. Please."

He dips his face to my neck. His whiskers scrape my skin when he pulls my hair away from my face with his chin and whispers, "Love you, baby. After giving two years of my life to this shit, I'm not willing to wait or take my time. I want everything with you."

"Yes," I moan. It's an answer to his words, his touch, and his grip on my heart. "Don't ever let me go."

He gives my clit more pressure—faster, harder—but it's not enough. I shift my legs farther apart.

"Fuck, I like that," he says.

I lose his hand on my breast as he rips his pants open to free himself. His hard cock is pressed to the small of my back.

Hot, thick, long. I want it. I want him.

"Please," I beg.

His hips press into me. "Not until I see you come. Fall apart for me, baby. Then I'll give you what you want."

His arm returns to me, and he holds me when I fall apart. My orgasm washes over me like a wave hitting the rocky cliffs. It's violent and aggressive, and I love every moment.

Cold hits my chest when he bends me at the waist and presses me to the marble. He wastes no time. My sex is still pulsing when he slides into me from behind.

Something new with Brax.

"Yes," I moan, with my cheek and breasts pressed to the counter. I push up on my toes to get more of him. "Love this. I love you."

His fingers bite into my hips as he pulls me to meet every single one of his firm, delicious thrusts. My orgasm lingers and lives to see a second life. I wish I could see him take me like this. Have visual proof of the pure possession that floods me.

Either he can read my mind, or he's feeling the same. His words are labored. "Never thought I'd want anyone so much. Making you mine and setting you free at the same time will be the best thing I'll ever do."

Every time he thrusts, his words and his cock hit a new place, taking me deeper in love and lust.

"Yes," I gasp. "It's all I want."

There are no more words. Just unbridled energy.

When he comes, he groans, holding my hips to him, burying himself inside me and staying there for many long moments while we both calm our beating hearts.

His hand slides over my ass, up my back, and into my hair before his muscled chest hits my back at the same time his lips touch my temple. "We're close, baby. So fucking close to the end. Stick with me, and I'll give you a normal, beautiful life."

I turn my head as far as I can to look up at him. "My life turned beautiful during a wedding massacre. It'll be blinding when we're free of this."

He tips his forehead to mine. "I can't wait."

34

JITTERY

Brax

I scroll back six years to scour Damian's email to see if there's anything I missed. I already have copies of every document, file, and electronic piece of information to be had from this house. If he ever used a phone, it was a burner, and he switched them out weekly.

If I've learned one thing about the cartel, nothing keeps them safer than pure paranoia.

The man was careful. His distrust and suspicion of everyone around him fueled him to never conduct cartel business electronically. It's why it took me getting shot to fully gain his trust.

In all I did, it ended up being that damn bullet. It was pure luck it didn't catch an artery. I was even luckier I didn't die from infection when some self-taught surgeon dug it out of me and left me with a scar to rival Frankenstein's.

I did what I had to do and built on that luck, but in the process, I lost two years of my life. I never thought about it that way until now.

I did what I came here to do in the eyes of the government. I have enough evidence to indict multiple organizations in the U.S., take down one of the main supply chains coming into the country, and Cole Carson has what he needs for the CIA to go batshit crazy the way it does outside of our borders ... the kind of crazy that never makes the news.

I'm done. Having a taste of home for just a few days and seeing my mom sick and fighting for her life pushed me.

But what has really sealed the deal is Landyn.

I've got to get her out of here. She easily could have freaked out and turned me away when I told her who I really am.

She accepted my reality and stayed for me.

For us.

There's only one thing I haven't accomplished.

Brian.

If I don't figure it out soon, I'm afraid I never will. I'm running out of time.

I have a new list of suspicions, but none of them make sense with the timeline. Whoever killed him was smart and careful. Taking him across the border muddied the waters enough that I find myself at a dead end every single time.

Figuring this out will be too hard. I need to exhaust every piece of evidence while I'm here. Make sure I haven't missed anything. I can't leave any rock unturned.

Aside from crossing the border and waltzing my ass back into Alamandos' compound to turn the place over to find his sick list, I'm out of options.

Out of options and out of time. It's the figurative double-edged sword I might die on if I can't sort it out before we get the hell out of this place for good.

"What are you doing up?"

I look over and Landyn is standing in the double doors to the bedroom. I left the doors open this morning so I could at least see her. The only time she's been out of my sight since we got back was when I dealt with Nic Decker for the last time.

"It's early, baby. Go back to sleep."

She lifts a shoulder before walking barefoot through the office.

She's wearing my T-shirt and a pair of shorts. She told me the cameras creep her out now more than they ever have. She understands that I did everything I could to protect her from them.

Even if I was an asshole about it in the beginning, which she didn't hesitate to tell me on the flight home.

She moves between my legs and my hand lands on her ass when she lowers it to my thigh.

I can't wait to get her out of here and away from the fucking cameras.

Her tired gaze hits mine, but it's different than it was. As much as I wanted to tell her the truth about who I was, I was worried it would take time to get to this point. I was prepared to beg and plead as long as it took to get her to accept me.

When she looks at me since we got back from New York, there's only truth, honesty, and shared secrets between us.

The only thing I love more than that is her.

She glances at the computer screen I don't bother hiding from her. "What are you working on?"

I lie to her for the purpose of the cameras, but she can see from the screen that I'm full of shit. "I'm finalizing the first payment to the Jackals. Rocco is making the drop this afternoon. They'll get the rest when the delivery is made."

She lays a hand on my face and leans in to kiss me. "I miss you when I wake up alone."

I pull her tighter to me. "There's a lot going on."

She nods and pulls in a breath. "Wake me up before you leave, okay?"

"I had the doors open. I was watching you sleep while I worked."

"Still." She traces my jawline with her index finger. "Wake me up."

"Whatever you want, chica."

Finally, a satisfied expression settles on her lips. "I'm going to go down and get some coffee before I take a shower. Can I bring you a cup?"

"I'll take anything you want to bring me."

She leans back and looks satisfied with herself. "Well, then. I might surprise you with breakfast if June allows me to touch her favorite skillet."

"Rocco should be in here at any minute to discuss the money drop."

"Rocco is here." We both look up as the man-boy announces his arrival, sauntering into the room as he scowls at us. He doesn't look like he's ready to work for me. He's back in ripped jeans, a tee, and his cut. "You guys seriously make me sick to my stomach. You're like a sappy couple from network TV."

"Network TV?" Landyn sits up straight in my lap, but I don't let go of her. "I'm offended."

"You should be," Rocco drawls smirking at Landyn. "Wait, not just network TV. Like late-night reruns from decades ago. You can't keep your hands off each other but it's so fucking syrupy sweet, it gives me a stomach ache."

Landyn gives me a peck on the lips before climbing out of my lap and heading for the door. "That's what happens when you're in love. I need coffee, and then I'm going to make breakfast for everyone."

She looks back with a satisfied smile before leaving me with Rocco. She knows the sooner we get this done, the sooner we'll get out of here for good.

I turn my attention to Rocco and hike a brow. "Are you ready?"

He glances down at his old clothes. "It's why I'm here, right? To be your go-between. My job is to drop the money. No biggie."

I rest my forearms on the desk. "Don't fuck around. Don't even miss a stoplight, Roc. If you see yellow, don't think about hitting the gas. I need you to make the drop and get back here with no altercation."

He rolls his eyes. "I might be a dropout, but I'm a fucking scholar in the school of hard knocks. I know not to roll through a stop light with hundreds of thousands of dollars in the trunk."

I look him up and down. "What's with the cut? You have an entire closet of clothes that won't get you profiled if you get stopped."

"Dude, I'm not going to get stopped. Last time I showed up in my Marino uniform, the club gave me so much shit, I had to think twice about going back. I can't do anything about the haircut, but I can make sure I don't meet my President looking like I just left a polo match."

"I'm just watching out for you. Don't be the dumbass who gets caught with a load of cash in their trunk. I need this drop to happen with no drama."

"Chill, Kingpin. I'm your man."

"Shut the fuck up. I'll let the kingpin comment slide because we have more important things to focus on." I lean back in my seat. "Get in and get out. Do you understand? I don't need you hanging around to shoot the shit. Make the drop and come straight back. It should only take a few hours."

He lifts a shoulder. "I got this. I'll be back in your damn khakis in no time pretending to let Landyn boss me around."

I pull in a breath and hold it too long before exhaling. I barely slept last night. The details are circling my brain like a team of fighter jets looking for the perfect place to drop a bomb.

Because that's exactly what's going to happen tonight. That bomb will fucking obliterate the Marinos and everyone who's ever worked with them.

Carson and Tim are handling it, and things are on track to go off without a hitch. I only know this because I got a text in the middle of the night saying we're still on. That was the plan—a check in once every twenty-four hours unless something goes south.

Going south isn't an option.

I force myself to relax into my chair. "Where are you meeting Logan?"

"Not sure. He said he'd let me know right before I leave."

I tip my head. "Is he jittery?"

"How the hell am I supposed to know? I've never made a money drop, let alone one for a cool half-mil."

"Fair enough. But it's Marino money. I want to know where it's going. That's non-negotiable."

"I'll ask Logan and see what he says."

"He'll understand. If he doesn't, I'll make sure he does. I deserve to know where our down payment is going." And follow the money to assure this thing is going to go down without a hitch, but I don't say that aloud.

Rocco pushes to his feet and stuffs his hands in his front pockets. "I'll do what I can."

"Appreciate you," I tell him the truth, but I also have to lie to him. "When you get back, we're going out. Late dinner. Landyn wants to celebrate you passing the test. I made reservations, and you can't wear your cut."

His brows pinch. "I don't need to celebrate anything."

"Try to explain that to my wife." I've thought this over for days. I have a feeling the way to turn Rocco will be Landyn. I've forced him to be here, but she's the one who's made the real connection.

He shakes his head. "I live here and eat here for free. You forced me to take that test. It's not something I would've done on my own. Why would anyone celebrate that?"

I haven't had an ounce of guilt in this job until I met Landyn.

And, now, Rocco.

I have a feeling he's going to be a harder sell. My conscience has eaten at me. No matter what I've done to make sure he has choices when we get out of here, he's used to being on his own. He might not come around easily.

"You worked hard and accomplished something." I pause for a moment and choose my words carefully. Who knows, maybe he'll remember this moment when he's sitting in an interrogation room, and he learns Boz Torres is a complete lie. "You'll always be rewarded when you work with me. Don't ever forget that."

He fidgets and looks like he's listening to nails on a chalkboard rather than someone praising him. "Whatever."

"Go find Landyn and help her with breakfast," I order. I can't risk saying more.

"Do you know how fucked it is that I've never had anyone tell me what to do until I moved in with the cartel?"

I wave him off and turn back to my computer, but not before I make one last point. "You're a prospect for the Jackals, and you're pissed about me telling you what to do? Think about how fucked that is, Roc."

He has no smartass response for that, so I know I made my point. I need him to remember this in twelve hours when he'll be given a choice to save his own ass.

"Check in before you leave," I call to him as he makes his way out the door.

"Yeah, boss."

I watch him leave and look around the office that's become ground zero for everything I've done since I got here.

It's been a long time. In less than twelve hours, I'm done.

Boz Torres will be no more.

I'm ready to bury him along with every other asshole who'll rot away in prison. Every minute that passes is a ticking time bomb.

I need to get Landyn out safely, but the uphill battle of getting Rocco to flip is a thorn in my side.

The thought of leaving here not knowing who killed Brian makes me feel like a failure.

If I didn't have Landyn, it would all be for nothing. I try to focus on that, because if I haven't figured it out by now, I don't see it happening before we leave for dinner tonight.

35

REALITY

Landyn

After being here all this time, I actually found a book in this house.
Shocker, it's horror fiction.
Not that I'm actually reading it. I'm doing everything I can to pretend to read it.
Today is tedious. After everything I've been through to get to this point, time has never crawled this slow. I have a feeling the next few hours will only get worse.
Rocco just left to make the money drop.
I walked him to the front door. It took all my willpower not to force him to hug me goodbye and promise to be more careful than he's ever been.
I didn't. I'm pretty proud of myself that I was able to keep my cool and act like today isn't life altering.
You know, normal.
I chatted on and on about going to dinner tonight to celebrate his GED. Little does he know, there will be no meal and no festivi-

ties. The night will consist of me freaking out that he won't make the right choice.

After today, I'm taking a huge step, but the choice is all mine. I'm crossing a line—one from being born into a life of crime and greed and being controlled by my father to moving over to the good—a new start with Braxton Cruz. My life will look completely different than it ever has. I cannot wait.

If Rocco doesn't make the right choice, I don't know what I'll do.

I'm proud of myself for holding it together since we got back. I've fought harder to be normal than I ever thought possible.

Normal has never been so hard.

Rocco leaving feels wrong. Our unit is no longer intact.

I'm on my way back to our room to pretend to read my book when I hear Spencer. His loafers quickly click against the marble and echo through the quiet house. He's speaking in Spanish. I might not understand his rushed words, but his tone causes me to still.

Besides a few phrases I pick up on here and there, all I understand is *Señor Torres,* and him agreeing over and over and over with whomever he's speaking to.

Dammit. My fluency in Spanish is a small step above ordering at an authentic restaurant. I regret not trying harder during those classes in high school.

I pause when Spencer's swift gait comes to a stop around the corner. I can't see him, and he has no idea I'm here.

But someone always knows where I am since the damn cameras pick up on everything.

I grip my book and take the steps one at a time, slow and controlled and...

Normal.

But I listen as my bare feet take me silently toward the stairs.

"Sí. No, señor. No entiendo..."

His words speed, and I understand even less than I did before. He's agitated and arguing with whoever is on the other line. So much, his words turn from conciliatory to angry.

Spencer talks on the phone all the time. He manages this house and coordinates with the guards. June and Miranda report to him. He's organized, professional, and kind.

And even though I don't understand ninety percent of what he's saying, something is...

Off.

"Sí, sí. Adiós." Spencer's voice is clipped and agitated, and he doesn't sound like he's actually agreeing with anyone on anything. That's when I hear, "Fuck!"

I hurry for the stairs, but his shoes hit the marble again, and this time he's not efficient or controlled.

Something is wrong.

Gripping my book in my sweaty palms, I turn the corner for the stairs, but that's when I come face to face with the butler who does so much more.

My heart pounds in my chest when I see the agitated expression on his face. The last thing I need is to appear *not* normal.

"Hi," I clip and raise the book two inches. "I'm going to read for a while."

Spencer's eyes narrow a touch, shifting to the back of the house before returning to me. "You should do that in Mr. Torres' office while he works."

Shit. What does that mean? "Okay."

"Go," he demands. "And don't leave his side."

When I take the last step, I forget all about trying to keep my shit together, no matter what I promised government agents in the backroom of a Manhattan bar that I would not do. If only I knew what Spencer was saying.

This isn't nothing. This isn't just me feeling off because Rocco left to deliver the down payment. It's selfish, but I don't want him anywhere near the Jackals. I'm desperate and anxious about the choice he has no clue he'll have to make tonight.

It feels like a marathon by the time I get to the open double doors of the office where Brax is sitting behind the desk frowning at his laptop.

"Hey."

The moment his eyes shift to me, they narrow, but just slightly. No one would see it but me, especially over surveillance. He sits back in his chair and echoes my greeting. "Hey, yourself."

I don't waste another moment. I do what I have done so often since we got back from New York. Hell, I did it when I thought I was Mrs. Boz Torres.

By the time I get to him, he's turned and widened his legs for me. I drop my book to the desk and go straight to him. With one hand on my ass the other snaked around the back of my neck, he pulls me to him when my lips land on his.

My fingers dig into his skin.

He feels it.

I pull my lips away from his to drag them across his jaw to his ear. My words are barely a breath for no one but him to hear. "Something's wrong. It's Spencer. He was talking to someone on the phone in the main hall just now."

Brax is better than me, but he would be. He's a professional and has been doing this for two years.

He fists my hair enough to pull my face from his just enough to look into my eyes. "You're in the mood. Do I need to fuck you before dinner?"

My teeth sink into my bottom lip. For the first time since we've become this, I'm too nervous for him to do anything to me.

But we do need privacy.

All I do is nod.

I stand to move, but he claims my hand tightly as he grabs his cells from the desk where they were sitting in front of him. He never looks away from me as he pulls me to the bedroom. When the sound of the lock clicks on the door, I pull my hand from his and rush straight to the bathroom. The need to distance us from the cameras overwhelms me.

I drag my hands through my hair and turn when he closes the doors behind him. My whispers become desperate with every additional word that tumbles from my lips. "I'm sorry. It's probably nothing. I just couldn't understand what he was saying. He was different, but he didn't see me. I thought I could do this, but every little thing has me freaking out. Then he told me to come to you and not leave your side. Something is wrong."

Brax listens to me, but he's also focused on his cell. He's tapping away at the screen, his focus zeroed in on whatever he's looking at.

"I'm sorry," I repeat. I can't control the tremble in my tone as I pace back and forth in front of him.

The next thing I know, Spencer's voice fills the room. I rush to the phone to see the surveillance of him just a few moments ago when we crossed paths.

I listen, still not understanding anything more than I did a few moments ago.

All I can do is focus on Brax's face. His laser-focused expression is intense as he takes in the words that are foreign to me. Finally, the scene I just witnessed ends as Spencer rushes off down the hall.

"Brax," I whisper even though there's no need to. "Please tell me I'm freaking out for nothing."

He barely has a chance to angle his dark, troubled eyes to mine when his attention is drawn away again. He pulls his second cell from his pocket—the one I now know is his direct line to the CIA and DEA.

He scans the screen.

His frown deepens.

"What is it?" I hiss, my heart speeds frantically to a level unhealthy for any human.

He sets both phones on the counter next to us and claims my face in his big, warm hands as his intense gaze lands heavy on me. "Your father and Ed Decker teamed up. They don't buy the fake-dead-cop story since they didn't hear anything in the news about it when it happened. That and the fact they haven't seen or heard from Nic in days. They suspect me. Alamandos confirmed I was told to bring him in. But, baby, I had orders not to kill him, and now he's missing."

I grip his forearms and squeeze. The need to hold onto him

tighter than ever is overwhelming—like he'll evaporate in front of me, slip through my fingers, and I'll lose him forever.

"They're coming here to get me. They have Alamandos' men with them. Their plan is to take me to Tijuana. Spencer tried to convince them not to come, but it didn't work."

"No." The word is a shallow breath on my dry lips.

He nods once. "Yes. We talked about this. Planned for this."

Tears race down my cheeks.

He swipes them away with his thumbs. "You can do this. I know you can. Get changed. Fast, baby. Cole and Tim are scrambling on their end, but we need to get out of here, and we need to be cool doing it."

It's hard to swallow over the lump in my throat.

He pulls my face to his for the fastest and most desperate kiss, stealing precious time before his tone becomes deep and gritty. I've never heard it before. I'm not sure whether it scares me or makes me feel better. "Love you, chica. I'm going to give you a real life. We just have to do this first."

My head bobs anxiously in his hands as I pull in a labored breath.

I need to get my shit together.

He presses his lips to my forehead. "Go."

Then he releases me. This plan was only for the worst possible scenario.

I prepare for what I never thought would be a reality.

An escape.

36

GO

Brax

She did what she needed to do, and she did it fast. If we make it out of this alive, I plan to remind her how fast she can get ready.

It took us four minutes to change, pack, and make it down the stairs.

With a hand at the small of her back, our feet hit the main floor of the house. It's all I can do not to pick her up and run out the door. Hauling ass through the main gates in one of Damian's cars is not an option. If they called Spencer, my bet is that the guards know too.

Their job is to make sure I don't leave.

"Sir, where are you going?"

I fist the material at Landyn's back that's barely covering her ass. I pull her to my side and look down at her as I turn us to face Spencer. "I have a few hours this afternoon, and the winds are low. We're taking the boat out. No better time."

Sunglasses sit perched on her head. The sheer, oversized shirt leaves nothing to the imagination. The bikini that shows through is the same one I lost my mind over and told her not to wear again.

She's weighed down with an overflowing bag of beach towels. She looks like she's leaving for a day on the water, but instead of a bag full of sunscreen and cocktail shaker, a small armory is hidden inside.

"I've only been begging for this for weeks." Landyn smiles up at me before turning to Spencer. "We'll be back in plenty of time to get ready for dinner."

Spencer's eyes shift between Landyn and me. He stands in the middle of the great room, between us and the terrace. Spencer can't stop me, but the guards could.

"I've been told that you should stay here, Mr. Torres." He turns his gaze directly on me.

Landyn leans into me, and I swear, I feel her heart beating through her chest. Besides that, she's cool and steady. "No way. I've waited long enough. Boz promised, and I'm holding him to it."

Spencer gives us a quick nod. "Of course. I sent June and Miranda out for the afternoon. Can I make you a picnic to send with you?"

"No," I answer, taking him in. Fuck, he wants us to go. "I'm glad you gave them the afternoon off. You should take it too."

He shakes his head. "I have things to manage here. The keys are in the boat. I had it serviced this morning."

"Thank you, Spencer." I drop my arm from Landyn and collect her sweaty hand in mine.

He steps to the side.

We can't waste any more time. My cell that connects me to Cole Carson is going crazy in the pocket of my swim trunks.

I look down at Landyn. "Let's get some sun, baby."

She squeezes my hand tighter than she ever has, but her smile is as light and airy as the weather outside. "I can't wait."

I pull her through Damian Marino's great room to the terrace doors as I slide my shades up my nose. I push her in front of me, but don't say a word as we make our way around the pool and to the back gate.

"Pick up the pace, Landyn."

Her flip flops smack her feet a bit quicker, and I widen my strides as I scan our surroundings.

Getting by Spencer was one thing. He and I share the secret of Nic Decker—a commonality that won him over. But if he sent June and Miranda away, he expects a showdown.

If the guards get orders from Alamandos' men, and we're still here, that's it. There's no way I'll be able to protect Landyn or fight for my own life.

We get to the stairs that take us all the way down to the docks off the back of Damian's property. The cameras can still see us, but they can't pick up audio from here.

"Almost there, baby. You okay?"

She doesn't look away from the steep stairway that leads to the ocean, and this time I hear the anxiety when she mutters, "Uh-huh."

"The second we board, you release the lines. The sooner we're out of sight, the better."

We make it to the last landing of the steep staircase. The sound of the rolling waves gets louder with every step as we approach sea level.

So when we hear a commotion coming from behind us, I know it's really fucking loud.

Cars screech to a halt.

Voices, angry and heated, increase in volume every second that clicks by. I fist the material at Landyn's back and pull her to me as I stop and look up.

She panics. "They're here already?"

I see bodies moving at the top of the cliffs.

"Go, chica. As fast as you can."

My cell vibrates again, and this time I don't ignore it. I'm forced to let her go and stay as close to her back as I can. I put the phone to my ear. "Yeah?"

It's Carson. "They're there. Literally on your ass. Move."

Landyn is running down the steps as fast as she can in those damn shoes. "Almost to the dock."

"It's bad, Cruz," Cole bites. "No one is holding back. They're chatty on the wires. They convinced Alamandos you killed Nic and aren't who you say you are. They're talking about the trip to New York. They think you've turned on them and are working with someone else. I've got the Coast Guard scrambling to get to you. Get on the damn boat and get out—now!"

"Fuck!"

"I'm trying to get satellite eyes on you," Carson clips. "Head north around the point and then out to sea. But not too far—you'll lose your signal and I won't be able to track you."

Landyn hits the landing to the dock, and I'm right behind her.

"There they are!"

I barely look back when I hear the words bellowed from the cliffs above us. All I see are silhouettes in the sun, but I can't make out whose they are.

But I do see guns.

And they're pointed at us.

Landyn has one foot on the stern entrance where the boat has been backed in when the first shot is fired.

She screams and stumbles forward.

"Fuck!" I yell. "Up the stairs and keep your head down."

The Vanquish is an almost sixty feet long yacht. Damian bought it right before I clawed my way into the family. It looks like it belongs on the Mediterranean more than the coast of California. It's the top of the line when it comes to luxury.

But, more importantly, it's fast, which is what we need right now.

He's got a deep-sea fishing boat docked in the next slip, but it hasn't been used since I got here.

More shots rain down from above, ricocheting at our heels.

I push Landyn into the seat at the helm. We're like sitting ducks inside the tempered glass roof and walls that were meant for three-hundred-and-sixty-degree views.

Perfect when you're cruising the ocean, but a fucking nightmare when you're being shot at.

With one turn of the key and push of a button, the monstrosity rumbles to life below us. I turn and look up the cliffs to see five men, two of them are guards who have reported to me for a long fucking time. They make their way down the stairs with their guns drawn, but at least the gunfire has stopped.

I turn back to Landyn's frightened expression and wrap her hand around the throttle. "When I get the lines off the boat, you hit it hard. Steer toward open sea. Do not hesitate."

Her eyes widen, but she nods. I run from what little safety the helm offers and stay low. But I'm out in the open when I get to the bow to release a line from the cleat, and that's when the gunfire starts all over again.

Shit.

It goes high and peppers the water over the bow.

"Brax!" Landyn screams.

I duck below the side rail along the port side where they can't see me to release two more lines.

When I make my way to the other side to release the last ones, they've hit the bottom landing, and there's nowhere for me to hide.

I pull my gun from the back of my shorts and cup the butt of my Glock in my other hand.

I fire three times.

One man drops heavy on the landing, but the rest duck out of my line of fire before I can get them.

I recognize one of the guards' voices when he yells, "Fucking traitor!"

They have no clue. To be a traitor, one has to actually be on your side at some point, which I never fucking was. The fact that they're not calling me a pig tells me they have no clue who or what they're dealing with.

One guy pops up to start firing again, but I let loose.

I empty an entire magazine on them as I run to the last line.

I drop to the deck after I release it and yell, "Go!"

Landyn must be freaked out and scared, but she handles this the way she's handled everything since the first day I laid eyes on her. She does exactly what I told her to do.

She doesn't ease into it. She hits the throttle fucking hard, proving Damian had good taste in his hobbies. Every single horse in the engine jumps out of the gate with all the power money can buy.

I'm thrown into the side of the hull as bullets ping off the side of the yacht and glass shatters.

I scramble. It's all I can do to keep my footing as we take off over the heavy surf, the boat jumps and wracks as we go.

I look over the stern as we take off into the blue and see the four who remain standing board the fishing boat.

Fuck.

I run up the stairs to the helm, broken glass crunching beneath my shoes, and find Landyn white knuckling the controllers. I pull the cell out of my pocket, push it at her, and have to raise my voice to talk above the engine and wind. "Talk to Carson. Tell him there are four in a fishing boat following us. Get the guns."

I take control of the boat as she turns her blue eyes to the California coast. They widen when she sees what I just described.

Fear and panic lace in her expression.

"Brax—"

"Talk to Carson," I demand. "And find me a loaded gun."

Landyn

"They're following us!" I yell as Brax takes over.

"Guns, chica. Get me a fucking gun."

I grip the railing with one hand to hold on for dear life and put the cell to my ear with the other. "Cole?"

"Landyn." His tone is not at all cocky or chipper the way it was when I met him in New York. "I'm tracking you through the cell. The Coast Guard is on their way."

"They're following us." The words rush out of my mouth as I run down the stairs to where I dropped the bag of towels and guns when they started shooting at us. "They're in the other boat."

I tumble to my ass when the boat jumps over a huge breaker. I scream and drop the cell. It slides across the deck. I have to crawl on my hands and knees to get it.

"Cole? Are you still there?"

"Here. How many are on the other boat?"

I pull myself to my feet, but scream when I hear gunfire.

I drop back to the floor. "I don't know. I think there were three standing in the front. Cole, make them hurry! They're shooting at us."

That's when I spot what I need. The bag slid under a dining table. I crawl and reach for the handle to drag it back to the stairs.

"What's happening, Landyn?" Cole demands.

The boat veers left and right, and I'm thrown into the side of the narrow stairway. My voice is desperate and sounds like I just sprinted a 5k. "I'm trying to get back to Brax. He needs a gun."

"Hurry, Landyn. He's got to keep them off your tail. The Coast Guard is on their way, but there's at least three miles between you."

Three miles? It might as well be thirty. I throw myself at the top of the stairs and turn the corner where Brax is steering the boat back and forth to avoid gunfire while looking over his shoulder. "Cole said the Coast Guard is still three miles from us."

"Shit," Brax hisses.

The sun peeks through bullet holes in the glass canopy. A side window is littered at our feet in shards. I drop the cell in a cup holder and dig through the bag for the guns where I packed them haphazardly before escaping Damian's house.

I hold out two handguns to Brax, but he only takes one. "Aim and shoot. Anywhere in their vicinity."

My eyes widen. "What? I don't know how to shoot."

He looks from the fishing boat to me and bites, "It's shoot or drive."

I almost topple over sideways when we bounce over another wave. "No. I don't want to drive."

"Point and shoot. That's all you have to do."

I nod and move to a sofa that's open to the outside. Wind whips my hair around my face. There's no way I could aim at the biggest target with the boat jerking around, so I do what he says. I steady it in both hands, point, and squeeze.

The machine in my hand fires.

The powerful discharge rocks through my body.

"No, baby. Unload on those fuckers," Brax shouts over the wind, waves, and engine.

I turn back and see they're keeping up with us.

Shit.

I grip the gun tighter and steady myself as best I can. Then I do what Brax told me to do.

I shoot.

Like really shoot.

Their guns are bigger. The long barrels are pointed at us from the bow of the fishing boat. The water behind us is littered with bullets, but the fishing boat starts to weave just like Brax is doing.

"Good," Brax yells for me as I feel the yacht increase in speed. "Keep going."

I nod and turn back.

I keep shooting until I hear an empty click.

"Dammit," I mutter and reach for the bag.

"Get down," Brax demands.

The moment I scrunch to my feet, Brax keeps one hand on the steering column and extends his other over my head.

His shots aren't defensive, random, or chaotic. He's intense and deliberate. His dark eyes narrow as he aims. His muscled arm flexes and tenses as he squeezes the trigger and fires out the back of the boat.

Over and over and over.

When he empties his pistol, he drops the weapon in the chair behind him and turns back to the open water in front of us.

I peek over the sofa, and the fishing boat has swerved to the side. One man is hanging over the bow of the boat with another trying to pull him back.

But the gunfire has stopped.

I turn to find Brax's stare heavy on me. He exhales a breath so deep I sense the anxiety leave his body.

I scramble off the sofa and move to him as we race across the open seas in Damian's yacht. He turns back to watch where we're going as the land has all but disappeared on the horizon and picks up the phone. "You still there?"

I can't hear what Cole says on the other side, but Brax looks down at me when I slide between him and the helm to wrap my arms around him. "Yeah, we're okay." He pauses two beats before I feel his entire body go taut. "Please tell me that's the Coast Guard barreling at us."

I crane my neck around and see two boats speeding straight for us. "Is that them?"

Brax pulls back on the throttle, and the boat instantly slows. He presses his lips to the top of my head. "Yeah, baby. That's them."

One boat speeds past us toward the fishing boat that has now completely turned around. The other slows as a voice comes over the speakers. "Turn off the engine. We're taking control of your vessel."

Brax reaches around me to switch a few knobs and levers. The rumble of the smooth engine that saved us comes to a halt.

I exhale, allowing all the tension in my body to dissipate completely... maybe for the first time since we got back from New York. I sink into Brax and never want to let him go.

He pushes me away just far enough to claim my face for a bruising kiss.

I'm not the only one with pent up anxiety.

When his tongue plunges into my mouth, the world melts away. Adrenaline laced with lust is an intoxicating cocktail. But when you throw in a shot of freedom, life feels new and fresh. Like it's turned on an axis in a matter of one life-or-death boat chase.

"Special Agent Braxton Cruz?"

Brax presses his lips to mine firmly before pulling away just enough to tip his forehead to mine. He looks straight into my eyes when he answers, "That's me."

"The CIA is looking for you."

I turn to the five men staring us down. They tied their boat to ours and four of them board.

Brax finally tears himself from me and holds his hands out. "There are empty guns here in the helm and more that are loaded in the bag. She held them off. I think I took down two in the chase before they gave up and turned back."

When Brax turns, my heart clenches. "You're bleeding!"

His white polo is stained red at the shoulder. He's been shot. I hadn't noticed with all that was going on. The love of my life doesn't move, and the officers don't seem to be worried about the blood. Two of them head below deck and the other two stay with us.

I try to go to him, but one of the men holds me off and speaks to Brax. "You know I've got to frisk you. It's procedure. I've got two federal agencies on my ass who are anxious to get you back, so let's get this done."

Brax gives him a chin lift and ignores his bloody shoulder. He turns a one-eighty as they make sure he's unarmed. Another officer holding a long gun looks me up and down, and mutters, "I'm pretty sure she's good. There's nowhere for her to hide anything in that ... get up."

I ignore him and finally get to Brax. I peel up his blood-soaked sleeve and look up at him. "You were shot."

He looks down at his shoulder. "I was grazed. Trust me, I've been shot before. I know the difference."

I try to breathe a sigh of relief but can't. I ignore the Coast Guard and Brax's bloody graze that would have me in fits at any other time. Now that we're out of Marino territory for good, I ask what I haven't had the time to focus on, but it doesn't mean I haven't thought about him every second since I heard Spencer on the phone.

"Brax, what's going to happen to Rocco?"

37

DÉJÀ-FUCKING-VU

Brax

"Déjà-fucking-vu," Carson booms when he enters the room.

Landyn is tucked under one arm glued to my side as an ER doctor stitches up my other shoulder.

I press my lips to Landyn's forehead before looking up to the CIA officer. "It was a graze."

"It takes a lucky fucker to know one. And you, my friend, should run straight to Vegas. I heard the whole thing. There were more bullets flying out there than monkeys in a Broadway musical. I'm afraid the sea life population took a hit during that chase."

I look up at Carson. "It wasn't as bad as the church on our wedding day."

"Did you tell your bride that when we met I was in your exact position getting stitched up in the middle of maple syrup country from my own graze?"

"Really?" Landyn asks.

I try not to roll my eyes. "If I remember correctly, they had to cut your pants off and you were the only man in the room in his underwear. I've at least kept my dignity."

Carson holds his arms out low. "Who wouldn't want to see me in my underwear? It's a gift and a privilege. You're welcome."

I'm not the only one who wants to get on with things, because Landyn asks, "Where is Rocco?"

Carson finally gets down to business and crosses his arms. "Your boy is in custody."

I can feel Landyn's freakout coming when she exclaims, "What?"

I hold her to me even though she tries to pull away. "This is a good thing."

"How is that a good thing?"

I focus on her worried blue eyes and try to calm her down. "Because it's the safest place for him right now. We don't need him to go back to Damian's or incriminate himself with the club."

She bites her lip, glances at Carson, and then back to me. "And Spencer?"

I pull in a breath and don't want to say too much here in an unprotected area. "Spencer is complicated."

That's when Micah enters the ER. "Are you about done? You both need to debrief, and we need to monitor the situation. The wire room went dead. As soon as we cut off communication, the cartel stopped talking. We're flying blind. I've got cars waiting outside to take us to the San Diego Division."

I look down at my left shoulder as the doctor snips what looks to be the last stitch. He sets down his tools and rolls back on his stool. "You're done. Keep it clean. No swimming or baths. We'll give you some ointment to take with you."

"Can I get a shirt?" I ask.

The doc stands and moves to the door. "I'll have the nurse get you some scrubs."

"Cute," Carson jibes. "You two will match."

The first thing I did when we got here was demand some clothes for Landyn. She might still be wearing that bikini underneath, but she looks like a hospital orderly in a set of scrubs that hang on her small frame. I don't have the mental capacity for her to be waltzing around in that see-through shirt that couldn't net fish if it had to.

I stand and collect her hand. "Let's go. I'll show you what it's like to be on the other side for a change."

I hold onto her tightly. We've been living in an alternate reality—a parallel universe. We made it to the other side. In all we've been through, we haven't talked about what's next. Where we go from here.

Hell, all we have is what's on our backs. We left with only a bag of towels and guns.

I've got to get us through today and figure out what's next.

Landyn

"We've cut off Alamandos' communication to most of his counterparts in the U.S. His teams are waiting for the load to cross the border. Damian's home is being seized as we speak. This isn't ideal since the product hasn't left Mexico yet, but we couldn't wait after the boat chase. At least you were the sole contact between the Marinos and the Jackals. The product is on the move, and Alamandos can't do shit about it." Tim's eyes shift to me as I stand next to Brax in my oversized scrubs. "Edward Decker and your father have been taken into custody. Their assets are frozen. The scene wasn't pretty."

I exhale.

And all eyes in the room follow Tim's to land on me.

I cross my arms and shrug. "What? Do you think I'm going to be upset about that after what he did to me?"

Carson glances at the men before turning to me. "Would you

be willing to testify to that? Human trafficking on top of everything else we have on your father would really put a nail in his coffin."

I only have to think about that for a moment. "If it helps to make sure he'll pay for everything he's done, then yes. I'll do whatever it takes."

Brax gives me a squeeze. "I'll be by your side the whole time."

"I just wanted to let you know." Tim pulls in a big breath after bringing us up to speed. "Rocco Monroe is here in the holding cell. We need to figure out what to do with him. His deal is already drawn up by the U.S. Attorney if he tells us everything he knows about the Jackals."

We've been here for all of ten minutes. The DEA San Diego Division is big, and we caused a stir coming in. Apparently, it's not common for DEA agents to work with the CIA. Brax looked more like a rock star as they shuffled us down the hall to this conference room. An American flag stands in the corner next to a picture of the President of the United States and the Administrator of the DEA. The only reason I know that is because I read the nameplate. I've never seen her or heard of her in my life.

"What does Rocco know?" Brax asks.

"Nothing," Micah says. "Other than the fact he's in deep shit. He's trying not to act like he's freaking the fuck out, but he is. I'm sure that's nothing compared to how he'll respond when he sees you."

"What about Spencer?" Brax bites and looks around the room. "He did everything he could to keep them from coming to the house. I told you this week I wanted a deal drawn up for him too."

Carson and Tim glance at one another, but it's Carson who says, "He's not a citizen and is here illegally. They're taking him into custody, because he was there. You need to be prepared for what could happen. I doubt he'll be charged, but it is likely he'll be deported. The Marinos didn't hire anyone with a visa or any U.S. citizens. It was their way to keep them loyal. They were threatened that they'd be turned over. They knew it was their ticket to staying quietly in the country. It was both their protection and their penitentiary."

I look up at the man who saved me from a life of abuse and misery. Everything about him bleeds good and just. And right now, his expression says it all. He's ready to dig his heels in and fight.

He turns to Carson and raises his voice. "I don't give a shit if you have to charm your way into the West Wing. Give Spencer a chance to turn and make it worth his while. We're standing here because of him instead of in the trunk of a car headed to be tortured just like my brother. I'll sign Spencer up as an informant, or you make him an asset. Backdate the damn papers, dammit. But make it happen."

"For June and Miranda too," I add, even though I'm in no position to be making demands or pleas for anything.

"Miranda is a victim," Brax adds. "I can attest to that, so she'd better be treated like one. And June has as much shit on Damian as Spencer. If you give her an offer in exchange for her testimony, I bet she'll take it. Miranda will follow whatever June does."

Carson answers immediately. "This isn't my decision, Cruz. You think I want them sent back? I've been listening to them the whole time you've been under. I'm going to do what I can, but I can't make any promises."

"I've given two years of my life to this. Uncle Sam can't pick and choose when to believe me. I've gotten this far, and I'll vouch for all three of them. Now I've got to go in that room and convince Rocco Monroe I'm not the bad guy for lying to him."

"It's not like he's got options," Micah points out. "The Jackals will be no more after today."

"We can only hope," Tim says.

I turn to Brax. "Can I talk to him?"

Micah butts in. "No way."

Brax wraps an arm around my shoulders and pulls me to his side. "Maybe."

"Are you kidding me?" Micah bites. "She has no business

inside an interrogation room unless she's the one being grilled. And that's not out of the question given who her father is."

Brax spears Micah with a glare. "No one is interrogating her but me."

"That's my boy," Carson quips.

Brax puts a hand to my chin and forces my face to his. "Let me talk to him. It's important that I'm the first face he sees since I was the one who forced him to live with us. I need to convince him to take the deal. He'll be angry. I don't want him taking that out on you."

"I don't feel good about this. I don't think he'll take the deal," I say. "He's never trusted anyone. No one has ever earned that from him. He's got to be scared, and when he sees you, he'll be so angry."

Just like always, Brax is resolute. "I can take it. This is nothing compared to bullshitting my way through a cartel for two years."

"Come with me," Micah says. "You can be a fly on the wall and watch."

I purse my lips, not wanting to go anywhere with Micah after our moment in the bathroom.

Brax is about to say something, but his friend puts a hand up to stop him. "I get it. You're in love with the mobster's daughter, and she's nothing like her father. I don't need to save you from yourself, and I'm back to being the guy who has your back no matter what."

Brax narrows his eyes. "You'd better be."

Carson looks from his cell to the group. "As much as I love a good bromance, we need to find out what we can from Monroe. The load should surface from the tunnel soon. Our teams are ready."

I turn back to Brax. "You have to convince him. I don't think he knows anymore about the club than what he's already told us. He has to come around. There's no other option."

"Ultimatums while you're still in the honeymoon phase," Carson says. "I like a strong woman. Nicely done, Landyn."

I turn to Micah. "Let's go. I want to watch."

We all head out the door, but not before Brax turns to Micah and warns, "Do not let her barge into the room."

Well.

It might come to that if Brax doesn't convince Rocco to step away from the dark side.

We're a unit. I'm not moving on until we save Rocco.

38

CHOOSE GOOD

Brax

"What the fuck?"

I ignore that and shut the door behind me. Rocco's expression morphs from shock to something deeper and darker when I move to the table and pull out the chair across from him. Metal scraping across the floor echoes through the room as confusion settles in his features.

The eighteen-year-old pushes to his feet. "What the hell's going on?"

I put a hand up, if for no other reason there's a decent chance he might come across the table at me. "We need to talk."

"What are you doing here?" he demands. His gaze shoots around the room before it travels the length of me, taking in the scrubs I'm wearing. "What happened to you?"

"I was grazed." I point to the table. "Sit."

His eyes widen. "You were shot? Where's Landyn?"

"I'm fine. Landyn is fine. I'll explain everything if you sit down and take a breath."

He falls to his ass but leans forward and lowers his voice to a hissed whisper. "They said I rolled through a stop sign, but I didn't. I did every fucking thing right, just like you told me to do. Then they arrested me because of some issue with the registration on the car. I call bullshit. Tell me you got a lawyer coming. I'm freaking the fuck out, boss."

"Calm down." I take a moment as he sits back in his chair almost violently. "We need to talk, and I need you to keep an open mind."

"How did you get in here? This is the fucking DEA, and the only reason I know that is because I caught sight of the sign before they brought me in the back through the parking garage. The DE-fucking-A, and you want me to calm down?"

I sit back and tip my head.

He pauses a moment, and his eyes widen.

Well, now.

I think he's finally getting it.

"No," he grits.

I start to fold my arms across my chest until it pulls at my stitches. That's going to suck for the next few days.

"Let me fill you in." I glance at my watch. "In the next thirty minutes, the Jackals will surface on this side of the border with one of the biggest loads the Marinos have ever tried to transport. But that load will never make it to the streets. It'll be taken down by federal agents."

He shakes his head and stares at me like I'm a stranger. "No. No fucking way. I don't believe it."

"Believe it."

He doesn't stop shaking his head as his fingers dig violently through his hair. "You're a cop?"

"You weren't arrested. You were taken into custody for your own safety. Damian's house is being searched as we speak."

The blood drains from his face. "You set me up."

I shake my head. "I didn't."

"You fucking set me up. You lied to me and used me," he seethes. "When the club finds out about this, they're going to kill me." He stands, and his words boomerang off the walls. "They're going to fucking kill me, Boz! That's after I get out of prison."

"No one is going to kill you, and you're not going to prison. At least not for anything you did while you were with me." I stay planted in my seat as he freaks out.

"You have no fucking idea. They're going to think I worked for you." His eyes narrow. "I'm no narc. Hell, they'll probably have me killed in prison."

"Sit down, Roc, and listen. You have options."

"Get the fuck out of my face, you lying sack of shit. I'm not listening to anything you say. I want a lawyer. I get one—I know I do. It's my right or some shit. Get the fuck away from me."

I lean back in my chair and don't move. "My name isn't Boz. It's Brax. And you don't need an attorney because you haven't done anything wrong. You have options—I made sure of it."

"I don't have options. Someone like me never does. By you pulling me into that fucking house and making me work for you, you made sure of it. No one will trust me ever again."

He finally sits. His elbows go to his knees, and his face falls to his hands.

"I can see where you think you have no options, but you do. What do you think would have happened to you if you stayed with the club? You'd be busted for drug possession, distribution, and any number of things the U.S. Attorney feels like throwing at you. When all is said and done, you can add money laundering to that list, and if I did my job right, club members will also be hit with RICO charges." His head pops up and widened eyes stare at me from across the table. "Trust me, you have choices. If you're smart, you'll walk away a free man."

"You lied to me. Why should I believe anything you say? You're probably setting me up again. Using me to get to my club."

"The club will be no more after today."

He shakes his head. "That's what you think. They're powerful. Someone will find me. I know they will."

"If you cooperate, you're a free man. I'll personally make sure you walk away from this. I'll make sure you're safe."

"You can't do that." He juts an arm between us showcasing the half-tat that proves he tried to tie himself to the Jackals. "This means something. I can't go back."

"It's a tattoo. It doesn't mean shit unless you make it mean something. You can also make it mean nothing and start a new life."

"How am I supposed to cooperate?" he spits. "This tattoo was still healing when they sent me to mow your fucking yard. Then you made the deal and made me stay there. I have nothing to offer, even if I did trust you, which I don't. I'll never fucking trust you again."

"Let me help you."

"Why the fuck do you want to help me?"

I mull that over, because I know my answer is important. I knew this wasn't going to be easy or quick. "I've been working the case on the Marinos for two years. I have backgrounds on everyone I met, including you. When I read yours, I saw a kid who had just turned eighteen and made a shit decision because he had no other options. I can't make you do shit, but I can make sure you have a second chance. What you do with it is up to you."

His jaw goes hard.

I lean forward and rest my forearms on the table. "You got your GED. Do something with your life that doesn't include anyone controlling you—especially a club. Make your own way. I'll help you if you let me."

He repeats his question, and this time it's laced with venom. "What do you get out of helping someone like me?"

"Do you think the Jackals give a shit about you? They don't. And no one else has your back." I jut my thumb into my chest. "I had your back, Roc. I also know how much of a difference it can make when someone supports you. I was lucky enough to have that, and I'm trying to pass it on to you. Don't shit all over an opportunity like this."

"You're a cop and you lied to me," he seethes.

"Get over it. I am a federal agent, but I'm also the man who made sure you came out of this squeaky clean instead of in handcuffs when everyone else who wears that tat will. If you don't trust me after that, then you're proving to make one shit decision after the other."

His anger has dissolved into something else as he goes silent. I betrayed him. Knowing his background, it's unfortunately something he's used to.

"Give me a chance to prove to you that I can make a difference. Do it for your future self. In a world of bad, choose good. Do you want to be on the wrong side of the law for the rest of your life?"

His jaw goes hard. If looks could kill, I'd be on my way to six feet under.

"We can hold you for twenty-four hours. We'll make sure you have everything you need. You can be pissed at me all you want, but you need to cool off and think with a clear head. Use the time, Roc. Think hard about the possibilities—the good and the bad. Because both are fucking extreme. Think about your time at the house. Think hard, Rocco. You know me. I'm the one who had your back." I stand and go to the door, but stop and turn back one last time. "Just so you know, you'll break Landyn's heart if you don't choose well."

That gets his attention. "She's in on this too?"

I shake my head. "No fucking way. She's a victim of bad just like you are. She had no idea what was going on until we went to New York. But she's all in now. As soon as this case is wrapped up, she's coming with me. She's just as much mine as she's always been."

He sits back and crosses his arms. "Do you know how fucked up this is? Just for your information, I hate cops."

I shrug. "You were raised to hate cops—it's time to act like a man and think for yourself. You didn't hate me yesterday. I'm the same man I've always been. I can prove it to you if you let me. But I'll leave you with this: I'm going to be pissed if you hurt Landyn. Her goal is to have you in our lives. My goal is to give her everything she wants."

He rolls his eyes.

"In a world of bad, choose good." I open the door. "You've got twenty-four hours. Use them wisely."

The last thing I see are his betrayed eyes before I shut the door on him.

I walk to the neighboring room. Landyn is standing in front of the one-way window staring at Rocco. Tears stain her face, but she doesn't look away until two agents show him out.

Micah, Tim, and Cole stand behind her, but I don't look at any of them. "Chica."

She turns to me and swipes her tears away. "I don't think he's going to choose us."

I hold my hand out and she comes straight into my arms. I dip a hand into her hair and hold her to me. "He might come around."

She nods where her cheek is pressed to my chest, but I don't think she believes it. Hell, I don't have much hope that he won't go the wrong way either. But for her, I'm determined to do everything I can to convince him.

I look over her head to the men. "Let's get to the wire room. I worked and sacrificed for two years for this. I want to hear it go down live."

39

GONE

Landyn

I feel it before I have a chance to open my eyes.
    His fingers slide through my bare sex as his tongue swipes my neck.

We didn't get to our hotel room until the early morning hours. Teams of DEA agents were busy into the night. What was planned to go down early this morning, was kicked into gear a day early thanks to my father and Ed Decker trying to come after Brax.

The shipment was confiscated as soon as every kilo hit American soil. Every Jackal in sight was taken into custody. Their compound was raided, as were all of Ed Decker's properties.

So was my childhood home.

There are still a few stray Jackals on the run who weren't helping transport at the scene. But they still have federal warrants—namely the president, Logan Pritchett. He apparently doesn't like to get his hands dirty. Brax said this isn't unusual and hopes to officially charge him since his rap sheet is a mile long.

Alamandos Marino, on the other hand, has gone missing in Mexico. Every tap the CIA had on his organization has gone dead.

Their direct source to him was Brax when he was acting as Boz, and that's no more. He's a ghost and will likely not come up for air soon. He's not a threat to us here in the States with his organization in shambles—at least that's what Brax says.

Even the Marino distributors on the east coast were taken into custody last night.

Brax and I have only been out from under the oppression of the Marinos for less than twenty-four hours, and I've never felt more at peace than I do right now.

My eyes open to our new surroundings when Brax's voice hits me low and gravely from sleep. "Baby, we need to talk."

I part my legs farther for him. "Do we?"

He presses his long, hard cock into my ass cheeks as he spoons me. We checked into the hotel last night, took a shower, and fell into bed—naked and exhausted.

I don't know what time it is, but Brax is officially rested. The proof is long and hard and ready for me. "We need to talk about what's next."

I exhale with a little moan when he slides a finger inside me. "I thought we already moved onto *next*. What else is there to talk about?"

"I'm assigned to the New York City Division office," he mutters against my skin before he nips my earlobe. "I have a place in Queens. You live here."

I don't know what to say to that. My heart skips a beat, and it has nothing to do with the heat he's creating between my legs. The only thing I do is wrap my hand around his free one that's angled up my body and splayed across my chest. I hold on tight in anticipation of what he's doing to my body and my heart.

He keeps talking. "Before your dad delivered you up to the Marinos, you had a life here. I need to know how anxious you are to return to it."

My job as a stylist at a department store was fun and something to do. It also feels like forever ago—another lifetime. That woman is a stranger to me.

I arch my back to press my bottom into his cock and push my

head to his shoulder. "I doubt I have a job after not showing up for all this time. I want nothing to do with my parents. If you're in New York, there's nothing left for me here."

His hands still on me for one moment before he cups my sex. Then he pulls away just enough to angle his hips and fills me in one firm thrust. His fingers part and his hand dips deeper between my legs, feeling our union.

"Does it make me an asshole for being fucking thrilled there's nothing here for you?"

I wrap my hand around his between my legs to hold him to me. "Does it make me needy and desperate for wanting you to take me with you wherever you go?"

He presses into me harder. I wonder if he's as desperate as I am. "That proves it."

Brax rips his hand from beneath mine. He claims my fingers and brings them between my legs. All of a sudden, he's puppeteering me, using the pads of my fingertips to work my own clit.

"What does that prove?" I ask.

He turns his face to the side of mine as he takes me from behind. "That you were made for me."

Oh, yes.

I feel that down to my toes. But I can't form the words to agree. My breaths are shallow and desperate as I try to move my hips. I want to come on his cock.

"Brax," I beg and try to circle my clit faster, but he won't let me. He proves he owns my heart and my body, controlling me with my own touch. "Please."

"We're going to come together, chica. Are you going to milk my cock the way you were made to? Your sweet pussy wants me, and your body wants my cum. It's begging for it, and there's nothing in the world I want more than to give it to you. Every time we're like this I think about what it means. What could be happening as we speak. I love you more every time we're together."

I move as much as he'll let me. "Take me with you. I'll follow you anywhere. I love you and don't want anything but this."

"Love you so much it hurts," he growls. "You're like heaven. Don't ever take this away from me. I might've survived the cartel, but I won't survive losing you."

His hips move faster. He loses all sense of rhythm, proving his desperation runs as deep as mine. Finally, his hold on my fingers eases, and together, we work my clit. I move on his cock and under my own fingers, loving every moment. Being surrounded by him and losing myself in what we've become together.

He pounds harder, our bodies sweaty and breaths shallow. My orgasm creeps in, and I try to still my fingers, but he doesn't let me. He circles my clit faster, pushing me to a higher cliff. My gasps and moans are not quiet. They're frantic—even eager—and I ride my orgasm longer than normal with him thrusting inside me.

He's right—my body wants everything about him. I feel myself spasm with him inside me. He thrusts even harder, his beautiful, strong body using all its strength to take me.

This is all mine. If he didn't just insist that I return to New York with him, I would've chased him to the ends of the earth.

He slams into me one last time on a growl when he comes. His heart pounds through his chest, keeping up with the pace of mine. We have to work to steady our breathing and don't move.

We relish in each other—connected and silent. I think about what's to come—what's set in stone and what's still unresolved.

Brax and I ... there's no doubt.

Rocco ... I don't have a good feeling about him.

"I'll do everything I can to make it a home for you, baby. Make you happier than you've ever been. I'm just an agent ... I might not be able to give you the lavish life that a mobster would, but you'll be loved like never before."

I turn my head to him. "You won't have to work hard. I'm happier than I've ever been. Any future with you is a perfect one."

He presses his lips to my temple. "We're going soon. My mom will be home from the hospital any day. I want to be there to help her and let you get to know my family."

I shift my hips to pull off his semi-hard cock and listen to him groan when I do. But I don't roll away from him. I turn in his arms and look into his dark eyes through the shadowed, generic hotel room. "You never found out who killed Brian."

He lets out a frustrated breath. "No."

I trace his square, stubbled jaw with the tip of my finger. "Is there a chance you still could?"

He shakes his head, and his eyes are filled with regret. "No. I found out too late that it was an initiation and ran out of time."

"I'm sorry," I whisper. "I know how important that was to you."

"It was. A year ago, the thought of leaving there without knowing who took Brian from us would have done me in." His fingers brush the hair from my face and his dark eyes roam my features. "But I'm okay now. My work will put a lot of people in prison. A shit ton of drugs won't touch the streets. And if Carson does his thing, the Marino Cartel will be no more. We also got the Jackals, the Deckers," he pauses, "and your father."

"It's all a tribute to your brother."

He shakes his head. "That's not why I'm at peace with it. The only reason I can sleep at night is because of you."

I blink. "Me?"

"In the end, I got you. I might've lost my brother who was more like a father after I lost my own, but I ended up with you. Brian would want me to be at peace, and be happy with you."

He leans in and takes my mouth for a slow, deep kiss—morning breath and all. Tears sting my senses. I hang onto his bare body and ignore the fact he's leaking from me.

When he lets go of my mouth, he tips his forehead to mine. "You're coming home with me."

I give him a small smile and try not to be sad about him not finding out who killed Brian. "Try to keep me away. When do we leave?"

"The day after tomorrow. I'll be writing reports on this case for weeks. I can do that from New York. I'll have to come back for court, but that won't be for a while."

I catch my lip between my teeth and admit, "My father's attorney is a shark, Brax. He's gotten him out of one predicament after another my entire life."

He rolls to his back and pulls me with him, framing my face with his big hands. "You let me worry about your father. You don't even need to testify to the deal he made with the Marinos if you don't want to. We have the whole thing recorded. He might as well be testifying against himself."

I'm steadfast in my answer. "I'm more than happy to testify against him. I want to, Brax."

He pulls me in for a soft kiss. "You can always change your mind. You might feel differently when the time comes."

"Can I go home before we leave? I have nothing besides the few things Micah brought us from Damian's house last night. That will only last me a few days, and I hate wearing the clothes that were purchased by Damian."

"I think I can make that happen."

"Thank you."

A slow smile creeps over his face.

"What?" I ask.

"I'm bringing you home with me. After the last two years, it's hard to believe. I can't wait."

I smile. "I can't wait either. But we're making a mess. You're leaking out of me."

"I love you messy. I'm tempted to see just how messy I can make you, but we need to get to the office. Go get in the shower—I'll clean you up."

"Yes. Rocco's twenty-four hours will be up soon. I want to be the one to talk to him."

"You know, it's not customary for non-law enforcement to question people we detain."

"Oh, I'm not going to question anyone." I say as I lean down to kiss him fast before climbing out of bed. "I plan to talk some sense into him."

Brax

"Wait. He's gone? We didn't have to release him until later this afternoon. What the hell happened?" I demand.

I look between Carson, Tim, and Micah, but it's Micah who says, "I drove you here. I know as much as you do."

Tim drags a frustrated hand down his face. "It was an oversight. We arrested over a hundred people yesterday. He was not on the list for questioning or charges. The U.S. Attorney didn't know about your pet projects. Agents were told first thing this morning to release him before we got here."

"Brax," Landyn whispers. "You have to find him."

Carson crosses his arms and rocks back on his heels. "He won't be found if he doesn't want to be."

Landyn frowns at the CIA officer. "You don't know that. I was going to talk to him and convince him to go to New York with us."

"Sorry." Carson winces. "I just hope he watches his back. There are still Jackals with outstanding arrest warrants. News tends to break when there's a boat chase and shootout off the coast of California—Brax's cover is blown. The world knows Boz Torres was really a fed working undercover. The DEA's takedown is headlining every news outlet in the country. We know from questioning the Jackals we arrested that they think Rocco flipped and was working for you. He'll be in deep shit if they don't kill him first."

Landyn's gaze shoots to me as fear laces her features. I pull her to my side and glare at Carson. "You're not helping."

Carson glares back at me. "What? She was tough enough to go back and immerse herself into the Marino Cartel after you told her the truth. There's no time to tiptoe through the tulips. We need to find Rocco before the Jackals do."

Tim crosses his arms. "He's right. And unless Rocco plans to run for Canada, we should assume the remaining Jackals are looking for him too. The agents returned Rocco's possessions to him, including his cell. We need to ping it."

"I need an emergency order on that ping and an updated

status on Logan Pritchett. Rocco is pissed and hot-headed. Not a good combination when the Jackals and Uncle Sam are looking for you at the same time."

"Give me your phone," Landyn demands. "I know he won't answer, but I can bombard him with voicemails and texts so he'll know it's me. I can't wait to have my own phone again."

I hand her my cell. "This couldn't have happened at a worse time. I just booked our flights for New York. We could stay longer, but I'll feel better having you there while everything settles here. At some point, your father will be out on bail. You were the center of attention from every organized crime group on both sides of the border. I promised you freedom, but I can't give you that here and know that you're safe. Putting an entire country between you and Dennis Alba will make me feel better."

Landyn purses her lips into a tense line and gives her head a little nod. "I know. But I can't imagine leaving here without at least trying to talk to him. He's got no one, Brax. You know that."

"We'll do everything we can to find him," I promise her.

"Onto your next project," Cole says. "I have deals drawn up for Spencer, June, and Miranda."

"Did they give me what I want?" I ask.

Carson widens his eyes and lets out a low whistle. "Gotta say, I'm shocked. I've never seen anything like this before. You didn't just reach for the sky, you asked for the stars and the moon."

"But did they do it?" I demand. He's not lying. I asked for a shit ton, but those three deserve every single thing I asked for and more.

Carson tips his head. "Evidently, there are some in Washington who think you walk on water after what you were capable of pulling off. If you would've asked for Taylor Swift to deliver the deals, you probably would've gotten it."

"No shit," I mutter.

"None of the shit, that's for sure," Carson quips. "June and Miranda have signed. We figured they would. I told the U.S. attorney you wanted to be the one to talk to Spencer. Word is, he's nervous. You should put him out of his misery."

I check the time and turn back to Landyn. "I was going to take you by your house to pack your things after you talked to Rocco. I wanted to do that before your dad has the chance to get out on bail, but that's going to have to wait."

"I can take her," Micah offers.

I narrow my eyes. "Do you want me to punch you in the face again?"

Micah shakes his head and holds his arms out low. "How was I supposed to know she's the real thing?"

I look down at Landyn. "What do you want to do?"

She's typing away on my cell. "I'm not going anywhere until I know where Rocco is. I just sent him about two-thousand texts begging him to come back or at least call me. Let me leave him a voicemail and see if he calls back. We can always go later."

I turn to the group. "Let's get the ping going on his cell. I'll talk to Spencer. But I'm not taking you back to your house if your dad gets out on bail. There's no way you're getting anywhere near him."

Her blue eyes angle to mine. Until now, I had no idea anyone could bring me to my knees with just a glance. "Please, Brax. I can't leave not knowing where he is. I'm so worried."

I pull in a deep breath. "Okay. But we're not putting it off much longer."

"It's official: Brax Cruz is officially a whipped man. Welcome to the club," Carson announces.

I frown. "Get the fucking ping running and find him before the Jackals do."

"We're on it. I'll have them bring Spencer to a room for you too," Tim says and stalks out.

Carson follows, but not before he winks at me and nods approvingly.

Freak.

"I'll hang with Landyn," Micah says. "Kiss her ass and stuff, for what happened in New York."

Landyn holds up a finger as she leaves a voicemail. "Rocco, it's

Landyn. Look, you have to come back. At least call me—let me explain. I'm so worried about you. Please call."

"Keep the phone, just in case," I say. "Stay with Micah while I talk to Spencer."

"Come on," Micah says. "I'll buy you a cup of coffee."

40

OFFER

Brax

I'm waiting when the door opens.

Spencer is wearing the same clothes from yesterday when he spoke in code to urge us out of the house.

He pauses for a moment to stare at me, but then moves across the table.

Ever the professional and gentleman, just like he has been for the two years we worked around each other. I was the liar about my job and true identity.

Spencer sits, and I look up at the agents. "Thanks. I'll take it from here."

"We'll be in the next room. Just say the word."

I look back at the man across from me but speak to the agents. "I appreciate it, but I'll be fine. Spencer and I have an understanding."

The agents shut the door and leave.

Spencer leans back in his chair. He's always put together, but not now. He's rumpled and looks like he can use a shower. "We have an understanding?"

I ignore his question. "I'm sorry I haven't gotten here before now. I've been waiting on something before I talk to you."

Spencer stares at me, but it's not like the shitshow yesterday with Rocco. He's controlled as he studies me.

What a difference three decades can make.

"I knew you were different," he admits. "But I never expected this. I never thought anyone would be good enough to infiltrate the Marino family. You managed to do the impossible."

I don't agree because he confirms what I already know. "You've been in custody, so let me catch you up. My name is Braxton Cruz. If this goes the way I want it to, you can call me Brax. I'm a special agent with the DEA."

"The DEA." He shakes his head in disbelief.

"The Marino organization north of the border is no more. Assets are frozen. Properties have been seized. And everyone—I'm talking the Deckers, the Albas, the Jackals, and beyond—are in custody. We've taken control of the Jackals tunnel to Mexico. Alamandos is on the run, but we'll find him."

I watch him listen to the series of events from the last twenty-four hours. He has no job and no protection. I'm sure he expects to be extradited for being in the U.S. illegally.

"It's a lot, and those are just the basics. If you have questions, I'll answer what I can, but I'd rather get down to business. You and I have things to discuss."

"We do," he bites. "Where are June and Miranda? When I learned Ed and Dennis were on their way with their soldiers, I knew the scene at the house was going to be bad, so I sent them away. I was arrested and have no idea where they are or if they tried to come back. They've done nothing wrong. They don't need to be mixed up in any of this. If you have any kind of power, convince them that those two women are innocent."

"That's what I want to talk to you about. June and Miranda were taken into custody yesterday for their own protection. In exchange for their statements that will be used against the Marinos in court, they've both been offered full citizenship."

Spencer's eyes flare. "That's not what I thought you were going to say."

I lift a shoulder. If that surprises him, then the contents of the folder sitting between us will blow his mind. "They were also offered contracts to become confidential informants. That contract is for them more than us. If they tell us what they saw over the last few years, they will receive a percentage of the cash confiscated from the property."

He only stares at me.

I hold up a hand. "Granted, that percentage is small. However, you and I both have a good idea how much cash is stuffed away in that house. Even a small percentage is a decent amount. It will be enough for each of them to start a life as U.S. citizens. They can get a job—a real job. Not one they're coerced into working for practically nothing because the cartel has them by the balls. Or lady balls—we both know June has them."

Spencer nods. "Did they take the offer?"

I hold his stare. "Miranda was scared, but we never separated them. June talked her into it. They both signed."

Spencer exhales a tense breath.

"Also, Miranda will receive victim's assistance for what she's been through. Counseling ... therapy. Whatever she needs."

I watch the man sitting across from me. His expression shifts into something I saw in the garage the night I killed Nic when he insisted on cleaning up the mess. I've always liked Spencer, but that was the night we bonded.

"I have three daughters," he says. "My oldest is almost Miranda's age. I worked for the Marinos for years, but watching what she went through and knowing I could do nothing about it if I wanted to live to see the next day was the worst."

When I think about what almost happened to Landyn, my insides churn. "I had no idea until you told me. It was bad enough knowing it almost happened to Landyn."

"If I make it out of this, Miranda is welcome in my home. It's modest, but it's safe and loving. June, too, though I doubt she'd come."

As if on cue, I push the contract sitting in front of me across the table. "This is for you."

He hikes a brow and looks at the file that's now sitting in front of him.

"Go on," I urge. "Open it. I don't think you'll hate it."

He doesn't waste another second and flips it open. He starts to scan the document, flipping the pages, one by one.

"Read that word for word," I say. He stops and looks at me. "But I'd be happy to summarize it for you since I was the one who outlined it."

He lifts his chin.

I lean my forearms on the table between us. "Like June and Miranda, in exchange for your cooperation and information about the Marino Cartel, you will also receive full citizenship. We included your wife since your kids were born here. But unlike June and Miranda, you will not receive a small percentage."

He nods slowly as that sinks in. His eyes wander back to the file as he starts to flip pages again.

Page after page after page.

I wait until he gets to the last one. He freezes.

"As you can see, your percentage isn't small. In addition, we're offering you a lump sum."

He stares at the paper. "Is this real?"

"Very," I affirm. "What it's not is common. But this is not a common case. From my investigation, you've worked for the Marinos for decades. Your knowledge is priceless. The government does not come across informants like you often. I'll never meet another one in my career. We need you."

His gaze shoots to me.

I lean forward and lower my voice, not so the cameras or anyone in the next room can't hear us, but to get my point across. "You're a good man, Spencer. I vouched for you. No matter what you did or were forced to do when you worked for the Marinos, if you sign this offer, you're safe. You're protected." His stare zips to me and unspoken words dance invisibly between us. Those words scream Nic Decker. "No one will ask you to incriminate yourself."

He holds my gaze and nods before turning back to the file. I lean back in my chair and let him read.

I sit and watch as he takes it in.

The room is silent besides the hum of the air conditioner. He studies every word and requirement and reward.

Finally, he sets down the file but doesn't say anything. He stares at it.

"Can I ask you something?"

He looks up and nods.

"Why do you work for the Marinos? The real reason. Because I know what they paid you. No offense. It was shit. If you had a choice, you wouldn't have been there."

His eyes dart to the two-way mirror behind us before landing back on me.

I coax him. "I'm curious. Whatever you say won't affect this deal. The Marinos like to own people and hang shit over their heads ... make them beholden to them. Did that happen to you?"

He sighs. "I'm from Tijuana and worked on the grounds at Alamandos' estate. I was young, stupid, and poor. I needed the extra hours and cash, so he sent me to San Diego and turned me into a dealer. I had a transaction go bad and lost not only the product but the money too. It wasn't anything like the loads you saw, but it was a lot and it was violent. There was a shootout. So many damn bullets. An innocent bystander was killed. I don't even know if I was the one to do it, but Alamandos had me by the balls and threatened to leak the evidence to the police. I've worked up and down the chain in the Marino Cartel for decades. It doesn't matter how much I might want out. The Marinos ... they have a way of making you indebted to them and wrapping their fingers around your throat for life. I'm stuck."

I take in what he said and shake my head. "You're not stuck anymore."

His gaze wanders to the file. "No. I'm not."

"You're a goldmine of information. You're also a good man, Spencer. Let the government pay you to start a new life for yourself and your family. I suggest putting some space between you and San Diego, though, just in case. You need help with anything, I'm a phone call away."

He nods. "Thank you."

"Thank you," I return. "You saved Landyn and me."

"Are you and Mrs. Torres—I mean, Landyn—a real thing?"

"We are. I'm marrying her officially as soon as I take her home with me. We have you to thank for making it out alive."

"It was the right thing to do. I tried to delay them."

"Which proves you deserve this more than anyone. Take the deal, Spencer." I slide a pen across the table at him.

He takes it and flips to the last page in the stack of papers. After he scribbles his signature, he slides the file back to me. "I'll do what you want, but I'd really like to see my family first."

I stand and offer him a hand. "I look forward to continuing to work with you on the other side of the law."

He takes my hand. "I never imagined this, but I'm grateful for the opportunity."

I lift my chin. "Go. Agents will drive you home and sit outside your house. Just as a precaution."

A relieved expression settles into his features. "I appreciate that."

I watch him leave and wish I had the same outcome with Rocco.

Damn kid.

We need to find him before the club does.

41

FLAMES
ROCCO

I fall to the concrete floor.

My head bounces like a bowling ball. My wrists are duct taped, and my ankles are bound. I couldn't catch myself if I wanted to.

You know your life is really going to shit when staying in a DEA holding cell would have been the better choice.

But I fucked that up. Just like I always do. Self-sabotage should be my middle name.

If I had one.

Which I don't.

That would've required too much effort from my lazy-ass parents. Or, in their case, meant no effort at all.

"You little prick," Logan seethes. "Torres is a pig, and you were working for him."

My head spins when I roll to my back and squint through the darkened warehouse. Hell, I didn't even know this place existed. I have no clue how many properties they have.

"I didn't do shit, Pres. Swear. Fuck, I had no idea he was a narc until he walked into the room at the DEA yesterday."

"I don't believe one fucking word that comes out of your

mouth. You told them where the tunnel is. They shut it down—it's ruined. Do you know how many streams of income we lost because of you?" His anger bounces off the metal walls and echoes down my spine.

Logan and another brother picked me up at home. I hit the house to get some clothes and was going to be gone. I don't even know where I was going or how I was going to pay for it. All I knew is that my options were trusting a DEA agent, getting killed by the Jackals, or running.

The choice was easy.

Though, given my shitty reality, it's safe to say I'm in over my head.

I groan. "Tell me what I can do to make you believe me. I did my job. I told you what Boz told me. Gave your messages to him. Other than that, I don't know shit."

He stalks across the room toward me and the other member who was with him. I've never even met him, that's how fucking new I was when Boz yanked me from the club.

Boz ... Brax.

Whatever the hell his name is.

I should've stayed at the club. Moving into the Marino mansion put me right here. Not that I had a choice. Logan and the narc made the deal, like I was some cow at auction or something.

The narc fucked everything up. Logan had his hand in it too. I was just there for them to toy with—to use—like the dumbass I am.

"Get him up," Logan demands. "I want him on the hook."

The hook?

I groan when I get a steel-toed boot to my ribs. The guy reaches down and yanks me up by my cut. He smells like stale cigarettes and week-old fried food. "Asshole. Do you know how many men want to wear this cut? You shit all over the tat we allowed you to wear. Now you're going to pay for it."

I start to struggle and writhe, but I can't find my footing to fight back.

The old man struggles with my size and weight. It gives me just enough time to get one foot flat to the ground and swing my arms.

They land square on his temple.

He tumbles to the side but takes me with him.

"Well, what do we have here?"

I try to roll away, but instead howl in pain. I'm stomach to the ground, my arms are pinned below me. And the side of my face is pressed into the dirty concrete by Logan's heavy boot pressed on my neck.

"Fuck," I yell.

I barely look up at him, but I do see a gun pointed in my face as he bends to hold the damn cellphone in front of my face.

It unlocks, betraying me just like everyone else in my life.

"I wonder what I'm going to find in here?" he mutters as he starts to scroll.

"Go for it," I rasp. "You'll see I didn't do shit wrong."

He starts to read, mocking me with every single word. "Rocco – This is Landyn. Please, call me. Rocco – You have to listen to reason. You left before I could talk to you. Please come back. Rocco – This is Brax's phone, but it's me. I know our friendship meant as much to you as it did me. You saved me once—I want to help do the same for you. Call me." He presses harder, and I feel the tread of his boot sink into my skin. His voice rises two million octaves when he finishes. "Rocco – Please. Brax wants to help you. You didn't do anything wrong. You can start a new life. You don't need the club. We're here for you. I can't leave without at least talking to you."

That doesn't prove shit, but it sure doesn't help my cause either.

"The messages just keep going. Are you sure the bitch isn't into you? There're voicemails too." Logan squats and even more weight bears down on my neck. "They want you to come back. Who were you running from, pretty boy? Me or them? This still doesn't convince me you're loyal to the Jackals. This only tells me someone was grooming you for something else, and it had nothing to do with the family you made a commitment to—the club. I need to do something about that."

My heart pounds in my chest like it's a constrained animal at the zoo and needs to escape to survive.

Landyn is the coolest chick I've ever met, and the only one I ever trusted. Sure, I've had girls in my life for years. We partied or fucked. If I was lucky, it was both. But no one was like her.

Like a friend who believed I could do something. She was proud of me for shit I'd be embarrassed by with anyone else.

"If this is the same Landyn I had dinner with when that pig was playing me, I might want a piece of that." Logan's tone drips with something I hate. It reminds me of that Nic guy all over again. I struggle to move, but there's no budging between my suspected broken ribs and his foot.

"Rocco, it's Landyn." Her voice breaks through the filth and grime, where it doesn't belong. Hearing her fills me with regret.

I made the wrong choice. As much as staying with the DEA seemed like the worst idea in the world, I should've stayed for her.

She keeps torturing me through voicemail. "Look, you have to come back. At least call me—let me explain. I'm so worried about you. Please, call."

Dammit. Yeah, I made the wrong choice.

The barrel of a gun is pressed into my temple. "I think it's about time to take back our fucking tattoo, *Rocco*. I'll see what kind of mood I'm in after that."

A welding torch ignites somewhere too fucking close to me. Feeling the heat at my back has a whole new meaning.

"When all this is said and done, I might look for Landyn. She has a sweet mouth I'd like to fuck."

No fucking way. A fire burns inside me that puts their fucking flame to shame. I'll kill Logan. If they burn me and riddle me with bullets, I'll still find a way to take down this motherfucker.

Landyn believed in me.

Hell, the narc did too.

Yeah, I fucked up big time.

42

COINCIDENTAL

Landyn

The day has dragged.
An emergency ping order isn't like dialing 9-1-1 and getting a human on the phone in eight point two seconds.

It makes me wonder how long it takes to get the approval for a non-emergency ping order.

I'm antsy.

Who knows where Rocco is. Honestly, I hope he is on his way to Canada. At least he'll be safe. I continued to text him while Brax was talking to Spencer. Finally, Micah took the phone from my hands, slipped it into his pocket, and told me I'd make myself crazy.

At least Spencer, June, and Miranda took their deals. I fell in love a little bit more with Braxton Cruz when I found out he insisted on taking care of the three people that made up our weird little family while living among the Marino Cartel. June is the only one of the three who worked there just to be near her grandchildren in the U.S. She was paid little to nothing in exchange for them smuggling her into the country. Now she'll be a full-fledged

U.S. citizen. She deserves it. The way I watched her take care of Miranda, even before I knew Miranda's story, was heartwarming.

They'll be free of the Marinos forever.

And Brax made it happen.

I feel a chill crawl over my skin despite the warm afternoon sun when Micah throws the car in park and looks over at me. "You okay?"

I can't look away from the house I used to call home.

I take in the contemporary California architecture that I barely recognize and see details that I've never seen before. To anyone on the outside, it's an upper-class house, with sprawling landscape, and windows for days. It sits on one of the biggest lots in the neighborhood. You can't even see the garage from the front of the house. My mother always said it would ruin the aesthetic.

I wonder what our neighbors thought when it was raided yesterday.

I wonder if anyone asked where I was.

I wonder if anyone noticed I was gone.

I'm living proof a person can drop off the face of the earth and life carries on.

"Landyn," he calls for me.

I turn back to Brax's friend. "Sorry. I haven't been here since Damian's men took us."

Micah checks the time. "We should be hearing back from the judge about the ping anytime. Let's get in there and get this done. Brax wants you back with him."

Since we were just sitting around waiting, we decided I needed to pack my bags sooner rather than later.

Micah did what he promised. He bought me a cup of coffee and never left my side while Brax talked to Spencer before sitting through meeting after meeting with his supervisors, their supervisors, and even the bigwigs who have their pictures next to the President and the American flag in conference rooms. This is the biggest DEA bust in over a decade and has garnered attention from everyone—including the media.

I pull in a deep breath. "I'm ready."

We're about to get out of the car when Micah gets a phone call. He looks at the screen and mutters, "It's your Latin lover."

I unbuckle and sit up in my seat. "Maybe they heard from Rocco."

He answers and listens for a second before saying, "They got the ping order. It'll be up and running any minute."

We need to get back. If Rocco is close, I want to be there when they find him. "You figure out what's going on. I'll be fast."

"Wait. Let me come with you," he calls.

But I'm already out the door.

I run up the walk and type the combination into the keyless entry. When I open the door, I pause.

The house looks nothing like it normally does.

Furniture is askew.

Drawers are emptied and strewn everywhere.

Nothing is where it should be.

I look to the side, and my father's office is even worse. Someone went through every inch of this house with a fine-tooth comb.

And that someone is the DEA.

Well. Good for them. It's about time.

I need to get this done. I turn for the stairs but stop in my tracks.

My mother.

She's standing between me and the great room holding a water glass. It's full, but she's not drinking water. The liquid is the color of amber, and from the way she looks, this isn't her first.

I was at the Marinos the last time I saw her. I was hopeful and homesick and so, so stupid.

But the thing is, I don't hate her today like I did then.

I feel sorry for her. And not because of the state of her house or because her husband is in custody.

I feel sorry for her because she has lived a pathetic life. Everything she loves is fake and funded by illegal activity.

When Brax told me he was worried about not giving me the

kind of life I grew up having, I wanted to kiss the foolish words right out of his mouth.

I don't care about anything lavish. Being here cements the fact I wouldn't want this even if we could have it.

I want a life completely opposite from what I grew up with.

"I can't believe you'd show your face here," she says, somewhere between a seethe and a slur.

"I came to get a few things." I look around. "If my room looks like this, it will be easy to pack."

She shakes her head. "You did this."

My eyes go wide, and I raise my voice. "I did this? You're hitting the bottle harder than normal, Mom. I'm the last person responsible for this."

She takes two steps toward me. I smell the whiskey when it sloshes over the rim as she talks angrily with her hands. "You're testifying against him. You're going to fucking stand up in court and tell them he sold you!"

"Yes, I am. That's exactly what he did, and you stood by and watched him do it. The only thing you were worried about was what your friends would think."

"When I came to the house that day, you were fine. Why are you doing this to us now? Your father is in custody, and his attorney is having a hell of a time getting him out on bail. It has nothing to do with drugs or money laundering. It has everything to do with you!"

I move past her, but she grabs my arm to stop me. "Where do you think you're going?"

I jerk out of her hold and take two steps back. "It's none of your business."

She stares at me over the rim of her glass as she takes a gulp. "When I saw you with him that day, you both acted like it was real."

There's something about the way she said that. It's more of an accusation than an observation.

I don't confirm or deny it. She lost the right to know anything about me a long time ago.

"For fuck's sake, you fell for him, didn't you? You're so fucking foolish, Landyn. Braxton *Cruz*," she tsks, emphasizing his last name in a way that's odd, even if she's on her way to drunk. Her tired, hooded eyes work hard at raising a brow when she adds, "You and the undercover agent. I'd think it was utterly ironic if it weren't so obvious."

"Ironic?" I spit. "Irony has nothing to do with the way I got to where I am today. Dad walked me to the gates of hell and hand delivered me to Damian Marino. If Brax hadn't saved me, my life wouldn't be what it is right now."

"Wait, he still wants you?" She's so surprised, she actually sets her whiskey on the hall table and takes another step toward me. "I get when he was undercover. I'm sure he'd do anything to get to us. But why would he want anything to do with you now? You're an Alba. The fact he can stand to breathe the same air as you is beyond me."

Anger bubbles inside me. "I'm nothing like my father, or you for that matter."

"That's not what I'm talking about." Her eyes widen and a hand flies to her mouth. "He doesn't know?"

"Doesn't know what?"

"We assumed he knew. When the news broke yesterday about his identity and your father was taken into custody, we thought for sure he knew. Why else would he target us?" Her eyes dart around and it looks like she's working hard to think. She turns for the kitchen and mutters, "I need to call the attorney so they can strategize. This changes everything."

I forget about packing. I rush after my mother, catch her by the arm, and twist her around to me just as she reaches for her cell phone. "What are you talking about? What does Brax not know?"

She struggles against me and tries to unlock her cell. It's easy to reach around and grab it since she's clumsy and drunk.

"Give me that!" she cries. "I need to tell your father. He has to know. He thinks he's going to be charged with murder."

I freeze. "Murder?"

My mother pulls out of my hold and fights to get her phone

back, but I manage to hold her off. "It's bad enough they're claiming distribution and money laundering. But that agent is a Cruz. It makes sense why he was targeting us to begin with. Your father thinks he instigated the deal for you to marry Damian just to get close to us."

I shake my head. "No, that's not the way it happened. Brax is the one who made sure Damian could never hurt me. He did the same when Nic Decker wanted to marry me after the bloodbath in the church."

There's no way I'm telling her what Brax really did to keep me safe. No one will know that he killed for me.

Twice.

"His brother, Landyn," she bites.

The oxygen in my lungs evaporates at the mention of Brian. I whisper, "What about Brax's brother?"

Her eyes are wide and panicked. "It all made sense when it came out in the news. His brother was the cop who was taken across the border and killed. Braxton Cruz doesn't want you, Landyn. You were just a way to your father. It's too coincidental. When we found out who he really is, your father's attorney started preparing."

Oh, God.

No.

No, no, no.

"Tell me ... what's coincidental?" I demand, needing to hear the words to make my brain believe them. This cannot be happening.

She shakes her head violently. "Give me my phone. I need to call our attorney so he can tell your father."

She tries to get her phone back, but I shove it into my back pocket and rush her. She yelps in surprise when I grip her by the shoulders and give her a hard shake. "Did he do it? Tell me he didn't do it."

She struggles to get away from me, but I'm stronger. And I'm sober. Her hand connects with my face in a weak slap.

I brush it away as desperation fills me.

"Tell me!" I demand. "Did Dad kill Brian Cruz?"

When her nails sink into the skin at my shoulders, I push her. She topples to her back and tries to roll to her side to get away.

There's no way I'm letting her go.

I grab her hair. Bending to get into her face when I crane her neck around to make her look at me, I repeat, "Tell me, dammit." Mom cries out in pain when I give her head a shake. I'm not a violent person. I've never hit or attacked anyone.

I don't recognize myself.

This is what desperation does.

I stare down at my own mother. I'm ashamed to share her DNA. "Brian Cruz was tortured," I say. Tears well in my eyes, unlike any I've ever shed before. But these are tears of anger and disbelief of what's unfolding before my own eyes. She howls as I pull her hair tighter. "He was kidnapped and tortured for days before they killed him and dumped his body. Are you telling me my own father did that just so he could run drugs for the Marinos?" I grip her jaw with my other hand and give her head a violent shake when I scream. "Tell me!"

"Landyn?"

Micah's voice cuts through the house. I didn't hear him come in.

I ignore him, ready to threaten my own mother until she tells me the truth. My fingers dig into her skin, but she's had enough. Tears stream down her face, and she can barely get the one word out that will change my life forever.

"Yes!" she cries. "He killed him. They required it. He had to."

I let her go instantly as if touching her singed me and take a step back. She falls to the floor and cradles her face in her hands. Mine shake and tremble, stained with her blood.

"What the hell?" Micah exclaims. He pulls me away from the woman who's in a heap on the ground. "I was only on the phone with Brax for three minutes. What happened?"

I shake my head, willing it not to be true.

My father killed Brian Cruz?

I'm turned, and the beast of a man who has Brax's back no

matter what is in my face. He holds me by the shoulders and bends to look into my eyes. "What did she do to you?"

I gasp for air as my tears come harder. Micah is blurry when I look up at him. "He did it."

Micah's brows furrow. "Who did what?"

"Shut up," my mother pushes to her knees and grabs a chair to pull herself to a standing position. "Shut the fuck up. Don't you say a word!"

Micah looks from my mother to me. His expression hardens. "What is she talking about?"

"Don't," my mother seethes and starts to come at us.

Micah puts out a hand and easily pushes her back as he focuses on me.

I still can't believe it's true. I stare into my mother's eyes as the words scrape like razors from my mouth. "My father—" I find Micah and tears fill my eyes. "My father killed Brian."

Micah's expression morphs into something that reflects how I feel.

Shock.

Disgust.

Fury.

"You little bitch!" My mother tries to throw herself at me, but Micah pulls me to his side.

"Stay the fuck away from her," he demands, when he stops to reach for his phone. He looks from the screen to me. "It's Brax."

I drag my fingers through my hair and shake my head. "He's going to hate me. When he learns this, he'll hate me. What am I going to do?"

He presses the button and puts the phone to his ear. "Brax, something has happ—"

But he goes silent, and his eyes dart to me.

I brace.

"Send me the location. We'll be right there."

"What is it?" I ask.

"Rocco's phone hit a tower. They have a location. We'll have to deal with this later. We need to go."

43

I'M A GUEST ON YOUR MERRY-GO-ROUND

Brax

It took all of five minutes for Rocco's phone to ping off a tower.

We're headed east out of town, away from the city, and into an industrial area that has seen better decades.

Tim and another local supervisor scrambled teams to search the area. We split up, cleared too many buildings, and came up empty.

Not one pissed-off eighteen-year-old to be found.

Rocco's cell hasn't budged. This could be good news or really bad news depending on your outlook on life.

I'm not thinking good things.

A voice crackles over the com. "We cleared two more buildings on the northeast side of the block. One was abandoned, and the other was a legit business. We're going across the street to search another one."

I lead the way with Carson and Tim on my heels as I respond. "Copy. We're south of you—almost out of tower range. Check in when you're done."

We're about to turn a corner when Micah calls. I don't have the chance to greet him when he starts talking. "I've got Landyn. We're almost there."

"Dammit," I bite. "Keep her away. I have no clue what we'll run into. We're breaching another building."

"I want to be close. Brax, we need to talk."

I hear Landyn in the background, and I swear she's crying.

I'm about to rip Micah a new asshole for upsetting her again, but I stop in place and hold my hand up. Tim and Cole see what I see, and we all shift behind the corner of the building.

"A bike. It's Logan's. And that cargo van looks exactly like one that's owned by the Jackals. Rocco is in that building."

"I'll find you," Micah growls. "Don't go in without backup."

"Do not fucking leave her," I hiss.

He doesn't answer and hangs up.

Damn him.

I look back at Carson and Tim. Their weapons are drawn. It's just the three of us since we split up.

"This is the DEA's playground," Carson mutters low. "I'm a guest on your merry-go-round, so it's your call. You want to go in or wait for backup?"

Tim's jaw goes hard, but he lifts his chin to me. "You know these people best. I'll let you make the call."

I've navigated the last two years on my own. Having two people at my back feels like an army in comparison.

Common sense and my background in tactical training tells me to wait. We have teams in the area and don't know what we're walking into.

But my gut...

If Rocco's cell is in there, it means he's likely there too. So is Logan and at least one other. Maybe more.

We'll have the element of surprise.

A commotion comes from the building followed by yelling and howling.

Shit.

I turn to the men who have had my back for two years and

trusted me every step of the way. I look between the two of them when I lift the com to my mouth. "Found them. Track our location. We need backup. We're going in."

I silence the radio and steady my gun. "Let's go."

Landyn

"We're going in."

I curl into myself in the passenger seat as I listen to Brax's voice over the radio in Micah's car.

"Dammit!" Micah bellows through the small space. "What the hell is he doing going in without a full team?"

I wipe the tears that won't stop since we left my house after learning the news my father is a murderer.

Not only that, he's a cop killer. My father caused the Cruz family the worst heartache anyone can experience.

How will I look them in the eyes again ... let alone be a member of their family?

I felt physically ill on the drive here. Now all I can think about is that Brax is *going in*. And whatever he's walking into, Rocco is there too. And from the sounds of it, he's in trouble.

"What do we do?" I ask Micah.

He huffs. "Since I'm stuck babysitting you, we sit and wait."

"I'm sorry I'm a mess. I'm so afraid of what Brax will do when he learns about my dad. And now he's trying to save Rocco without backup, which means Rocco is in trouble. You should go. I'll wait here. I promise."

He spears me with an irritated glare. "My best friend already came at me once because of you. He told me not to take my eyes off you—which I fucking did—and you got into a catfight with your own mother. You have the blood on your hands to prove it."

I cradle my forehead in my hand as I lean into the window. "Don't remind me. And I'm sorry Brax kicked your ass over me."

"Whoa." He puts a hand up. "Let's get something straight. Brax did not kick my ass. That was what you call a colorful discussion between friends. All I'm saying is you're not leaving my sight. You'd better not have to go to the bathroom, or else we're about to become better friends than either of us wants."

I lean my head back on the headrest and close my eyes. I think Micah appreciates the quiet, because he doesn't try to make me feel better about anything, and the way I see it, my list of things that have gone to shit is long.

There's no activity on the closed-circuit radio. I glance at the clock on the dashboard and realize it's only been a couple minutes. "Micah?"

I swear I hear a barely-audible groan.

"You've known Brax a long time, right?" I ask.

"We've been over this. Since the academy."

I unbuckle and turn in my seat. "I love him. I told him I'd go anywhere with him. But we're new. You know him better than I do."

"You're right," he deadpans. "I do."

"What do you think Brax will do when he finds out about my father?"

He pauses for a moment before turning to me. "There are a lot of variables. I don't want to make you an accessory to what might or might not happen. Plus, your dad is in jail as we speak. Despite what you see on HBO, it's not easy to"—he takes his hand and slices it across his throat—"take care of your problems from afar."

Shit. I wish Brax would've figured this out while he was still undercover. He did it with Damian and Nic. There's no doubt he would've taken care of my father in the same way.

And I wouldn't be upset about it.

"I'm worried that he'll hate me, Micah." My voice is small and shaky in the quiet car as I admit my biggest fear to Brax's friend. "Do you think he'll hate me?"

He stares out the windshield, surveying our surroundings.

"Since I've known Braxton Cruz, I've never known him to fall in love with a woman whose father killed his brother for a fucking initiation." He throws me a sarcastic glance. "So, no, I have no idea how he'll react in this exact situation."

A lump forms in my throat so thick it threatens to choke me. I'm about to beg him to talk to Brax for me, but I jump when the radio crackles to life. I brace as I hear Brax's clipped, demanding voice boom across the frequency.

His words are dreadful enough.

But they're coupled with gunshots in the background.

I pray he walks out of this alive to hate me.

Right now, I'll take the hate.

44

JAMMED

Brax

"I need backup and medical," I boom into the radio.

Bullets are flying.

As far as I know, it's Logan and one other on the other side of this warehouse. I'm hunched behind a bar. Tim and Cole are twenty feet away. They're taking turns drawing the fire while I move in.

I talk over the bottles breaking—raining liquor and glass all around me. "I've got a burn victim who needs immediate attention. Stand down until I give the all clear, but get units on the way."

There was no sneaking in. Every door we tried was locked, and the place is a cave—not one window to pry open. The door and frame are metal, so there was no kicking it in.

We came in guns-a-blazing since I had to shoot the lock until it finally gave way. Our entrance might as well have been announced by the King's Court.

Cole peeks around the corner, arm extended, shooting while Tim reloads. Another bottle falls next to me.

I hunch over and look around the corner.

Rocco is sprawled in the middle of the chaos. He's writhing in pain.

When we got in, we saw what was causing the howling.

A blow torch.

They were in the process of burning that damn tattoo off his arm.

Logan and the other guy ran, leaving Rocco in the middle of the open space. He's spread eagle and cuffed, stretched as far as his body will allow so they could torture him.

Logan makes a run for it as the other guy tag-teams us, but Cole is good. He might have a desk job now, but he's as sharp as ever. I watch his eyes narrow as he takes aim.

The incoming bullets immediately come to a halt.

"Move," Tim yells. "Pritchett went into the backroom and shut the door. I'll get Monroe out of here. You get Logan."

Cole catches up to me, and we both hurry past a groaning Rocco. I barely take my eyes off the room ahead of me to see the flesh melted on his forearm.

Shit.

"I'm on your right," Cole mutters close to me.

We're swift and light on our feet. The door Logan entered is swinging. I nudge it with my foot.

A stairwell.

Cole and I move in, covering for each other as we start to climb the stairs taking in our environment through the sights of our guns. We're on the third and last flight and slow when we get to the only door.

It's closed.

I turn the handle.

And locked. Dammit.

This door isn't metal. I motion for Cole to take a step back. With all my force, I put my foot to the door right beside the locked handle.

It busts open at the jamb.

The moment the door swings open, bullets fly.

Cole and I put our backs to the wall on either side of the door. That's when we hear it.

Nothing.

Just ... silence.

Followed by a hissed, "Fuck."

I take the opening and turn.

The room is empty. Bare. No furniture, no doors, no closets.

Just Logan Pritchett.

And guessing by his panicked expression, his gun is jammed.

I walk in and never take my sights off him. "This is an interesting development, Logan."

His hands shake as he rattles his gun—pulling, yanking, and prodding.

"It's no use. Drop the weapon and kick it to my partner so you can walk out of here alive. You keep fucking around with that, this will end differently."

His eyes flit from me to the gun. "Don't talk to me, pig. My brothers are in jail because of you. The club is practically dead—"

"The club *is* dead," I interrupt, never taking my eyes off his hands. I stop ten feet away and aim. "You've got one dead downstairs. That leaves you. If I had to guess the few stragglers didn't stick around to fight to the death. They ran. Not very loyal."

He shakes his head as his movements are vicious trying to get his gun to work.

"I'm going to kill you," he rages. "I'm going to kill you and that punk-ass kid who turned on us. If he thinks that burn is bad, wait 'til I get my hands on him."

"Drop the gun, Logan. I was undercover for years. I'm a patient man until someone starts shooting at me."

"I can take him out from here," Cole drones. "I only need one bullet, Logan. Drop the fucking gun or its new home will be in your tiny, pathetic brain."

"It's your last chance," I warn.

His struggles with the weapon intensify.

I take a step, but that's when it happens.

A click.

The air in the room goes tense.

It takes a beat for Logan to realize, but when he does, everything happens at the speed of light.

"Brax!" Cole yells.

Logan raises his gun.

It's pointed at my knees and moving up, making it very fucking easy for me.

I pull my trigger.

Logan's gun hits the floor before his head does.

Blood slowly pools beneath him. I take two steps forward and kick his gun to the side of the room. Then I pull the radio from my tactical belt and take a breath. "The building is secure and both subjects are down."

The DEA com center replies, "Do you need additional medical assistance at the scene?"

I pause before pressing the button. "No. It's just the burn victim."

I turn, and Cole holsters his gun, but never shifts his frown from me. "You, Cruz, are a drama queen and a bullet magnet. I think you and I need to take a break. I have a wife, two kids, a cranky cat, and a farmhouse. I'd like to grow old with them ... and in them, if you catch my drift. I'd give you the whole *it's not you, it's me* bit, but I'm no liar. It's you—totally you. You need to rethink your priorities."

And with that, I watch the CIA officer turn and clomp down the stairs.

Wow.

After two years and all we've been through, Cole actually broke up with me.

Whatever. He'll get over it when he needs his next action fix. I have no doubt he'll be back.

Plus, my priorities are just fine. I'm counting on the unprotected sex to blow my life up into a big, fat cloud of normal that lives forever and ever until death do us part at a really fucking old age.

Shit. I think Cole Carson is rubbing off on me.

I shake that off. I have an intern to check on and an illegitimate wife who's probably about to lose her mind.

45

LUCKY

Landyn

Rocco lies in the hospital bed with his good forearm draped over his face. The patient gown is barely hanging on, otherwise he's bare from the waist up. They're treating his burn

He's lucky.

Lucky he's not dead.

Lucky Brax, Cole, and Tim got there when they did.

And lucky his burns are second degree for the most part.

They got there just in time. There are a few spots on his forearm that are third degree, but they're small enough, the doctor said he won't need a graft. He's being treated for an infection just in case and needs someone to help dress the wound until it heals.

That's where Brax and I come in.

Rocco needs us. We're back to where we wanted to be when we were going to take Rocco to dinner but really talk him into coming to New York.

Okay, so we might've had a detour that included Rocco running, being attacked and thrown into the back of a cargo van by his own club, and a homemade tattoo removal. It was downright scary, and I never want to experience anything like it again.

Tim managed to help Rocco out of the building while Brax and Cole were dealing with Logan Pritchett. Once we heard they were clear over the radio, I made Micah take me to them and rode with Rocco to the hospital.

I haven't seen Brax since. Micah said there's a procedure following a shooting. It's taken all day.

I guess when you're undercover, it's a different ballgame. He didn't do that after our wedding day.

Micah hasn't left my side, and I haven't left Rocco's. I'm a mess of anxiety. I need to get Brax alone to tell him about my dad.

I dread it more than anything.

For the time being, I'm focusing on Rocco. I've decided I'm going to be the best older sister he never had.

Honestly, I have no clue if he really has a sister or a brother. He's never told me. But if he does, they're horrible for not wanting to be a part of his life.

I won't mother him. I'm not that old, and with all the unprotected sex I've been having, the only other thing on my mind—besides Brax hating me or forcing Rocco to move across the country with us—is babies. I do want to be a mom, but not to Rocco.

Just no.

"How is the pain?" I'm sitting by my newfound brother's side. "Should I ask the nurse if you can have another pain killer?"

He pulls in a deep breath and shakes his head. "I'm an idiot. If I'd been at the tunnel with them, my ass would be sitting in jail right now. I deserve the pain."

"Don't say that. You're lucky. The doctor said other than a scar, you'll make a complete recovery and won't suffer any long-term effects."

"What the hell am I going to do in New York?" He scrapes a hand down his face and stares at the ceiling. "I've never been out of California. I have no experience other than fucking up with a motorcycle club."

"You and I are so similar. I worked at Nordstrom's dressing people. Before I was sold to the Marinos, my biggest problems were if my coffee order was wrong or if I'd need to worry about seasonal fashion rules in SoCal since the temperature hardly changes. I want to do something, but I don't know what that is."

He turns his head on the pillow toward me. He looks younger than he ever has. There's no bravado or swagger or brave face to impress anyone with. He's a man-boy barely old enough to vote or join the armed forces. Hell, he can barely buy a lotto ticket in the Golden State.

He's lost, and he needs a family.

I reach for his hand and give him a squeeze. "We'll figure it out together. You don't need a club, and I don't need to be supported by organized crime."

Rocco rolls his eyes. "Yeah, but you've got ... whatever his name is."

"Brax," I stress, trying not to let it show how just saying his name makes me nervous. The longer I hold this piece of information that he's been so desperately searching for, the worse I feel. I swallow over the lump in my throat. "Yes. I have him, and you have us. He took care of June, Miranda, and Spencer. He'll do the same for you."

"I will do the same."

I turn quickly when I hear his voice. Brax is standing in the doorway of the hospital room. Micah is behind him, arms crossed leaning a shoulder to the door jamb.

For as long as I've known the man I've called my husband, he's always dressed like he could walk into a boardroom or a fancy cocktail bar. Very rarely would he put on a pair of jeans.

But I've never seen him like this.

Brax is dressed from head to toe in black. Tactical pants fit him too well and have more pockets than I can count. His T-shirt stretches across his chest and his biceps bulge from beneath screaming at the world that he's DEA. His hair is messy, and his short-clipped beard is thicker than normal.

And he's safe.

I didn't know it was possible to love someone so much that it would make me desperate with fear with the possibility I might have to live without them.

My voice is raw. "You're back."

His warm, dark eyes never veer from me as he takes the few strides across the small room. His hand dips into my hair, and he gives it a slight pull to tip my face to his. When his lips touch mine, warmth fills me. I do everything I can to push away the dread of the conversation that needs to happen soon.

So very soon.

When he bumps my nose with his, I fall deeper in love. "Did you convince Rocco to switch coasts?"

"I didn't give him a choice. I told him we'll figure out everything when we get there."

Brax stands and looks down at our young friend. "We will. You got a second chance today, Roc. We'll make sure you don't fuck it up this time."

"Poetic as ever," Micah mutters. "When are we blowing out of California? Everyone here is so perfect, I'm starting to get a complex."

Brax looks down at Rocco. "How bad are those burns? Can you travel?"

"They said there was a chance of infection if I didn't keep it dressed. But I'm taking so many meds, I don't know how that would happen."

"I'll make sure he's okay. The nurse taught me how to take care of it," I say.

"I've never been on a plane before," Rocco adds. "I'm gonna need at least a six pack."

Brax huffs. "You want government agents to buy a minor alcohol at the airport? Not happening."

"You'll be fine," I assure Rocco.

Micah scrapes a hand down his face. "I'll stay with the ex-biker tonight. Take Landyn back to the hotel and get some rest. We have a meeting first thing in the morning at the Division. Tim wants us there before we head back to New York."

"Where is Carson?" I ask.

"He grabbed the first flight he could find back to D.C. Apparently, I pushed his boundaries, and we're on a break. But really, he was done. Somehow, he weaseled his way out of the procedures I sat through all day. It's either his level at the CIA or Officer Cole Carson doesn't give a fuck. It's probably the latter."

"Go," Micah stresses, but this time spears me with a stare that speaks a thousand unspoken words. "Rocco's got to be sick of you fussing over him. I'll grab a pizza, and we'll talk football like real men."

Brax holds his hand out to me. "Let's go. I'm starving and need a shower. Are your things in Micah's car?"

"I ... um." I bite my lip before shaking my head. "I never got around to packing a bag."

There. Not a lie.

He frowns. "Okay. I'll take you tomorrow on the way to the airport. We'll be tight on time, but I'll make it happen."

It's all I can do not to look at Micah. "It's okay. I don't want to go back there ever again. I'm ready for a whole new start."

He pulls me to my feet and straight into his arms. "So am I."

After the quickest goodbyes to Rocco and Micah, we're on our way.

And dread fills me from the toes up.

Brax

I PULL on a pair of sweatpants and T-shirt from the bag Landyn and I share, and run a hand through my wet hair. I have no idea what's so important about this meeting in the morning that it has to be done here and not back in New York, but Tim was insistent. I also know Landyn is all woman and used to shop for a living. I can't move her across the country with five changes of clothes to her name. We've got to swing by her house.

She's staring out the window at the shitty view. Talk about a downgrade from the blues of the Pacific Ocean out the back of Damian's estate.

I've never appreciated a parking lot view, but I do this one.

I fucking love it.

I pull in a breath, and it smells like freedom. No one is watching. I'm not worried about sleeping too deeply. I can take a shower without literally feeling naked because I don't have my gun on me.

I cross the room, and Landyn jerks in surprise when I pull her back to my chest. There's hardly been a time that she hasn't relaxed into my touch. It didn't take her long after we said I do for her to come around and be mine.

But not right now.

Her body is tense when I wrap an arm around her. "Chica, it feels like you're in another world. Are you worried about leaving California?"

She shakes her head before turning herself in my arms. Her eyes are cold and flat—not at all like my Landyn. "That's the last thing I'm worried about. You could take me to Timbuktu, and I'd be thrilled. I don't even know where that is, but if it's where you were, I'd go."

"Something is off. I don't like the look on your face."

Her eyes instantly glass over. Her heart races where our bodies are melded as one. "I have to tell you something and I don't know how to say it."

I bring my hand up to her face and swipe the tears that spill over. "Baby, why are you upset?"

She tries to pull away from me, but I don't let her. This reminds me of when Nic got to her all over again. I find my own heart racing to meet hers from the memory.

My tone hardens. "Did someone do something to you?"

She gives her head a small shake, and her voice trembles. "No. Not to me."

"Landyn," I bite. "I don't like seeing you this way. Who did this to you?"

She exhales a shaky breath, and her tears come harder as she white knuckles my shirt. With every moment that passes, she's more and more distraught, and my anxiety spikes right along with it. "Micah took me to my house today."

I frown. "You said you didn't go."

"No. I said I didn't pack a bag, but we went." She shakes her head. "I'll never lie to you, Brax. I love you too much."

That confuses me more than anything she's said so far. I've never worried about her lying to me. "Why didn't you pack a bag when you were there?"

The words come out in a rush. "My mom was there."

Fuck. Now I get it. My tone dips. "What did she do to you?"

"She didn't do anything." Her gaze falls to her fingers mauling the material at my chest. "I mean, she did, but it's more of what she said."

I've had enough.

I bring my hand to the side of her face and nudge her chin until she looks me in the eyes. "No shit, chica. Tell me what she said that made you like this. I'll take care of it."

"She knows who you are," she blurts. "I mean, everyone knows who you are now. Your case is all over the news."

"I don't give a shit what she knows."

She swallows hard, and her tears come faster. "She was surprised that we're still together."

"Why?"

"Because of who I am." She looks up at me. "And who you are."

"Baby, you're not telling me anything. I'm about to lose my patience. You're not making sense."

Her face screws up. "Brax, I don't know how to tell you this. I've been dreading it all day, but I can't keep it from you. You have to know—you deserve to know."

I put my hands to her shoulders and push her away, far enough to look her in the eyes. "What are you talking about?"

Her face is red, tears are falling from her cheeks, and she can't control one emotion seeping from her beautiful body. "It's about Brian."

I freeze.

"What?" I bite.

She nods. "I'm so afraid, Brax. I'm afraid you'll never look at me the same again. I'm just—"

My fingers dig into her shoulders. "What about Brian?"

She looks into my eyes, and the expression on her face is worse than after Nic attacked her. That pain was nothing compared to what's storming through her veins. "My father ... he..."

Wait.

My hands drop from her body and take a step back to stare down at her.

She hugs her middle as if to hold herself up from crumpling to the floor. "I didn't know. I swear I didn't know."

I bring my hands to my head and thread my hair before fisting it. I turn and give her my back.

I can't breathe. My body begs for oxygen.

"He killed Brian." I utter the words out loud, unable to believe them.

"I'm sorry," her broken, tortured voice hits me from behind. "My mom was drinking. She let it slip. She said they thought you knew, and that's why you were targeting my father. She said his attorney is already working on a defense."

I shake my head and drag my hands down my face. "How did I miss it? I looked through everything. There was nothing."

"Brax?" Her voice is pleading. "Brax, please say something."

"Fuck!" I bellow.

I can't look at her. Not right now.

Dennis Alba killed my brother. Ripped him away from us ... just for the chance to work with Alamandos.

"Please look at me," she cries. "I don't know what to do or say. I wish I could change it. Change who I am for you. If I could kill my father myself, I would. Please. I'm so sorry."

"I've got to get out of here," I mumble.

"What?" she shrieks. "No! You can't leave. Brax—"

She tries to come for me, but I'm already at the dresser grabbing my keys, badge, and gun as I stuff my feet into a pair of tennis shoes.

Landyn grips my arm. "No. Stay and talk to me."

I shake my head and turn straight for the door. "I can't breathe."

"Oh my God," she cries. "Don't go. I'm begging you."

I don't look back. I can't.

I yank the door open and slam it behind me. I'm down the hall and hit the stairwell, the only thing on my heels are her cries.

46

ALONE

Landyn

I'm alone.

So very alone.

I don't even have a cell. All I have is the stupid hotel phone. But even if I wanted to use it—or hell, even worse, touch it—I don't have anyone's phone number.

Who remembers phone numbers?

That's when I realized not knowing anyone's phone number makes me feel even more alone.

The first thing I'm going to do when I get Brax's phone number is memorize it.

There's so much I don't know about him.

I need to know it all—burn it on my brain for the rest of my life.

Every inch of his body.

What makes him tick.

Every corner of his beautiful heart.

And if he finds it in that heart to love me after learning that my father ripped his family apart, I'm going to love him more than any human could love another.

But I'm not sure he can. Or, if he could, why he would. The reality of it is, no one wants to look at a woman every day for the rest of their lives knowing that her father killed his brother.

Then there's the unprotected sex.

So much sex.

I fall to the bed we shared last night and bury my face in a pillow. When I press my hand over my tummy, I know there's no chance he'll be back.

He won't want his children to share genes with an Alba.

I can't blame him.

Tears overcome me, and my body wracks with sobs.

Just yesterday I was planning the rest of my life as Landyn Cruz.

Today, I'm paralyzed by the thoughts of life without him.

I MUST'VE CRIED myself to sleep.

My eyes are swollen, my sinuses are clogged, and my heart is shattered.

A click of the lock turns, and my broken heart seizes. I freeze. I'm not proud of myself, but I'm a coward. I can't look at him. If he's here to get his things and leave for New York without me, I'll pretend to be asleep.

I'll fall part later when I'm alone, like any self-respecting, obsessed woman who will be forever heartbroken.

The familiar sound of keys and a gun clank lightly on wood across the room. I try to even my breaths, but it's impossible.

There's rustling. A whiff of material sounds before hitting the carpet.

Then the bed dips behind me right before his warm hand sneaks up my shirt and splays itself on my tummy.

His lips brush my temple, and his voice is as exhausted as I feel. "I know you're awake, chica."

My eyes open to the dark room shadowed only by the lights peeking through the closed curtains. I hate that his touch brings me to tears yet again.

Dammit.

I think anything would bring me to tears right now.

But he's back, and he didn't just grab his things and leave. At least there's that. "Where did you go?"

It's his turn to tense. He wraps me up tighter, and I realize he stripped down to nothing. I wish I were naked, too, just to feel his skin against mine. "Don't ask questions you don't want the answers to, baby."

I grab his wrist to loosen his arm and roll to face him. Framing his jaw in my hands, I take him in.

His expression is raw.

His dark eyes are exhausted.

But not like spending hours at the gym exhausted.

Emotionally exhausted ... like he could sleep for a hundred years and his soul would never recuperate.

I tell him the truth. "I want to know everything. I'll always want to know everything. Where did you go?"

"I went to the shore—where I took you for tacos and beer after the funeral. I needed a minute. I needed to process what you told me. After all this time, I didn't think about how I'd feel when I found out who really killed Brian. I was too set on finding the truth. I knew what I wanted to do to them. Hell, I planned it out for years. I wanted more than anything to deliver justice in my own way."

"I don't blame you. I want to kill my father, too, and not for what he did to me. He can rot in jail for that. In some twisted way, him using me as payment for his debt brought me to you. At least, it's how I've rationalized everything that I've been through. But that isn't the case. We're here because my father killed your brother. There's no way to rationalize that."

He shakes his head. "I called Tim and told him what you told me. We decided to bring your mother in for questioning."

My face falls. "What did she say?"

"She was angry and hung over. I think she'd been passed out for a while, but she was coherent enough to talk. At first, she denied everything and said you were a liar. Then we explained that if she has information about a murder and says nothing, she's an accessory. When I detailed what would happen to her, she let loose. And once she started, she didn't stop."

"Holy shit."

"Yeah," he agrees. "It's been a long night. Let's just say, your dad is racking up the charges. He needs to get comfortable in a jumpsuit, because he's not getting out on bail, and he'll live out the rest of his days in prison."

"Good. But it isn't what you wanted or what you planned."

"No, it's not. For years, there was nothing more I wanted to do than dispense revenge in the same way they killed my brother. And it's not that I couldn't do it. I was fucking thrilled to take out Damian and Nic to protect you. But when I was sitting at the shore, staring out at the waves, I realized something."

My heart skips a beat in anticipation. "What?"

"I don't need that kind of revenge. Not anymore. I'm content with letting your dad rot in prison for the rest of this life and watching your mom lose everything they ever had."

"But why? I didn't even know Brian, and I can't help but want the worst for my father for what he did. Prison seems like summer camp compared to what he deserves."

"Maybe. But I'm okay with it." He frames my face and presses his lips softly to mine—softer than he ever has. "I have you. I've never believed in this shit, but who the hell knows, maybe Brian knew what I needed. He sent you in a bloody wedding dress and threw you at my feet."

I close my eyes and plant my face into his neck. "Did Brian have a dark sense of humor?"

He wraps his arms around me, and I relish in his embrace. I thought I lost this forever. "Brian knew I was hard headed. He knew me better than anyone. If this was him, he sure did a bang-up job getting my attention."

"I thought you were going to leave me," I admit.

He gives my hair a tug and kisses me again. This one is familiar. It's my Brax. "You're going to have to try harder than that to get rid of me, baby."

Relief floods my soul. "What's your phone number?"

He leans back and frowns. "Why do you want to know my phone number? You don't even have a phone."

"The moment we land in New York, I'm getting a phone, Brax Cruz."

He slides a thick thigh between my legs and closes his eyes. "Whatever you say, Mrs. Cruz."

I sink into him. "You're going to make me cry again."

"We have a couple hours before we need to check out. I'm wiped."

I settle into him, because I'm exhausted from the rollercoaster of a day. "Thank you for coming back to me."

"I'll always come back to you. Love you too much to live without you."

47

MORNING PERSON

Brax

I feel it before I have a chance to open my eyes.
 I usually wake up hard.
 But not like this.
All the blood in my body has traveled south and settled red-hot in my dick.
 I groan and lift my hips for more.
 This is new.
 I feel lips on the tip of my cock.
"I thought you were going to sleep through this and give me a complex," she murmurs.
I look down my body. All I see is a mess of beautiful blond hair from my waist down. I run my fingers through it before twisting a chunk around my fist. She ditched the clothes she was sleeping in and is as naked as me. "How could I sleep through this?"
"Last night when you left." She pauses to drive me crazy, dragging her wet tongue up my shaft, from root to tip, before blue eyes peek up at me. "I promised myself I'd memorize everything about

you. Part of that was your phone number, but the other part was every inch of your body."

Her suck on my tip is lazy and slow and maddening. It's all I can do to keep myself from holding her still and surging into her mouth. "I'd say take your time, but if you do, there will be hell to pay."

"Why is that?" There's a playful smile in her tone. I hear and feel it on my cock.

"Because I'm coming inside you, but not in your mouth. We're not wasting grade-A, baby-making sperm as a morning snack."

"Grade-A," she echoes.

"Only the best for you, chica."

"And our baby."

"And our baby," I agree. "Are you going to get down to business or do I need to flip you over?"

I lift my head and pull her hair at the same time. I look into her eyes that are still a little swollen but not anguished like they were last night.

She bites her lip as she nods.

"Good. Up on your knees and spread your legs. Play with yourself while you suck me off."

I was in a shocked haze and shouldn't have left her last night. I realized that when I was sitting by myself at the shore. It felt wrong being there alone, even though it was instinctual.

I've spent two years going it alone.

Literally.

But not anymore. The last thing I want to do is be alone.

I don't care who Landyn's father is. She's not an Alba.

In my heart and soul, she's a Cruz. We'll make it official in the eyes of the law eventually. It doesn't matter when. She's mine now and forever.

She does as I say. Her bare, heart-shaped ass rises, and her knees part. With one hand wrapped around the base of my cock, she slides the other between her legs.

"You're so fucking beautiful."

She sucks me deep in her mouth. I rock my hips up and watch her hollow her cheeks.

Fuck.

In and out and in and out.

When my tip touches the back of her throat, I'm afraid I might blow my load.

Her moan vibrates through my body before her mouth goes slack.

"Baby," I warn. "You might have to get acquainted with my cock another day. I'm going to have to flip you and fuck you soon."

She looks up at me, and her tits rise and fall with labored breaths. She's close too.

That's it.

I bend at the waist and do a sit up, yanking her up my body. Her legs part, falling around my hips.

I slide my fingers through her wet pussy once. She shudders when I circle her clit. I never take my eyes off hers when I put my hands to her hips and sink her onto my cock.

Wet.

Tight.

And all mine.

She rides my dick, fucking herself and me into a combined state of utopia, while I put my thumb between her legs. She moves faster, taking us to a new place.

Her head falls back, and I get to watch as she comes. Her gasps fill the room, and I take over, gripping her hips and pounding into her.

I groan when I come, and hold her down on me.

She falls to my chest, exhausted and sated. I put one hand on her ass and the other on her head that rests on my chest. "If you wake me like that every day, I'll live a perfect life."

She huffs one laugh. "I'm actually not a morning person."

I dip my hand farther to cup her at our connection. "I bet I could convince you to like mornings."

"I bet you could convince me of anything." She turns her head and presses her lips to my pec. "We need to get up. We're going to be late."

"I have a surprise for you."

She looks up and frowns. "I'm not sure I can handle any more surprises after yesterday."

"After we took your mother into custody last night, I packed your shit. I stuffed as much as I could into every bag and suitcase I could find. We might have to rent a tractor trailer, but we'll get it across the country somehow."

Her expression transforms into the happiest shock I've seen on her so far. "You did?"

"Baby, you've got a lot of shit. I think you underestimate the size of the closets I can afford in Queens. I don't know where we're going to put everything."

She surges up to press her lips to mine. "I don't care. Thank you!"

I pull her to me for one more kiss. "Let's go home."

48

BREAKING UP THE BAND

Landyn

"I put in for a promotion and got it. I'm leaving the New York Division."

"What?" Brax clips.

"The fuck?" Micah bites. "You're breaking up the band?"

I watch Brax and Micah glance at each other before turning their glares back on Tim who wears a sheepish wince. You can tell this conversation isn't an easy one for him.

"Um, congratulations," I offer since no one else in the room has. "Where are you moving to?"

"Yeah," Micah echoes. "Where *are* you going?"

Tim crosses his arms after pointing at the two agents in the room. "Don't make me eat shit. You know Annette wants out of the city."

"Where are you going?" Brax demands.

He sighs. "Miami."

"Wow." Micah rolls his eyes. "You're really taking her to small-town America. I hope you don't run into traffic at the four-way stop after grabbing a coffee at the corner store. Sounds quaint."

"She's from Florida, asswipe. It's close to home for her, and the kids can be close to their grandparents."

"That's great," I offer since no one else in the room is happy for Tim. "Don't take your family for granted."

"Ditto," Rocco mutters from the side of the room where he parked his booty in a conference chair. His arm is bandaged and he's holding it gingerly. I can tell he's hurting even though he won't admit it. He refuses to take a painkiller.

"I just found out yesterday and wanted to let you know before the news spread. But there's more," Tim says.

"That was plenty," Micah complains. "Getting a new supervisor is going to be a pain in the ass. I feel like we just trained you."

Tim ignores Micah and looks straight at Brax. "You're the shiny new star. You might as well be the mascot for the DEA at the moment. The Administrator was here for the festivities, and I talked her into rewarding you for your hard work and time given to the job. She's giving you your choice of offices—in case you want a change of pace."

I look up at Brax who's as surprised as I am.

I was mentally prepared to move to New York.

"Whoa." Micah raises his voice and turns to his best friend. "We work together. It's bad enough you left for two years. You can't leave."

Brax shakes his head but not like he's saying no. Like he might actually be considering it.

"Fuck me, you're going to leave?" Micah booms.

Brax's grip on my hand tightens and he scrapes his other down his face. "It's a lot to think about. I wasn't expecting this."

I give his hand a squeeze. "What about your mom? You've been away for so long and she's recovering."

He gives me a little nod. "I know. But she could come. She hates the cold. She always has."

Tim smirks. "Patty might like Florida. Lots of retirement communities down there."

Micah throws out his hands. "This is hell. Like literal fucking hell."

Brax looks down at me. "What do you think about Miami?"

I lean into his arm. "I told you I'd follow you anywhere. And it seems as if my stuff is already packed."

Brax turns to the side of the room. "Roc?"

Rocco shrugs. "It's not like I have a lot of options. I guess I'll go where Mom and Dad go."

"Hey," I snap. "I'm only four years older than you."

"Whatever," he mutters. "Sure, Miami. Girls in bikinis. Sounds like a party."

Brax looks back to Tim. "As long as my mom wants to move, I'm sticking with you. I'll take Miami."

Micah glares at Brax. "When did you turn into a selfish asshole?"

"But." Brax glares back at his best friend before turning to Tim. "Tell them Micah is included."

Micah crosses his arms. "Dude."

"I figured," Tim says. "I already asked. He's part of the package."

Micah shakes his head. "Are you even going to ask if I want to move to Miami?"

Brax shrugs. "You went to college in Florida. You loved it. Why wouldn't you want to go back?"

"It would be nice to be asked, that's all I'm saying," Micah huffs and moves to the door of the conference room we took over. "Let's go, Roc. We've got to get to the airport. And, evidently, I need to give notice and pack every belonging I own. It's just shits and giggles being your friend, Cruz."

Micah stalks out, and Rocco groans as he pushes himself up to follow.

Brax turns to Tim. "I appreciate it."

"I'm selfish. Braxton Cruz and Micah Emmett make me look good. I was hoping you'd follow me. I knew you and Emmett would be a package deal." He tips his head to where Micah and Rocco just left. "That was fun though. But if we don't leave soon, we'll miss our flights. You two were late."

He's right. Brax and I were not in a hurry after our morning festivities.

Tim leaves, and I turn to Brax. "Miami. I'm excited."

"I'm shocked. But it's a new start for us. It'll be good."

I step into his arms and press my front to his. "I don't care where we are. I can't wait for a lifetime of adventures with you."

EPILOGUE

Brax
Four weeks later

Landyn and I were packing the apartment last week when I got a call from Cole Carson.

His exact words were, "We're still on a break, asshole. But turn on the news—you're going to want to see this."

Landyn and I stood side by side among stacks of boxes, staring at the TV as the news reported how Alamandos Marino, leader of the Marino Cartel, was killed in a roadside explosion. Authorities thought he was being transported from one safehouse to another. His entire caravan was taken out. The Mexican government speculates it was infighting with the Lazadas.

That was it. The CIA did their thing.

The Marinos are no more. I did what I set out to do.

Talk about a whirlwind.

Six weeks ago, we were living in a mansion owned by the Marino Cartel. Two weeks later, I moved Landyn into my place in Queens—though moving her in is a relative term. She lived out of boxes and suitcases scattered in every corner we could fit them during our time there. I spent my days wrapping up the case in San Diego and planning to move. Landyn spent her days with my mom and Rocco.

Getting Landyn to the point where she was comfortable with my family wasn't easy. She was a mess all over again when we saw my mom and sisters for the first time.

I get it. She was a ball of nerves. Her dad killed my brother. He caused more heartache and pain for my family than anyone should have to endure.

But my family loves me, so they love her. And after the last few weeks of bonding with my mom, they'd love her regardless. They experienced what I fell in love with no matter how hard I tried not to. They couldn't hate her if they tried.

We pulled into Miami late last night. My mom will join us before winter. We're going to start checking out retirement communities this weekend for her to visit. She wants to be outside, play bingo, line dance ... whatever else they do. She can fully recover and my sisters can help her pack. It will be hard for her to move from Queens after living in that house for thirty years, but not as hard as it could be.

Brittney and her husband are buying the house we were raised in.

Our memories with Brian will live on, and my sister and her family will have the space they need. It worked out perfectly.

The government is moving our things, but they won't arrive until next week. We rented a small apartment, but only signed a six-month lease. We're going to get the lay of the land and figure out where we want to live. I thought we were going to have to get a two bedroom so Rocco could have a place to settle until he got on his feet, but Micah stepped up in a big way.

Rocco starts taking classes at a small university next month.

Micah played in college as an offensive guard—not at a small school, but at one of the strongest Division 1 football programs in the country—and has contacts all over Florida. He called a few old coaches and they called their friends. Within a week, Micah was wheeling and dealing like Jerry Maguire and landed Rocco a partial scholarship with a small program who'd just lost a wide receiver recruit at the last minute. Rocco's high school videos and stats spoke for themselves, but it was Micah who put his neck on the line for the kid we've all adopted.

If memory serves, I think Micah's exact words were, "If you fuck this up and make me look bad, I'll quit claiming you as my illegitimate son. Work hard, and don't be an asshole."

Words to live by.

And to think Micah gave me shit about being *poetic*.

Things are finally settling down.

I start at the Miami Division next week, and Landyn starts cosmetology school the same day. She thought about going back to college for about five minutes before telling me she always thought about standing behind the chair. I told her to do anything she wants, as long as she comes home to me at the end of every day. The program takes about a year. She said she didn't want to wait any longer to start something she loves.

We rolled into town last night, and Landyn has made two million lists of to-dos. The first being a trip to the grocery store.

I'm elbows to the cart, trudging behind her. This is one part of "normal" I didn't miss when I was undercover. There's little in life I hate more than grocery shopping. Personally, I'd rather be shopping for a TV, but here I am.

She's standing in front of me wearing a tank, short-shorts, and plastic flip flops. I love that she wears this when she has enough clothes to fill a dozen closets. She stops to read her list before looking back at the shelves to search a wall of sauces.

I stand up straight and take her in. This reminds me of another moment that feels like it happened a lifetime ago.

I push the cart to the side and say, "Hey."

She doesn't look at me and frowns at a collection of salsas. "Hmm?"

"What's your name?"

She throws her frown at me for a quick second before picking up a jar from the shelf. "What are you talking about?"

I walk closer and look down at her bare left hand. "You're not wearing a wedding ring. I hope that means you're single."

Her frown deepens. "We haven't been here even twenty-four hours. Has the heat made you delirious already? You know why I'm not wearing a ring."

She's right. After the Coast Guard picked us up that day, we were nearly to shore when I slid the same gawdy-ass ring off her finger that I put on it when I married her under the name Boz Torres. I never took my eyes off hers when I chucked it into the Pacific Ocean and told her the next time I put a ring on her finger, it'll be mine and not a dead man's.

I knew she loved that when she surged to her toes to kiss me in front of the entire team from the Coast Guard.

"You should give me your phone number."

She adds the jar to the cart with the rest of the shit and puts her hands on her hips. "I think you've lost your mind."

"I'll beg if I have to."

"Brax—" she starts and sucks in a small breath. She blinks once before a small smile touches her full lips.

I rest an elbow next to the green chilis, lean closer, and lower my voice. "I can't let you leave here without knowing if I'll get to see you again."

She tips her head back just enough to look up at me. "Is that so?"

I nod. "I never believed in love at first sight, but after seeing you shop for peppers, I'll die if I don't get to stare into your blue eyes for the rest of my life."

She bites back a smile. "You like peppers?"

I lean in closer—so close my lips almost brush the skin of her ear. "I like them spicy. I see we have that in common."

She splays her hand over my heart and pushes me back just enough to look into my eyes. "I love spicy. But I'm afraid I can't give you my number on that alone. We need to have more in common than chilis."

I glance at the cart. "I see you like ... sausage. I have some epic sausage. I feel like we belong together."

She can't bite back her smile any longer. "How do I know if you're telling the truth? Men lie about their sausage all the time. I mean, there's sausage and then there's"—she glances around before lowering her voice to match mine—"*sausage*."

"Mine is the latter. Give me your number, and I'll prove it to you."

She shrugs. "Not everyone has a phone, you know. Apparently, they're a luxury. And I decided a long time ago I'm not giving my number to just anyone. I want everything. I want trust and protection and a connection so deep that words aren't needed. I want to simply look into a man's eyes from across the room and feel his love."

"I'll prove to you I'm that man."

She gives my shirt a playful tug. "How will you do that?"

I pluck the grocery list from her hand. "I can't do that in the grocery store, but I can if you give me your number. I'll prove to you how much we have in common."

I scan the list for something random to keep the game going, until I hit the bottom of the page.

I freeze and read it again.

Her hand on my shirt fists.

I look into the blues that I literally cannot live without. "No shit?"

Her head and shoulder tip toward one another. "I don't know. That's why it's on the list."

I throw the list in the cart and claim her face in my hands. In the international aisle, I kiss the woman who has been my wife since the first day I laid eyes on her.

I kiss her like I never have before.

When I tip my forehead to hers, we're both breathless. "It doesn't matter where we met, who sent you to me, or what our names were when we said I do. We were meant to be together. And now you're pregnant."

Her eyes glass over. "We don't know that. It's why we need to buy a test. I'm afraid to get my hopes up."

"But you're late?"

"Very. I didn't want to take a test too soon."

I kiss her again. "Chica, why are you shopping so slow? Let's get this shit done and get home."

She smiles. "I love you."

"Love you too." I pull in a deep breath and think about being a dad. I think about my own father that was taken from us too soon and Brian who was ripped away when he never should've been. I can't wait to try to be half as good as them. And to think about doing it with Landyn ... I'm the luckiest man on earth. "This is one time I love that you're late."

Landyn
Four years later

"WHERE IS HE?" I look down at my three-year-old sitting fidgeting in my lap as he searches the crowd. Brian is a miniature version of his father, and I wouldn't want it any other way.

Dark hair and dark eyes, but his complexion is only a shade darker than mine. He's ornery, energetic, and carries a baseball with him everywhere he goes.

He's perfect.

"I don't know, bud. They all look the same." Brax's arm is stretched out across the back of my seat. His mom sits next to me, Micah next to her, and Tim and his family are flanking our group. We're sandwiched in, and it's hot. It's only May, but it is Miami. The humidity is no joke.

This is my family now. My father is serving a life sentence in prison for capital murder, and that doesn't include all the other charges he was found guilty of. The last I heard, my mother had moved to Vegas and was working at a casino. Beyond that, I haven't checked in on either of them.

I just don't care.

Particularly today.

Rocco graduates today. I promised him I wouldn't cry. It was a lie. Graduations are miserable to sit through, but I made everyone attend this one. I even had to force Rocco to walk across the stage instead of collecting his diploma through the mail.

He turned his life around, and we're going to celebrate him—even if we sweat to death doing it.

Rocco isn't graduating with honors, nor is he in the top of his class. But he got his diploma and played football for four full years. He made friends, went to parties, and acted his age.

It might have taken him almost a year to fully come around, but Rocco embraced Micah, Tim, Brax, and me as his family. Brian adores him and calls him Uncle Roc.

Rocco surprised us two years ago when he came to the house and wanted to talk to Brax alone. He hadn't declared a major, and it was time.

To say that Brax, Micah, and Tim have had an influence on Rocco's life is an understatement.

"There he is." Brax leans in to Brian and points to the side of the stage. "It's almost his turn."

Two more graduates walk across the stage before his name is called. "Rocco Monroe, bachelor of science, degree in criminal justice."

Brian claps so hard, his ball drops to our feet, and he doesn't even care. Micah hollers obnoxiously, and Tim's family gives him a standing ovation.

Rocco raises his arms and walks across the stage like a prize fighter.

I don't move aside from wiping my eyes. And despite the heat, Brax wraps an arm around me and presses his lips to my temple like he does every time I shed tears for any reason.

"I'm sorry. I'm just so happy," I mutter.

"You should be," my husband says. "He wouldn't be here without you."

I shake my head. "That's not true. He's a good one. I just annoyed him enough to let us be a part of it."

"True. It'll be interesting to see what he does."

"He'll do amazing things. I can't wait to see," I say before turning to my husband. "Brax?"

He doesn't take his eyes off Rocco as he mutters, "Right here, baby."

I put my fingers to his shades and pull them from his face. His brows pinch and his eyes squint in the sun.

I lean over and press my lips to his. Just like always, he wraps a hand around the back of my head to extend my kiss. When he finally lets me go, I say, "Love you. Without you, none of us would be here."

Brian steals his father's shades and shoves them on his face, but Brax doesn't look away from me. "I'm the luckiest man on earth. Love you, chica."

From the bottom of my warm, squishy author heart, thank you for reading Possession.
Read Cole Carson's book, Scars – A Killers Novel
Read Ozzy Graves' book, Souls – A Killers Novel
If you enjoyed *Possession*, I invite you to read Deathly

Keep reading for a sample of Vines – A Killers Novel by Brynne Asher

ACKNOWLEDGMENTS

If you're in the Beauties Facebook Reader Group, then you're familiar with Emoji, my dear hubbalicious of almost three decades. A couple of years ago, I went to him with an idea for a new series.

His first thought was that hits a little too close to home. See, Emoji spent his career as a Special Agent with the DEA. I respected that, and The Agents were shelved.

Then hubbalicious retired and took a job in the private sector. It was his idea to dust off my many ideas for this series and write The Agents. But, being me, I took fiction to the power of infinity and threw all the drama and emotions at these characters that I could fit into one *thick-ass book*. (Thank you, George, for nicknaming The Agents, Book 1.)

First and foremost, thank you to my husband for providing me with a lifetime of ideas and knowledge. When you told me you wanted to work for the DEA, I said I'd follow you anywhere. It's been a ride, and I wouldn't have it any other way. Love you.

Hadley Finn, thank you for the endless hours of brainstorming, editing, and friendship. There's no way I could do this without you.

Michele and Karyn, thank you for reading my words raw and being my biggest cheerleaders. You pushed me when I needed it and were patient when I struggled. Your support means the world.

Layla and Sarah, you're my OG author tribe. As the years click on, I can't imagine you not in my life. Our daily chats and laments keep me going. I wouldn't be able to do this without you.

Carrie and Beth, what would I do without your eagle eyes? Thank you for your edits and willingness to read at the very end.

MSB Design – Ms. Betty's Design Studio absolutely killed it with *Possession's* cover. Betty, thank you for your patience and knowing exactly what this book needed more than I did. The cover is absolute perfection.

I don't hand out many ARCs these days, and it's for a reason. My review team is the best. Thank you for always wanting my words and crazy love stories.

And finally, thank you to my Beauties for hanging with me on a daily basis. There are anywhere between 362 to 363 days a year I do not release a new book. That's a lot of time to talk about things other than new releases. Thank you for all the chats, cow posts, and collective love for Jason Kelce. You make every day bright and happy. Love every single one of you!

ALSO BY BRYNNE ASHER

Killers Series

Vines – A Killers Novel, Book 1
Paths – A Killers Novel, Book 2
Gifts – A Killers Novel, Book 3
Veils – A Killers Novel, Book 4
Scars – A Killers Novel, Book 5
Souls – A Killers Novel, Book 6
Until the Tequila – A Killers Crossover Novella

The Killers, The Next Generation

Levi, Asa's son

The Carpino Series

Overflow – The Carpino Series, Book 1
Beautiful Life – The Carpino Series, Book 2
Athica Lane – The Carpino Series, Book 3
Until Avery – A Carpino Series Crossover Novella
Force of Nature - A Carpino Christmas Novel

The Dillon Sisters

Deathly by Brynne Asher
Damaged by Layla Frost

The Montgomery Series

Bad Situation – The Montgomery Series, Book 1
Broken Halo – The Montgomery Series, Book 2

Betrayed Love - The Montgomery Series, Book 3

Standalones

Blackburn

ABOUT THE AUTHOR

Brynne Asher lives in the Midwest with her husband, three children and her perfect dog. When she isn't creating pretend people and relationships in her head, she's running her kids around and doing laundry. She enjoys decorating and shopping, and is always seeking the best deal. A perfect day in "Brynne World" ends in front of an outdoor fire with family, friends, s'mores, and a delicious cocktail.

Made in the USA
Middletown, DE
03 January 2024

47171612R00261